Praise for Anne Marie Forrest

"The ending offers an emotional punch-line that few romances will risk nowadays. Forrest's debut is a rare thing, a story which captures the irresistible make-believe of falling in love"

THE IRISH TIMES

"A fresh and heart-wringing twist to the boy-meets-girl theme"

PUBLISHING NEWS

"A minor miracle, a masterpiece. From the very first page we feel the full force of Forrest's originality, humour, humanity, craftsmanship and sheer daring – a mix that surely means a touch of genius"   GAYE SHORTLAND, AUTHOR AND EDITOR

"Charming, heart-warming and funny – a modern-day fairytale"

MARIAN KEYES

"A lively, surreal, dark read"   IT MAGAZINE

"A special warm Irish ingredient which is highly infectious . . . it's well written and unexplainably sad. My reader loved it"

THE BOOKSELLER

"This novel is fresh and interesting, unsentimental and very funny"

IRISH FARMER'S MONTHLY

"*Something Sensational* is Anne Marie Forrest's new book and it certainly lives up to its title"

IRISH NEWS

"*Something Sensational* is hilarious"   WOMAN'S WAY

"Forrest can certainly write"   IMAGE MAGAZINE

ii

The Love Detective

Also by Anne Marie Forrest

Who Will Love Polly Odlum?
Dancing Days
Something Sensational

The Love Detective

Anne Marie Forrest

POOLBEG

This novel is entirely a work of fiction. The names,
characters and incidents portrayed in it are the work of the
author's imagination. Any resemblance to actual persons,
living or dead, events or localities is entirely coincidental.

Published 2006
by Poolbeg Press Ltd.
123 Grange Hill, Baldoyle,
Dublin 13, Ireland
Email: poolbeg@poolbeg.com

© Anne Marie Forrest 2006

The moral right of the author has been asserted.

Copyright for typesetting, layout, design
© Poolbeg Press Ltd.

1 3 5 7 9 10 8 6 4 2

A catalogue record for this book is available from the British Library.

ISBN 1-84223-119-7
ISBN 978-184223-119-7 (From January 2007)

Typeset by Patricia Hope in Bembo 11.3/14
Printed by Litografia Rosés S.A., Spain

www.poolbeg.com

About the Author

Anne Marie Forrest began her writing career with the publication of her first novel, the bestselling *Who Will Love Polly Odlum?* This was followed by *Dancing Days* and *Something Sensational*. *The Love Detective* is her fourth novel. Anne Marie's novels have been translated into French, German and Spanish.

Anne Marie lives with her husband, Robert, and her two young daughters, Lucy and Sylvie. For more information, visit: www.annemarieforrest.info or email Anne Marie at am_forrest@hotmail.com.

Acknowledgements

Heartfelt thanks to my parents Claire and John, sisters Hilary and Louise, brothers Ian and Richard; Una, Peter, Lenka and Bob; my parents-in-law Helen and Bob; Liam, Sheila, Una and Barry (whose vast knowledge of all things musical I called upon); Matthew, Clara, Conor, Fintan, Robert, George, David, Deirdre, Sinead and Rory.

Many thanks to Paula, Gaye, Linda, Niamh, Claire and everyone at Poolbeg.

A big thank you to my fellow Irish writers, for their friendship and for being such an inspiration; in particular: Tina Reilly, Sarah Webb, Martina Devlin, Marisa Mackle, Marita Conlon McKenna, Jacinta McDevitt, Claire Dowling, Catherine Daly and Tracy Culleton.

Thanks also to Kevin, Mairi, Marie, John, Pat, Niamh, John, Louise, Deirdre, Derry, Deirdre and Jackie. Our address may have changed many times over the years, but their friendship has been a constant. And to Judy and Cuddles (AKA Mr **** ****. See, I told you I'd put you in a book!).

A big, big, big thanks to my daughters Lucy and Sylvie (even if they were more of a distraction than a help, but a very entertaining and lovely distraction).

Much thanks also to all my readers whose letters and

emails I've very much enjoyed receiving. I hope you enjoy *The Love Detective*.

And the biggest thanks of all to Robert, once again, for everything. Four books down, and you're *still* with me!

To Sylvie, this one's for you . . .

1

"I want to know what lo♥e is . . ."

"I'm telling you, weddings are just one big swiz. You'd have to wonder why anyone would be foolish enough to go through with one, you really would."

It's Sunday night and I've just picked up my friend and flatmate Caroline at the airport after her flight home from the wedding of one of her colleagues in London, and we're driving back into the city in her car which she let me borrow for the weekend. Or rather, we're stuck in a line of stationary cars pointed in that direction. We haven't moved in over fifteen minutes and all the time I have Caroline yap-yap-yapping into my ear. She hasn't paused for breath since she hopped into the passenger seat and there's no sign of it happening anytime soon. She's in one of her famous rants.

"Till death do us part!" She's practically spitting with indignation. "You mean until the next bit of skirt do us part – bridesmaid skirt in this instance!"

I glance across at her. "What *are* you talking about?"

"Don't you ever listen, Rosie? I'm talking about the groom

1

and bridesmaid — *obviously.*"

"And what? Are you trying to tell me the groom went off with the bridesmaid?"

"Yep." She nods emphatically. "I sure am."

"On his wedding day?"

"Oh, yes."

"Oh, come on! That sort of thing only happens in movies."

"Hah! That shows how little you know. In actual fact, it happens all the time."

"And you know this. How?"

"I just do."

"No, you don't."

"Yes, I do."

This could go on all night but, not wanting to feel like a character in a pantomime, I drop the matter and revert to our original topic. "So go on, tell me, what *did* happen between the groom and the bridesmaid?"

"Like I said, they went off together."

"I still don't believe you!"

"I'm not lying! I saw them!"

"You saw them — what?"

"You know . . ." She raises her eyebrows suggestively.

"No, I don't *know*! Like, what are you saying? That you saw them having sex together, is that it?"

"Yeah —"

"No!"

"— or as good as."

"Caroline! You either did or you didn't. Which was it?"

"I saw them going up the stairs in the direction of the honeymoon suite. *Together.*"

I wait to hear more but, when there's nothing else forthcoming, I glance over at her again. She's sitting there, a smug Hercules Poirot look on her face, like she's just delivered the most conclusive proof imaginable.

"That's *it*?" I demand. "That's the sum total of your evidence?"

"Well, yes."

"Oh, for crying out loud! There could be dozens of explanations."

She throws me a dismissive look. "Sure!" She brushes away a non-existent speck of dust from her immaculate cream trousers. Who else but Caroline would choose to wear a cream suit when flying? *And* how can it be still so spotless, and totally creaseless?

"They could have been putting presents away for safe-keeping," I go on. "Or freshening up. Or fetching something. Who knows?"

"God! Rosie! You are so naïve! If there's one thing I know, it's human nature and –"

"And I don't?"

"Well, come on, you're not the most perceptive. No, those two were definitely up to something, believe me."

I let the dig pass. That's just Caroline. She speaks without thinking but I know her well enough not to take too much offence and, anyway, she has a point. I may not be the world's most perceptive but, then, she won't be lining up anytime soon to collect her award for sensitivity. In fact, she's just the kind who would go up to a bride on her wedding day and –

"Oh God! Please don't tell me you said anything to the bride."

"What do you take me for? Of course I didn't."

"Good."

"Well, not exactly."

My heart sinks. "Well, what *exactly* did you say?"

"I don't really remember. Come on, Rosie, can't you

start passing some of these cars out?"

I don't know what she's seeing out through her side of the windscreen but all I'm seeing is two lanes of bumper-to-bumper traffic – nothing is moving. "We're never going to get home at this rate," she grumbles.

She's avoiding the subject, of course, and if she's embarrassed enough to do that then I fear the worst. This must be bad.

"What did you say to her?"

"Nothing – nothing much."

"Nothing much?"

"I just warned her to look out, that things aren't always as they seem."

"Caroline! You sound like you were threatening her!"

"Funny you should say that; she said exactly the same thing."

"That's all a bride needs on her wedding day – unhinged guests going around making threats." I love Caroline, I really do, she's one of my best friends, but sometimes I have to wonder about her. "Remind me not to invite you to my wedding."

"Your wedding!" She laughs.

"What's so funny?"

"Rosie, you can't keep a boyfriend for any length of time so don't you think talking about your wedding is just a little premature?"

"That's not fair!"

"But it's true!"

"No, it's not!" I protest though, of course, she's right. It is true. I've never gone out with anyone for more than a few months. What am I saying? Not even that long – my dismal average is about a month.

"What was it Shane said about you the other night, before I went to London?"

"Shane? *Shane*?" I explode. "Like what does he know?"

Then I mumble, "Anyway I don't remember." But again, I lie. Of course, I remember. How could I not?

"You must remember," Caroline insists. "You went storming off in a huff!"

I stormed off, yes, but not in a huff. I stormed off because I was afraid of what I might say if I stayed. Like, what the hell gives Shane the right to say things like that? What makes him so sure that when everyone else has settled down, I'll still be lurching from one disastrous relationship to another? And does he really think it's by choice? Does he really think I like starting off each new relationship full of hope, full of that excited feeling that – maybe – this could be the one – and then to see it all fall apart – just like all the others before it?

"Rosie, what's the matter?"

I shrug. "Nothing," I snap.

The thing is, all I really want in life is to fall in love, live in a wonderful house, work in a fulfilling career, have two perfect children, and to live happily-ever-after. Is that too much to ask for? Okay, maybe it is quite a lot but I don't believe it's that much different from what most people want. But to live happily-ever-after with my perfect man in our perfect life, I first have to meet him. It's fine for Shane. He may have struck lucky by finding the love of his life but not all of us have been so fortunate and we end up – or at least I have – kissing an awful lot of frogs in the process.

"Come on," coaxes Caroline, "don't get into a puss on me."

"I'm not in a puss!"

"Good.

I try explaining: "Shane's wrong, you know."

"About what?"

I shrug, then I look over. The thing about Caroline is that

she has the attention span of a goldfish and I see I've lost her. She's moved on. She has her phone out and she's checking her texts.

I sigh. "It just seems – well – you know – you have to kiss a lot of frogs to find out that they are just that – frogs."

She laughs. "Haven't you learnt by now that all men are frogs?"

Now she's just being stupid. I look over at her again. Her eyes are glued to the little screen and her fingers are going like the clappers. I sit silently and stare out at the depressing sight of the tail-lights of the car in front of me. It begins to drizzle. I flick on the wipers. And then I begin to think of Killian and I smile to myself. Now here's a man who I've good reason to suspect may not turn out to be a frog. Part of me wants to tell Caroline all about him, but another part of me is reluctant to; I should just keep the thought of him to myself for a while, dwell on it, enjoy it, savour it.

"Actually," I blurt out, like there was ever a chance I wasn't going to, "I met someone nice at that party Shane and I went to last night."

"I don't believe you!" she cries.

"What?" I glance over at her. Swish, swish, swish goes her blonde, shoulder-length hair as she shakes her head in disbelief. It looks so sleek, so glossy that it could be the hairdresser's I collected her from, not the airport. But then, that's Caroline. She likes to be in control of her appearance, of work, of every aspect of her life. I guess that's what makes her so successful. "Rosie," she goes on now, "the reason you were going to that party was to catch up with Shane. Your plan was to spend some quality time with him, remember?"

That's true and I am embarrassed by the way things worked out but I didn't know that, as soon we arrived in the door, I'd literally bump into someone like Killian.

"Yes, well, plans are made to be broken."

"I think that's promises, actually. Anyway, go on, tell me about him."

At first I'm reluctant to but then I start thinking about him and that gets me talking.

"Okay, he's tall, good-looking —"

"So far so exactly the same. Rosie, you don't go for any other kind!"

I ignore her. "— and smart and creative. He works as an architect. He has a cat and — "

"But you *hate* cats."

"I don't hate them — I just find them a bit spooky. You know, the way they stare at you, like they can see into your very soul. But at least it shows Killian has a caring side. Plus he's musical. He plays the trumpet."

Caroline laughs.

"What?" I demand.

"You really think you could stick someone who plays the trumpet? When Dana started on the violin you never gave over moaning about the racket."

"A trumpet is different. It's not whiney and screechy."

"Okay, but you still haven't told me what makes him so special."

I think. "Well, he has this great smile and these eyes, these gorgeous, really gorgeous big bright blue eyes."

"So what are you saying? That if his eyes were a fraction less blue or a fraction smaller then you wouldn't fancy him, that he wouldn't be special?"

"No, I'm not saying that. I just — just — just, oh forget it."

All the things I said about Killian are true but what I really liked about him was the fact that he was so easy to talk to. From the moment we met we never stopped – it was like we'd known each other for years. There was none of the usual awkwardness; we were tripping over one another with all we had to say. I kind of felt this guy got me, *really* got me. He even laughed at my poor attempts at humour. But I know if I try to explain all this to Caroline it will come out all wrong.

I shake my head. "I just like him, all right?" I leave it at that and change the subject. "Anyway, apart from your belief that the groom ran off with the bridesmaid, did you enjoy the wedding?"

"What was there to enjoy?" she grumpily snaps.

"It was a wedding!" I snap right back.

"Exactly. Cringe-making from start to finish. Everyone doing 'a little bit of this and a little bit of that and shaking their ass, da, da, da da'! All the single lay-deez scrumming like rugby players for the bouquet. Crabby old relatives moaning at the end of the night how the music's too loud, the cuppa tea's too cold, and how there's nothing but cheese sandwiches left to eat. Enjoy it? I don't think so. Especially when the whole thing is a farce anyway, a big sham, a big celebration of love when everyone knows there's no such thing!"

"No, they don't!"

"Well, they should! They should know that love's just a delusion to keep us all procreating in order to ensure the survival of the human species."

"Rubbish! Just because you've never been in love doesn't mean there's no such thing. Of course, there is."

"All right then, give me an example of two people you know who you really and truly believe are in love with one another."

"That's easy," I say as the traffic *finally* begins to move.

"Go on so."

I think for a while. I must know dozens. Mentally I go through all the people I know but find that surprisingly few are in serious relationships. When I think of those closest to me, the situation is even worse. I've known Dana and Caroline since our first year in college and their love lives could best be described as non-love lives. As for our other good friend Mick, as an actor an on-stage kiss is the nearest he's got to romance in the time we've known him. That leaves Shane. Shane and Loretta.

"So?"

"I'm thinking."

"See, I told you!"

"Okay then, Shane and Loretta."

She laughs. "They're the best you can come up with! Oh please! You don't think they're in the least suited!"

"I never said that."

"No, but you've made it pretty obvious."

"*If* I do think it, it doesn't make it true. They've been going out together for a while now. They seem to get along."

"Is it because you don't like Loretta? Is that why you think they're unsuited?"

"I said I thought they *were* suited. Aren't you even listening? God! You can be annoying! Now, can we just drop this whole stupid conversation?"

"Fine by me."

"Good."

"Good."

Her phone beeps and after reading the incoming message, she begins texting a reply. The traffic is moving nicely now and, finally, some fifteen minutes later, I pull into the drive of the 1960's semi-d Caroline and I share with Shane and Dana.

"One couple, that's all," she repeats as we get out of the car.

"Just give it a rest," I answer crossly.

2

*"All you need is lo♥e, lo♥e;
lo♥e is all you need . . ."*

As I walk to the bus stop the next morning to catch my bus into work, the conversation with Caroline keeps going round in my head. What if there is no such thing as love? It's true I've never been in love, not really. Infatuated perhaps, for short periods of time, but I've never felt anything remotely close to the real thing. What if it doesn't really exist? What if it is just a myth, a great big conspiracy to keep us all happy?

But this myth is everywhere. I turn my iPod on, press random select, and what do I hear? The Beatles telling me that all I need is love, love; love is all I need. When they penned that song, were they really in a position to know anything about love? Four young fellows with funny haircuts from Liverpool? Or were they cleverly pandering to their audience, to those gaggles of screaming teenage girls who probably believed they were in love with John, or Paul, or all four?

11

I get to the bus shelter and notice the advert on the side of it. In contrast to this cold January morning, it shows a glorious red sunset on an exotic beach with a silhouette of a couple walking hand-in-hand. *'Summer brochure out now!'* I study the happy, hand-holding couple. Are we supposed to believe that we too can have that, if only we hurry down to our nearest travel agent and shell out for two weeks in the sun? Then I notice that the woman ahead of me in the queue is reading a glossy magazine and on the cover there's a photo of some soap celebrity declaring how she found love with her new boyfriend. I can't help thinking that within the year that same magazine will have a photo of that same woman but, this time, with a caption telling of her private hell with her love rat. It seems Caroline's cynicism is infectious.

My bus comes belching along and I shuffle on with everyone else. I find a seat towards the back. Once settled, I furtively eye up the other passengers feeling like – I don't know – some anorak-wearing detective maybe, except I'm not looking for evidence of a crime. I'm looking for evidence of love. Caroline *has* to be wrong. Love *does* exist. But here in our little crowded microcosm everyone is on their own. But then a young couple come on and sit down together in the seat facing me. The girl is pretty and dark and very cute-looking in her bright red hat and matching scarf. With the scars of teenage acne still evident and a closely-shaven head, the boy is no oil painting but the girl is looking at him as if he's Brad Pitt.

I feel optimistic. This looks promising. Maybe this is the real thing. I notice the girl keeps giving him sidelong, almost shy, but very loving glances. Then, she takes off her gloves, takes one of his hands in hers and begins to stroke it.

"Stop!" he says and roughly pulls away. "Why do you have to be so clingy all the time?"

Okay, maybe these two don't present the evidence I'm looking for after all. I turn from them and to the window.

I arrive at my stop and file out of the bus, pop into a coffee shop for some takeaway coffees, then continue walking for another couple of minutes until I reach work.

Work is a boutique called Elegance, not far from Grafton Street. I've been here for about four months, which is approximately two months longer than I expected. After I *finally* finished my science degree in college I took the job as a stop-gap until I got something more in my own line, as my mother always puts it. The trouble is, I'm not sure 'my own line' really is 'my own line'. If only Caroline especially, but Dana and Shane too, weren't doing so well in their careers then my mother wouldn't have such a yardstick to judge me by. But until I figure out what it is I want to do, this job suits me fine. I don't have to work weekends or nights. The pay covers all my immediate needs. I get a twenty-five per cent discount on anything I buy which would be marvellous *if* I wanted to dress like a woman twice my age with absolutely no taste. Caroline says that Monica, the owner, should be brought up on a charge of false advertising for calling the place Elegance. She has a point. Far from cutting edge, it serves a well (if not very stylishly) heeled clientele, women of a certain age – 50 plus, and of a certain size – 14 plus. Caroline says I should tell Monica to rename the shop, *Yes, Your Bum Does Look Big in This!*.

"Morning," I say to Monica and Fay as I hand them a coffee each. We've a nice little system worked out. I'm always a little late but Monica is happy as long as I bring the coffees.

The very early mornings are generally quiet and now we sip our coffees and have our customary chat as we ease ourselves into the day. It's odd to think I spend more time

13

with these two women than I do with my own friends or family. It's just as well I like them both.

Sallow-skinned and with thick black hair tied in a bun, Monica is in her fifties and still a fine-looking woman, if, as she puts it herself, 'a little on the stout side'. The old-fashioned word 'buxom' comes unbidden to my mind when I see Monica first thing each morning, standing behind the counter and behind her enormous gravity-defying bosoms. And these are bosoms. A more modern word like breasts just doesn't do them justice.

Monica has run the shop for over twelve years and I think in its heyday it probably was the biz but it's a bit of an anachronism now, surrounded by glass-fronted shops catering for twig-like girls who dress to reveal rather than conceal. Monica has been a widow for even longer but has three sons and a lot of our chats centre on her 'boys', or rather she chats about them and we listen. We know all about them. She fears that the youngest, Tim, aged 15, is sleeping with his girlfriend. She bemoans the fact that the middle one, Doug, aged 20, is "as thick as a plank, won't get out of bed for love or money" and she "can't imagine anyone ever offering him a job," as she put it one day when I think she was at her wits' end with him. She lives in terror that the oldest, Roy, aged 24, will arrive home one day and announce he's going to marry his – as Monica puts it – 'wagon of a girlfriend'. From time to time the three sons come into the shop and it's kind of strange knowing so much about them when they hardly know my name and, though Monica may moan about them, she's always delighted when they do come in. Giving out about them to us is, I think, just her way of letting off steam.

Roy, the older one, is nice enough I guess but – I don't know – he's a bit condescending, especially when his girlfriend comes with him. They stand at the door – like visiting gentry – and Monica goes rushing over to them, all delighted to see them, but then they'll invariably say something that will upset her. I don't think they mean to, or even notice. The last time they came in, she hurried off to get a dress she'd put aside for the girlfriend that she thought might suit her for an upcoming dinner but the girlfriend just took one look at it and said, "I just don't think that's really my sort of thing, Monica." Tim, the fifteen-year-old, is hardly distinguishable from the gaggle of friends who come trooping in with him: iPods permanently plugged into their ears, all baggy jeans hanging around their crotches and hoodies pulled up over their heads in case anyone might, loike, see them or something? If it wasn't for the fact that his own mother owns the shop, but even more because there isn't a single thing in it any one of them could possibly want to nick, I'd be inclined to keep an eye on them. The first time I saw Doug – that's the middle one – I remember thinking, how come Monica hasn't mentioned how good-looking he is, which he is – in a dark brooding kind of way, but I soon lost sight of that. The problem is his personality – or absolute lack of it. His visits are short, and he never says a word, not to his mum, or Fay or me, not so much as a hello – he just stands there sullenly as Monica chats at him.

Fay is roughly the same age as Monica but there the similarity ends. She is slender, tall, graceful and very distinctive-looking. She wears her snow-white hair cropped really short which suits her. She has the loveliest skin and these amazing cheekbones. She's quite beautiful, really. It's weird but young guys don't even seem to see her but it's totally different with men her own age who come in with their wives – you can see they just love her. Especially when she talks – she has this husky voice that rarely rises above a whisper. Shane says that whenever he rings the shop he always hopes she'll answer. He says she should quit work and instead make her fortune on one of those sex phone lines: "Do you want me to tell you what I'm wearing?". No, I can't see her purring into the phone any time soon. She may have the voice for it, but that's about all. She's far too much a lady.

It's funny how little I know about her. She never talks about anything personal and I'm not great at drawing people out — not like Caroline. If Caroline worked with Fay she'd probably know every little detail of her life but I never know what to ask her. She's so private that I'd be afraid she might think I was prying.

The little I do know is that she lives on the top floor of an old redbrick overlooking a park in one of the city's older, better suburbs. She talks about the park sometimes, about new birds she's spotted, that kind of thing, but as I say she never, ever talks about herself.

All the more opportunity for Monica to talk about herself and hers.

". . . so then I look in my purse and the €100 note has disappeared," she's telling us now in between sips of coffee. "At first I think I must have spent it but you'd remember breaking a note that size, wouldn't you? So I'm in a temper now and I go marching upstairs and of course Doug's still in bed even though it's nearly one in the afternoon. So I storm in, pull back the curtains, fling open the window, whip off the duvet, and demand to know if he's taken the money. And you know what he does? He tries to make out that he hasn't touched it and tells me to go and ask Tim about it. I mean to say, if taking it wasn't bad enough but then trying to blame his younger brother as well! I swear, when I think back to when he was a baby, I could cry. He was the sweetest little boy: huge brown eyes, a head full of thick curls, always chuckling. He could charm the birds off the trees, still can, when he puts his mind to it, but lately he's a right pain . . ."

Coffee and the latest update on Monica's sons out of the way, we settle down to work. Fay and I begin sorting out and pricing some newly arrived stock while Monica attends to our first customer of the morning, a chubby woman in her fifties accompanied by her skinny husband: a real Jack-Sprat-and-his-wife coupling.

Without Monica to keep up the flow of conversation, Fay and I lapse into silence. She checks the invoices, and prices everything, and I make room for the new items on the floor.

Meanwhile, Monica is serving the woman and having a very difficult time of it. The problem isn't the woman but rather her overbearing and very obnoxious husband who's commenting on every single item Monica suggests to his wife for a forthcoming wedding.

"No, no, she can't wear pink, not with her complexion. Something darker would be better. Have you anything in brown or navy?" he asks Monica.

"Séamus," protests the woman weakly, "it's a wedding – I want something a little more exciting."

"Don't be stupid, Maura!"

"But Seamus, I just think th –"

"Maura, look, with the weight you've carrying you need something to disguise it, not draw attention to it."

In the end, despite him, Monica does give the woman several outfits in some lovely shades to take into the changing cubicle but, while the woman is trying them on, Jack Sprat goes around the shop, makes his own selection, and brings them back to the dressing-room.

Now he has his baldy head cocked in between the curtains, and is allowing his wife little peace.

"Jesus, Maura, you're never going to fit into that!" he hectors at the top of his voice. "I'll get the lady to give you a bigger size."

He goes marching across the shop to Monica.

"So, how is your wife getting on?" Monica asks politely.

"She needs that grey suit in a bigger size," he snaps back impolitely.

"Really? I'd have thought the size eighteen would be plenty big enough."

"Well, it isn't. She's bursting out of it."

Monica looks like she's about to protest but then thinks better of it and goes and finds the suit in a twenty and hands it to him. Grabbing it from her, he marches back to his wife, pulls back the curtain and joins her in the cubicle.

"Be careful now. Mind you don't burst the zip."

As I listen to him haranguing her from behind the curtain, I wonder how, why, when these two got together. It's hard to imagine they were ever in love and impossible to believe they still are. I wonder if they once had their own big white wedding. I wonder if his heart was bursting with love and pride that day as he stole glances as she walked up the aisle towards him. Or was he thinking – even back then – that she looked a right state?

Finally the two of them emerge from the cubicle. The woman goes to the mirror and stands there looking at her reflection while he looks over her shoulder. In her stockinged feet, with the hideous grey suit hanging off her, she looks vulnerable and thoroughly miserable.

He stares at her critically. "Stand up straight, why can't you!"

Automatically she obeys him but I notice her bottom lip has started to tremble. I'm not the only one who's noticed. Monica looks as if she's about to explode but before she gets a chance to say anything, it's Fay – quiet Fay – who erupts.

"How dare you! You little – little –" she searches for a fitting description, "– you nasty, nasty little man! There is nothing the matter with your wife only she has the misfortune to be married to you! Just who do you think you are? Standing there, belittling her like this?" She turns to the woman. "Lady, if I were you, I'd go home and think about packing my bags . . . or rather think about packing *his* bags. No one should have to put up with this . . . crap!"

With that, she scoops up a bundle of clothes and marches back to the stockroom, leaving us all gaping after her.

3

"Why do fools fall in lo♥e?"

". . . and the thing is I've never heard Fay so much as raise her voice until today."

Needless to say, Jack Sprat left in a temper, dragging his wife behind him, and now I'm recounting the whole episode to the girls. With Shane over at Loretta's, it's just Dana, Caroline and me at home, and we're ensconced in the living room. Caroline and I are cosied up on the couch with our feet tucked underneath us. Dana is sprawled on the armchair, her slippered feet propped up on the coffee table. We've microwave dinners on our laps, glasses of white wine close at hand, the television is on mute and I'm coming to the end of my tale.

"I mean Fay is the quietest, most ladylike woman you could ever imagine."

There's silence for a moment.

It's Caroline who speaks first. "What is it about men? If you ask me, they're all worms and –"

"Wasn't it frogs they all were yesterday?" I ask but she doesn't hear.

She goes on: "You know, I bet Fay's talking from experience and that's why she lost it today. Obviously she was in a bad relationship once and seeing that woman being treated like that brought it all flooding back to her."

"Hmm, maybe," I murmur, finding myself in the unusual position of being in agreement with Caroline. But for once I think she's making sense. Fay was very upset.

"Maybe the relationship is still going on," Caroline goes on. "Is she married?"

"No, not as far as I know."

"Has she ever been?"

I shrug.

"Is she in a relationship?"

"I don't think so."

"You don't think so! How can you not know? You spend half your life with her! Don't you ever talk?"

"Yes, of course we do. But she's a very private kind of person. She doesn't volunteer much information."

"Well, why don't you start asking her questions then?"

I wonder just what questions Caroline expects me to ask: "Hi, Fay, lovely morning isn't it? You know, I was just wondering if you were ever in a bad relationship?"

"No, no, no," Dana suddenly pipes up. "You're all wrong, Caroline. She was in a relationship all right but it was nothing like that. I'd say she was deeply in love but then something happened, something tragic – maybe he died or something – but she still loves him to this day. It's *because* she's known true love she couldn't bear to see another woman unhappy."

"Yes, maybe." I have always thought there's something a little lonely about Fay. Sometimes, when the shop is quiet, she stands there, looking out the window, deep in thought like – I think now – some tragic heroine, reflecting on her life, remembering the man she once loved but sadly lost.

But Caroline's not buying Dana's theory.

"Oh for God's sake! True love, my arse!"

"Very nicely put!" I say.

"There is no such thing as true love!"

"Oh, not this again!" I moan, recollecting our conversation on the way back from the airport.

"But there isn't," Caroline persists. "So why do people waste half their lives looking for it and then, when they think they've found it, convince themselves it's the real thing. That woman in the shop probably thought she was in love when she married. She didn't know he was going to turn out to be such a pig. Love – hah! There's no such thing!"

"Of course, there is!" Dana shouts back at her. "You're being ridiculous!"

"All right then, name one couple you believe are totally in love with one another."

"Not again. We've already had this discu –" I begin but don't get a chance to finish.

Without a moment's hesitation Dana comes back with her answer. "My parents. They've been married for almost twenty-five years and they're as mad about each other now as they were the day they married."

Now, why didn't I think to say my parents?

"But how can you know that?" Caroline is demanding.

Oh yeah – maybe because they fight so much.

"Of course, I know," Dana insists. "Why wouldn't I? I see the way they are. They can't do enough to please one another. My mother thinks my father is the sun, moon and stars and he thinks the same of her. Every single day for the last twenty-five years he's brought her up a cup of tea in the morning and they can't get through the day without ringing each other three or four times. He still thinks she's the beautiful young woman he married and, in her eyes, he's still the man with the film-star looks who swept her off her feet all those years ago. To this day, they're besotted with one another."

"But you can't know that for sure!" insists Caroline.

"I can. I do, and that's all there is to it!"

Not quite, it seems.

"For all you know," Caroline persists, "your dad could be having affairs left, right and centre.

"He's not!"

"Or your mum, for that matter."

"She's not! Neither of them are!"

"You can't know that!"

"I do!"

"Caroline, why can't you just let it go?" I butt in.

"Because *she's* being ludicrous."

"I am?" laughs Dana. "*You* are, you mean."

"If Dana believes her parents are in love, then why are you so desperate to convince her otherwise?" I ask. But straightaway I think I know the answer. Caroline's dad left her mum to move in with his girlfriend when Caroline and her brother were young. Maybe that's where all this is coming from but, even so, it doesn't give her the right to go on at Dana like this. "Can't you just let Dana think what she wants?"

My words go unheard. They're both far too wound up to pay me any attention. Dana is yelling at Caroline now.

"If I thought for one moment that I'd live my life without ever having what my parents have, then, really, just what is the point of it all?"

"But what makes you so sure you *will* have what you *think* they have?" demands Caroline.

"Because I want it so much. And despite what you say, I think that's what you want too. Isn't that what everyone wants?

To have someone to love. To be loved by them in return. To be the most special person in their whole world. To be their whole world. To be the first thing they think about when they wake in the morning. To be their very reason for living."

I mightn't have put it quite so floridly but, yeah, I'm with Dana on this one. Caroline, however, definitely is not.

"That's not what I want! What I want is someone who's compatible, who's successful, not too hard on the eye and who's seriously rich. That's what I want. Love doesn't come into it."

Dana is staring at her, as if she just can't believe what she's hearing. Five, ten, fifteen seconds pass.

"What? What?" demands Caroline. "Why are you staring at me? Stop looking at me like that!"

"That's just the saddest thing I've ever heard. You really are . . . sad!"

"If I'm sad then you're pathetic!" shouts Caroline.

"Caroline, Dana, come on!" I try again. "Why can't you just leave it? Dana, you know you can't win an argument with Caroline, so why are you even trying?"

But I may as well be invisible. They pay me no heed. They've regressed back to the playground.

"Sad!"

"Pathetic!"

Suddenly I lose my temper. "Just listen to the pair of you! You're like children! Sitting here squabbling about love. The thing is, I don't know how you can claim to know anything about it in the first place. I can't remember the last time either of you went on so much as a date. Dana, with the greatest respect – *not* – your prince on a white horse isn't going to come galloping into this sitting-room to sweep you off your feet and, Caroline, your millionaire in a Rolls-Royce will have a hard job tracking you down to that armchair."

Suddenly they both turn on me.

"Just listen to you!" shouts Caroline.

"Oh please!" cries Dana.

"What?" I ask.

"It's just so easy for you!"

"What is?"

"All you have to do is walk into a room and you have every man swooning at your feet," says Caroline.

"That's not true!"

"Yes, it is," insists Dana.

"Have you any idea what it's like for the rest of us?" asks Caroline. "In the end of the day looks are what it's all about. That's all men see. *You* should know that!"

"What do you mean by that exactly?"

"You know."

"No, I don't. Why don't you tell me?"

"Okay, let's take this guy you met at that party the other night – what's his name?"

"Killian."

"Yeah, Killian. Well, why do think he asked you out?"

"Ahhm – because he liked me."

"But *why* did he like you?"

"I don't know. Because we just got on well together."

"Bullshit! You could have been talking Klingon to him all night and he wouldn't have noticed. You'd still be going on your hot date with him."

I stare at her. Has she any idea how hurtful she can be sometimes? Is it that hard for her to believe that someone might actually find me interesting?

"Hang on a second!" I'm angry now. "How come this is suddenly all about me? This was *your* fight."

But Caroline goes on: "I've seen you at parties, Rosie,

and all you have to do is bat your long lashes at them and they're all over you like flies. Don't tell me it's the inner you they're attracted to!"

"That's not fair!"

"No, it's not fair. It's not fair that you got the catwalk legs –"

"Oh, come on!"

I stare at her. "Listen to you. You're going on like you're plug-ugly!"

"I'm not saying that," protests Caroline. "But all the make-up and grooming in the world isn't going to turn me into you!"

"Actually," interjects Dana, "I probably am."

"What?"

"Not plug-ugly but, you know, more ugly than pretty."

"Oh please!"

"I have eyes, you know. I can see what I look like."

"But . . . but . . ." I falter.

Until this moment, I never once thought Dana was concerned in the slightest by her looks. Unlike Caroline, who wouldn't dream of setting foot outside the door unless she was looking her absolute best, Dana pays scant regard to how she looks. Her hair she keeps permanently scraped up in an eyebrow-stretching ponytail, she's never in anything other than jeans and baggy sweatshirts, and those dark-framed glasses she wears scream out: "I am an academic! I am too busy with my research to bother with frivolous concerns like my appearance! Take me as I am."

But she is pretty, probably prettier than Caroline. She has lovely blue eyes, long shiny chestnut hair, and a fantastic figure. But only I and those who have seen her first thing in the morning shambling to the bathroom, only those of us who've seen her before she's had a chance to put on her ugly disguise, could know this. Funny – as soon as most women get out of bed in the morning they start on the task of prettifying themselves. Dana does the opposite.

"But, Dana, you're lovely," I tell her.

"Don't be so bloody patronising!"

"Pardon?" I feel like I've been slapped across the face.

"It's all so easy for you! All last week we had to listen to you going on and on about how good it was going to be for you and Shane to get a chance to catch up at that party but, almost as soon as the pair of you arrived, Shane says you disappeared off with that hunky architect and he didn't see you for the rest of the night. The irony of it all is that the poor guy would probably have been better off with any of the other women in the room."

"That's a mean thing to say!"

"But it's true. That dumb fool has no idea what he's dealing with, has no idea you're going to dump him in a couple of weeks."

Where *is* all this coming from? I'm really taken aback.

"That's not fair," I protest. "I only want what you want, someone special, except you seem to have this daft idea he, whoever he might be, will find you slumped on the sofa in your tracksuit, glued to the telly."

"Oh, that's mean!" says Caroline.

"No meaner than the stuff the pair of you are saying to me!" I shout.

"Do you think I'd be here on the sofa if I had any better offers?" demands Dana. "And no, Rosie, despite what you say, you're very different from me. How could you possibly expect to fall in love when you don't give anyone a proper chance? They do one thing wrong and you cast them off without so much as a second thought. At least Caroline is honest. She admits she's just looking for some rich fellow but it seems to me that, despite all you say, you're just looking for a good time and don't care who you hurt along the way!"

"Is that so?"

"Yes."

They have got it so wrong. "I see." I look from one to the other. Right now, I really hate them. I've had enough of this. Without another word, I turn and leave the room, slamming the door as I go.

Once outside I stop. I think about storming back in but then I hear Dana.

"Do you think we went too far? Should we go after her?"

"She does seem very upset."

"Let's give her some time. Let her settle down. Then we'll go in to her. Knowing her, she won't stay mad for long."

"Is that right?" I mutter to myself and make up my mind to show them just how long I can stay mad.

I pound up the stairs and storm into my room. Actually that's not quite right. It's not really possible to storm into a room that measures five foot by seven with barely a square foot free of furniture.

More accurately, in *attempting* to storm into my room, I fling open my door but it hits the open door of my wardrobe and flies back in my face so that I then have to stretch my hand in through the gap, somehow manage to close the wardrobe door, then open the bedroom door, go in, take one step, and that brings me to my bed on the far side of the room – I'm using the word 'far' loosely here. Ah yes! My room. Rectangular though it may be, it is deservedly called the 'boxroom' of the house.

But there are some advantages to a room this size. I can close my bedroom door without getting out of bed. With just one movement in the morning, I can be sitting at the end of the bed, washing my teeth in the little basin which is ingeniously, if bizarrely, squeezed into what little space there is between the foot of the bed and the wall. (If I slept with my head down that end, I could even manage to wash my teeth without lifting said head from the bed.)

But the room's only genuinely redeeming feature is the big picture window with its view of the Dublin mountains. During the daytime, the faraway view of these hills with a foreground of rooftops, aerials, roads and other urban paraphernalia might not be of interest to an artist but I love it. It's mine. But at night I like it better – I can see all the little lights scattered along the foothills, all twinkling prettily way off there in the distance and, I don't know, I just find it comforting. But not now. Now, I feel thoroughly miserable.

Caroline and Dana are my friends, my best friends, along with Shane and Mick. I met them the week before I started college when I arrived on their doorstep having phoned them about their 'room to rent' ad in *The Herald*. That was over five years ago.

It doesn't seem like that.

"It's only the boxroom," I remember Caroline apologising as we all crammed in, which probably wasn't the best way to show it off: three people into one tiny room do not comfortably go. As I tried to turn to look around, I remember her saying something like, "I'm not sure if it'll suit you," as if there were others out there that it just might, to a tee. Like, maybe a dwarf.

I was nervous, so I did what I always do when I'm nervous, I made some stupid comments that were meant to be funny: about dwarfs, and how there couldn't be too many around this neck of the woods and how, in any case, there'd be nowhere for Snow White to fit. But of course none of this made any sense to the girls – they didn't know *where* I was coming from. I remember the furtive exchange of worried glances passing between them. I don't suppose they were holding out for best friend material, but reasonably sane and not too objectionable would be good. So far I felt I'd been doing well:

Likely to use a glass rather than drink straight from the milk carton – *tick*.

Unlikely to use other housemates' toothbrushes – *tick*.

Unlikely to steal from other housemates – *tick*.

Appears to be able to hold' reasonably intelligent conversation – *did babble on about Snow White and the Seven Dwarfs??????????*

"I was joking," I laughed. "No, really it suits me perfectly. I love it." I should have just left it at that but I was anxious to compensate for the stupid joke – I really wanted them to like me. "Honestly – it's exactly what I was looking for – exactly. I can't imagine I could find anywhere more suitable. Why would I want anything bigger?"

I remember the two of them staring at me, thinking maybe: what a coincidence, here we are with the smallest room in Dublin and here's a girl who's looking for exactly that.

Or maybe they were thinking: just why is this girl so desperate?

And I was desperate – not for the boxroom but to move in with them.

When Dana first opened the door and smiled her frank, warm smile and brought me into the kitchen, I began to feel a twinge of optimism resurge after my countless encounters with weirdos of every description in my search for a place to live. When I met Caroline in the kitchen and she called out a cheery hello and asked did I want a cuppa, I began to think, maybe, that the long depressing search might be coming to an end. As I looked around the bright comfortable living room with framed prints I might have chosen myself, I thought, yes, definitely, I want to move in here; I want them to want me to move in. As Caroline and Dana chatted on, telling me what they were going to be studying – Caroline, marketing, and Dana, psychology, and asked me what I was doing – science – I thought, yes, I really like these girls. But, then, when we got to the boxroom my heart did sink but not enough to put me off.

"So you're interested?" asked Caroline doubtfully, as we squeezed back out again.

"Yes, I really am."

"It's my brother's house," she explained. "He has one of the bedrooms but he rarely stays in it but, the thing is, he is quite fussy. He'll want to see references."

"No problem."

"And he'll need a month's rent in advance and a deposit."

"Yeah, sure."

"Plus we split all the bills."

"Okay."

"Okay then." Apart from my willingness to take the room and my ramblings about Snow White, everything else must have seemed in order. "Well, I guess you can move in whenever you want. I hope you enjoy living here with us."

And I did. I do. I love it. I love them but sometimes it's like they don't know me at all.

Now I pull the curtains and get into my pyjamas and then sit cross-legged on my bed, thinking.

How can they believe things are easy for me?

My love life is a joke – literally – but one thing the others *always* choose to ignore when making fun out of it is that I've been dumped as often as I've dumped. I don't deliberately set about picking the shallowest, most selfish and stupid men around but the truth is my choice in boyfriends has been pretty dire.

I made a mess of college. I think I only did science because I wanted to prove to everyone – including myself – that I wasn't some dumb blonde. And didn't I show them! Oh yeah! By taking five years and still coming last in my class. I showed them big time!

Now I'm working in a clothes shop not because I particularly want to but because it doesn't have anything to do with science. I wish I burnt with ambition. But maybe it's better that I don't. To fulfil ambition you need talent. I don't have talent. I don't have a vision. I don't have some well-thought out career plan. How could I, when I don't know what it is I want to do? Unlike the others.

Dana may not be earning that much from the part-time tutoring she's doing while she's finishing her Master's but she knows exactly where she's going in her life. So does Mick, and Shane. And Caroline is doing so well that she's already talking about getting a place of her own – actually buying a house – and the way Shane and Loretta have got so serious, so quickly, Shane will probably announce some day soon that he's moving in with her.

What will happen to me then?

The only real friends I have are the girls and Shane and Mick, but they have all these other friends and colleagues who they're forever heading out after work to meet up with. I never meet Monica and Fay outside work. Where would we go? What would we do? Two fifty-something-year-olds and one twenty-three-year-old? I can see us now, being turned away from one nightclub after another by burly bouncers because they're 'full' then tramping through the damp dirty night in our glad rags until we end up, sodden and bedraggled, in some fluorescent-lit burger joint with plastic trays of greasy food, surrounded by drunks. Okay, there could be other things we could do, but the thing is we just never do. That's the way it is.

Most of the time, I don't feel I need any more friends but sometimes I get scared of being left behind. Sometimes, I think I'm far more dependent on the others than they are on me. I'm not like Caroline. I'm not funny and interesting and the life and soul of every party; when I try telling a joke or a story, all the reaction I get is a puzzled gap in the conversation, then everyone continues on again, not exactly sure what that was all about. I'm not like Dana. She can sit in her room all evening, reading, totally contented but, if I'm the only other one at home, I have to stop myself from going to her door and shouting, "Come out here now! I need someone to watch the telly with me!".

My love life is a disaster. My work life is absolutely directionless. I spend half my day on the bus to and from work. I have no money. I'm terrified of being left behind by my friends. And yet they — Caroline and Dana — seem to believe my life is a breeze just because they think I'm good-looking.

Now I catch sight of my grumpy-faced reflection in the mirror above the basin and study it. All through my early teens I wore braces, was gawky and flat-chested and a head taller than most boys in my class, idiot boys who just so happened to think that asking me "What's the weather like up there?" was uproariously, rolling-about-on-the-ground, side-splittingly funny.

Then, when I was sixteen, my mum and I went to London for a week's holiday soon after my sister Sarah left for Australia. So there we were coming down the stairs in some high-street store on Oxford Street when this woman approached us. She said she thought I might have something, and somehow she persuaded my mum to bring me along to the modelling agency she worked for the very next day. There, I was looked at from every angle, made-up, discussed, and photographed to within an inch of my life but, in the end, it came to nothing. The agency didn't think they could place me after all: I was too short for the catwalk, they told my mum, not busty enough for Page Three work (please!) and not pretty enough for magazines.

So am I pretty? Possibly. But not *that* pretty – just pretty enough for my friends to believe it makes my life easy.

I turn off my light, climb under the covers and snuggle down but I can't sleep. Then, some time later, there comes a gentle tapping on the door.

"Rosie?" It's Caroline. "Look, I'm sorry if we upset you. I was just spouting off as usual."

I don't answer.

"Rosie, it's me, Dana. I'm sorry too. Okay?"

"Maybe she's asleep," I hear Caroline whisper.

I hear them shuffling outside, and more hushed exchanges.

"Rosie?" calls Dana again.

"Come on, let's leave her be."

Then there's silence. They're both gone, I think, and I turn the pillow over to the cool side and shut my eyes again.

Then I hear Dana whisper: "Sleep tight, Rosie – love ya."

4

"Could this be lo♥e?"

When I arrive at the restaurant I see Killian sitting on a stool at the bar. Before he sees me, I stand for a moment at the door, studying him. All this talk with the girls of love has me so bamboozled that I'm even more nervous than usual. I'm reassured to see that he's every bit as handsome as I thought I remembered: thick brown wavy hair, tanned skin, dark blazer, snow-white shirt, cream trousers – all very smart, all very casual. And all very normal – there isn't a discernible hint of the psycho about him. Not that I thought there was at the party – obviously, or I wouldn't be here – but I'm calmed now by what I can objectively see, before I get sucked into the evening.

I take a deep breath and walk over.

"Killian, Hi!"

He stands up. "Rosie! Wow! You look amazing – really amazing!"

"Thanks."

"So, would you like a drink at the bar, or shall we go straight to our table – your choice."

"I don't mind."

"Let's go to the table then. I could eat a horse."

"I don't think they serve them here," I laugh nervously.

"Pardon?"

Just then the waiter comes over and I'm relieved that my rubbish joke has gone unheard. The waiter takes Killian's drink, puts it on a tray, and leads us to our table. Killian has now taken me lightly by my arm and is sort of guiding me across the room, like I'm elderly or something, but I guess he's being gentlemanly, and that's good. Gentlemanly is good. And way, way better than shooing me on ahead so that he can watch me walking from behind. Yes, I think, I like this guy: handsome *and* gentlemanly. We get to the table, sit down, and the waiter hands us menus and a wine list and then leaves us.

Killian smiles at me.

Handsome, gentlemanly *and* with a really nice smile, and those amazing eyes – they're just so big and blue and full of expression. Now he leans forward and fixes those blue eyes on me.

"Now, what were you saying? Something about horses?"

Damn! *Damn!*

He's waiting for an answer.

"Oh – just – ahmm –" If I say "nothing" I'll come across as rude. If I point out that he was in fact the one who brought up the subject of horses and how he could eat one – ditto. "I was just saying I don't – ha-ha – think they serve horse here."

Immediately, I know he's forgotten his throwaway comment. I watch his brow furrow, his blue eyes narrow – he's confused.

"Do you like horse?" he eventually asks.

"God! No!"

There's a silence that is just that teeny bit longer than is comfortable. I could – should – jump in and try explaining it was *meant* to be a joke but I know I'd make things worse but then I'm saved by the return of our waiter. I'm glad to see him, happy that we can let the subject of horses die a death.

"Are you ready to order?" he asks.

"Just give us another moment," says Killian.

I smile at the waiter to promptly find he's not the smiling-back kind, but rather the kind who'd seem to regard being in any way pleasant as a sign of gross unprofessionalism, likely to get him unceremoniously kicked out of the Snotty Waiters' Association. Great! Him hovering and glowering is really going to make for a romantic evening. But now he turns his grumpy face from us, and walks away.

"I ate horse once," Killian suddenly announces.

Hang on a second, didn't we kill and bury the subject of horses?

"Just the once – when I was in France."

Seemingly not . . .

"Yes," he goes on. "I was staying with my sister Madge and her husband Billy. They have this fabulous old farmhouse in the Dordogne and one night they brought me to this restaurant. It was some local place and Billy – and he may have been joking – suggested I might try the horse. So I called his bluff and I did. It wasn't bad – actually. It was like . . ."

"Chicken?"

"Pardon?"

"That's what exotic meat always tastes like."

"Really?"

"Yeah – you know, crocodile, emu, zebra, snake – all kinds."

"And you've tasted these?"

"No, no!" What kind does he think I am? What kind of life does he think I lead? "Of course I haven't tasted them *personally*," – as if there were other ways of tasting – "but you know, whenever someone comes back from holiday and they tell you that they've tried some exotic animal like, say, monkey – if you can eat monkey that is, I don't know – but say you can, and say they have, and then, say, you ask them what it was like, then they always, always say chicken."

This is all sounding like nonsense, even to me. But that doesn't stop me. Does it hell! Time to crank it up.

"Cannibals even say that human flesh tastes like chicken." I don't believe it! We've barely begun our date and somehow I have managed to introduce cannibals into the conversation. How can this be? Those blue eyes are looking a little anxious now, next they'll be scanning the room for the nearest exit. Time to rein myself in. I smile, then shrug. "Anyway, all I'm saying is that from what I've heard a lot of exotic animals taste like chicken – that's all."

Another over-long silence.

"Actually, the horse tasted more like beef."

Okay – we're not exactly connecting here and I'm so relieved when I see our unsmiling waiter coming back again to take our order that I almost smile at him. When he's written down what we want, I sit back and look around thinking this place is nice, I guess, but it's a little too formal and sterile. Then, suddenly, Killian reaches out and takes my hand across the table. He smiles. He does have a lovely smile and, with the white cloth, the flickering candle, the single red rose, it's well – quite romantic after all. This is good – I think.

There's a silence.

He's smiling at me.

I'm smiling at him.

Then he begins: "I feel like I told you all there is to know about me the other night but I don't know anything about you – hardly anything. So tell me about yourself. What do you do?"

"Well, I work in a women's clothes shop in town – Elegance – you might know it."

He shakes his head. "I don't think so. My sister would though."

"Madge?"

"Hhm?"

"Your sister with the house in France?"

"No, another one – Melanie, the youngest girl. She adores clothes – absolutely adores them. She designs for a living, you know."

"Really? That's exciting. Anyway, apart from the part-timers there's just myself and two others working in the shop. They're older than me but we get on qui –"

"Melanie's been out of college for two years now and she's been working as a cutter with Stella McCartney in London but I think ultimately she'd like to set up on her own. She'd like to concentrate on the top end of the market. Maybe even do couture but that could be . . ."

While we're waiting for our starters I hear all about this sister. I think it's nice that he's so close to her and so interested in her work, I do. But the thing is – I'm kind of finding it hard to share his enthusiasm. It's not like she's my sister, although I'm beginning to feel I probably know more about her than I do about my own.

"Sir, madam, your starters."

Hurray! Saved by the grumpy waiter who puts a plate of crab cakes in front of me and Killian's tomato and basil soup in front of him. We begin eating in welcome silence. But not total silence I soon realise. The talking may have stopped but

39

it's now replaced by slurping sounds each time Killian takes a spoonful of his soup. I glance over at him. *Slurp. Slurp. Slurp.* He's hunched over his bowl, his mouth barely inches from his soup. *Slurp. Slurp.* Where are his manners? Does he not know he can bring his spoon to his mouth rather than the other way around? Perhaps sensing me looking at him, he glances up, and smiles a great big smile, big enough to show a great big blob of something green − a basil leaf, maybe − wedged between his teeth. I think before saying anything. I really don't want to have to point this out to him, but I realise I have to if I don't want to be looking at this green thingy − whatever it is − all night.

I point to my teeth. "I think you might have a little something stuck just there."

"Oh!" He runs his tongue over his teeth, then grins widely. "Gone?"

I shake my head.

Now he rubs his finger along the top, then bares his teeth again. "Now?"

"Not quite."

Now he scrapes between his teeth with his nail, then suddenly leans forward and bares his teeth in such an alarming manner that I instinctively pull back, like I'm Little Red Riding Hood and he's the wolf.

"Now?"

I shake my head again, caution myself to hold my tongue but immediately throw caution to the wind: "My, what great big teeth you have!" It's out and I can't do a thing about it.

He looks me, clearly not certain what to make of this remark. Maybe I can salvage it, reconfigure it, turn it into a compliment somehow.

"You must have a great dentist."

"Ah – thanks." He's distracted from the basil leaf – but just for a moment. "Where exactly is it?"

He's still leaning forward. Is he expecting me to put my finger on it? Maybe he's even expecting me to get rid of it for him? His sisters would, I guess, in the same situation; the way he keeps going on about him – they're obviously close. But I'm not ready for this kind of intimacy. I hand him a knife.

"Maybe you should take a look in this."

He narrows his eyes and peers at his reflection in the knife. Then he picks up another knife, pokes out the bit of basil and pops it back into his mouth, swallows it, then resumes eating his soup.

Slurp. Slurp. Slurp.

Suddenly my appetite is gone. I shove my half-eaten crab cakes aside.

After he's finished his soup, he pushes away his plate and then leans forward and gently strokes my cheek.

"You have a lovely face." Then he spots my half-eaten crab cakes. "Didn't you like them?"

"Not very much."

And before I know it, he's picking away at my food. Noticing me looking at him, he even offers me a forkful but I shake my head.

"So, you work in a shop – that much I know," he says when he's done eating my starter. "Do you like it?"

"Yeah, I guess. I enjoy the day-to-day of it but som –"

"Did I tell you I work as an architect?"

I nod.

"It's quite an old practice but in the last few years it's really expanded." And he's off. A lot of what he says to me – how the practice now specialises in restoring and adapting old buildings, how it even won an RIAI Silver Award for

Conservation last year – sounds familiar to me and I remember I heard it all that night at the party. It was all fairly interesting the first time but not so much this second time around. My mind begins to wander . . .

"Rosie?"

"Pardon?"

"I was asking you do you live on your own?"

"No, I share a house with three of my friends. Dana and Caroline and I have lived together for ages and then, Shane, an old friend of mine from school, moved in with us last year. He took over Caroline's brother's room which is brilliant really because –"

"Did I tell you I live with Fergus, my brother? We're renting an apartment together but we've just bought this house in Ringsend."

Jesus! What's with all this interrupting! He was like that too the other night. It's coming back to me now. The way he kept cutting in every time I started to talk but I guess I thought – I don't know – that he was just over-excited at meeting someone he liked.

"Well, it's more a cottage really, quite small, but that's okay because we've ended up having to gut the whole place – like all of it, from top to bottom."

"That's a big undertaking."

He laughs "I don't think we had any idea what it was going to be like – not an idea."

When our main course comes, he carries on telling me all about this cottage, and the work they're doing.

" . . . so I say to Fergus there's no way we're paying this guy what he's asking for the fireplace – no way.

And so he goes on, and on, and on. After a while it occurs to me that I haven't said a word for maybe ten, fifteen minutes – there hasn't been an opportunity, much less a need, and what's even worse is he hasn't noticed my lack of input.

". . . at the minimum it would take me and Fergus a week of hard graft to bring the fireplace up to scratch."

This whole evening is beginning to get tedious. I really should try to steer the conversation around to something interesting but I've kind of lost heart. I'm not sure I can be bothered. And how come I never noticed the way he repeats himself at the end of practically every sentence? What's that all about?

". . . course it was the genuine article, circa the 1900's which was exactly what Fergus and I were looking for – like, exactly."

There he goes again! I wish I hadn't noticed. Now, it's going to drive me crazy. Worse still, all this repetition is making his stories take even longer than they might otherwise and they're long-winded enough without him repeating bits. This story about his brother and the fireplace seems to be going on forever and I begin to wonder what exactly is the point of it, and wonder if I'll ever actually find out. But then, do I really care?

My attention begins to wander again and, as I look around, I notice our po-faced waiter drop a bread-basket on his way out from the kitchen. He goes to pick it up, pauses, then furtively looks around and, with the toe of his foot he sneakily pushes the whole mess under a side table. He catches me watching him, gives me a snooty 'it's-none-of-your-business look', turns on his heel and heads back into the kitchen, head cocked in the air.

I'm about to draw Killian's attention to this little scene but change my mind. It'll probably only prompt him to launch into some other vaguely related story involving one of his family members – like maybe the time his brother worked as a waiter. Or met a waiter.

". . . so Fergus took one end and I took the other and then we heaved it into the back of the van. Don't ask me how we managed, the weight of these things is something else – really something else. Then Fergus throws me a rope and says to me . . ."

God, this story really is endless. My eyes are beginning to droop. I stifle a yawn. I sit there, watching him, and I begin to think that whatever attraction there was, it's fading fast. I have no interest whatsoever in meeting him again. And as he talks on and on, I begin to think he's not even that good-looking after all. In fact there's even something rather odd about his eyes: they're just a bit too glassy – too glassy, too wide-eyed, and too starey. Funny how one of the first things that attracted me to him was his eyes but, now that they've begun to bug me. They've really begun to bug me. There's simply no ignoring them. I don't know. Maybe the lighting was different at the party, dimmer perhaps, or maybe I was drunk, or maybe I did notice but subconsciously put this wide-eyedness down to the initial stirrings of love or lust. Now, I'm thinking that maybe it's more of a genetic thing. I wonder if Fergus's eyes are like that. Or Marge's. Or Melanie's. Or Martha's. Or Martin's? Or the one who's working in the States – I can't remember his name right now but I'm sure I'll hear it again, many times, before the night it out. How many brothers and sisters does this man have?

Buggily, his eyes are also buggily, I decide, and shudder. They're beginning to give me the willies.

And that's when I decide that this has got to end – tonight. Fragments of the previous night's conversation with Dana and Caroline come flitting into my mind but I push them aside. Whatever merit their arguments had, now is not the time to consider them. All I know is that there is no way I'm going through another evening in the company of this –

this – this – slurping, renovating, buggily-eyed bore. There! It had to be said.

He takes a pause long enough to notice the untouched plate in front of me. "Don't you like your lamb?"

I shrug. "I guess I'm not as hungry as I thought."

I feel better now that I've made up my mind. I even feel a little kindly towards him, even as he's reaching out to take a slice of meat from my plate. It's not his fault, I tell myself. It's not like he's doing any of these things to annoy me. He's just being himself. If it's anyone's fault it's mine. I should never have gone out with him in the first place. Why did I then? Because, like every time I go on a date with someone, I hope there's a chance it'll work out, that it'll turn out to be something real. It seems that, for me, going out with someone is the only way I can find out if they're someone I *don't* want to go out with.

Caroline and Dana are wrong. They don't know what they're talking about. I do want to find love. But I won't find it here tonight.

I manage to get through the rest of the night and, with my decision made, I find I'm nicer to him and happier to put up with his endless, totally self-absorbed stories. I can see there's a lot to recommend him. He is smart, creative, hardworking, *loves* his family – all seven of them and, not withstanding my problem with his eyes, good-looking. I imagine lots of women could be happy with him, just not this one.

Our meal finally draws to a close and the waiter places the folder with the bill tucked inside on the table.

"I really enjoyed tonight," says Killian as he helps me on with my coat. "Tell me, are you free on Thursday? My brother has spare tickets for the new play in the Abbey. Do you fancy coming? I'd like you to meet him."

"Killian," I begin, "the thing is . . ."

5

"I'm in the mood for lo♥e . . ."

After, well . . . dumping . . . Killian, I begin heading home but on my way I get a text message from Shane. He's in some pub where a guy he knows is playing a gig tonight with his newly formed band. Shane wants to know if I feel like joining him. Since I could do with some cheering up and I'm not especially keen to go home to the girls, not after last night, I text him back and tell him I'll meet him there.

I head in the direction of the pub.

The place is jammed and I squeeze through the crowds until I see them all sitting around a low circular table: Dana, Caroline, Shane, and Loretta. I wasn't expecting to see Caroline and Dana; I guess I should have thought to ask Shane if they were coming. I'm surprised to see Loretta here too. She hardly ever comes out with us. She's a junior doctor and it seems like she's always either working or studying. On the rare occasions when she's doing neither, Shane and she prefer quiet nights in together at hers; or she prefers them and he's happy when she's happy. What exactly Shane sees in her is a total mystery. Shane is everything she's not. He's great looking – in a dark Italian kind of way, he's full of personality, and he's tremendous fun to be around, whereas she's as quiet as a mouse and even looks like one – kind of. Okay, some might think she's pretty – I know Caroline and Dana do, and I guess Shane must – but I just don't see it. Sure, she has this really neat little figure and this dainty little face eclipsed by those huge brown eyes of hers but, whereas Caroline sees Bambi, I just see a little mouse. A pale little mouse.

The thing is, I can't help thinking Shane is wasted on her and it's not like she even knows the real Shane. Instead of his usual life-and-soul-of-the-party self he turns into a little lapdog, happy to sit quietly by her side all night, whenever she's around.

Perhaps sensing me looking at her, she turns and is the first to see me. She smiles but it seems a forced kind of a smile. Sometimes I get the impression she doesn't like me very much even though she's never anything but polite to me.

"Hi, Rosie," she says, prompting the others to look up and they all call out their hellos.

"Hi, Loretta! Hi, Shane!" I don't say anything to Dana and Caroline. I don't feel ready to talk to them just yet.

"Anyone sitting there?" I ask, pointing at the empty stool beside Shane.

"Just Mick," says Shane. "He's gone to the bar."

"He won't mind." I take off my coat and sit down.

"I take it you enjoyed the party on Saturday?" says Shane.

"Yep." I nod but say no more. I see his smirk. I know what he's getting at. I'm not going to rise to the bait.

With Loretta working, Mick at night class, Caroline in

London and Dana visiting her parents, it was just Shane and I who went to that party where I met the ill-fated Killian and, as Caroline rightly pointed out, the reason I went was to spend some time with Shane even if it didn't quite work out that way.

You see, Shane is my best friend, has been forever. We grew up on the same road, went to the same Montessori, the same primary, the same secondary, started college the same year (but he did law) and then, late last year, he took over Caroline's brother's room when the house he was sharing with some friends was put up for sale. But, the funny thing is, since we've been living together, I seem to spend less time with Shane than ever, partly because I don't have to make a point of arranging to meet him but also because he now has Loretta. And, of course, I'm happy he's in a relationship but – and this is the weird thing – I kind of miss him. Before, nothing was so trivial about our respective days that it didn't warrant telling the other. Now he has someone else to talk to and it seems days pass with little more than a hello between us.

Mick arrives back from the bar.

"It is my lady," he announces in an exaggerated theatrical manner when he sees me sitting there. *"O, it is my love! O, that she knew she were!"*

"What?" I ask crossly.

He puts his hand up to his ear.

"She speaks, yet she says nothing: what of that? Her eye discourses; I will answer it."

Maybe I should explain Mick. Mick moved from Cork to Dublin over a year ago to realise his 'epiphanic decision to become the world's greatest actor – a Sir Laurence Olivier for the twenty-first century,' as he puts it – hiding his light under a bushel is not a phrase Mick would hold much store by. An obvious first step in his quest for greatness would be to overcome his impediment (not that he'd regard it as such – badge of honour more like) of a Cork accent so thick that, if he were ever to appear on telly – in a speaking role which has eluded him so far – they'd need subtitles running across the bottom of the screen.

But until greatness visits him, he's keeping busy: he's taking acting classes by day, elocution classes by night, going to every audition in town and, in between, he drinks copious cups of tea and pints of beer in the city's hundreds of pubs and coffee shops.

"*I am too bold, 'tis not to me she speaks.*" Mick's still going on in this ridiculous manner.

"Mick, stop it!" I snap at him now. "You're annoying me."

"All right, all right." He reverts to his normal self, pulls up another stool and squeezes in beside me. "It's just that I had my audition for our end-of-term production of *Romeo and Juliet* today."

"Oh, and how did you get on?" I ask.

"Not so good. I didn't get the part I wanted."

"Which was?"

"Romeo, of course. They gave it to some child of fifteen."

"Someone like the real Romeo, you mean?" remarks Dana.

"Yeah, yeah, remind me of my age. But I did get a second reading for the part of Mercutio."

"That's good – isn't it?"

"Perhaps." He shrugs. "If I resign myself to a fate of always playing support and never the lead."

"Can we all go along to see you?" Caroline asks.

"I should think you would."

"It's such a wonderful love story, isn't it?" I say. "A wonderful love story of a pair of star-crossed lovers."

Mick looks at me dubiously. "The operative word being 'star-crossed". You do remember the end, don't you?"

"Yeah?" I respond a little uncertainly.

"*'For never was a story of more woe, than this of Juliet and her Romeo.'* Myself, I'm more partial to '*And they all lived happily ever after'*."

"Are you saying they *didn't* live happily ever after?" I ask.

Mick throws his eyes up. "Ah no, not quite."

"Are you sure?"

"Definitely."

"Don't tell me you've never read *Romeo and Juliet*?" cuts in Dana.

"No, but I watched the video with Leonardo di Caprio in it."

"Then you must remember the end?" Mick demands. "To get out of her marriage with Paris, Juliet takes a sleeping potion to make it seem like she's dead. Learning of her death, Romeo goes to Juliet's crypt, swallows the poison he's brought with him, and dies. Juliet wakes, sees her love lying there, tries to poison herself with the remains of Romeo's poison but there's not enough so she plunges a dagger into her heart."

"Really, is that what happened in the end?"

"How could you *not* know?" demands Dana.

"Maybe the ending in the film was different."

Mick shakes his head.

"Well, maybe I feel asleep then."

Mick may be fast acquiring friends at every turn since his move to Dublin but us lot have first dibs on him. It was Caroline who first met Mick, on the train back from Cork. There Caroline was, minding her own business, relaxing after a day of back-to-back high-powered meetings, when this giant of a man, this handsome if somewhat red-faced Corkman with a thatch of fair hair, squeezed into the seat beside her.

"Howrou?" he bellowed at her.

"Pardon?" asked Caroline wondering – as she says – if it *was* English this man was speaking.

"Howrou?" he bellowed again.

"Fine, thanks," replied Caroline, hazarding a guess at a likely answer. Then, out of the corner of her guarded Dublin eye, Caroline watched the red-faced giant settle himself on the seat beside her and, once settled, proceed to search through an enormous bag of clothes until he found what he was looking for. From amongst the underwear and socks he unearthed a sliced pan's worth of sandwiches repacked in the original baker's wrapper and a tartan-patterned flask big enough to quench the thirst of an entire parish, as Mick himself might have put it.

"Wouldoulikewanofmesangwiches?" asked the countryman, or so Caroline figured, seeing him nod towards the mound of unwrapped sandwiches now sitting on the little fold-up table in front of him.

"Well . . ." she hesitated, mindful of childhood warnings of sweets and strangers but these were sandwiches, not sweets, and very delicious-looking sandwiches they were too. "Well . . . if you're offering . . ." she reached out a greedy hand, "don't mind if I do."

"Mmm-mm-mmmm."

Together they munched contentedly.

"Would you like an udder?" invited Mick.

"Pardon?" spluttered Caroline. Sure, she'd heard of people – especially country people – eating all sorts: pigs' tongues, sheep's intestines. Her own dad – a countryman himself – was quite partial to drisheen and what was that only sheep's blood in the form of a thick, dark, and disgustingly smelly sausage.

But she'd never seen anyone eating cow's udders, and most certainly not on the 5.30pm City Gold service from Cork to Dublin.

"Go on," coaxed Mick nodding again towards the sandwiches. "Have an udder wan. There's plenty there. I'll never ate 'em all."

Steadily they worked their way through that mound of sandwiches. Caroline still swears they were the best she'd ever tasted.

After the sandwiches came the tea and, along with pouring out cup after cup, the countryman poured his heart out too. At first Caroline found it hard to know what he was saying with his up-and-down singsong accent but gradually her ear tuned in (so much so that she found herself responding in kind).

To make a long story short (most certainly made longer by Mick's rigmarole telling), Mick told Caroline that he'd been working in the family farm ever since leaving school but then, one day, his premature midlife crisis – for want of a better term – came to a head. All fired up, he marched straight into the kitchen where his mother and father were having a mid-morning cuppa and announced that, with his thirtieth birthday looming, life was too short to spend it working on their dream and he was off to pursue his own: to become an actor.

To his surprise his parents weren't quite as devastated as he'd expected they would be. If anything he thought they looked slightly relieved.

For some reason I always picture him leaving home with his belongings tied up in a spotty red handkerchief dangling from a stick, Dick Whittington style, but it wasn't quite like that. In fact a week later his mother and father drove him to the train station to wave him off to Dublin, all set with the brand new collection of luggage they'd bought for him, plus the sandwiches and flask, plus a nice cheque for a few grand to help him get on his feet.

By the time the train pulled into Dublin's Heuston Station, Caroline couldn't help feeling responsible for this countryman. Reluctant to let such a seemingly guileless soul off on his own to be chewed up by the big bad city, she – quite uncharacteristically – invited him to stay with us until he got sorted. He didn't stay long – after a few nights on the sofa, he found himself a little apartment on the top of a six-floor block overlooking the Liffey but we've all been friends with him ever since.

So, that's the story of Mick and how he came to be part of our lot.

"Does anyone want a drink at the bar?" I ask now.

They shake their heads

"I've just been," says Mick.

"Right."

Getting up, I can't help noticing the way Shane is holding Loretta's delicate little hand in his and for some reason I find it annoying. They're just so settled-looking, like some old married couple and suddenly I feel like holding up a placard and demanding the real Shane back. I don't, of course. It's not like I have a handy placard on my person. Instead, I head to the bar.

Ten minutes later, I struggle back through the crowds, place my drink on the table and sit down.

"So have you given him the elbow yet?" Shane asks once I'm seated.

"Who?" I ask crossly. I know exactly who he means, of course, but under the watchful eyes of the others – Caroline and Dana especially – I feign ignorance. I don't want to give them the satisfaction of being able to pass each other smug 'See, see, now weren't we right?' looks.

"Old blue eyes, the guy from Tony's party," Shane expands. "That architect?"

I think about pretending that everything is going swimmingly well. What business is it of his – of anybody's – anyway?

"Why should you think I've given him the elbow?" I demand.

Shane laughs.

"What's so funny?" I ask, then looking around I see his is not the only laughing face.

"Oh come on!" protests Shane. "You know what you're like. None of your boyfriends last long."

I throw Dana and Caroline dirty looks. "So you've all been talking about me then?"

"Actually, we haven't," Caroline snaps. "We've more interesting things to discuss."

"So where is he now? Weren't you meeting him for dinner earlier?" Mick asks. "How come you didn't bring him along?"

I shrug. "Maybe he had to go home."

"So you are seeing him again?" asks Shane.

I shrug again

"So you're *not* seeing him again?"

And I shrug again. I look around the table. They're all smirking.

"No! I'm not!" I snap. "All right? Satisfied now?"

Again they burst out laughing. And these are supposed to be my friends!

It's Shane who gets the ball rolling.

"So what was it this time? You didn't like the hair on his knuckles?"

He's referring to Paul, second boyfriend from last, lasted three weeks who, as it happens, did have the hairiest knuckles I've ever seen outside the confines of Dublin Zoo.

"Don't be stupid," I protest. "That's not why I broke up with Paul."

"That's what you said," pipes up Caroline.

I give her a withering look. I am *so* not friends with her right now. "Well, I was joking, all right?" And I was. It was easier to make a joke out of that whole mortifying episode of my life than to go into the real reason.

Sure, the knuckles weren't the most attractive I've ever seen on a man but the real problem was that this guy – and there's no kind way of putting this – was thick but it took me three weeks to figure that out even though all the others could see it straightaway – which I guess makes me pretty thick too, and I think that's the part I find so embarrassing.

At the start I was flattered to be with someone who seemed to find me so incredibly interesting. Whenever I talked, no matter what I said, he sat there nodding so earnestly, so vigorously, that I began to feel like Stephen Flaming Hawking. But hang on, even I knew I wasn't *that* interesting. So, what was going on? Would he keep nod-nodding away like one of those dogs with the loose heads that people have on their dashboards no matter what I said? No matter what nonsensical rubbish I came out with? I decided to see. "Imagine, Kylie Minogue has been made President of France!" I told him one night, just to see his response. And what was it? The usual nod, nod, nod. Okay. I tried another one: "And did you hear the Americans are going to start building the first satellite town on Mars this summer?" And again – nod, nod, nod.

Maybe I'm doing him an injustice; maybe he wasn't thick at all, just too polite to demand, "What idiotic nonsense are you talking about now?" Either way, there could be no future for us.

55

"Maybe it was because of the way he runs," Dana is now suggesting and of course I know exactly who she's referring to: Anton – three, maybe four boyfriends ago – lasted two months.

"Don't be stupid. I never broke up with anyone because of the way he runs."

"You did! You said Anton ran like a turkey."

"Well, he did, and it probably didn't help but there were other reasons too."

Because, in the end, I realised that he was most obnoxious guy ever born, without exception. At the start – fool that I was – I was bowled over by him. He was so confident, so successful, so incredibly rich but the problem was that I was little more to him than his new Lexus – just some *thing* to reflect his success to the world. Even now I can imagine him standing before the mirror thinking to himself: "I'm successful, I'm rich, and I'm pret-ty good-looking now that the second hair transplant has taken root. I *deserve* a fancy-piece hanging from my arm." Okay, maybe he never had transplants and he mightn't have used the word fancy-piece (Does anyone actually say fancy-piece? Is it even a real phrase?) but you get the picture. It is true however that, one day, when I turned up for a date he looked me up and down and announced that I "sure was candy for a sore eye", a slip of the tongue maybe but it said a lot about where he was coming from. I split up with him that same night.

Hearing myself being called Bubblehead was worse though, much worse – as much the circumstances as the word itself. I was in my last year in secondary school and I'd just started going out with a guy called Jude. Despite the name I really liked him and I thought he liked me too. There we were one night in my parents' house watching a video when his phone rang. As he went out to the hall to answer it, I pressed pause at the point where Thelma and Louise's car descends over the edge. As he chatted on, I sat there, all warm and glowy, kind of missing him already as I idly stared at the frozen close-up image of Geena Davis's mouth open wide enough to swallow a truck.

"Okay, okay," I heard him, "yeah, okay. I'll be leaving Bubblehead's as soon as the video is over. I'll see you then."

That he should call me Bubblehead was bad enough. That he didn't need to explain to his friend who Bubblehead was was even worse. I finished with him the next day. I was too mortified to tell anyone the real reason. When people asked why, I just gave them some flippant answer. It's easier that way.

I look around. They're still laughing – even Loretta. Okay, I know I go along with it usually but now I'm getting annoyed. I'm sick of them thinking it's okay to laugh at me and to make fun of my love life – that I won't mind.

"Give over!" I suddenly shout.

"Hey, come on," says Caroline. "We're only having a laugh."

"Well, go and have a laugh at someone else's expense."

"Why are you getting so upset?" asks Shane, bewildered by my reaction.

"Why shouldn't I? Why is it that all of you think it's okay to laugh at my private life? Do you think I have no feelings?" Apart from laughing along with the others, Loretta is the only one who hasn't said anything but she's the one who gets it first. "It's all right for you, Loretta, sitting there all cosied up to your boyfriend!"

She opens her mouth to protest but I don't give her a chance. I'm only warming up.

"As for you, Shane, I'm getting sick of you. You act like my life is something I play out to give you laughs. Well, it's not. And Mick, tell me, when was the last time you even asked a girl out? And you," I turn to Dana, "all you do is moan about not having a boyfriend and *you*," I'm pointing my finger at Caroline now, "isn't it about time you changed the record and stopped harping on about men and how they're all worms and frogs and all manner of wildlife and stopped going on and on about how there's no such thing as love? It's an easy cop-out."

Now that I've said my piece, I feel better and I sit back and take a sip from my drink.

I'm aware they're all staring at me, stunned by my reaction no doubt. Yes, taking the mickey out of me and my love life is just one of the things they do and, yes, normally, I'm quite happy to go along with it, just not tonight.

It's Caroline who speaks first. "Well, they *are* all worms, aren't they?"

Everyone – bar me – bursts out laughing.

Mick speaks next. "Never," he announces.

"Never, what?" demands Caroline.

"Rosie asked when was the last time I asked a girl out."

"And what are you saying?" Caroline's eyes widen as she realises just what it is he *is* saying. "No! You're telling us you've never asked a girl out?"

He nods.

"Never? In your entire life?" asks Caroline in disbelief.

Mick nods again but then, glancing around the table, he sees all the astonished faces gaping at him and his own habitually red face begins to redden further.

"I can't believe I just said that," he mumbles.

"Is it that you've never fancied anyone?" demands Caroline.

"No," he shakes his head. "No, it's not that."

"What is it then? I just don't get it! Are you shy?" Caroline demands. "Or gay? Or what?"

"I dunno. Yes. Maybe."

"What? Maybe you're gay?"

"No, no, maybe I'm shy – "

Caroline bursts out laughing. "You!"

"You know, when it comes to women," finishes Mick.

"But *we're* all women!" cries Caroline, waving a hand around the table.

"Excuse me," protests Shane but nobody pays him any heed.

"And you're not shy of us," persists Caroline.

"Yeah, but I know you. That's different. You're my friends."

Caroline is shaking her head. "I don't get it. How can you be shy? You're an actor for crying out loud!"

"I know, I know. But it's different. Going up on stage in front of hundreds of people is easier than going up to a woman and asking her out. By doing that, you're telling her so much, you're laying yourself wide open. You're setting yourself up for rejection."

Caroline looks like she's at a loss for words. "But you're an actor!" she repeats finally. "You've chosen a life of rejection!"

"It's not the same! And you're making it sound like I chose acting because I like rejection – I do hope to actually make a living from it some day."

Caroline is staring at him in total bewilderment but, before she gets a chance to say any more, there comes an interruption.

"Hi there."

We all look around. Some guy, a cute-looking guy I've never seen before, is standing by our table. He's got curly black hair, dark blue eyes and a great big smile on his face. My first impression of him is that he seems nice but not really my type. He's a little on the muscly side to start and he's small – I'd guess he's a couple of inches shorter than me.

"Finn!" Shane stands up, takes this stranger warmly by the

hand and with the other claps him on the back. "Everyone, this is Finn. He's the reason we're here tonight. Finn is the drummer with Dove. He set up the band. Finn, this is my girlfriend, Loretta, and my friends – Dana, Caroline, Rosie and Mick."

We nod in greeting and call out our hellos but he's come at a bad time. Caroline isn't finished with Mick just yet.

"You've never had a girlfriend?" she persists.

"Pardon?" asks the newcomer.

"No, no, not you! I'm asking *him*!" She points at Mick.

"Not really," Mick answers with a shrug.

"You've either had or you haven't? Which is it?"

"I guess I have to say I haven't then."

"At your age? I just don't get it!"

"I've met women at parties and that but I've never had, like, a serious girlfriend."

Caroline's shaking her head from side to side in disbelief.

"Look," says Mick, "I wish I'd never said anything. It's no big deal. Can we just drop it? You're making it sound worse than it is."

"How could I? God! You know, you should write in to that woman in the *Sunday Independent*, the one with the problem page."

"Maybe I did."

There's dead silence for a second. We all, Shane's friend included, stare at Mick.

Beetroot has nothing on him.

"What do you take me for?" Mick manages to gather himself sufficiently to give a unconvincingly dismissive laugh. "Of course, I didn't." We're all still staring. "I was kidding, right?"

"Right," says Shane.

"Of course," says Caroline.

But neither of them sound convinced.

"Listen, I'd better go," interrupts Finn. "We're on in a few minutes."

"Good luck!" says Shane. "Listen, we'll catch up later on, after you're through."

"Yeah," says Finn. "Anyway, thanks for coming, everyone. Hope you enjoy it."

The rest of us wish him good luck.

"Shush," says Shane. "They're starting."

The lights go down and the place is in near darkness except for the stage which is spotlighted. First on is Finn. He bounds on like a sprung coil, gives a massive wave to the crowd, then climbs up onto his stool behind a huge drum kit. He's kind of cute, sitting up there, grinning down at the crowd, and he has got the biggest, dirtiest, ear-to-ear grin ever.

Next come the two guitarists who take up their positions to the front of the stage and then, finally, the lead singer. I pause drinking, mid-sip. This man is truly gorgeous – a vision. He's like an identikit of all I want in a man. He's lean and tall and tanned, with long curly fair hair, perfect white teeth, and cheekbones any supermodel would die for.

"Hello, Dublin!" He calls out.

"What? I thought he *was* from Dublin!" Caroline shouts across the table.

"Tank youse all for coming here tonight!" he shouts.

Yep, he's from Dublin all right, no doubt about it.

But then, when he starts singing, his voice changes completely. It's deep, powerful, rough and without accent. The first song is a fast-paced rock number and, right from the start, the crowd love it. They follow it up with a few more pacey songs. I look around – nearly every head in the place is bobbing along to the music.

"What do you think?" Shane shouts.

"They're brilliant! He's brilliant!"

Now the tempo changes and the band slows right now. The next song is a soulful one. All the roughness is gone from the singer's voice as he sings of the awful emptiness of a day stretching out in front of him after having just been dumped by the woman he expected to share his life with. At times, his voice is barely a whisper. Holding the microphone right up to his mouth he tells of all their dreams she's taken with her: of the exotic places they'd planned to visit together, of the timber cottage they'd hoped to build overlooking the lake, of the children they'd dreamed of having. All these dreams he tells us, in the most heart-rending voice, are now replaced with bleak nothingness. Then, without the backing of his band, he ever so softly repeats the chorus one last time. When he finishes the room is in complete silence. He stands there, with his eyes shut. Everyone is utterly spellbound. I am utterly spellbound. I feel a lump rise in my throat.

It's the singer himself who breaks the mood.

"Thank youse all!" he shouts into the microphone. "Now we're going to take a break of fifteen minutes so stick around."

I turn to Shane. "They're amazing!"

"Aren't they?"

"So how do you know them?"

"Through Finn. I did some legal work for his old man. He has a chain of hardware stores and Finn works with him during the day."

And just as we're talking about him, Finn comes back over.

"Grab a stool and squeeze in there," Shane urges him. "You know, you were bloody brilliant!"

"You think?"

"Yeah, weren't they, Rosie?"

"Definitely."

"Thanks."

"Have you been together long?" I ask.

"For over a year now, but we've only started gigging in the last few months."

"So how did it all start?"

"Well, I've been drumming for years and I'd been with a few other bands but then I decided to put a band of my own together. Mark – that's our lead singer – is a great friend of mine, we go way back, and I knew he'd a fantastic voice, so I talked to him first, and he was really keen to give it a go. As for the other two lads, the two guitarists, the band they were in broke up so they were happy to join us when I asked them."

"I see." I'm trying to concentrate but I keep looking over Finn's shoulder, hoping to catch a sight of Mark, or hoping he'll catch a glimpse of me chatting to his mate and, maybe, come over. Then I spot him across the bar, talking to a couple of girls. They're obviously telling him how good he was. He looks so animated, so full of life and I fancy the pants off him.

Then I get the feeling someone is looking at me. I glance around. It's Shane. He's smirking. He winks suggestively in the direction of Mark and mouths something I don't catch but I can guess. Damn him. He knows me better than I know myself. I feel annoyed.

I give him a haughty look and turn my attention back to Finn.

"So have you any more gigs lined up?" I ask.

"A few. We've one next Friday, in another pub – The Stag. Anyway, I'd better go," he says, getting up. "We'll be going back on soon."

"Right, nice meeting you." I'm disappointed I didn't get to talk to Mark.

The second part of the gig is as good as the first and Mark is every bit as brilliant and it seems like no time at all that he's singing his last song, then wishing everyone goodnight.

As we're gathering up our coats, Finn comes over again.

"Will we see you all at our next gig?" he asks.

"You bet!" says Caroline.

"Next Friday, isn't it?" Shane asks.

"Yep."

"See you then so," I say.

6

"That old devil called lo♥e . . ."

"Do you really think Mick wrote into that problem-page woman in the *Sunday Independent*?" asks Caroline.

It was getting lonely being in a huff and a little pointless since the girls weren't taking much notice and, besides, I was beginning to feel I'd overreacted a little so I'd decided to go back on speaking terms with them again. Now, the three of us are in town having coffee.

"Dunno," I answer, not really registering her question. We're sitting on high stools by the window and I'm watching the crowds passing by on the street outside.

"I know you don't know, but I'm asking you, what do you *think*?" asks Caroline.

"What do I think about what?" I ask absent-mindedly.

"Oh, for crying out loud! Are you listening to a word? I'm asking you do you think Mick wrote into the problem page of the *Sunday Independent*?"

"How should I know?"

"What do *you* think, Dana?" demands Caroline.

Dana looks up from her newspaper. "Don't know," she shrugs. And couldn't care less, she might well have added for all the interest she shows.

"Do either of you ever remember reading a letter that could have been from him?" Caroline persists. "You know – lonely boy, moved to the city, outgoing personality but shy around women, never had a girlfriend, and what should he do?"

"Aren't they all kinda like that?" asks Dana.

"Hmm . . ." Caroline is thinking. She's not going to let this go.

"Why don't you go into the newspaper office some day and check out the back issues if it means that much to you?" I suggest jokingly.

"Now there's an idea!"

"No, no, no, no, no!" I immediately regret opening my mouth. "You can't do that!"

She shrugs. "Why not?"

"It's prying into his privacy," points out Dana.

"What privacy? Writing into a newspaper is hardly a private thing to do."

"But I don't think he meant to tell us about it – it sort of slipped out," says Dana "He'd die if he thought we went in and read what he wrote – *if* he did write anything."

"He need never know."

"It's just sneaky. And anyway, why are you so interested?" Dana asks.

"Why wouldn't I be? He's our friend and I just find the notion of him never having had a girlfriend weird. Like, when he says he never had a girlfriend, what do you think he means – exactly?"

We both look at her blankly.

"Do you think he never slept with a girl or – or – or even kissed one? God! That would be just . . ." she searches for the right word, ". . . tragic."

"He didn't say that."

"But I wonder. Like, if he was living at home with his parents in the middle of nowhere, then it's not like he'd have had that many opportunities."

"There are girls in the country too," I point out. "And towns, with nightclubs and pubs. It's not like he never saw a girl before coming to Dublin."

"Why are we *still* talking about Mick?" Dana asks. "Do you fancy him, Caroline? Is that it?"

"No! Of course not! Don't be ridiculous!"

Dana looks at her keenly. "I think you do."

"I *so* do not!" Caroline repeats adamantly.

"All right, if you say so."

We lapse into silence. I go back to staring out at the passers-by. Dana goes back to her newspaper. Caroline goes back to her thoughts.

"Like, why would I?" she suddenly bursts out. "What is there to fancy? Yes, he's funny and he's generous and he's great company and he's good-looking – "

"Good-looking? Do you think?" I interrupt.

"Yeah. Don't you?"

"I never thought about it. He's a bit . . . I don't know . . . burly, isn't he?"

"Of course, he's burly. What do you expect? He did work on a farm for years."

"I guess. That would account for his high complexion too."

"What do you mean 'high complexion'?"

"Well, he's a bit red-faced, isn't he? Like he's just come in from the cold, having herded the cows back up the field after milking."

Caroline throws her eyes to heaven. "I swear, Rosie, nobody could please you! If Tom Cruise were to wander in here right now, sit down beside you and declare his love for you, you'd probably start picking faults with him."

"No, I wouldn't. Tom Cruise is a fine thing," I tell her. "Except . . ."

"Except what?"

"Except for his feet."

"His *feet*?" Caroline explodes. "What on earth is wrong with his feet?"

"Well, they're a little on the dainty side, aren't they? You know, for a man?"

"See! See!" she explodes. "Nobody could please you."

"How did we get on to the subject of Tom Cruise?" I ask. "What was it we were talking about?"

"Caroline was telling us why she doesn't fancy Mick," Dana reminds us. "Even though she thinks he's generous, great company, fun and good-looking."

"Yeah," says Caroline. "And he is all of those things but none of them count when you weigh them up against the disadvantages."

"Which are?" I ask.

"That he's thirty and doesn't have a job but instead he's chasing some wild dream at this late stage of his life. If you ask me, anyone foolish enough to be interested in Mick would have a dreadful life, a life of abject poverty and complete uncertainty."

She pauses and Dana and I look to one another, wondering if she's finished or if there's more to come. There is.

"Like, what's the good in being generous if you don't have anything to be generous with? And good-looking and funny only go so far. They wouldn't be much comfort in some dingy, slummy, grimy-windowed, dark, dank little home too small to swing a cat in, let along a couple of children. Interested in him? No way!"

"You seem to have given the matter a lot of thought," observes Dana.

"No, I haven't! I'm just answering your question. Now can we finish this conversation? Who wants another coffee?" she asks, getting up.

Minutes later, she comes back down with three fresh coffees and we sip in silence and I'm staring out the window again. Town is jointed. Then something strikes me about all the couples I see filing past the window, how nearly all of them seem to match. Short men pass by hand-in-hand with short women, tall men with tall women, good-looking with good-looking, even bespectacled with bespectacled. And it's the same when it comes to race: white with white, Asian with Asian, and so on and on. I do notice some exceptions but they're rare enough to prove the rule and it strikes me that if love truly is this random thing, this overwhelming force that we're led to believe, then I can't help thinking it odd that it so often happens between similar-looking people. I think about mentioning as much to the girls but decide not to. I don't fancy another tirade from Caroline and there's no knowing what will spark her off.

"And what," Caroline suddenly pipes up, "if he did get involved with someone? And the whole acting thing didn't work out for him? What then? When he's heading back down to Bogland to spend the rest of his days milking cows and living in some half-derelict old farmhouse with his ageing parents, would he expect the poor girl who's had the misfortune to fall in love with him to go trotting after him?"

"Oh, for crying out loud!" Dana begins folding up her newspaper crossly. "We're not going to get any peace with you jabbering on and on about Mick. I'm going shopping."

7

"Lo♥e the one you're with . . ."

It's Monday and I'm back at work. Monica rang in sick, her back's been giving her trouble and her doctor advised her to take a few days' rest. It's funny how dead the place is without her and her near-constant chatter about her troubled sons. It's just me and Fay, and Fay doesn't do chitchat — *really* doesn't do chitchat. It's only now with Monica out of the mix that I begin to notice how very quiet Fay is as she goes about her work. She just hums gently to herself and gets on with things with the minimum of fuss, which is fine but it doesn't exactly help make the day fly by.

In fact it drags. It is desperately, desperately quiet. I feel like going out onto the street and begging passers-by to "please, please step inside," but don't. Instead, I try to think of things to say to Fay to pass the time but it's hard going.

"Did you go anywhere nice at the weekend?" I find myself asking.

"Not especially." Fay looks up and smiles but carries on with her task in hand — dressing one of the window dummies.

"So it was quiet then?"

"Yes, quietish."

"I see."

Pause.

"I went to see this new band," I tell her, for want of something to say.

"Really?"

Pause.

"Yeah, really."

The thing about Fay's quietness is that there's nothing rude about it; it's just the way she is – very pleasant, but also very quiet. Unlike the rest of us, or me at any rate, she has no compulsion to jabber aimlessly for fear of silence. So now I begin telling her about the gig, how the band had been set up by this drummer guy called Finn, how there's two guitarists and a singer called Mark who's really brilliant and gorgeous, how the crowd loved them, how they're playing again on Friday, and how I'm definitely going to go and see them. And all the time I can see she's really not that interested even though she's listening politely but I keep rambling on regardless.

But then my phone beeps and I break off. It's a text message from my mum.

I'm coming 2 town 2 do some holiday shopping. R you @ work?

I text back: *Yes.*

Beep-beep! Another text from Mum.

I'll call in 2 c u.

Do.

Beep-beep!

C u so. B there in 10 min.

Great.

Beep-beep!

R maybe 20, the traffic is v heavy – barely moving.

Okay.

Beep-beep!

CU then so.

Okay.

I wait for her next beep-beep but none comes and I put my phone down. "That was my mum," I tell Fay. "Just telling me she's coming into town and that she might pop in."

Fay smiles and nods but says nothing. Then the front door opens. It's a customer. Thank God! I practically bound over to her, so pleased am I at the distraction but the woman tells me she's 'just looking' and doesn't need my help. I go back to the counter and look around for something to do, for something that needs tidying, but everything's in order and I stand there, drumming my fingers and humming that song Mark and his band played at their gig – about the long day stretching out and, even though I haven't just been dumped by the love of my life, I too am beginning to feel this day is truly interminable.

Then my phone beeps again. It's Mum again.

Just looking for a parking space now.

I don't bother replying. What's there to say? Except that she'd be better served keeping her eyes on the road even if the traffic is crawling. And even if I had been going to, she doesn't give me much time; already my phone is beeping again.

Can't find a parking space anywhere.

I think about texting her back to tell her that if she wasn't so busy texting, she might stand a better chance of finding a space but I don't get a chance.

Another beep-beep.

Town is crazy!!!! Where are all these people coming from???

Not for the first time I begin to regret my decision to buy her the phone as a birthday present. Little could I have known she'd become the addict she has.

Another beep-beep.

Parked & on my way.

Two minutes later, another beep-beep.

Nearly there.

Almost immediately the door is flung open and my mother — a smiley-faced, fluffy-haired, round ball of a woman, almost as fat as she is tall — comes sweeping in accompanied by the familiar musky smell of her favourite perfume. I see she's dressed in her serious shopping clothes — trainers and a purple velvety leisure suit. She's carrying an oversized handbag in one hand and her phone in the other. And she's *still* texting.

"Mum, Mum! Hello! There's no need to text me to tell me you're here. I can see you."

"Don't be silly. I'm just telling Geraldine I'm meeting you." She gives Fay a wave. "Hello there, Fay!" she calls out.

"Hello, Mrs Kiely."

"It's Nora! Don't mind your Mrs Kiely."

"But why?" I demand to know.

"Why what, love?" she asks, looking at me puzzled.

"Why are you texting Geraldine to tell her you're meeting me?"

She looks at me like my question is just about the stupidest thing she's ever heard.

"Because she doesn't know."

"But why does she need to know?"

"God! Rosie! She doesn't *need* to know. I'm just . . . chatting."

I don't know why I simply don't let it go but I'm in that kind of mood.

"You're texting not chatting. There's a difference, or there should be. There's no law to say that just because you've a mobile phone on you, you have to be on it all the time."

"Well!" My mother throws her eyes up to heaven. "It seems *someone* got out of the wrong side of the bed this morning, eh, Fay?"

"There *is* only one side to get out on," I snap. "My bed's up against the wall." I don't know what it is about my mother but I always seem to end up acting like a petulant teenager around her.

"So what has you in such a bad mood then, hmmm?" she asks in a very annoying tone.

"I'm not in a bad mood. I'm fine," I snap.

"No, you're not. You're in a dreadful mood."

"I'm not or I wasn't although the one sure way of putting someone in a bad mood is to point out to them that they're in one."

She sighs wearily. "I was going to ask you to come to lunch before I head off to the other side of the world but maybe I'd be better off going on my own even if I won't get to see my youngest daughter for four whole weeks," says my mother, the martyr.

"Mum, I'd love to come to lunch. You know I would."

"All right then." She turns to Fay. "Fay, is it okay with you if I take this young lady to lunch?"

I cringe. Young lady? Why does my mother have to say things like that?

"Of course," answers Fay.

"I hope she isn't causing you too much trouble," says Mum conspiratorially.

"Mum! Fay's my colleague, not my baby-sitter!" I snap, then grumpily head to the store room to grab my coat.

When I arrive back out my Mum is giving Fay the first degree.

"So you never went to Baggot Street Commercial

College?" she's asking, referring to her own alma mater.

"No, never."

"Maybe you were friendly with some of the students there?"

Fay shakes her head. "No."

"That can't be it so. Hmm . . . let me see . . . you say you're living in Rathgar . . . you don't know Jack and Mary Molin by any chance?"

"No, no, I don't think so."

"So you won't have been to any of their parties then?"

Fay shakes her head.

"Just as well, awful affairs. But you definitely look familiar. Like I said to Rosie the last time, I'm positive I've met you before, maybe way back. I never forget a face – hopeless with names, but great with faces."

Fay gives a smile and shrugs.

"Mum! You're embarrassing Fay. Can't we just get going, please?"

"Of course, of course." She smiles at Fay. "Anyway, Fay, lovely to meet you again and I'll be racking my brains until the next time."

My mother links my arm in hers.

"Isn't this the life?" she says as we walk down Grafton Street. Irrespective of how busy the footpath is, my mother always walks in a dead straight line leaving it up those coming in the opposite direction to manoeuvre their way around her. "You know, I'm beginning to think your dad and I should have retired years ago."

For thirty years the pair of them ran the garden centre they'd built up from a little shed to a big business. But this year, having finally come to accept the fact that none of their four children had the slightest interest in taking over their empire, they've sold it in order to enjoy an early retirement. And they've big plans for their golden years (as Dad insists on calling them much to Mum's annoyance) starting with a trip to Australia to see my sister who's living there. They're leaving on Wednesday.

I'll miss my mum when she's gone. Growing up, she was always so busy running the garden centre and raising all of us but, now, with my brothers and sister scattered around the globe and with more freedom since selling up, she and I have had more time together than ever.

We arrive at the restaurant.

"This way, ladies," says the waiter weaving his way through the tables. We follow after him – Mum first, then me – and she's chatting back to me at the top of her voice, unaware that all the other diners in the place are turning to see just who is this terribly loud woman.

"Isn't this lovely! A real treat. You know, I could never understand how so many people seemed to be free during the week when we were running the garden centre but now, look at me," she booms, totally oblivious to the fact that everyone is doing just that – looking at her, "I'm one of them. Here's me out to lunch and your dad's out golfing." As she squeezes her bulk between the backs of two chairs much to the annoyance of their discommoded occupants, she carries on chatting and I follow behind her. "You know I was worried when we decided to sell. I was afraid we'd drive each other crazy but we've never got on better."

It's true. Growing up, they seemed to be always squabbling – the pressure of the business, I guess. Things were especially fraught between them when I was in my early teens. They'd carried out a massive expansion around that time and it seemed as if they were forever worrying about how they'd make the repayments.

"Ladies, your table," says the waiter, showing us our table, right at the back, in a gloomy dark corner, beside the kitchen. So of course I'm about to start complaining but it's Mum who speaks first.

"Lovely, just lovely."

We sit down and take the menus from the waiter. Moments later Mum looks up from hers.

"Maybe we should order a couple of glasses of wine. What do you think?"

I hesitate. "I'm going to have to go back to work. And you're driving."

"Oh come on, a glass won't do any harm."

Wine-drinking during the day is a new thing with my mother, something she's taken to since retirement as part of her whole enjoying-life-while-she-can philosophy, as if she's going to pop her clogs at any minute. Now, without waiting for my answer, she beckons the waiter over.

"Tony," she begins, (she's the only person I know who actually listens when the waiter introduces himself), "can you recommend one of your house wines?"

"Were you thinking of red or white, madam?" he asks.

"White, something sparkling. I'll leave it up to you." She puts her head slightly to one side and gives him a coquettish smile. "I've no doubt you'll choose something nice," she tells him.

Tough businesswoman she may be, women's libber my mother most certainly isn't. In fact she's a truly outrageous flirt but a very manipulative one. While sisters may be doing it for themselves, my mother doesn't understand why on earth they'd want to bother when they can get a nice man to do it for them. And the truth is, she can get men to do anything for her. Except maybe my dad.

"So a glass each for me and my daughter," she tells the waiter but of course she can't leave it at that. "We're having a special lunch before I head off on the trip of a lifetime to see my other daughter and her family in Australia."

That's another thing my mother always does – tells people working in shops and in restaurants all about her business, as if they'd be interested.

"Has she been living there long?" asks the waiter.

"Almost eight years. She's married to an Australian. They live in Melbourne."

"Really? I have a brother in Melbourne."

"You don't say!"

"Yes, he's been there for a couple of years now. He keeps saying he's going to come home one day but I think he's far too settled. He's working in this . . ."

And as he pours out his brother's life story to my mum, I sit there, shuffling in my seat, wondering if he's ever going to get around to serving us, or if I'll be going back to work hungry.

Finally, he remembers what he's meant to be doing.

"I'll get your wine. We have a lovely house white, a 2004 Sauvignon Blanc from –"

"Perfect," says Mum. "Just perfect.".

He heads off.

"What a nice man," she says, as she sits back into her chair. She looks around. "Now, isn't this the life?"

She's looking very well, I notice, relaxed and younger than she's seemed for years; her fluffy golden hair is even fluffier and more golden that usual.

"I see you've been to the hairdresser's," I remark.

"Yes," she answers, and pats the back of hair. "I got it

done this morning, for the holiday."

"It suits you. You're looking very well, Mum."

"Why, thank you, Rosie. What a nice thing to say."

"You look – I don't know – very happy."

"And why wouldn't I? Life is good. My children and grandchildren are all well and healthy, with the garden centre off our hands your dad and I have no financial worries and our time is all our own and, on Wednesday, we're off to Australia."

The waiter arrives down with our two glasses of wine.

"Are you ready to order?" he asks.

"Well, let me see," begins my Mum. "I'll have the home-made vegetable soup to start, with some bread, of course. And then . . . hmmm . . . it all looks so lovely . . . I think I'll have the 10oz fillet – medium rare – with vegetables and a baked potato. Actually, no, I'll have the chips. In fact, I'll have the chips and the baked potato, if that's okay and . . . hmm . . . a side order of deep fried onion rings."

Then it's my turn.

"I'll just have the chicken stir fry for main course."

I go to hand the waiter back the menu but notice my mother is staring.

"What?" I demand.

"No starter?"

"I'm not all that hungry."

"No wonder there isn't a pick on you. You need to look after yourself."

"How? By ordering a starter, and a main course with chips *and* potatoes *and* onion rings?"

She ignores me. "So, tell me," she begins now the waiter's gone, "how are things with you?"

"So–so."

"Any romance?"

I groan. "Oh please!"

"What about that nice American you were seeing?"

"That was ages ago and, like I told you before, he's gone back to America."

"Pity. And how's Shane?"

"Fine."

I know exactly where this is heading.

"A lovely boy."

"Boy? He's twenty-three!"

"And how's he getting on at work?"

"Fine, as far as I know."

"You know you could do worse."

"Mum! He has a girlfriend. He's been going out with her for months now."

"That's a pity but maybe it's not serious. I wouldn't give up on him yet."

"We're just friends."

"Friends? So you say."

"Well, we are."

"I'm not sure I hold with the theory that men and women can ever be just friends."

"Whatever." I've heard it all before.

"And tell me, are you still sending out CV's? You'd want to find yourself a job before the next crop of graduates come out."

"I *have* a job!"

"Yes, but you're not exactly using your qualifications."

"Mum, I'm *never* going to use my qualifications."

"Don't say that."

"It's true.

"It seems like an awful waste."

"The waste was doing my degree in the first place."

"You don't mean that."

"I do, you should never have made me do it."

"Oh, so it's my fault now, is it?"

"No, I don't mean that. Look, I'm still young. I've all the time in the world to figure out what I want to do."

"Young? You're twenty-four now and –"

"Twenty-three. I'm twenty-three."

"Twenty-three, twenty-four, either way you're no spring chicken."

"If I'm no spring chicken, then what does that make you?"

She ignores me. "You'd want to be thinking seriously about the future."

"Oh God, I can't be doing with this."

Before she retired, before all my brothers and my sister went away, I sort of snuck under the radar and I think I preferred it that way.

"When I was your age I was married with a baby and another one on the way."

"Are you saying that's what you want for me?"

"No, no, I'm just saying that –"

"Is this your idea of a nice lunch out? It's beginning to feel more like an interrogation."

"I can't help worrying about you, Rosie."

"Well, don't. Just concentrate on your holiday and leave my life to me."

She takes another sip then resumes her onslaught. "You see, the thing about you, Rosie, is that you're too picky."

"Is that right?"

"Especially when it comes to boyfriends."

"Do you want to me to settle for the first man who comes along? Is that it?"

"No, but you could spend your whole life waiting for Mr Perfect."

"And so what if I do? Wouldn't it be better that settling for Mr-I-guess-he'll-do-in-the-absence-of-someone-better?"

"I'm not so sure. If you ask me, there's far too much talk about love these days. Take your dad and me."

"What about you?"

"I can tell you now that there were no bells ringing or cupids flying or violins playing when he and I got together but, you know, he was decent, I liked him, my parents liked him, or at least my father did, and they were happy when we decided to marry."

"How depressing! You make it sound like an arranged marriage."

"It wasn't. But maybe there are worse things. It's all about compatibility."

"Compatibility? Then how come you two used to fight so much?"

"That was just our way of getting along."

"But you *didn't* get along. You fought all the time. I love my dad and all, but don't you think that maybe you settled for the wrong man. Don't you think you should have waited for the love of your life?"

"God, Rosie! They were different times. Your father is cantankerous, set in his ways and he has a short temper but you know, he's a good, kind man, he's been a good provider, a good father to you and your brothers and sister and a good husband to me."

"A good provider! You did most of the work in the garden centre!"

"Now that's not fair."

"But it's true."

"We're a good team and that's what's important. As I say, we're compatible."

"Compatible. That's it? You make it all sound so dreary!"

"Well, excuse me, I don't mean to."

"But don't you think you missed out?"

"Missed out on what exactly? Look at you – your head is so full of nonsense you're never going to be happy. You're forever picking fault with perfectly decent men and you let the likes of poor Shane slip through your fingers –"

"Slip through my fingers?" I interrupt. "What is he? A fish?"

She ignores me. "And you know what'll happen to you?"

"Oh please!"

"You'll end up with no one, that's what."

"Please, Mum, can't you give it a rest? Why don't you tell me about your holiday instead? Have you decided on an itinerary?"

"Well," and she's off, "as you know, we're flying into Melbourne and Sarah will meet us at the airport and we're going to spend the first week with her – just getting to know the boys and catching up. Then Sarah and Rod are taking us on a trip down the Great Ocean Road. After that we're going to fly to Perth and . . ."

As we carry on eating our meal she does most of the talking.

"Of course your dad is worried he'll die from the heat but Sarah says that all the houses and hotels and cars have air-conditioning and we won't notice it too much. He's worried too about the food but according to Sarah it's not that much different to what you get at home." She pauses and looks around for the waiter. "Will we order dessert?"

"I'd better not," I say. "I should be heading back to work. Fay will be wondering what's happened to me."

"I guess I should be going too. I've a lot of shopping I need to get done before the trip."

"We've got couple of new lines in the boutique. Why

don't you have a look?"

"Ah no, Rosie. Sure, that shop is for old women."

I haven't the heart to point out to her that, at sixty, she's exactly who the boutique is aimed at.

After paying the bill, we leave the restaurant and head back in the direction of the boutique.

"You know, I'm sure I know her from somewhere."

"Who?"

"Tell me, is she married?"

"Who?"

"I'll be driven mad trying to place her."

"Who?" I demand again. "Who *are* you talking about? I'm not telepathic, you know."

"Fay. Do you know if she's married?"

"Not as far as I know."

We reach the boutique.

"Well," I say, "if I don't see you again before you head off have a brilliant time and be sure to give Sarah and the family my love."

"Of course, I will," she says. "Come here," she commands and, being a head taller than her, I bend down and she gives me a great big bear hug. "Take care of yourself now, love," she whispers.

"I will. I'll miss you." I kiss the top of her soft fluffy hair.

"Send me a postcard!" I shout out as I watch her carrying on down the street, those coming against her moving this way and that to avoid her.

"I will!" she shouts back, then adds, "If I have time," and gives a happy little laugh.

8

·

"When I fall in lo♥e, it will be forever . . ."

I'm not back in the shop ten minutes when I get a text from Mum — so much for our goodbyes.

Ask Fay did she ever work in Haughton and Knowles — the solicitors."

She's gone to get a sandwich.

Ask her when she comes back.

Why?

Just ask her.

No.

Then the phone rings — it's Mum, of course.

"I thought you were gone to Australia," I say crossly.

But she's too excited to take any notice: "I remembered how I know Fay. It came back to me."

"Really?"

"Yes. After I finished at Baggott Street Commercial College I went to work for Haughton and Knowles as a secretary, before I married your dad."

"So?"

"Well, the reason I got the job was because one of the

86

junior solicitors, Anthony Knowles, a nephew of Christopher Knowles who was a partner in the firm, ran off with my predecessor – she was called Fay and I'm almost sure it was your Fay."

"Really?" Now I'm interested, if a little confused. "But how could you know what she looked like, the Fay who ran off, if she was gone by the time you started working there?"

"Because I remember bumping into her later a couple of times with Mary O'Donnell. You remember Mary? She worked with me at Haughton and Knowles. We were great friends. I don't see much of her now but one time Mary and I were inseparable, but then she married Bobby Walshe who was at least twenty stone back then so heaven only knows what size he is now. Anyway they went to live in Wexford where they opened a –"

"Mum, Mum!" Time to reel her in, otherwise she'll go on all day. "It's Fay you're meant to be telling me about."

"Yes, well, like I said, she – Fay, that is – and Christopher Knowles' nephew ran off together to London. It seems they'd been carrying on for a while and everyone guessed as much but not for one moment did they imagine he'd leave his wife and young family but he did. He left his job and his home and his family and set up house with Fay in London which was unthinkable back then. Nowadays that sort of thing happens every day of the week but in those days it was considered a terrible scandal."

I'm still confused. "But if they ran away to London, how come you used to bump into her during your lunch break?"

"If you don't keep interrupting then I'll tell you. They did run away to London but things didn't go well for the pair of them over there. Fay had a little baby girl but the poor little thing died and, soon after, he left her and came back to his family and back to work. Fay didn't stay in England long after – I suppose there was nothing left for her there. It would have been after she came back that I'd have met her with Mary when we were on our lunch breaks. I remember feeling very sorry for her whenever we bumped into her. Mary used to tell me what a beauty she'd been but the Fay we used to see around was a very different woman: a bit down at heel and always a little distracted. Mary used to say the poor thing suffered from her nerves."

"And you think this was our Fay?"

"I'm sure of it."

The door of the shop opens: it's Fay. She smiles at me and goes to the stockroom to put her coat away.

"Mum, I have to go."

"*You* have to go? You mean *I* have to. I have a hundred thing to do, I can't be wasting time like this, chatting. But listen, just ask Fay did she ever work for Haughton and Knowles."

"I will not!" Fay's come back from the stockroom. "Mum, I really have to go, all right, I'll talk to you soon."

"Just ask her."

"No!"

"Rosie! Rosie!" She's calling into the phone but I hang up.

The afternoon is almost as quiet as the morning and every now and then I find myself looking over at Fay, wondering about her.

It occurs to me that she must have been very good-looking, the kind of woman who'd have drawn more than her fair share of admirers in her day, including this junior solicitor it seems. Even now she is very striking but there is also, I think looking at her now, something a little sad about her. If what my mum says is true, then that would account for that. People are always saying time is a great healer but maybe there are some things even it can never fully heal, like losing a baby and the man you love.

She gives me a funny look.

"Is something the matter, Rosie?" she asks.

I realise I'm staring. Someone less polite would probably have demanded to know what I'm staring at.

"No, no, I'm sorry, I was just daydreaming."

I want to ask her if she was in love with this solicitor fellow, if she lived with him, had his baby, if that baby died, if he then went back to his wife? I want to ask her all these questions but I don't.

How can I? I've never shown much interest in her private life before. To start now with: "So tell me, Fay, is it true that you ran off to London with your boss's nephew and that he then deserted you after your baby died?" would probably be a bit much.

9

"She's in lo♥e with the boy . . ."

"Hi everyone!" shouts Mick, letting himself into the apartment. "Tonight's the night! Are you lot ready? Come on, come on! You don't want to miss the chance to see me outshining Colin Farrell, do you?"

Everyone – that's me, Dana, Caroline and Shane – are in the kitchen, all in the middle of eating. It's seldom we're all here at the one time and the place is like a bomb hit it – there are dirty dishes and pots everywhere. Of course it would be far more sensible for each of us to take turns cooking for everyone else but, so far, we've just not been that organised. What am I am saying? "So far" – like we will be one day?

I notice Mick is looking very well. He's wearing a classy dark suit and has managed to put some control to his unruly mop of hair. The reason he's here now is because we're all off to see him in his first speaking role in a 'major motion picture' as he puts it. This is a big deal for Mick. On the couple of other occasions he's been in front of the camera as an extra in the soap opera *Fair City* he's been mute. But now, he actually has a real role, a very small role admittedly but a speaking one, in a big-budget Irish-American movie filmed just after he first arrived in Dublin but only now released.

No wonder he's looking so excited, if a little anxious. He's clearly keen to get going but none of us makes a move – we're not quite finished eating yet and we do have plenty of time.

"Mick?" begins Caroline between mouthfuls of pizza.

"Yeah?"

"Given that you were in the film – ah – how come you weren't invited to the première? How come you had to wait until it came out on general release?"

I notice the grin on Mick's face slips but Caroline ploughs on obliviously. Trust her to ask the question we've all been wondering about, but didn't like to ask.

"What I mean is, how come you had to wait to go and see it along with everyone else?"

"Look," begins Mick, sounding somewhat annoyed, "the whole point of a film première is to promote a film, to sell it to an influential audience not to the actors. Our work is done. If" he carries on defensively, "every single person involved in the making of the film were to be invited then there wouldn't be room for guests, for the people who are important now – you know, the critics and distributors and other film types. They're the people who matter at this stage."

"So none of the cast got to go to the première?" asks Caroline.

"The stars, obviously. But not the whole cast."

"I see but –"

"But what?"

"Nothing. It's just that, well, isn't that a little disappointing?"

"Disappointing, how?" snaps Mick. "I've a speaking part in a major motion picture – how can that be disappointing?

So what if I didn't get to go to the première?"

"Of course," Caroline goes on. "It's just that –"

"There'll be other premières," interrupts Mick. "Mark my words, one day I'll be walking down the red carpet – Angelina Jolie on the one arm, Hilary Swank on the other. This is just the start. So now, are you lot coming or am I going on my own?"

Despite his brave words he sounds really annoyed and I notice Caroline has the good grace to look like she regrets ever opening her mouth.

I put my plate in the sink and go to get my coat. The others too begin to get ready. But then, just as we're about to head out, Caroline pipes up:

"Just a moment," she tells Mick. "Rosie, Dana, come with me!" she says, beckoning us over.

"Ah, Caroline, no!" Mick cries. "We'll be late." He glares over at Dana and myself. "Don't you dare go with her!"

"Relax, Mick. We won't be a sec," Caroline promises and, grabbing both Dana and me by the hand, she ignores our protests and drags us across the landing and into her room.

There, she begins pulling bits and pieces out of her drawers.

"Right! Here, you wear this," she says to me, handing me a pink feather boa.

"This ridiculous-looking thing? Why would I want to do that?"

She ignores me. "Here, Dana, this is for you – now put it on!"

She throws over a gaudy silver scarf with tassels and Dana catches it, then holds it up by the tip of her fingers and stares at it disdainfully.

"What on earth do I want with this?" she demands.

"Hush! Just put it on," orders Caroline and goes on poking in her drawers until she finds what she's looking for. "And this will do me just fine," she says, pulling out a purple crocheted shawl. She drapes it around her shoulders. "See? It pays not to throw things out. Now, let's see."

She catches us both by the hand and pulls us over to the mirror, then studies our reflections.

"I look completely ridiculous!" grumbles Dana, frowning at herself.

"You wouldn't if you took that scowl off your face," Caroline tells her. "Hmm . . . But we do need something more to glam us up."

She picks up her make-up bag where it's thrown on the bed and begins rooting through it, then pulls out a stick of bright red lipstick and some baby-blue eye shadow.

"You first," she says to Dana and Dana begins to protest but Caroline is having none of it. "Hurry on, or I'll do it for you," she threatens.

"Caroline, what *is* all this about?" I demand but she ignores me.

"Come on, come on! Mick's waiting! You next," she commands.

"Did you ever think about a career in the army?" I mutter.

"Come on, hurry now!"

"Yes, sir!"

"And here –" she throws me an eyebrow pencil "– give yourself a couple of beauty spots while you're at it."

She puts some – a lot – of lipstick on herself and then, seeing I haven't got very far, she grabs the pencil from me and draws in a beauty spot the size of a one-cent coin at the corner of my eye. Then she gives herself a couple.

That done, she studies Dana and me and is not at all happy with the modest amounts of make-up we've put on, so she takes the task in hand, ignoring our squirms and protests. Me first. Then Dana.

"There!"

"What are we meant to be?" asks Dana, staring at her face in the mirror. "The ugly sisters?"

"Nonsense!" Caroline is making kissing faces at her own reflection. "Perfect! If I do say so myself. Now all we need is something for the boys." She flings open her wardrobe. "A hat, we need a hat. Ah-ha!" She spots what she's looking for. "Here – give me a leg-up, Dana." Reluctantly Dana obeys and from the top shelf Caroline pulls out a black gangster hat she wore a couple of months ago for a fancy dress. "This will do for Shane." She hops down. "That leaves Mick. We need something special for him." She thinks for a moment, looking about as she does. "I know!" She rushes over to the top drawer of her dressing table and pulls out a pair of star-shaped shades. "Perfect!"

Reluctantly I, in my pink boa, and Dana, in her gaudy silver scarf, follow after an exuberant Caroline who's wearing that purple shawl as proudly as if it were a velvet ermine-trimmed royal cloak. All she's missing is the crown. We arrive back into the living room. The two boys stare.

"Please, just *don't* laugh," pleads Dana.

"What's all this about?" Shane asks, looking from one of us to the other.

"I wish we knew," grumbles Dana.

"Here, take this," Caroline orders, handing him the hat. "And Mick, these are for you." She gives him the shades.

"I don't understand," begins Mick. "Why are –"

"Look, this mightn't be *the* première but it is *your* première," Caroline tells him. "So it's only fitting we should dress for the occasion."

We all look to Mick to see his reaction. He's standing

there staring at Caroline.

"I – I –" he begins.

"Oh God! You're mad at me, aren't you?" cries Caroline. "You think the whole idea is stupid!"

"No, I . . ." I notice he's blinking a lot and it suddenly occurs to me that he's close to tears but, just as I'm thinking how I simply can't bear to witness such an excruciatingly embarrassing moment, he puts on his shades.

"How do I look, *dahling*?" he asks.

We all burst out laughing, as much out of relief as anything.

"Perfect," Caroline laughs. "Right, let's go," she commands.

Back in her stride again, she begins ushering us all out but when we're in the hallway, she turns and orders us to "Stay there, for a second," and then disappears into the kitchen.

"Oh, *come on*!" mutters Mick. "What's she doing *now*? We're going to miss the start," he frets.

Moments later, Caroline reappears with a bag slung over her shoulder and a delighted grin on her face.

"What's in the bag?" asks Dana.

"Sssh!" Caroline puts her finger to her lips. "You'll see. Now, come on, come on, or we'll be late." She gives Mick a push to get him going but he stumbles.

"Hell!" he mutters and puts his hand up to his star-shaped shades. "How am I supposed to see where I'm going with these bloody things?"

"You don't need to see," Caroline tells him. "Just hold on to me."

So, with Mick holding onto Caroline and the rest of us trailing after the pair of them, we make our way out of the house and out on to the street.

"Can't we go in one of the cars?" asks Dana.

"No, we'll get a bus, or flag a taxi," says Caroline.

"But why, when there are two cars just sitting there?"

I know what Dana's thinking because I'm thinking the same — she's worried she might bump into someone she knows.

"No, no, taking a car into town would only be a hindrance," says Caroline. "Have you ever heard of anyone going straight home after a première? No, I'm thinking of Dawson Street first — do some high-class pub crawling and then over to Reynard's afterwards — find ourselves a nice little corner in the VIP section where we'll drink champagne and dance until dawn, or at least until they kick us out. What do you think, Mick?"

"Sounds good to me — if we get in."

"Are we really likely to — looking like this?" asks Dana doubtfully.

"Course we'll get in," insists Caroline. "Aren't we with one of the hottest up-and-coming Irish actors who just happens to be currently starring in a film alongside Colin Farrell? Besides, I know all the guys on the door."

When we arrive at the cinema, we find Caroline isn't quite finished.

"Close your eyes," she barks at Mick.

"What?"

"Just close them, all right!"

"I don't need to. It's not like I can actually see."

"Just close them!"

Caroline quickly whips out a red beach towel from her bag.

"What are you doing now?" Mick demands to know.

"Just keep your eyes closed and stop talking," she tells him as she lays the towel between him and the front steps. "Now you can open them," she announces. "*Da-da!*"

He's staring down at the 'red carpet' before him but,

before he can say a word, Caroline takes out a bottle of champagne from her bag.

"Hey," cries Dana, "where did you get that? Isn't that the bottle I've been saving for a special occasion?"

"Occasions don't get more special than this," Caroline tells her then pops the cork and it goes flying into the air. "Here's to Mick and a red-carpeted future!" she cries. "*Hip hip hurrah!*"

"*Hip hip hurrah!*" the rest of us cheer.

Except Mick. He's standing there silently. With the shades on, it's hard to gauge his reaction.

"Speech! Speech!" cries Caroline.

We all look to Mick but he doesn't say anything. I'm not sure he could even if he wanted to and, perhaps, sensing as much, Caroline shows a modicum of sensitivity for once.

"*Hip hip hurrah!*" she shouts out again.

And again we all cheer.

"Here, Mick! Take a slug!" Caroline cries as the bottle bubbles over. "Quick!"

Mick does, then passes the bottle on to Dana.

"A slug?" mutters Dana. "A slug of the most expensive bottle I've ever owned! It's not some cheap cider, you know." But, despite her protests, she puts the bottle to her lips. "Hip hip hurrah to Mick!"

"Come on," says Caroline when Shane and I have taken our turn. "We can finish this later." She takes the half-full bottle and hides it under her coat, then grabs Mick by the arm. "Okay, I may not be Hilary Swank or Angelina Jolie but I'll do for tonight. Now let's get going. We don't want to miss the start."

"So tell us, what is it you say again?" Caroline asks Mick as we go in search of Screen 5, where the usher has told us the film is about to start.

"'Oi! Watch it!' to Colin Farrell when he brushes past me in the street. Three small words maybe but, as Colin put it after we finished shooting, 'Mick, my friend, there are no small parts, only small actors.'"

"Did he really say that?" asks Caroline.

"No. But he might have, if his people hadn't ushered him back to his trailer."

Just then, a bunch of guys push past us, knocking into Caroline.

"Oi! Watch it!" cries Caroline.

We all burst out laughing. The boys turn and stare at us and, for a second, I worry there's going to be trouble but then, probably deciding we're a bunch of weirdos, they think twice and carry on walking.

The film is just starting when we arrive into the auditorium but Caroline insists we go right up to the front. So, there we are, all in a row, in the dark, necks craned up, staring at the screen.

The film is an action one with Colin Farrell playing the lead role of a recovering-alcoholic cop with anger-management issues. In a nutshell, Colin's wife and children have been taken hostage by a criminal just released from prison who believes Colin is responsible for the deaths of his family and – surprise! surprise! – he wants revenge.

For some reason the filmmakers have decided this story warrants a whopping two hours and fifteen minutes and, as we watch, it occurs to me that they've managed to make every minute feel more like an hour despite the presence of Colin in nearly every scene. The film drags and drags and drags.

Every now and then, Caroline leans across me to Mick who's on my other side.

"How long more before you're on?" she whispers loudly.

"I've told you, my scene is right at the end."

"Are you sure there's actually going to be an end?" Her words get swallowed up by a great yawn. "It's looking less and less likely."

On and on this everlasting film drags and Caroline begins to get more fidgety and then, just as she leans over me to ask the question for the umpteenth time, Mick whispers.

"It's coming. Sssshh!"

So we watch as a frantic Colin Farrell races down a busy road in hot pursuit of his arch nemesis.

"Any second now," whispers Mick.

We watch as Colin almost trips over a dog. We watch as he nearly knocks over a blind woman.

"Any second."

We watch as a little kid on a bike brakes suddenly to avoid colliding with Colin and then goes careering to the ground. And we watch as Colin turns the corner.

"Here's me coming up!" Mick whispers.

We watch as Colin catches up with the guy he's been pursuing, jumps on him and wrestles him to the ground, then holds him down with the weight of his body. Then, almost immediately, half a dozen squad cars with sirens blaring and blue lights flashing arrive from all directions.

And we watch as Colin hauls the man up roughly, pushes him up against one of the squad cars and tells a guy in uniform: "Get this scumbag out of my sight or, God help me, I won't be responsible for what I do to him!"

Then, the credits role.

We sit there, confused. What happened to Mick? What happened to the part where Colin Farrell bumps into him and he shouts, "Oi! Watch it!" And as the penny drops –

they've cut Mick's scene – none of us move, or say a word. We just stay sitting there in the dark.

The lights go up and Mick puts on his star-shaped shades, stands up and walks back up through the rows of seats towards the door at the back of the auditorium.

By the time we see him again, he's already halfway down the street.

"Mick!" Caroline calls after him. "Come back! Let's all go for a drink!"

He turns and shakes his head. "Nah! I wouldn't be much company!" He carries on walking.

"Hang on a second!" shouts Caroline and she runs to catch up with him.

"Should we go after them?" Dana looks at Shane and me.

Shane shakes his head. "Come on," he nods in the direction of a nearby pub, "let's go for a drink. Mick doesn't need all of us crowding around, staring at him in sympathy." He glances down the street to where Caroline and Mick are standing at the traffic lights; neither is talking and there's a good foot between them – a casual onlooker would never guess they were together. "And anyway, he has Caroline."

10

"Fifty ways to leave your lo♥er . . ."

The next evening, I get home late to find Dana in bits. She's huddled up on the couch, clutching a cushion, and she's bawling her eyes out. I've never seen her in such a state. I don't think I've ever seen anyone in such a state and, straight away, I worry that something awful must have happened – to her parents, maybe. What else could have her like this?

"Dana, what's the matter?" I ask but she doesn't answer, she just carries on sobbing.

I sit down beside her and try to put an arm around her but she shrugs me away.

"Dana, hush now, hush," I say.

But she can't hush. It's like her tears will never dry up. She's crying and crying and crying, uncontrollably, more like a child than an adult, with all the messiness of a child. There's snot coming from her nose and the tears are streaming down her face. A pretty sight she is not, but heartbreaking, yes. Poor Dana. She's holding a sodden ball of tissue in her hand and now she wipes her nose with it but the tissue is already saturated and of little use.

"I'll get you some tissues," I tell her and quickly get up, glad to have a purpose.

I come back with a roll of toilet paper – it's all I can find – and I hand it to her, then I sit there, as she pulls off one long strip after another, and wipes away her sadness.

Gradually the tears subside.

"Do you want to talk?" I ask.

This only sets her off again. I feel completely helpless in the face of such misery.

"It's my dad," she says – eventually.

"Your dad? Is something the matter with him? Is he in hospital?"

She shakes her head. "He's . . . he's . . ." She can't go any further. "He . . . he . . ."

"Take your time."

"Oh, Rosie! He's been having an affair!"

I'm dumbstruck. How can this be? For as long as I know Dana I've heard accounts of her parents' devotion to one another: how he brings her up a cup of tea each morning, how they ring one another half a dozen times a day, how he's happy to drive her from one shop to another and patiently sit outside in the car for hours on end.

"Can you believe it?" she sobs.

I'm finding it hard. Only the other night, when Caroline was complaining that her feet were like blocks of ice, Dana – jokingly – suggested that Caroline should hop into Shane's bed and warm them on his back, the way her own mum always warms her feet on her father's. Too much information to be sure, but the kind of intimate little detail we've always been privy to.

And they did seem rock solid, a devoted couple so close

they'd even begun to physically resemble one another in their middle age; the kind of couple you'd imagine you could depend on to live out their lives together and then, when one died, the other could be expected to soon follow, no longer able to go on with a broken heart.

"It's been going on for over a year," she sobs.

They even finished one another's sentences. They even held hands with one another — I've seen them.

"Are you sure, Dana?" I ask.

"It gets even worse! I have a stepsister! She – *his girlfriend* – just had a baby!"

I'm staring at her. "Ah no, Dana! That can't be true."

"It is!"

"But how? When? I don't understand . . ." I trail off.

"She's a work colleague. Half his age. You know, I thought my parents really had something special but it's all been one big fat lie. His life, my mother's life, my life, our little family – just a joke!"

"But Dana . . . God! I don't know what to say. When did you find out?"

"This evening." She bursts out crying again.

I tear off a strip of loo roll and hand it to her but she doesn't see it and wipes her nose with her sleeve.

"I always go to dinner on Wednesdays but when I went over tonight the house was in darkness. I just thought they weren't back yet so I used my own key to get in, thinking I'd wait for them but I found my mother upstairs in her room, curled up in bed, like a baby, sobbing her heart out. This other woman . . . this bitch . . . had called around in the afternoon *with* the baby. She wanted my dad to leave my mum and come to live with her and I guess she thought by telling my mum what was going on, showing her the little baby, my mum would throw him out."

"And did she?"

"Well, he's not there now. But he's not gone to *her* either. He's staying in a hotel in town. He says he doesn't want to leave Mum. He told her she's the one he loves, that he never meant for any of this to happen, that it was all an awful mistake. But how can he not have meant for it to happen? How can it be a mistake? A mistake is forgetting to take the bins out or letting the bath overflow. How can a mistake go on for over a year? And how could he have a *baby* by mistake? He's not some teenage boy who half-believes it himself when he persuades some stupid girl she can't get pregnant if they do it standing up against a wall!" She shudders. "A mistake! Him with a lover! And with a baby! At his age! They were going to be celebrating their twenty-fifth wedding anniversary next month! It makes me want to vomit. The whole thing makes me want to vomit. It's all so utterly disgusting. My mum had no idea! I had no idea! How could he do this to the people he's supposed to love? To my mum? To me?"

I have no answers and even if I did, Dana isn't in the mood to hear them, but then, right at that moment the door bell rings. I look to Dana. She looks to me.

"Oh God, Rosie, do you think it could be him?"

"I don't know."

The bell rings again.

Neither of us budges. We're like statues. We go on staring at one another, like we're compelled to, like there's some magnetic force between us.

The doorbell rings for a third time but this time it doesn't stop – it goes on ringing and ringing like someone – he – has his finger pressed to it.

"Rosie, I couldn't handle seeing him."

"Will I go? I can tell him you're not ready to talk to him."

She doesn't answer. I don't think she's capable of making a decision.

"I'm going to go, okay?" I repeat.

She's staring at me, with frightened eyes the size of saucers but she doesn't try to stop me.

I open the door. Mr Vaughan is standing there. He looks utterly pitiful. His tie is hanging loose and askew. The top buttons of his shirt are open. One of his shirt tails hangs out over his trousers. His suit jacket is wrinkled and is falling off one shoulder. His greying hair is tousled and the bald is peeking through a thin patch I never even knew existed. He stinks of cigarette smoke.

"Rosie, is Dana here?" he asks, looking over my shoulder, desperately scanning that bit of the house that's in his view.

"I'm sorry, Mr Vaughan. She doesn't want to talk to you."

"But I need to speak to her. I need to explain things."

"I think it might be better if you come back when she's calmed down."

Before I know what's happening he's charging past me.

"Hey!" I hurry after him.

"Get out!" Dana screams at him as he comes into the living room. *"Get out!"*

"Dana, please!" he pleads.

"Get away! How could you do this?"

"Please, Dana," he comes towards her, "just let me explain – "

"No!" She backs away.

"You've got to understand. I never meant for any of this to happen. It's your mother I love. It's your mother I'm married to. My affair, if you can even call it that, with Ann –"

"Stop! I'm not going to listen to this!"

"It meant nothing. What happened between us never

105

should have happened. It started with the Christmas party, and then, I don't know, it carried on. It shouldn't have, none of it should have happened – I was stupid and then, when I tried to finally put a stop to it she told me about the baby and –"

"*Stop it!*

"I don't love her! You have to believe that!"

"*Shut up*! I'm not listening!" Dana blocks her ears. "You're pathetic!"

But he ploughs on.

"You don't know how many times I tried to break up with her –"

"I'm not listening!"

"– when she told me she was expecting Cathy, it became all so much more complicated."

Dana takes her hands down from her ears. "Cathy?"

He nods. "Yes, Cathy – your sister."

"Cathy?" repeats Dana.

He nods again. His face softens. He looks like he oh-so-foolishly thinks he's finally connected with Dana. He looks like he just might be insane enough to take out baby snaps to show her but, before he gets any such chance, Dana picks up a heavy picture frame from the mantelpiece and hurls it at him. It hits him in the side of the head. Immediately blood begins pouring out. His hand goes up to his forehead and when he takes it away again it too is covered in blood. He looks at it, then back at Dana. He begins walking towards her.

"Dana, please – ?"

"*Get way from me!*" screams Dana. Then she runs from the room and up the stairs.

I hear the door of her bedroom slam.

He goes to follow her.

"I think it might be better if you gave her some space," I

say and find myself putting a hand out to stop him.

He looks down at me, and then stares at me – like he's never seen me before and isn't quite sure what I'm doing here. Suddenly he slumps down on the corner of the coffee table, hunches over, puts his face in his hands and he begins to sob.

"Oh what I have I done?" he cries, rocking back and forth.

I stand there, not knowing what to do. I wish the others would come home. The sobbing and the rocking goes on and on. My sympathies are one hundred per cent with Dana but I can't stand here, just looking at him, doing nothing.

"Mr Vaughan," I hear myself ask, "would you like me to get you something for that cut?" Like I think that will actually solve anything, but it's all I can think of to say.

He doesn't respond.

"Mr Vaughan, will I get you something for the cut?" I repeat.

He lifts up a tear-stained and bloody face, stares at me blankly and then, without a word, he gets to his feet and makes for the door.

I stand outside Dana's room and call her name. She doesn't answer. I put my ear to the door and listen but I can't hear a thing.

"Dana? I'm here if you need me, all right?"

But there's no response.

When Caroline and then Shane come back, I tell them all that's happened. In turn, each of them tries to coax her out of her room but with no luck. She won't talk to either of them.

We three sit up late into the night, going over the evening's events – trying to make sense of it all. We talk about Dana. Caroline tells us about the night Dana first moved into the house, how her parents came with her, to check everything out (including Caroline, most probably) and then how, a couple of nights later, her dad came back with a telly for her room, an extra duvet, and a microwave.

We talk about how close she is to her parents. She rings them every day, both of them On the rare occasions I think to ring my dad, his immediate response is one of worry that something must be up, or that I must be in need of a loan. Much as I love my mum and dad, I'm happy to see them when I see them, and haven't really missed them since they headed down under. Shane's more or less the same and I think Caroline would be happy if she didn't see her mum or dad from one end of the month to the next. But Dana visits hers every Wednesday evening and Sunday afternoon. Caroline tells us that only yesterday Dana was talking of going on a weekend break to Paris with them later on in the spring. They are – were – that kind of family.

Dana is still barricaded in her room the next morning when I get up for work. Again I call through her door but I get no answer. Before I reluctantly go, I leave a tray with tea and toast for her outside her door but I don't even know if she hears me when I tell her.

11

"You don't have to say you lo♥e me . . ."

I'm lying on the couch, hungry but too lazy to do anything about it. I'm just not in the mood to cook. After work I bought all this veggie food Dana likes so much thinking I might do a stir-fry for us but when I rang her on her mobile on my way home, she told me she wouldn't be back until late. She said was planning to stay in college to catch up on some research and she'd get something in the canteen. I was surprised she even went in today. I didn't think she would, given the state she was in last night. But when I tried asking her how she was, she just said she was fine and immediately hung up which I think is a fair indication that she isn't fine, but then I'd hardly expect her to be.

It's funny, but on the bus home I remembered how Dana had nominated her parents as her happy couple and I can't help feeling utterly depressed by that thought.

"Hi!"

I look up. Shane has popped his head around the door.

"Are you on your own?" he asks.

"Looks like it." I sit up. "Shane, I was going to cook up some dinner for Dana but she's staying late in college to do some research. Are you hungry?"

"Yeah, but I'm going out with Loretta to eat. She should be here any minute."

Right at that moment the doorbell rings and I think, that's a bit freaky. Are they so close they've become telepathic?

"That's probably her," he says.

"Okay, well, see you later."

But, just as he turns to go, a thought strikes me: here is one half of the happy couple I nominated. True, it was only because I couldn't think of anyone else but now I wonder what is the story with them? I know Shane as well as I know my own brothers, better even, but I hardly know Loretta at all. I don't *not* like her. I just don't really *get* her, in the same way I guess she doesn't get me. I've never understood the attraction between her and Shane. He never says much to me about their relationship or how he feels about her but then, why would he? I'm hardly the most receptive audience when it comes to the subject of Loretta. But, like, what makes them tick as a couple? What do they talk about? Could they *actually* be in love? Could they be the proof I'm looking for? The proof that love exists? I have my doubts about them but maybe it's time I put them under closer scrutiny and find out if their relationship offers the evidence I'm looking for.

"Hey! Can I come with you?" I shout after him.

"Ah – are you sure you'd want to?" he sounds a little dubious but I'm so taken with my great idea I hardly notice.

"Yeah."

He hesitates. "The thing is, I was more telling you we were going out rather than actually inviting you to come along."

"So you don't want me then?" I pout.

110

"It's not that, Rosie. It's just that –" He breaks off.

"What?"

"Nothing."

"Look, Shane, I'm trying to make an effort here. Loretta is your girlfriend. I'm your best friend. I just thought – you know – that maybe it was time I got to know her better." Okay, that wasn't my original reason, but it sounds good.

"O-kay . . ." He still seems a little doubtful.

"So can I come, then?"

"And you'd be nice to her?"

"Of course, I would – I'm always nice to her."

He looks at me for a moment before answering. "All right then." He's still sounding a little dubious.

"What? I can come?"

"Sure. Yeah, I guess it is about time you two started getting to know each other properly."

"Great! That's what I think too. So just let me tidy myself up and I'll follow out after you."

"Don't take too long. The booking is for 7.30."

When I arrive out twenty minutes later, Loretta is sitting in the driver's seat with Shane in the passenger seat beside her. I'm relieved when I see the two of them laughing. At least they're not annoyed that I kept them waiting. I didn't mean to. I just couldn't decide what to wear. I didn't want to be too underdressed – Loretta's always so smart – but then I didn't want to be too dressed up either. They're laughing so much now they don't see me and I stand there, looking at them, wondering *what* could be *that* funny. Then, when they eventually stop, Shane smiles at Loretta, then leans over and kisses her. What begins as a little peck turns into much more and I start to get a little uncomfortable. Suddenly Loretta spots me and pulls away. She says something to Shane who looks up and waves at me.

He opens the door and gets out.

"So what's the joke," I ask him, noticing he's still smirking.

"Well . . ." he begins, then changes his mind. "Oh nothing much – I was just trying to cheer Loretta up. It won't sound half as funny if I try telling you now." He pulls the seat forward to let me into the back.

"Hi, Loretta," I say, as I clamber in. "I hope you don't mind me tagging along."

As I'm struggling with my seat belt, Shane gets in and then we're off.

I sit back and look out the window but there's not much to see, just the occupants of other cars stalled in the lane beside us. I notice that a little girl in the back of the car alongside ours is staring in at me and – automatically – I smile at her. She's just so cute with her little pigtails and her little round glasses, but she doesn't react, she just keeps right on staring. I turn from the window. Ah, yes, this is nice I think. Yes, indeedy. Here we are – me, my best friend, his girlfriend – all out for an evening. And, despite Shane's concerns, we're all quite comfortable with one another. Why, we don't even feel the need to talk. Yes, this *is* very nice. This *is* a good idea – I don't know why I didn't think of it sooner. Very adult indeed. I turn to look out the window again but the little girl is still gaping in at me. I turn back. Shane and Loretta are both staring straight ahead. In silence. Hum-de-dum-de-dum. The stereo isn't even playing. There's just silence. Hmm. Why isn't the stereo on?

"You don't have the stereo on, Loretta?"

"Oh! Do you want it on?"

"No, no – not at all. It's nice to get some peace at the end of a busy day."

"Yeah, that's what I think too – and today was hell."

But that's *not* what I think – what am I saying? The last

thing I want at the end of a day is silence. The busier the day, the more I need some loud music to blast away the petty concerns of work.

"Don't you like music, Loretta?"

"Yes, of course I do. I can turn some on if you want."

"No, honestly, the quiet is just perfect. Just perfect."

I sit back. We travel along. Then Shane looks over his shoulder.

"What?" I ask.

"You're humming."

"Oh, sorry, I didn't even realise. Is it bothering you?"

"Not at all," says Loretta.

"Yeah," laughs Shane, "you're way off tune."

"Sorry."

"I *can* turn the stereo on if you'd like," says Loretta.

"No, It's fine. Yes, this is just fine. Just fine."

It's around then I notice I'm sitting on something. I look down and see Loretta's coat sticking out from underneath me, a coat she must have carefully laid across the back seat so that it wouldn't get wrinkled. I lever myself up and pull it out and cringe to see it's a right crumpled mess. I'm about to tell Loretta but the sight of her sitting there so silently, so composed, so concentrated on driving makes me change my mind. Maybe it would be better to wait until we're all getting out of the car – yeah, it'd be easier to tell her face to face. I try to brush the wrinkles away but with no luck so I carefully lay the coat back down on the other half of the seat.

I sit back and notice that I can hardly see out the front. This back seat is *very* low. I feel like a little child.

"So, Mammy and Daddy, where are we going?" I ask.

Loretta looks at me quizzically in the rear-view mirror.

I laugh. "I feel like a child in the back here. You know, out for a Sunday drive with Mammy and Daddy but, of course, it's not Sunday, it's a weeknight, and we're not going for a drive but for something to eat."

And while I'm on the subject of the blatantly obvious . . .

"And you're not my mammy and daddy either, are you?"

Enough! Enough! I will *not* babble this evening. I don't want Loretta thinking I'm a few slices short of a full sliced pan. *If* she doesn't think so already – which I often feel she does. I look out the window. That car has caught up with us again and that kid is still *staring* in at me. What *is* her problem? She's not cute. She's just freaky now.

"So anyway, where *are* we going to eat?"

"Dino's," answers Loretta.

"Great!" My heart sinks. It's the same restaurant I went to with Killian, the one with the snotty waiter.

"We just thought we'd try it out," Loretta goes on. "They've done it up recently."

"I've seen it. It's quite nice." There's another silence, a silence I have an overwhelming urge to fill. "But a little too formal maybe."

"Really?" asks Loretta.

"But overall it's nice. Yes, lovely in fact." The last thing I want Loretta thinking is that I'm criticising her choice. I remember Shane's warning to be nice. I *can* be nice. I *will* be nice. I *am* being nice. "Yeah, it's one of my favourite places."

Shane cranes his neck around. "Have you actually ever been there?"

What? Does he think I'm lying?

"Yeah, of course I have. I go there *all* the time."

"Really?

"You could say I'm a regular." Why did I say that? It's going to be obvious the minute we set foot in the place that I'm no regular. The only person who might remember me is the grumpy waiter who served us that night and I can't see him cheerily calling out when he sees me. Well, I'd better get rid of him then. "Yeah, but they have a problem keeping staff – you know."

"Really?"

"So the maître d' was saying."

Shit! Now they'll expect me to be best buddies with *him*.

I lapse back into silence. It's better that way. And again it's a total silence. Neither of them say a word. I wonder if this is the way they always are with each other, or is it because I'm here. I wonder what they were laughing about before I got into the car. Would they be laughing now if it wasn't for my presence? And just why wouldn't Shane tell me what the joke was? And – come to think of it – why did Loretta need cheering up? Was it because I was coming along? Was the joke about me?

But these are all questions I can't ask and this maddening silence goes on and on and bloody on. Then I notice Shane reach out his hand and place it on Loretta's knee. But still they don't talk to one another. I want to scream at them to say *something*!

"Shane?" begins Loretta obligingly.

I lean forward to catch what she's saying. She glances back and is a little disconcerted to see me so close behind her. I quickly sit back again.

"Did you get a chance to collect my clothes from the dry-cleaner's?"

"Sorry, hon – I forgot. I'll do it tomorrow, okay?"

"Yeah, that's fine, thanks. I wouldn't ask but I'm up the walls."

"I know."

And that's it. Silence again. I look out the window again. And that stupid kid is *still* staring and, without thinking, I stick out my tongue at her. When I look back I notice

Loretta's eyes fixed on me in the rear-view mirror but I say nothing. What explanation could I possibly give?

Finally we pull into the carpark and we all hop out of the car. Loretta goes to get her coat and it's immediately obvious it's a right mess.

"I'm sorry," I say, "I may have sat on it."

She looks at me and I begin to worry that she might think I did it deliberately.

"I didn't do it on purpose."

"I didn't think you did, Rosie." And she probably didn't either – at least not until I put the idea in her head.

When we arrive into the restaurant, we're met by the grumpy waiter.

"Hello," I smile.

"Ah, you're back again." He doesn't smile or anything like that, but his recognition is more than I could have hoped for.

I give Shane a self-satisfied, see-I-told-you look, then turn back to the waiter.

"Yes – I'm back again." And that's when it comes to me – his name, it's Tony. "I can't keep away from the place – Tony."

Because three people arrived when only two had been booked, there's some confusion but matters are solved when Tony begrudgingly sticks an extra chair at the side of the table and lays an extra setting. We sit down.

"Sorry," I say, as my knees bump against Loretta's.

We take our menus and I read through mine. I decide to go with crab cakes and the lamb again – this time I might actually get to enjoy them. But then I worry. I thought we were heading to somewhere cheap and cheerful. I don't have much money with me. I could skip the starter and order one of the less expensive main courses but I'd have to insist we all

116

pay separately. But I can't do that. There's no way I'm going to sit there dissecting the bill at the end of the evening, quibbling over who had the extra coffee. Not in front of Loretta – no way! To hell with it – I'll just use my Visa card. *If* I have it with me. I'm pretty sure I do but I can't suddenly pick up my bag and start poking in it to see – what would Loretta think?

I look up from the menu and happen to glance over at Loretta. She has a funny look on her face.

"Are you okay?" I ask.

"Fine."

"You look a little odd, that's all."

"Gee, thanks."

"I just meant I thought you looked down."

"Loretta had a foul day at work," Shane explains.

"How come?" I ask.

Loretta shrugs again. "I don't really want to get into it."

"One of the consultants was on her case all day," explains Shane. "He's being a real bastard to her ever since she started working with him. And then one of the patients died on the operating table."

"God! What happened? Tell us the gory details."

She stares at me for a long time. "Like Shane said he died and no, I'm not going to get into the gory details as you call them. He was a real person, with a real life, a real wife, a real family. Not some character out of *ER*. I knew him. I looked after him for the last week. Nobody expected him to die. If the operation had gone as we'd hoped it would he'd be going home to his family by the end of the week – to his wife and two-year-old son."

"Sorry, I didn't think."

"Rosie never does. Sure you don't?" laughs Shane.

I give Shane a dirty look but don't say anything. Okay,

maybe he is trying to lighten the mood. Okay, maybe I sounded stupid but I was just trying to make conversation. I am trying to make an effort. Nobody else seems bothered. Shane should be helping me. I need his help.

As the waiter pours out the wine, I notice Loretta glance over at Shane. She gives him a cheesed-off look and he looks back with a cheesy-apologetic grin. Is that because I'm here? When the waiter is finished pouring, Shane raises his glass.

"Cheers!"

"Cheers!" I call back. I'll be nice even if it kills me. I take a sip. This is *very* tasty. I pick up the bottle. It looks very expensive. I wonder how much it costs. Never mind, I have my Visa – I hope. Then I see that Shane and Loretta are staring intently at one another, their glasses still raised.

"Cheers to the next six months," says Shane, softly.

"To the next six months!" says Loretta and clinks her glass against his.

I look from one to the other. Suddenly everything falls into place. No wonder they picked such a fancy place. No wonder they ordered such a good bottle of wine. It's their six-month anniversary! And they have me – the moppet that I am – stuck here at the edge of the table. Why didn't they tell me? I could die. I have never been so embarrassed.

"I'm sorry. I didn't know it was a special occasion. Shane should have said."

"You're right. He should have," laughs Loretta. "But it doesn't matter."

"Of course, it matters."

"It doesn't, really, Rosie. We two can go out together any night. Look, I'm a bit preoccupied with what happened today at work but I'll try and put it aside. I'm glad you're here."

"I'm sorry," says Shane.

At first I think he's apologising to me but then I realise it's to Loretta. He reaches out and takes her hand. I feel so *so* small.

I get up.

"I think I'll go and leave you two to your meal."

"There's no need," says, Loretta. "We're happy you're here."

"Thanks but I want to go home. Besides, I'm worried Dana might be on her own. I shouldn't have come out."

"Are you sure?" asks Shane.

I look at him and suddenly feel like shouting: What do you bloody well think? Yeah, sure, I got glammed up, drove all the way here with you, made them set an extra place, then sat down, drank some wine and waited until the waiter was just about to take our order before deciding, that, yeah, I didn't want to be here in the first place. Do you know me at all? What has happened to you? What has happened to us?

But I don't.

"Yeah, sure I'm sure."

As I make for the door of the restaurant, I glance back. The two of them are deep in conversation. Shane is looking contrite. I can imagine what they're saying:

"How could you have asked her to come?"

"I didn't. I swear. She asked herself along."

I bump into the waiter.

"Goodnight, Tony."

"Goodnight. And, by the way, the name is Michael."

I walk home. It's a long way but I feel I need the exercise and the fresh air.

So are Loretta and Shane in love? I don't know. Yeah, sure, she's in love with him – anyone can see that and it's true that he seems fond of her, maybe loves her even – but I can't quite believe he's *in* love with her – that she's *the* one for him.

But whether or not he's in love with her, one thing's for sure – *her* presence has completely changed what's between Shane and me. I remember all those long ago days when he and I used to walk home together from school and the walk was never long enough to say all we had to say – the minute we got home we were on the phone to one another again. Now we'd probably walk the whole way in silence. She's done that. She's changed what's between us. Since she came along, Shane hardly feels like my friend any more.

12

"You've got to hide your lo♥e away . . ."

I try ringing Dana several times during the course of the morning but her mobile is switched off. I really want to talk to her, to see how she's doing. I didn't get a chance last night. She wasn't there when I finally got home after my aborted dinner and by the time she did get in, I'd fallen asleep. I didn't see her this morning either. She was gone before I got up.

During a quiet moment, I decide to try her mobile again but, just then, the shop phone rings. I answer it:

"Hello, Elegance Boutique, how can I help you?"

"Hello, can I speak to Fay O'Neill, please?" a male voice asks.

"Who shall I say is calling?"

There's a brief silence on the other end.

"Anthony."

"Just — Anthony?"

My interest is piqued. If he was one of our suppliers, he'd say as much and, anyway, he'd be more likely to ask for

Monica. Yet he doesn't sound like a customer either, or the husband of a customer. No, this sounds personal. Fay doesn't get many personal calls.

"Yes – Anthony," he repeats.

"And will Fay know what it's in connection with, Anthony?"

"Pardon? No, I just need to speak to her." Then adds urgently. "*Please* can you just get her for me?"

"One moment."

I put my hand over the receiver. "Fay!" I call over to her. "There's a gentleman caller on the line by the name of Anthony. Won't give his second name, and won't say what it's in connection with. In fact he sounds very mysterious."

I actually see the colour drain from her face.

"Fay, are you okay?" I ask.

Fay nods. Slowly she comes towards me, takes the phone, holds her hand over the receiver and stands there waiting until I go away. But I hover.

"Excuse me?"

I turn to see a customer standing at the counter, holding up a dress. "Have you this in a size fourteen?"

I tell her I think there may be one in the stockroom and that I'll go and check. When I come back, I notice Fay is no longer on the phone.

After I've served the woman and she's left, happy with her purchase, I ring Dana again, but again I have no luck. Then I ring both Shane and Caroline to see if they've been able to contact her, but they haven't. Maybe I should call by the college to see if she's there.

"Monica," I say, "would it be okay if I nipped out for an hour? It's pretty important."

"Sorry, Rosie, Fay's not well. She's getting her coat. I already told her she can go home so I need you to stay."

Without Fay there, Monica and I have to work that bit harder and in the end it turns out to be a very busy day. It's not until closing time, when Monica is doing the till, that we get a chance to speak again.

"I'm throwing a twenty-first on Friday," Monica tells me. "Will you come?"

"I know you look brilliant for your age," I joke, "but still I don't think anyone is going to believe you're twenty-one."

"It's for my son, Doug."

"But, Monica, I don't really know Doug."

"But you've met him. Please say you'll come, Rosie. Do it for me, as a favour. The thing about Doug is he doesn't seem to have many friends. When he was at school it was different. He was very popular but, then, when he left, he got in with a bad crowd but he seems to have lost touch with them too which is no bad thing in itself, but I'm afraid no one will turn up."

Of all Monica's sons, he's the one I like least. He's always so sullen when he comes into the shop and I know he has Monica's heart nearly broken. But how can I refuse?

"Okay," I say.

I go by the college on the way home but there's no sign of Dana in any of her usual haunts and when I do get home, I'm relieved to see her on the couch even if she is lying there in her pyjamas, even if she is watching *Emmerdale*, (which I know she hates), even if there is a mound of balled-up tissues beside her. She's not interested in talking and I tiptoe around her. I bring her in some soup and a toasty and she mutters thanks but I see they're still there, untouched, when later I come back in to sit a while and watch telly with her. They're still there when I head off to bed.

I wake in the middle of the night. It takes me a moment to figure out what woke me but then I hear sobs coming from the living room.

I go out and find Dana still where I left her and I sit down beside her and stroke her hair. After a long time, she looks up at me.

"How could he do this to us?" she asks. "How will Mum ever cope?"

"I don't know. I don't know."

And I don't. If someone as unlikely as her dad is capable of cheating, then what hope is there?

Neither of us has any more to say. I keep on stroking her hair. Then I hear little snores. I get up, go to Dana's room, take her duvet off her bed, and bring it back and lay it on her. I give her a kiss on the crown, then go back to bed myself.

13

"Can you feel the lo♥e tonight?"

The first thing I see when I go into the kitchen the next morning is a note from Dana propped up on the table. *Gone to my mum's,* it reads. That's good, I think. Spending some time with her mum is probably the best thing for both of them.

When I arrive in to work, I see Fay is back again.

"Feeling better?" I ask her even though she looks pretty washed out.

"Pardon?"

"You went home sick yesterday. Are you better now?"

"Fine," she says in a tone that tells me that that's an end to that particular conversation.

Just after lunch, the texting starts. I get a text from Shane asking me am I going to Dove's gig tonight. Between one thing and another, I'd forgotten about it but now I text him back to tell him I'll see him there (like I'd miss out on an opportunity to feast my eyes on the handsome Mark – not that I actually say that in the text). Straightaway, Shane texts back to say he's going there directly from Loretta's and that they'll meet me in the pub. Next I text Caroline to ask if she's going. She texts to say she is but that she's tied up after work and will also meet me there. When I text Mick, it's the same with him. Then I text Dana in the hope of persuading her to come along but I get a short reply back – *Not in the mood* – and I guess she isn't.

After work I decide not to go home since there's nobody there. Instead, I take a walk down Grafton Street. I wander into a bookshop. I'm not looking for anything in particular, just passing time really, and I browse from one section to another until I find myself in the relationships section. Standing there, looking at the rows and rows of books, I'm suddenly overwhelmed by the choice. I don't even know what to pick out to flick through. It strikes me just how many – hundreds, thousands, hundreds of thousands – self-help books have been written about love: how to find love, how to know it's real, how to keep it etc, etc, etc – *ad infinitum*. Since when did finding love become so complicated, complicated enough to have spawned all this? Maybe I should write my own self-help book, I think, but then again, maybe not. But I could write a book called *How To Pick The Wrong Guy* or *Unlucky In Love: Ten Rules To Guarantee You Are!*

And then there are *all* these accounts of people's own real-life love experiences, piled high on tables – in this bookshop, in every bookshop, in every town, in every city. The mind boggles. I pick up one book. Some guy has given himself a year to find a wife online. I pick up another. This woman has written about her experience of saying yes to every man who asked her out during the course of a year.

Hey, I could have written that! Except I could have called it – *"Saying Yes, Because You Haven't Learnt To Say No!"*

I move on and come to the fiction section and soon I begin to think that those factual books are just a molehill compared with all the imaginary love stories ever written. Since the very first boy-meets-girl story was created (and what was that first story, anyway? Adam and Eve – but that wasn't fiction, was it?) how many billions and billions of words have been written on the subject? How many hours have been spent making up these tales of love, how many millions more have been spent reading them? Is there any topic so pervasive? Is there any subject more written about, sung about, talked about, thought about? It's like a global obsession.

I leave the bookshop – empty-handed – defeated by choice – and decide to go for a bite to eat. And as I sit there, I wonder about that woman who wrote the book on saying yes to every guy – did she manage to find love in the end? I look back on all the hours I've spent with boyfriends over the years. All those intense early hours, when I really believed this could be *it*. And then, the disillusioned hours when the realisation that this is most definitely not *it* begins to sinks in. Has that woman managed to stay friends with any of these guys? Or, like me, does she go from all to nothing? One day I'm pouring my heart out, and mentally planning a future with him and, then, it all goes belly-up, and all that's left between us is an uncomfortable hello – if even that – when we pass each other on the street.

Despite all the time I had on my hands, I still manage to be late and the band is in the middle of a song when I arrive. I find Caroline, Shane, Mick and Loretta already there, sitting towards the front. Shane calls out and points to the empty seat beside him and I squeeze in. I look to the stage.

Ah, Mark! Looking as good, better even, than he did the last night. He's wearing jeans and a white T-shirt that show off his perfect body to perfection. Yes, I think to myself, I could sit here all night, watching him. And listening to him too – of course.

He finishes the song, brings his mouth close into the microphone and tells us that the next song he's going to play is a brand new one and he hopes we'll like it. The other guys begin to play and he then starts to sing. It's a slow song with a catchy tune but I'm paying more attention to what he looks like than to how he sounds and I don't even notice the words at first. It's not until he repeats the chorus again that those words begin to sink in.

"Blue eyes upturned, blonde hair flicked,
Tight jeans crinkled, purple shirt gaping,
And light –
Bouncing off a silver pendant.
No reason, no rhyme,
It takes no time, just a first glimpse of you,
To fall in love.
No reason, no rhyme,
Light –
Bouncing off a silver pendant.

That song is about me! But it can't be! But it is! Me at their last gig: my favourite pendant, my new purple shirt, my best jeans, my blue eyes and my blonde hair. It's me – it has to be. And if I'm in any doubt I see that Mark is staring straight at me as he repeats those words – *"It takes no time, just a first glimpse of you, to fall in love"*. I'm flustered. I give a puzzled half-smile back and he winks.

But then, the song ends, the band take a break and I watch them file off the stage. I look around the table to see if any of the others might have noticed but there's no sign that they have. Am I imagining it? I haven't ever even spoken to this guy. Why would he write a song about me? Then I think of that other song, the Carly Simon song, *"You're so vain, you probably think this song is about you?"* Am I being vain? I don't know but I do know the others are very likely to think so if I tell them my thoughts. I can imagine the hoots of laughter. Maybe it is all just a coincidence. But then I think of the words, the wink, the smile – it can't be a coincidence.

Then Caroline leans over to me and I'm sure she's going to say something about the song, that she's noticed too. But instead she asks: "Any word from Dana?"

I shake my head. "No – nothing, just a text saying she didn't want to come."

"Same here."

Maybe I am being foolish. I don't know Mark. Why would he write a song about me? I should just put all this nonsense out of my head and settle down, talk to the others. I realise I haven't even spoke to Mick since his big film debut and his famous non-scene with Colin Farrell.

"Hi, Mick, how are you?" I shout over.

"Fine, Rosie," he calls back.

"Pity about the other night."

He gives a shrug.

"So why do you think they cut your scene?" I ask.

"Don't know."

"You must have been very disappointed."

Before he can answer, Caroline butts in. "Rosie, keep your trap shut!" she snaps.

"Pardon?"

"Time and place, time and place," she practically hisses at me. "Just let Mick enjoy himself tonight."

"Well, excuse *me*!"

I turn away and ignore the little intimate whisperings going on between the pair. I can just imagine: *"Don't mind her, Mick. You know what she's like. She just never thinks."*

And I guess I didn't but I didn't mean any harm either – Mick knew that. Caroline is just being over-protective. But soon I forget all about them – sucked in by the vision of perfection that is Mark. I've spotted him again in the crowd. He's coming this way. I watch him as he moves confidently through the people. He sees me looking at him and he holds that look as he comes closer and closer. Every now and then, someone stops him for a chat so his progress is tortuously slow but, even when he's talking his eyes are on me. I stand up, leave all the others engrossed in conversation – Shane with Loretta, Caroline with Mick – and I begin making my way over to Mark. When I'm nearly there, I hear someone call my name and I look around.

It's Shane's friend – Finn – grinning over at me. Damn! Not now!

"Hi there, Rosie!" He comes over. "Glad you could make it."

"Yeah, so am I. You were even better than last time."

"You think?"

"Sure."

"Have you heard we've been asked to play support to Damien Rice when he comes to Dublin later in the year?"

"You're kidding! But that's brilliant!"

He nods his head excitedly, causing one of his thick black curls to fall over his eye. He reminds me of a lively puppy. He brushes the curl back. Finn, I think, would know if Mark wrote that song about me,.

"I love your new song," I begin.

"Yeah?"

"Yeah."

While Finn stands there smiling, I'm trying to work out exactly how I can ask what I want to ask but subtly enough so that if I'm way off the mark he won't think I'm some egotistical freak. But I take too long, I lose my chance.

"Hey, Finn!" Someone shouts out.

We both look around. Some guy is coming over. I make my excuses and move away quickly. I don't want to get caught up in introductions, in a conversation.

I turn to see where Mark is now, to find him standing there, right behind me.

"Hi!" I stammer.

"Rosie, isn't it? You're here with Shane?"

I nod.

"I saw you at our last gig but I didn't get a chance to talk to you." He's standing so close to me that I can feel his breath on my face which is handy since I might be in need of his oxygen as I can hardly breathe myself. Anyone else and I might ask him to back away a little but I'm okay with this. He's even more gorgeous up close. He has the most perfect skin.

"I'm glad you're here again tonight," he says.

"Yeah?"

He nods his head. "It's easier to sing when there's someone like you in the audience."

"Someone like me?"

He reaches out and brushes a hair away from my cheek. "You know, someone special, someone my songs could be about."

There! He's practically admitting he wrote the song about me. "Really? And –"

"Hey, Mark!"

We both look up. It's Finn, still grinning and now

beckoning Mark over. How many of these grinning Finns are there? It's like he's bloody everywhere.

"I'd better see what he wants," Mark sighs. "Don't go away now."

"Oh no, I'm not going anywhere." Okay , cheesy I know, but it's all I can come up with.

And I do stand there, right at that spot. I can't see Mark or Finn now. They've probably got caught up in some band stuff and I begin to think that surely he didn't mean I had to wait in this exact spot. I could, I suppose, go over and sit with the others.

I go back to the table. Nobody has even noticed I was missing. Shane has his arm around Loretta and they're deep in conversation, and Caroline and Mick are in the middle of an argument. I sit down

"I'm not doing it," Mick is telling Caroline, "so stop going on about it, all right!"

"But why? It's perfect."

"What are you not doing, Mick? What's perfect?" I ask.

"Nothing," mumbles Mick.

Caroline looks at him. She's clearly annoyed. "Mick has a screen test for a TV advert."

"Wow!"

"Wow – nothing," snaps Mick.

"What's the problem?"

"I don't want to be stereotyped."

"I don't think you have to worry about that just yet," points out Caroline.

"So what's the ad about?" I ask.

Caroline explains: "Mick would be playing the part of the adult son to this old country couple. He's just got a job in the city but he's reluctant to go because, as he tells his parents, he'll miss all the comforts but, really, the only obvious comfort amidst all the domestic mess in this rundown little kitchen is a fancy china butter dish in the centre of the table with a half pound of *Cork Glory* on it —"

"What's that?"

"This new butter, and that's the reason he doesn't want to go — because he'll miss it so much when he goes to the city."

"The eejet! Have you ever heard anything so stupid?" moans Mick.

"So what?" demands Caroline. "It's money for jam — butter even. You wouldn't even have to act. You could just play yourself."

Mick looks at her. "You have it all worked out, don't you? You probably think the production company could simply decamp down to my parents' house and film it there."

Caroline shrugs. "It's an idea."

"That's exactly how you picture my home, isn't it?"

"No, not at all," she protests weakly, looking a little shifty-eyed. "Well, maybe," she admits.

"You think they live in some stone-floored, 1920's kip with chickens roosting in the dresser. And I suppose you think my mother goes to bed in her wellies every night and my father in his cap and they sleep with a goat between the pair of them to keep warm."

"No, no." She's looks over at me and I can't help smiling because I know that's exactly the kind of thing she thinks.

"You know, you really haven't a clue," snaps Mick. "As it happens my parents live in a six-bedroom Georgian farmhouse set on three hundred acres."

"Is that big?" I ask.

"Ah — yeah. About the size of, say, County Leitrim. And

they farm more cows than there are probably people in Leitrim."

"Oh!" Caroline digests this information. "So you could say they're big farmers?" she asks.

"You could."

"If the farm is that big then how do your parents look after it all?" I ask.

"They have people working on it."

"So it's like a business?" asks Caroline – translating it into language she understands.

"You could say that."

"Then what are you doing here in Dublin, struggling to be an actor?" she demands.

Mick looks over at her. "Jesus, Caroline! I thought you of all people actually had some idea what I was about. I don't *want* to be a farmer. I want to be an actor."

"Well, then, why are you being so bloody unprofessional? If you're that serious about acting, then aren't you stupid turning down this ad? Think of the exposure, think of the money for goodness sake!"

"Yeah, and think about how every week, for years to come, I'd be beamed into people's home, playing a gobshite who won't leave home because he's so thick he doesn't know he can buy butter in a supermarket. For the last time, I am *not* doing it."

"Well, I think you're being stupid."

"Fine."

"Fine."

They both sit there with stubborn, scowling faces on them but then the band come back on stage which is just as well as I can't think of a thing to say to lessen the tension.

I relax back into my seat. For all of the second half Mark sings his songs directly to me. I swear it's like there's no one in the room but just us two. At one point, I do manage to drag my eyes away from him to take a sip from my drink and I notice Shane looking over at me. He raises his eyebrows questioningly, nods in the direction of Mark, but I shrug and pretend I don't know what he means. I see that Loretta too is smirking knowingly. The other two – Caroline and Mick – are so busy scowling at one another that Mark could jump down from the stage and do a striptease in front of me and they wouldn't notice.

And then, at the very end of the night, he sings that song again – my song – and as he does he never takes his eyes off me, not for a second.

And then it's all over. Before I know it, the others are gathering up their coats, getting ready to go.

I look around for Mark.

"Are you coming, Rosie?" asks Shane. "Loretta is driving. She can take us all home."

"Doesn't anyone feel like going on to somewhere else?" I ask, thinking I could maybe casually invite Mark to come along.

"No," snaps Mick – looking crossly at Caroline.

"No," snaps Caroline – looking crossly at Mick.

"No," says Shane, "I'm knackered."

"And I've an early start," says Loretta.

I look around. I can't see Mark anywhere. I could hang about on my own but I don't want to come across as desperate. I reluctantly put on my jacket and follow out after the others as slowly as I can but there's no sign of Mark.

14

"Crazy little thing called lo♥e . . ."

A couple of days later, I meet Caroline after work in a little restaurant around the corner; a cheap and cheerful Chinese with really quick service. So we're sitting there, eating and chatting. We talk a lot about Dana. She hasn't been back to the house since but both Caroline and I have been in contact with her by phone. She says she'll come back in a day or two, when her mum is feeling better. I guess she means when she's feeling better too.

"Speaking of mums and dads," says Caroline, "have you heard from your own parents since they went on holiday?"

"Have I what? Mum keeps sending me these text messages."

"Are they having a good time?"

"Well, that's not what these are about." I pick up my phone and scroll it until I find what I'm looking for, then I turn the screen to Caroline. "Look."

She leans forward to read it: *"Don't get taxis home on ur own late @ nite."* She looks up at me quizzically.

I shrug. "There are loads of them – they're like her little

commandments to me, instructing me to do or not do this or that." I start reading out old ones. *"Don't leave ur drink unattended in pub — people spike them"* . . . *"Don't ever walk home on ur own at nite."*

Caroline laughs. "I guess she's worried about you, being so far away."

"Yeah. She probably read some dreadful article in an Aussie paper about some unfortunate girl who was raped by a taxi-driver, or had her drink spiked. The thing is, it's been years since she worried like this — not since I was a teenager. The last words I'd hear then as I headed out the door to the local disco were — *'Stick with the crowd!'* I guess she thought that as long as I didn't wander off on my own, or with a stranger — i.e. a boy — then I couldn't get into trouble. But I used to pretend I didn't know what she meant and I'd ask her all these annoying questions. Like, if I needed to go to the toilet, did she want me to bring the crowd with me? All of them? All the couple of hundred people at the disco? Even the people I didn't know?" I look back down at the text again. "But you're right. I think she is worried. They've had a lot of problems since they left — not least being faced with their own mortality. The other morning when I rang my sister's house they were both in bed asleep so I only got to talk to Sarah but she said they went through the worst turbulence ever on the plane over — not that they told me, in case I'd worry I guess, but Sarah said Dad really thought they were going to die."

"The poor fellow!"

"The thing is, he was reluctant to go in the first place. My mum had a job to persuade him. Heaven only knows how she's going to get him back onto the plane when it's time to go home."

"Maybe she won't! Maybe he'll refuse to come back with her and decide to live out his days down under."

"After what happened between Dana's parents nothing would surprise me."

Suddenly Caroline's phone rings and she looks to see who it is. I notice her smile in recognition but then she looks up and shakes her head in annoyance.

"It's just Mick but I'd better get it." She answers her phone. "Hi, Mick. What? Oh, that's a shame. I know. I know. Come on, there'll be others. Yeah, I know. Of course, you are but you've just got to put it behind you. Don't dwell on it – it's a waste of energy. Okay, give me a ring later. I can call over if it suits. All right, then. Bye."

She looks up. "He was at an audition for an ad but he didn't get the part."

"That butter ad?"

"No, he refused to even think about that one. He can be very stubborn. And maybe he was right. Maybe he would be selling himself short. But that's the fourth audition in a row he hasn't got."

"Selling himself short? You've changed your tune."

"Maybe I have," she replies casually but almost too casually it strikes me.

I look at her but she's looking down at her cup as she thoroughly stirs her sugarless coffee. I'm about to start teasing her but then I stop myself. It wouldn't go down well, I suspect. I don't fancy getting my head bitten off. She does seem a tad touchy on the subject of Mick.

"You know, I went to see him last night in rehearsals for *Romeo and Juliet* – their end-of-term play," she tells me.

"Yeah?"

"Yeah."

"And was he good?"

"Good? He was brilliant!" She finally puts down the spoon. "You know, he's a really, really great actor. Way better than any

138

of the others that were there last night. That Romeo was pitiful. And Mick's accent – well, the thing is, he has no obvious accent when he's on the stage. It's the weirdest thing. And he has this amazing presence. Every time he came on stage it was like he owned it. I'm telling you this acting thing isn't such an off-the-wall idea after all. He's got real talent."

"Good. It would be great if he made it."

"Yeah, there's no doubt but that he will. He just needs a good agent."

"Is that hard to get?"

"Seems like it. The one he's with is rubbish. She seems to thinks that all he's suitable for is things like that stupid butter ad. And, of course, there's loads of competition but I know he'll make it. I'd bet my life on it."

She sees me smirking. "What?" she demands.

"Oh, nothing." But I can't take the smirk off my face.

"What?" she demands.

"So what *is* the story with you and Mick?"

"Rosie! How many times do I have to tell you, there is no story, there never was a story, and there's never going to be a story. We're just friends. Is that so hard for you to understand?"

"The lady doth protest too much methinks."

"Oh shut up, Rosie!"

"All right, I'm sorry. I'm just teasing."

"Well, don't!" She looks at her watch. "Come on, we'd better get going."

We both go to the till but Caroline insists on paying the bill.

"My treat."

"No," I protest. "Let's split it."

"Look, Rosie, let me! I got a bonus today. A big one. I'm feeling generous and you're probably broke as usual."

She's right there, so I let her go ahead. Then, I tell her that I need to use the toilet before we leave and she says she'll hang on for me outside.

On my way, I notice Fay in a corner at the back of the restaurant and I wave over at her but she doesn't see me, or so I think, so I make my way over to her.

"Fay, hi!"

"Rosie!"

I see she's with someone – a good-looking man about her own age. He's wearing a dark well-cut suit, white shirt and a red tie. He has a thin tanned face and white wavy hair. They make a very handsome couple, if they are a couple. On the one hand, like a couple they are sitting in a romantic little booth – a perfect lovers' hideaway. On the other hand, their manner is far from couple-like. They're both sitting bolt upright now, with several inches between them but I wonder if this is because Fay saw me coming.

"Hello," I say to the man.

He nods at me. "Hello."

I stand there, waiting for an introduction but none is forthcoming. In fact, neither of them says anything and their demeanour doesn't exactly invite chitchat from me. I feel awkward. I realise they're waiting for me to go.

"See you tomorrow," I say to Fay. "Nice meeting you," I say to her boyfriend or whatever he is.

"Nice meeting you too," he says.

When I get outside, Caroline is waiting for me.

"What kept you?" she demands.

"Nothing," I murmur. I'm too preoccupied to say any more. I'm thinking about Fay and her dinner companion. Just who is he? What were they doing there together? Why didn't she introduce him to me? Was he – by any chance – the same man who rang the shop the other day? And why was she so flustered when she took that call? And, just why did she go home so suddenly afterwards?

Such a lot of questions – *but* the biggest question of all is: was that a wedding ring on his finger? And the answer to that is – yes.

And *that*, I think, answers a lot of the other questions.

15

"Lo♥e is in the air . . ."

Just when I think I have everything – phone, bag, keys, money – and am finally about to head out, I hear a key turning in the lock in the front door. It's Dana.

"Hi, Dana! You're home!"

"Hi." She puts down her big holdall and throws off her coat.

"How're you?" I ask warily.

She shrugs and says nothing but she's not looking too great. In fact I'm shocked by her appearance. She's wearing her usual uniform of jeans and a sweatshirt, except this sweatshirt can't possibly belong to her. It's humongous. It's hanging off her and reaches down as far as her knees. She looks like one of those people in an ad who's shed a whopping amount of weight, something like 90 kilos in six months, but who's wearing their pre-diet clothes to illustrate the difference between now and then. I can't even imagine who the sweatshirt could belong to or where she found it. But her face *is* very gaunt and she has lost some weight that she could ill afford.

She makes straight for the couch and flops down. Her hair is a greasy mess. I notice her glasses have a band of tape around the bridge.

"How's your mum?"

"Devastated." She looks up at me and notices I'm all dressed up. "Are you going out?"

"Yeah, Monica from work is having a twenty-first for her son at her house."

"Where are Shane and Caroline?"

"Shane is over at Loretta's. I'm not sure where Caroline is." I notice the look on her face. She clearly doesn't relish the prospect of being left here on her own for the evening. "Look, I don't have to go," I tell her. "I can stay with you. I'll ring Monica and tell her something has come up." My suggestion isn't entirely altruistic; I'd much prefer not to go.

"I don't need baby-sitting," she says, crossly.

I sit down beside her. "I'm not saying that but I know you've gone through a lot –"

She gives a bitter laugh. "You don't know the half of it."

"But I do know how close you are . . . were . . ." I'm not sure what tense to use "to your father. Of course you're upset."

She shrugs. "You should see the state my mum is in. Since he left she's done nothing but sit at the kitchen table in her dressing-gown, just smoking cigarette after cigarette and drinking cup after cup of coffee and –" Suddenly she breaks off and looks up at me. "Oh, she's in such a mess. She keeps asking me how he could have done this to her like I should know. She's never, *ever* going to get over this."

"She will – given time."

"Rosie, you don't know what you're talking about – she *won't* ever get over it. He was her whole life. Their twenty-fifth wedding anniversary is next month. They'd planned to renew their wedding vows in front of all these people who were guests at the original wedding and then they were having this huge party afterwards. They were even going off on a Mediterranean cruise together to celebrate. They'd been planning it for months, years even. Dad even made Mum buy a whole new wardrobe. It was going to be a second honeymoon for them."

"Your poor mum."

"And all along he was having this grubby little affair. I don't understand how he could do this to her. He really did adore her. I never, ever heard him argue with her. I never heard him criticise her. He was always there for her, all down through the years whenever she needed him. They were as close as any two people could be, so close that sometimes I felt like an outsider, that my problems didn't matter. I always thought Mum was so lucky to have someone who loved her so much in spite of everything. Someone who stood by her. How could she have seen this coming? You know, when his brother left his wife, Dad didn't talk to him for years and years but, in the end, my dad is no better than him."

She takes a tissue from her pocket and blows her nose. I can't leave her in this state.

"Dana, I'll ring Monica and tell her I can't come, and you and I can have a quiet night in. We can get a video if you want or we can talk – it's up to you."

"I'm sick of talking. It's all Mum did the last few days – talk, talk, talk – the same old stuff over and over and over." Suddenly she looks at me. "Can I come with you?"

"To the party?"

"Yeah."

"Okay – ah, great!"

But then Dana's face clouds over again. "Only I look a mess and I don't have anything to wear. I haven't done a wash in ages."

"You can borrow something belonging to me."

"Rosie, there is the issue of height difference."

"Hmm, well, let's go and raid Caroline's wardrobe then. We can put some of her hoard of designer stuff to good use. We'll pick out something really nice."

"No! What if I ruin it?"

I laugh. "There are few perks in having your beloved dad run out on your mum but one is that Caroline wouldn't dare say a word even if you brought it back in tatters."

She manages a smile. "Okay then." She puts her hand up to her glasses, to where they're bound with tape: "But I'll need to find my contacts."

"What happened to your glasses?"

"Oh nothing – they just fell."

All things considered, Dana looks great. She's wearing a really pretty little top, tight jeans and boots that I know cost Caroline something ridiculous like €500 – not that I told Dana that, otherwise she'd never have dared put them on. After she washed her hair, I managed to persuade her to let me comb it out and now it hangs in this beautiful shiny mahogany curtain down as far as the tiny waist I'd forgotten she had. She even let me do her make-up and, without her glasses, her eyes look incredible – big and soulful, her recent trauma making them even more soulful than they might otherwise be.

But I feel kind of guilty for dragging her along to this party; it's a pretty depressing affair. It seems Doug – who we've yet to set eyes on this evening – is a real Johnny No-Friends and there can't be more than thirty people in total rattling around this huge double drawing room. Aside from the gaggle of hooded youths – the youngest son and his friends – everyone else is either a neighbour or relative with an average age of about fifty, here to please Monica, I imagine, rather than out of any affection for the birthday boy.

It was Roy, the older son, who let us in and, once he gave us both a drink, he hurried back to his girlfriend. Now as we stand there, sipping our glasses of wine, Monica comes towards us with a reluctant Doug trailing behind her.

"Rosie!" she calls. "Welcome! You know Doug," she introduces her surly son.

"Hi, Monica! Hi, Doug!"

Monica may have a great big smile on her face but Doug looks like he'd prefer to be anywhere else but here; such a long string of misery, I can't help thinking. Handsome, yes – but too sullen to be attractive, and he's deathly pale, like he hasn't seen sunlight in a very long time. I remember Monica telling me how he spends hours and hours in his room with the curtains drawn. I can well believe it.

"Happy birthday!" I say to Doug and he grunts in response and I can't help wondering – Monica, or no Monica – what possessed me to come here to celebrate his birthday. I never liked him when he came into the shop to Monica, and I'm liking him even less now. I should have just said no.

"This is a friend of mine – Dana," I say.

"Hi, Dana," Monica smiles. "You're very welcome. Rosie, Fay's here too, somewhere. She arrived a little while ago."

"Did she come on her own?" I find myself asking, suddenly thinking of that man she was with in the Chinese restaurant.

"Yes, she did," Monica nods and then looks around. "Ah, there she is," she says, spotting Fay sitting on a couch on her own on the far side of the room. She's nursing a drink and looking decidedly uncomfortable, like she's wondering how soon she can politely take her leave.

"Will we go over to her?" asks Monica.

"Sure." I turn to Dana. "Are you coming?"

But Dana doesn't hear me. She's just standing there, staring at Doug and he's staring back at her. It's the weirdest thing. I swear they're like Meg Ryan and Tom Hanks in *Sleepless in Seattle*, in that scene where they first set eyes on each other and they keep looking at one another in puzzled amazement. Or like Leonardo di Caprio and Claire Danes in the film version of *Romeo and Juliet*, when they're gazing at one another in wonderment through the fish tank: I might have drifted off before the end of the film but I do remember that scene. And still Dana and Doug are staring at one another as if they just can't believe what they're seeing. Their eyes aren't even blinking. They can't get enough of one another.

"Rosie, are you coming?" Monica calls back.

I don't budge. I'm staring at them staring at one another and trying to figure out what's going on.

"Rosie?" Monica calls again.

"Yeah, I'm coming."

We make our way over to Fay.

"Hi, Rosie! You're looking very nice," she says when we reach her.

"Thanks. You are too. That's one of ours, isn't it?" I ask, noticing that the dress she's wearing is one from the shop. It seemed like nothing on the hanger but it looks great on her slim figure.

Monica thinks so too. "It's wonderful on you. Much nicer than on that woman who tried it on this afternoon."

"But you told her it suited her," I point out.

She shrugs. "What can I say? I lied! She'd already tried on about a hundred outfits. I thought if I persuaded her to buy this one, then I might finally be able to get rid of her."

I laugh.

Soon, all three of us are talking about this nightmare customer and then about shop stuff in general. I look over and Dana and Doug are still staring at one another in that freaky way. Five minutes later, when I look over again, they've disappeared. I scan the room but I can't see them anywhere. What is going on?

After a while, Monica says she needs to go and check on the other guests and she leaves me and Fay on our own.

We sit back into the couch. Silence reigns. One thing I admire about Fay, even if I don't always necessarily like it, is the way she doesn't try to make small talk for the sake of it but there are times, like now, when small talk serves a purpose. I do like Fay but even with the crutch of work we have little to say to one another during shop hours. So what can we talk about now? I look around the room. There is absolutely no one I can pass the time away by fantasising about, just all these middle-aged people, Doug's older brother and his girlfriend, and the bunch of hoodies. Apart from these guys (who I'd guess would put up with just about anything to get their mouth around a free bottle of booze), I doubt there's a single person here who's not willing the hours away, who's not desperately hoping for that time to come when they can decently make their excuses and rush away home. This is without doubt the worst party I have ever been to in my whole entire life.

"This is the worst party I have ever been to," mutters Fay.

I look over at her and then burst out laughing. "I was thinking exactly the same."

"And so is everyone in the room – except perhaps those young fellows. I'd give them another hour before they're completely legless. Free booze is a great draw. It beats sitting in some park somewhere, or in a graveyard, bemoaning how life sucks!"

I laugh.

"Ladies, would you like a drink?" It's Doug's older brother again.

Both of us reach out, put our empty glasses on the tray he's holding out to us and take a fresh glass of wine. I look over at Fay, who's looking around the room. I think about that man in the restaurant she was with and, again, I begin to wonder just who he is and what he means to Fay. Maybe now's the time to ask her about him when we're both sitting here like this, relaxed, getting along so well.

She looks over at me and smiles.

"Fay?" I begin.

"Yes?"

I lose my nerve. "You haven't seen Doug anywhere?" I say instead, scanning the room.

"I think he's gone upstairs."

"Alone?"

She shakes her head. "With the girl you came in with. Dana, isn't it?"

I groan. "The last thing she needs is to get involved with someone like him."

"I'd say that's the last thing any girl needs. I know he's Monica's son but –"

"You don't like him either then?"

"It's not that. I do like him, I've always liked him but well . . . I think, he's got a lot of issues."

"Like what?"

But she clams up. "He seemed very taken with Dana, and she with him."

"I think she's lost her reason. Why him? Now? Of all people?" I demand. "I know she's had a rough time these past few days but even so." I notice Fay is looking at me quizzically so I go on to explain. "Her parents have just split up – she's found out her father has been having an affair and that his girlfriend's just had a baby girl."

"Oh dear!"

"'Oh dear' is right. The thing is, it's all been a big shock. Dana thought her parents were rock solid and they did seem to be besotted with one another. I can't understand how he could have an affair. How could he go and do that?"

I look to Fay, like she might have the answer. She doesn't say anything for a while

"Relationships are complicated," she says eventually. "Does anybody ever really know what's going on between two people, even the two people themselves?"

"Ah no, I guess not."

Fay laughs. "Listen to me, like I know anything about relationships. The wine must be going to my head."

I think it must be going to mine too because suddenly I hear myself blurting out: "That man I met you with in the Chinese restaurant, is he your . . ." I try to think of a word less absurd when applied to a middle-aged man but at this moment I can't ". . . boyfriend?"

"Boyfriend?" She laughs. I'm not sure if she's laughing at the question or at the ridiculousness of the word. "Ah no, Anthony's – he's – not my boyfriend, no," she says, and then her whole face closes up – completely. She stands up. "I should go to the bathroom."

She leaves me sitting there, staring after her.

Fay doesn't come back and the party really goes downhill from there on. First, Monica starts looking for Doug to blow out the candles but he's nowhere to be found. Then she sends Roy up to try his room and when he comes back down I hear him telling Monica it's locked. Then Monica goes upstairs but returns Doug-less and the birthday cake – HAPPY BIRTHDAY

DOUG! – surrounded by 21 candles remains unlit, sitting in the middle of the table, in the middle of the room, until it's sent flying to the floor when a fight erupts amongst the hoodies – two of whom are drunkenly pushing and shoving each other while the others stand around saying things like, "Guys, calm down!" "Vic, come on!" and "Easy, Rhino, take it easy!". Within moments of the cake smashing to the ground, some of the older guests band together and eject all of them, bar Monica's Tim, and it's off to the graveyard with the lot of them I guess, where they can sit around and moan about how the whole world is against them, and nobody understands them.

But there's more to come. I go out to the hall determined to find Dana but, just as I begin to climb the stairs, I hear the sound of crying coming from underneath and a mixture of concern and nosiness prompts me to see who it is.

It's Monica, sitting on the little telephone table.

"Monica, hey, hey, what's the matter?"

She looks up at me and I see the tears are streaming down her face. She's in bits. There isn't a trace of the composed woman I'm used to at work. I crouch down beside her and take her hand.

"Oh Rosie! You know, twenty-one years ago this very night I gave birth to that boy. I still remember the nurse coming in later, saying I must be tired and asking if I'd like her to take Doug to the nursery but I wouldn't let her. I'd prefer to keep him with me, I told her. Then she said that, maybe, she could put him in the cot but I wasn't having that either. I'd been waiting long enough to hold him. There was no way I was letting him go – the cot seemed far too lonely and big a place for such a little fellow. I remember I spent most of the night lying with him in the bed, cuddling and whispering to him; telling him about how I'd been dying to meet him, and about his little room waiting for him at home, and about his big brother and his daddy."

I'm stroking her hand now; there's little need for me to say anything, she just needs me – someone – to listen.

"You know, I've done my best since their father died but it's impossible. I can't cope. I miss him. He should be here with me tonight. Not dead. It's not fair. We had everything, everything. I loved that man to bits. Even still, I miss him as a husband, but as a father too. I can't help thinking how all our lives would be so different – so much better if he hadn't died. The boys need a father. And I thought Doug was finally getting himself together, that all the bad times were behind him, but I don't think he'll ever change."

Suddenly she gets up and roughly wipes away her tears and with it her momentary weakness, as she's brushed it aside – no doubt – time and time again, throughout the years.

"I'd better see to the guests," she says.

For the second time that night, I'm left sitting on my own. It's then I notice the picture on the wall opposite: it's Monica and her husband on their wedding day. The bride and groom. I think how strange that there should even be these two words – bride and groom. There's no other term or title for something that lasts so short a time – just a day, but such an important day, such a life-determining day. In the photo, the bride and groom are standing at the steps of the church, laughing into the camera. The wind has caught Monica's veil and it's flapping in the wind. All the guests are in the background, great big smiles on their faces, delighting in the happiness of the occasion. I notice Monica and the groom are clutching hands ever so tightly and suddenly that little gesture, that momentary manifestation of perfect and reciprocated love, makes me feel like crying. I turn from the picture. I wonder what Monica's husband's name was – I realise I can't remember it if I've heard it, but now it seems important to know.

I resume my search for Dana. I climb the stairs to find only one door is closed and I hear what I think is the low steady murmur of Dana's voice coming from behind it. When I knock, the talking stops.

"Dana?" I call but no answer. I knock again.

I hear the door being unlocked from the other side. It opens just a little, and then Doug peers out. He doesn't say anything, just stares.

"I want to tell Dana I'm heading home now," I say.

Without a word he closes the door. How rude can someone be! Just as I'm about to knock again, the door opens. It's Dana.

"Dana, I'm about to head home. Are you coming?"

"I think I might stay."

"Don't you think you'd be better coming home? You've had a rough week."

"And that's why I want to stay."

"I see." What can I do? She's an adult. I can't force her. "I'll see you at home then."

"Okay ."

And then, just as she's about to close the door, I call her back: "Dana, can you ask Doug what his father was called?"

She looks at me like I'm crazy but, maybe, figuring it will be the quickest way to get rid of me, she turns and asks Doug. I don't hear his answer but Dana comes back and tells me it was Trevor.

Trevor and Monica. Monica and Trevor. I mull over these two names on the way home in the taxi. Yeah, I think, they go together. They suit. They belong. It's just such an awful, awful pity they're not still together.

Mick and Caroline – not bad, but of course there is no

Mick and Caroline.

Doug and Dana – no, *no,* awful, they don't go together – at all.

Shane and Loretta – definitely not, but then what name would go with Loretta? Something like Lorcan, maybe. Yeah, a smug polo-neck-wearing Lorcan with glasses. *"Hi, my name is Lorcan Lyons. This is my wife, the lovely Loretta, and these are our children, Lottie, Lola, Larry and Loughlin."*

Fay and *what*? What did she call her maybe / maybe not (married) boyfriend tonight? Albert? Andrew? No, it was Anthony – I think. Yes, it was definitely Anthony. Anthony and Fay – no, that sounds dreadful. Anthony is far too staid to go with a whimsical name like Fay. But it's definitely Anthony. In fact – now that I think about it – I'm pretty sure that that was the name of the man who called her at work, that day she got all flustered and then suddenly had to rush home. So just who is this Anthony, and what *is* the story with them? Are they in love?

And Mark and Rosie – does that have a ring? Or would it be Rosie and Mark? No, Mark and Rosie is definitely better. *"Yeah, that's Mark and Rosie – they've been going out together for years,"* I imagine some imaginary person telling some other imaginary person in some imaginary situation in some imaginary future.

When I get to bed, I find I can't sleep. There's too much stuff in my head. I'm worrying about Dana and what the hell she's doing with Doug. I'm thinking about Fay and her mysterious man, and about Monica too, lying all alone in her bed. And I'm imagining Mark in his bed – and hoping he is all alone. But then, when I'm finally drifting off to sleep, I suddenly sit bold upright in a *Eureka!* moment. Anthony is the name of the guy Fay ran away to London with all those years ago. I'm nearly positive. Is that Anthony of long ago the same

Anthony of today? I'd bet anything it is – I just know it is.

I reach for my phone:

– *What was the name of the man Fay (from shop) was going out with long ago?*

I press SEND and the message goes whizzing off to my mother on the other side of the world.

I lie down again. But then I sit back up again. I pick up my phone again.

– *And, btw, I hope u & dad are having a brilliant time. Love you loads. XXX*

16

"Making lo♥e out of nothing at all . . ."

The next night sees me at another party – a hastily arranged one at Finn's house to celebrate the news that Damien Rice has officially asked Dove to play support, with the invite coming via Shane. But, unlike last night's dreadful affair, a massive crowd of people fill the place with the sounds of laughter, chat, amenable drunken discussions (not *fights*) and there's music so loud that the floorboards are vibrating. The drink is flowing, there's dancing too, of a sort, and couples getting friendly.

I've just arrived with the usual crew – Shane (but without Loretta – she's working), Caroline, Mick, Dana plus Doug. Yes, Doug. When I'd tried describing Doug – sullen, mute, rude – to the others they assumed I was exaggerating. But then they met him.

"What does she see in him?" hisses Caroline, when he and Dana are out of earshot.

"Ah come on, he's not bad," says Mick, kindly

"Yeah, he's just very quiet," says a charitable Shane.

"But can he actually talk?" asks Caroline. "No, really, I

mean it. Like, have you actually heard him say anything?"

Leaving the others, I decide to go in search of Mark – he is the main reason I'm here after all. Tonight's the night: the time has come to turn those flirty looks between us into something more. So now I'm pushing my way through the throng in search of him and, as I "Excuse me! Excuse me!" my way through the crowd, pushing a path between people's sweaty backs to gently – or not so gently – guide them out of my way I suddenly feel a hand on my own shoulder.

I swing around. It's Finn, beaming at me.

"Finn! Hi!"

"Hi, Rosie. Good to see you here."

"Thanks for inviting us. It's a great party."

"Glad you think so."

All I want to do is ask him where Mark is but I can't just blurt the question out straightaway.

"You have a great place," I say, instead.

"Thanks."

And it is. From the outside it's just a regular old anonymous 1950's corporation house in the middle of an estate of hundreds like it but the inside is something else. All the little downstairs rooms have been knocked into one to create a big open space, made even bigger by the brilliantly white walls – the perfect backdrop to some outsized paintings that provide dashes of tremendous colour. The wall to the back garden has been replaced by a series of glass doors running the width of the house and the original staircase has been traded for a very modern one made out of glass blocks that descend into the main area.

"I love those stairs," I say, and that's when I see Mark across the room, standing at the foot of them. He's surrounded by three girls all smaller than he is, and all three have their heads craned up, listening while he talks. He looks like some god-like figure and they look as if they're worshipping at his feet.

". . . blood, sweat and tears . . ."

"Pardon?" Distracted, I've missed whatever it is Finn is saying.

"The house – it took blood, sweat and tears. It was a wreck when I bought it."

"You did all this!" I look around in amazement. I remember now Shane telling me that Finn works in his dad's DIY store during the day. Clearly his talents stretch to more than serving at the counter.

He nods. "Yeah."

"Wow!"

If ever I had my own place, I think, looking around, this is exactly what I'd like. "I really love the paintings. Especially that one with all the reds." I point to one on the far side of the room. "It's just got such colour, such life."

He smiles at me. "Do you think?"

"Yeah. Where did you get it?"

"It's my own. They all are."

"What? You mean you painted them yourself?"

He nods.

"Gosh – you play the drums, you paint, you renovate houses! Ahh, what do you do in your spare time?"

He laughs. "I don't have much."

"I bet."

"But I like to travel too, and I like books, and going out with friends and going to the cinema – the usual." He smiles but then he looks embarrassed. "But that was more of a rhetorical question, wasn't it?"

"Maybe," I laugh. "But I am interested." And I guess I am. The night's long. Mark's not going to disappear. And Finn is nice. "So you like movies? Have you been to see any good ones lately?"

"Breakfast on Pluto. Have you seen it?" I shake my head. "Well, you *have* to go! I swear I was blown away. The reason I went was because I thought I should – you know, because of Patrick McCabe and Neil Jordan and Cillian Murphy – they're all so brilliant – but I was afraid I'd be disappointed. But I swear it was just fantastic – the best film I've seen in years. Ever, maybe. The character of Kitten is incredible. There's a point in the film when you realise that he really doesn't care whether he lives or dies and suddenly he has no fear and that makes us fear for him because he doesn't care what awful situation he gets into. It's really powerful stuff. But funny too. And really, really sad." He smiles. "Anyway, talk about a long answer to a short question. Sorry, I tend to babble when I'm excited about something."

"I don't mind. It makes a change. I'm usually the one babbling. Not that I'm saying you're babbling, of course, and, even if you are, at least your babbling makes sense whereas no one ever knows what I'm babbling about. I'm probably babbling now. Am I babbling now?"

He laughs, then nods. "Yeah, you're babbling now."

"Oh."

"But you're making sense – sort of."

He smiles and I smile back and then I think, yeah, I like him. He's cool. He's interesting. I could be friends with him. I would definitely be happy hanging out with him, if, say, Mark and I were going out together. But we haven't *quite* got to that stage yet.

But then, suddenly, Finn lobs a bomb into our conversation:

"Would-you-like-to-go-and-see-*Breakfast-on-Pluto*-sometime? I-wouldn't-mind-going-to-see-it-again."

"Pardon?"

"Ahmm . . . well . . . this is difficult . . . I'm not very good at this sort of thing but I . . . I wanted to ask you that ever since I first saw you. Not to go to see *Breakfast on Pluto*, of course, though we could go to see it, but, well, I just wanted to ask you out. So, would you like to go out sometime?"

I stare. "Go out?"

"Yeah . . ."

"You mean with you?"

"Yes, with me. Is that such a silly notion?"

"No, no, of course not." I don't believe it – Mark's best friend is asking me out. "Ah, Finn . . ." I hate the idea of hurting his feelings. I do like him but he's just not Mark. "Can I think about it?"

"Sure, sure."

The disappointment on his face is obvious. In the sometimes incomprehensible language of love, I guess, "Can I think about it?" is universally understood to be a chicken way of saying, "No way!"

We stand there, awkwardly, neither knowing how to put an end to this awful situation.

"I'm going to get a drink. Do you want one?" he asks, breaking the impasse, and retreating into the role of host.

"Sure."

"Beer, wine, champagne?"

"White wine is fine."

Finn heads away and I stand there staring after him. I like him. I do. He's fun, nice, interesting, clearly very talented, and good-looking too, I guess. He has the best smile ever – a whole face smile, the kind of smile that leaves no choice but to smile right back. He probably wakes up each morning smiling. It's hard to imagine him ever being sullen or dull or cross. But – the big *but* is – he's just not the kind I'd ever imagined myself with. He's an inch or two smaller than me for a start, and I've never gone out with anyone whose head

I can see over. Okay, maybe I can't quite see over it but he does lack that crucial couple of inches. But he is a very nice guy. If there was no Mark, *maybe* I would consider going out with him. But there is a Mark. And he's the one I want. I look over to where Mark is now. The three girls are still fawning all over him. Suddenly he senses me staring at him, and he looks over and gives me one of his slow sexy smiles.

Automatically I smile back but then think – Christ, I have to get out of here! His best friend has just asked me out and I've turned him down. Now is not the time for me to be flirting with him. I hurry out into the garden and sit down beside a little Zen-like pond and try to achieve some Zen-like calm as I consider this recently complicated situation.

And it is complicated. Until tonight I had no idea just what Finn and Mark meant to each other – I guess I thought they were just two guys – two buddies – in a band. But, on the way to the party, Shane began telling us all about their history and it goes right back to the very day they were born. He told us how their mothers first met in the maternity ward when they were both in labour. How – somehow – between their contractions and their screams – the two women discovered that they lived on the same street. How by the time they left hospital, the women were firm friends and the boys were destined to be friends too – whether they liked it or not. How when Finn's own mum died when he was four, Mark's became like a second mum to Finn and he spent as much time in their house as in his own. How it was Mark's mum who brought them both to school on their first day. How even when his father was too busy to go to school plays and concerts, Finn always had Mark's mum and dad in the audience, cheering and clapping for him too.

These guys are way more than friends. They're like blood brothers. I can see them as eight-year-olds, making little slits in their skin, and mixing their bloods together.

How can anything ever happen between me and Mark now?

"Hi, gorgeous! Are you waiting for me?"

I jump at the sound of Mark's voice. I swing around. He's smiling down at me.

"Hi! I brought you a drink," he says, holding out a champagne flute.

I take it. It's empty. I look up at him quizzically.

He sits down beside me and, from inside his jacket, he takes out another flute and a bottle of champagne. He pops the cork, takes my glass from me, fills it, hands it back to me, then fills his own.

"Cheers!" he says holding his glass up.

"What are we celebrating?" I ask.

"Our first kiss." He takes my glass from me.

"But we haven't . . ." I begin but he puts his finger to my lips, then pulls me in close to him and gently kisses me.

"We haven't what?" he murmurs.

I stare at his face, so close to mine. I've been waiting for this moment since I set eyes on him.

"We haven't what?" he repeats.

"Nothing."

I close my eyes. He kisses me again, longer this time. My foot knocks over my drink but I hardly notice.

When he takes me by the hand I don't object, but I follow after him and he leads me back inside and up those glass stairs which now feel ridiculously public – anyone at the party who cares to notice can see where we're headed, and what's on our minds. When I glance down I see only one face upturned. In the middle of the madness, one person is statue-still, staring up at us. And that person is Finn. Our eyes meet. He's holding a glass of white wine – my white wine? – in his hand. He raises it to me and I see him mouth the word, "Cheers!" He's not smiling now. He turns away.

Mark tugs at my hand to hurry me along and, at the top of the stairs, he pulls me into a bedroom. He leads me to a bed, sits down on it and positions me in front of him. Without a word, he slowly begins to take off every stitch of my clothes until I'm standing there in front of him, totally naked. Then, ever so slowly, he looks me up and down and then he reaches out and traces a finger down my body – I feel it move over my forehead, down my nose, it pauses on my lips, then carries on down, circles one nipple, then the other, and ever so gently on over my stomach it goes and then it stops. I want to scream at him to keep going. He raises his face up and stares at me.

"You are beautiful."

I can't answer. That one part of me his hand hasn't touched yet feels like it's going to explode.

"Take your clothes off," I manage to whisper. "Quick!"

I stand there, staring at him as he does. In one movement he's pulled off his T-shirt, in another, his jeans and now he's standing naked in front of me. I step back and look at him.

"So are you," I say. And he is the most beautiful man I've ever seen outside the confines of magazines, television, or the big screen. He's like a male model, all glistening hairs, six pack muscles and an even tan. Who says men can't be beautiful?

He sits back down on the bed and pulls me on top of him. My legs wrap around his waist, and I feel his hands lightly running up and down my back.

But suddenly I pull away.

"Whose room is this?"

"What?"

"Whose room is this?" I repeat.

"Mine. Why?"

I'm relieved. For a second I thought it might be Finn's. I feel guilty enough (but not enough to call a halt) about the inescapable fact that I'm about to sleep with Finn's best friend, mere minutes after he asked me out – but I don't think even I could have gone through with it if it was Finn's room. I think that would be too tacky for even me to contemplate.

We begin to kiss again, but once again, I pull away.

"You live with Finn?"

"Yes." He's beginning to sound exasperated.

Oh fuck! What am I doing?

"Now enough of questions." He turns my head around so that his lips can reach the nape of my neck and I feel him begin to kiss it ever so softly. And then I feel him slip inside me.

"Oh fuck!"

I wake to daylight flooding in through the window. I look over. Mark is curled up beside me, his head resting on me. I stroke his golden hair and I smile at the memory of last night. It was perfect. Absolutely perfect. But then, like someone with temporary amnesia, earlier memories come back and I cringe when I remember Finn and the way he stood there, looking at us as we climbed the stairs.

Suddenly, I don't want to be here. I don't want to be lying here, at eight-thirty on a Sunday morning, waiting for Mark to wake, then going through breakfast together, with Finn and his disapproval hovering over us. I want to go home to my own house, back to my own bed.

Quietly, I get up, collect my clothes from where they lie

on the floor, dress and tiptoe down the stairs.

The place is a mess. Bottles, glasses, streamers, flaccid balloons, and overflowing ashtrays are scattered all over the place. There's even a body sprawled on the couch – like some lost item someone has forgotten or not bothered to take home with them. I find my coat and bag but, just as I'm about to ring for a taxi, I remember to check my wallet first and find I haven't enough.

I ring Caroline.

"Caroline, will you come and get me?" I whisper into the phone as soon as she picks up.

"What?" She sounds sleepy and cross. "Where are you?"

"At Mark's."

"At who's?"

"Mark – you know, from the band."

"Finn's friend?"

"Yeah."

"You're joking! Will you ever learn?"

"Give over!"

"Can't you get a taxi?"

"I haven't enough money."

"Get one and I'll pay when you get here."

"All right."

"Or better still, stop at the bank machine."

"I hadn't thought of that." I hang up and then call a taxi. The phone rings and rings until finally a bad-tempered woman answers. I have to think for a moment before I remember the address, and then she tells me it'll be half an hour.

As I put my phone back in my bag, I see legs coming down the stairs and then Finn's face follows.

"Hi." He looks surprised to see me – and not especially happy. I guess I'm no longer privy to his smile.

"Hi."

"You're leaving already?"

"Yeah, I have a lot I need to do today. There's a taxi on its way."

He puts on the kettle, then pops some bread in the toaster. Maybe these open-plan homes aren't so great after all – there's nowhere for me to go – except outside into the freezing morning.

"Want a cuppa?" Finn asks.

I hesitate. "Thanks."

"Tea or coffee."

"Tea, please."

Silence reigns, except for the sounds he makes as he moves about.

"So are you going to see him again?" he suddenly asks.

"I – I beg your pardon?" I stutter.

"Are you going to see him again?"

"That's none of your business. Look, about last night, I'm sorry about what happened between you and me, but I don't think I led you on. I didn't mean for things to turn out the way they did." He's just standing there, coolly staring at me. "I didn't mean to hurt you. Do you think we could be friends?"

"I have plenty of friends, thanks."

"Look, there's no need to be rude."

"Sorry." He hands me the cup of tea.

"Thanks."

"Rosie?"

"What?"

"Do you really like Mark?"

"Excuse me?"

"Or do you do this sort of thing all the time?"

"How dare you! Of course, I like him."

"Good. He's like a brother to me so don't go hurting

him, all right?"

"I've no intention of hurting him! Why should you think I'd hurt him?"

"I'm just saying, all right?"

"And I'm just not listening, all right! What happened between me and Mark is our business. What are you? His father? You'll be asking what my intentions towards him are next."

I slam down the cup of tea, pick up my bag and storm off out into the frosty morning.

Fifteen minutes pass. My feet are like blocks of ice. There's still no sign of the taxi. Maybe I should walk, it's not that far but in these heels I'd soon be crippled. Worst of all, I'm conscious that Finn can see me standing here, looking like an idiot. Then I hear my phone beeping in my bag and I reach in and take it out and see that it's a text from my mum. I open it.

– *Anthony Knowles cod you should get co alarm fitted go your house! Love u loads 2. XXX*

What? But that makes no sense whatsoever! What's she talking about it? I stare at it. What *is* she trying to say? That somebody called Anthony Knowles said I should get a co alarm, whatever that is, fitted in my house? That I should get someone called Anthony Knowles to fit this co alarm thingy? Or is she saying she's arranged to get Anthony Knowles to go to my house to fit it? I don't know. I can't figure it out – I think my brain is thoroughly addled from the late night and the cold. I wish I had a hat. Maybe it simply means she's finally lost the plot. In the absence of anything better to do, I keep staring at the message until, finally, I begin to see it's actually two messages not one, but made confused by her (un)predictive texting and the absence of punctuation. What's she's trying to say is:

— *Anthony Knowles. And you should get an alarm fitted in your house!*

Anthony Knowles — *that's* the name of Fay's old boyfriend. And the rest is just one of her keep-safe commandments.

"Hey, Rosie?" I look around. Finn is calling from a downstairs window. "You can wait inside, you know. I wouldn't like you to lose a couple of toes to frostbite."

"I'd sooner risk that than getting my head bitten off."

He disappears.

Another five minutes slowly go by and then Finn arrives out with a cup of tea. "At least have this to keep you warm while you're waiting."

Ungratefully, I take it from him. He stands there for a moment looking like he wants to say something, but then he leaves and goes back inside

Just as I'm finishing my tea, the taxi arrives. I leave the empty cup on the garden wall and hop in.

17

"Let's fall in lo♥e . . ."

As soon as I open the front door, I hear Caroline laughing. Caroline has this great laugh. It's a right dirty laugh, real kind of bawdy, like Ken Williams in an old *Carry On* film and totally at odds with her classy appearance. People are always a little taken aback when they first hear her erupt. Now, I stand there listening, wondering what can possibly be *this* funny. I swear she's as hysterical as a kid getting the soft soles of their feet tickled. I find myself smiling. The laugh goes on and on and on, punctuated every now and then by cries of: "Stop it! Oh stop, stop please! I can't listen to any more! Too much, too much!" I wonder who's with her and decide it must be Mick – he and she are as thick as thieves these days. But then my ears pick up another voice, a female one, murmuring away in the background, but too low for me to identify. Now, Caroline's laugh reaches a crescendo. Then it stops, abruptly.

"You're priceless, you really are," I hear her say. "I've never laughed so much. You know, you can be very funny sometimes, Loretta."

Loretta? Funny? These are two words that don't belong in the same sentence.

I walk into the kitchen.

"Hi."

"Hi, Rosie," they say in unison.

Loretta gets up: "I think I'll have another tea – does anyone want one?"

We shake our heads.

She puts the kettle on, then stands there, cup in hand, waiting for it to boil. Caroline goes to the bin, clears the crusts of her toast from her plate and dumps it in the sink. Why this sudden change from lounging to purposefulness the minute I appear? I am suspicious. I feel like a schoolteacher who's come into a classroom of angelic-faced children, all sitting quietly at their desks – *now* – but whatever mischief they were up to still hangs in the air.

"So, what's going on here?" I ask. I mean it in an all-friends-here-together sort of way, but somehow it comes out differently, like I'm demanding an answer.

"Oh Rosie, you should get Loretta to tell you about some of the things that go on in that hospital. Honestly, you couldn't make the stuff up!"

"Really?"

It seems I remember that when *I* tried asking her, Loretta was at pains to remind me that it was real life we were talking about, and not an episode of *ER*. Humph! From the way she and Caroline were laughing, I'd say we're talking more *Scrubs*.

Caroline looks at her watch. "I'd better get going. See ye later."

"Hey, Caroline?" calls Loretta after her.

"Yeah?"

"Good luck!"

"Thanks, and thanks for everything. I mean it."

Seconds later the front door bangs shut.

I think for a moment before speaking.

"Ah – what was all that about?" I ask Loretta, quite casually.

"What?"

"You wished her good luck."

"Yes?"

"But why?"

She stares at me for a moment before answering, slowly, like I might have difficulty following her. "Well, good luck is what people say sometimes when one or the other is leaving. It's a term commonly used as an alternative to goodbye. It probably stems from long ago, when people's journeys were genuinely arduous and fraught with danger."

What? Does she think I'm here to learn English as a foreign language?

"Of course, it being a Sunday morning, the roads are very quiet, and Caroline is a safe driver so the odds are that –"

"No, no, you wished her good luck in a *different* way."

"Oo-kay," appeases Loretta, as if I'm a crazy she's wary of upsetting.

"And, why did she thank you for everything?"

"I don't know. Could it have been the toast I made for her?"

"She thanked you and *really* meant it."

She shrugs. "Maybe I got it just right – a surprisingly difficult thing when it comes to someone else's toast."

I'm not convinced but if I persist I'm in danger of appearing somewhat unhinged. But, like the schoolteacher, I just know there's something going on but Loretta is a tough nut to crack. I'll tackle Caroline later

So I sit down at the table and start pouring some cornflakes into a bowl. I notice Loretta's eating a fruit salad. It looks delicious. Especially compared to my cornflakes. I look down at them now and it strikes me that I don't particularly like cereals. And yet morning after morning I eat them out of routine, because I can't be bothered making any effort. From time to time, I do struggle home with bags of fruit determined to juice my way to health and happiness but then the fruit sits in a bowl on the counter, a rotting reminder of my good intentions, until someone finally throws out the mouldy mess.

"Where's Shane?" I ask.

"He's gone for a swim. He's decided to train for a triathlon. I'm going to collect him when he's finished."

"Shane doing a triathlon? Ha! That'll be the day!"

"Why not, if he trains hard enough? He's pretty determined."

She picks up one of the Sunday newspapers from the table, selects a supplement and begins to read. It seems she's decided that that's the end of our conversation. I sit there, thinking. When did she start talking like she knows Shane better than I do? He's been my friend for years and years, she's only been going out with him for a couple of months – well, okay, six months. And since when did she and Caroline get to be such great buddies? Caroline wasn't supposed to like her either. And does Dana sit around laughing with her too when I'm not here, telling her she's *so* funny.

What do they all see in her that I can't?

She looks up from her paper, and gives me a quizzical look. I realise I'm staring.

Maybe it's time I tried a little harder. Tried, full stop. Apart from that disastrous night of their six-month anniversary, I never really try with her. But where to begin? No need to start with anything heavy. Chat is what we want, not heartfelt exchanges of our deepest thoughts.

"Were you working last night?"

"Yeah, I just got off."

How can she possibly look this good then? I bet she spent most of it snoring her head off in the on-call room.

"Busy?" I ask.

"Mayhem. I swear I've had about two hours' sleep since I got up on Thursday morning. I'm exhausted."

"I know how you feel – I didn't get much sleep myself last night." I cringe. I could bite my tongue off. I sound like I'm boasting. Quick, quick, I need to change the subject. "You and Shane are getting along very nicely."

Not the smoothest change ever but I can't take the words back now. She looks up from her paper again and then hesitates as if she's wondering if I'm expecting an answer, or if there's more to come.

"Yes, we are," she says finally.

"It's funny . . ."

She looks up. "What's funny?"

"Well, you don't seem like an obvious couple."

"Don't we? Why's that then?" There's steel in her voice.

Another quick change of subject would be the sensible way to go, but – oh no – not the one I take. "You just don't seem suited. You know he's – well – quite lively and outgoing and – well, you're – ahmm – not so much." I'll soon need a bigger shovel for all this digging but still I can't stop. Down, down, down I'm going. "I'm not saying you're *not* suited. No, no, just nobody would ever think it at first." I'll be eye-to-eye with a kangaroo before I know it. "I mean you clearly are suited but like, if, say, someone put fifty boys and fifty girls in a room and then brought a stranger in and told this stranger, that he – or she – whichever – had to pair everyone up, I just don't think that he – she – would necessarily put you and Shane together." What the hell am I rabbiting on about? Just shoot me with that shovel right now!

"So why would they be doing this?" Loretta wants to know.

"What?"

"Why would they be putting all these people in this room – these fifty boys and fifty girls?"

She's mocking me and there's not a damn thing I can do about it. I deserve it.

I shrug defensively.

"Would it be, like, a scientific experiment?"

"I'm just saying – if. Look, I know I'm making a mess of this but I'm trying to make an effort here. Shane is my best friend. You're his girlfriend. It would be nice if we could get along. I just think we should try to get to know one another. Maybe you and I could do something together some day."

I can't believe I just said that.

From the look on her face, neither can she.

"Nothing big," I add hastily. "Just a coffee or, say, the pictures. We wouldn't need to spend the whole day together, or anything."

"Well . . . I . . ." She looks like she's desperately searching for an excuse.

I am mortified. I should never have bothered trying. It was fine the way things were. We're not cut out to be friends.

"I . . . I –"

Suddenly there's a tremendous bang on the ceiling. We both look up, then we stay looking, and listening to the rhythmic banging that's now coming from the room above. The lightshade begins swinging back and forth, back and forth, back and forth and the two of us sit there, heads upturned, watching it sway to and fro, like we're hypnotised.

I feel my face going red. How excruciatingly embarrassing! *We* are listening to Dana having sex.

And very good sex it sounds like too. We could be in the room with her.

There comes the highest pitched scream ever and we both jump. Then the grunting starts. Unmistakable sex-grunting, unmistakable man-about-to-come grunting. And then a shout, a male shout: "God-oh-God-oh-God-oh-God-oh-God! Oh God! Oh God! Oh God!"

Loretta and I look at one another.

"You know," says Loretta, "they're the first words I've ever heard him speak!"

We both burst out laughing.

Then all is quiet. We sit there, our necks craned upwards again, wondering if that's it. It seems it is. There isn't a peep but then we jump at the sound of the kitchen door opening. It's Doug, wearing nothing but a pair of jocks, tight, *very* tight jocks. He looks mildly surprised to see us but says nothing, having reverted to his habitually mute manner. Neither do we say anything. We just there in silence, our eyes following him as he goes to the fridge, takes out a carton of juice and drinks directly from it. I realise I'm staring and force myself to look away. My eyes meet Loretta's and it's about all we can do to stop ourselves laughing.

He crosses the floor, goes to the bin, squashes the carton in, then mooches back out again, without so much as a glance at us.

"Well, lucky old Dana," says Loretta, once he's gone. "I think I can see now what the attraction is."

And that starts us laughing again.

When we do finally stop, she looks at her watch, then gets up to go.

"I'd better go and get Shane." She pauses for a moment or two. "Maybe we could go for that coffee sometime."

18

"Stop in the name of lo♥e!"

It's late that afternoon and Caroline and I are in town to do some shopping. Or rather, she's in town to do some shopping and I've been dragged along to fulfil a number of roles. These are:

(a) To agree that – yes – she definitely does need yet another red wool coat / cream mohair polo / black suede boots, or to persuade her that – no – she does *not* need yet another red wool coat / cream mohair polo / black suede boots – depending on whatever answer she's looking for.

(b) To nod in agreement when she bemoans the fact that sizes are definitely getting smaller, and what used to be a size ten is now a size twelve, or even fourteen.

(c) To patiently stand outside dressing-rooms throughout the city until she comes out, and to then nod my head in approval, or shake in disapproval – as required, as indicated by the expression on her face.

(d) To agree that, no – €100 is not a ludicrous amount for her to spend on a face cream – (which clearly it is, but it's *her* €100 not mine).

(e) To carry her bags when she's talking on the phone, browsing through racks, clocking up another bill, or when she's just too damn lazy to carry them all herself.

(f) And, finally, to wrestle her to the ground and grab her Visa card from her *if* she totally loses the run of herself. Fortunately it hasn't come to that – yet.

For my efforts, she's now treating me to coffee and cake and I'm telling her *all* about Mark. Finding her with Loretta in the kitchen this morning delayed this outpouring but now I'm in full flow.

I haven't been going on *that* long – ten, fifteen minutes maybe – when she suddenly heaves this enormous sigh.

"Rosie, can you just give it a rest – *please*?"

"What?"

"It's been nothing but Mark, Mark, Mark since we sat down."

"That's *not* true."

"*Is* true!"

"Well, I'm sorry! I can't help being excited. I just really, really like him."

She sighs again. "How many times have we been here before?"

I look around the coffee shop. "I don't know – a dozen times maybe?"

"I don't mean *here* here. I mean how many times have I sat listening to you going on about some guy, telling me how he's the one, how special he is, how you really like him?"

"I'm sorry if I'm boring you. Given that you dragged me along to go shopping with you on a Sunday, I think the least you can do is listen to me. Did you think I wanted to come? Have you never heard of the phrase 'busman's holiday'?"

"Look, all I'm saying is, can't you take it a little more slowly this time?"

"Why, when I really like him?"

"But you hardly *know* him."

"Of course I know him."

"Okay," she sighs and wearily invites me to, "Tell me what you know about him, then."

"Well, he's good-looking and –"

She interrupts with another great big sigh.

"Caroline, *what's* with all the sighing?" I demand.

"Rosie, *I* know he's good-looking. Anyone who's ever set eyes on him knows he's good-looking. *He* knows he's good-looking. The very fact that you're seeing him means he's good-looking, otherwise he wouldn't get a look-in. It's the same thing again and again with you. Can't you tell me something, *anything*, that will allow me to understand why this time it might be different?"

I think for a moment. "Well, he's intelligent and deep and sensitive," I tell her, thinking of the lyrics of all the songs he's written, and I sit back, feeling quite pleased with my answer.

"Mark?"

"Yes. And passionate, and I don't mean in a sexy way, although he's that too. But just listen to his voice, the way he sings, the words he sings, they're just so full of passion."

"He does have an amazing voice – I'll give you that. But intelligent, deep and sensitive? Sorry, honey, I'm just not seeing it."

"But you've never even talked to him."

"That's true. Okay – next time I see him, I'll make the effort to get to know him."

"Good."

"Maybe I'll be pleasantly surprised."

"You will."

She stands up. "Come on, I want to get over to Tower

Records before they close. Here, will you carry some of these bags for me?"

We make our way through the crowds. Caroline is leading and I'm trailing behind but I'm beginning to feel a little disgruntled by the fact that I seem to have far more than my fair share of what are, after all, *her* bags.

"Do you know who I think is really something?" she turns around to ask.

"Who?"

"Finn."

"Finn?"

"Yeah. What do you think of him?"

I hesitate. "He is nice." I think about telling her what happened between him and me last night at the party but decide not to. I don't want to have to listen to her going on at me about how mad I am to choose Mark over Finn.

"Nice? He's more than nice. He's gorgeous!"

"Let me get this straight. It's okay for you to fancy someone because of the way they look but for some reason I'm not allowed."

She isn't listening. "His eyes are just –" she shivers "– oh, I could dive into them – now *there's* deep. And that grin of his, it is wicked. I bet he has a great sense of humour. You'd just know by the look of him that you'd have a brilliant time on a night out with him."

"Don't let Mick hear you saying that."

"What's it to do with Mick?" she snaps.

"Oh – you know . . ."

"Leave it out! How many times have I got to tell you – struggling artistic souls are not my thing. All I'm saying is I can't understand why, if you're going to fall for one of the band, you'd fall for Mark rather than Finn. I'm not saying *I* fancy Finn, I'm just remarking on how nice he is."

"Yeah, he is nice but –"

"I mean, if I were going to hook up with a struggling creative type, then I might as well stick with what I know best and hook up with Mick. But I'm not – that's not part of my life plan. No, a nice dot.com millionaire, that's what I'm holding out for."

"You really are such a romantic," I remark.

When we reach the music store, she hands me the rest of her shopping bags.

"Hold these while I take a look," she tells me.

So I trail around the shop after her like I'm her own personal servant but, in a way, it suits me to have my hands full. I don't want to be tempted into buying CD's I can ill afford at the moment.

"So why won't you tell me where you disappeared off to this morning," I ask when she stops to flick through some CD's that have caught her eye.

"I don't know what you're talking about."

"You do and what I can't understand is why you told Loretta but you won't tell me."

"I really haven't a clue what you mean."

"Why was she wishing you good luck? And why were you thanking her, and really meaning it?"

"What are you on about? You know, you can be *very* peculiar sometimes."

We leave the shop finally – thankfully – my arms are almost wrenched from their sockets, and we start walking down Grafton Street and back to the carpark.

"Oh my God!" I grab Caroline's arm and drag her over to the nearest shop window.

"You have got to be kidding. Jesus, Rosie! You've only just met him!"

"What are you talking about?"

She nods towards the window. It's only then I notice that we're standing outside Weir's Jewellers.

"No, no, I'm not interested in that!"

"Well, then, do please tell me why you have your nose pressed against a window full of trays of engagement rings?"

"Do you see that couple over there?" I ask, peering over my shoulder in the direction of Brown Thomas.

She looks around, and then looks back at me. "Rosie, we're on Grafton Street. It's a Sunday afternoon. There are like about ten million couples within eyesight."

"That middle-aged couple standing by Brown Thomas. She's wearing a long fawn-coloured coat."

She goes to look around again.

"Be discreet!" I hiss.

"Loudly hissing 'be discreet!' is hardly the best way of being discreet yourself!" she snaps.

"They can't hear me."

"No, but everyone else can."

And she's right; those nearest are beginning to stare at us.

Caroline cranes her neck around again and scans the people.

"That woman you work with, is that who you mean? Fay, isn't it?"

"Yes, yes!" In my excitement I'd forgotten that Caroline has met Fay in the shop. "Tell me, what are they doing?"

"Well, they're both staring over in this direction and she's saying something to him, like maybe, why is that very peculiar girl I work with standing up against a shop window, pretending to be invisible? For goodness sake, Rosie, what do you *think* they're doing?"

"I mean, does it look like they're together?"

"Of course, they're together."

"But do they look intimate? You know, like a couple?" I demand. "What's their body language like?"

Suddenly her eyes open wide.

"What?" I demand.

"Ooooh!"

"What? What?" I go to turn around but she stops me.

"Don't! You don't want her to see you, do you?"

"But what are they doing?"

"What *aren't* they doing?"

"What do you mean?"

"Well, he's got his hand under her coat, and she's nuzzling into his ear, kissing him and . . . oh my!"

"What? What?"

But Caroline's just staring with her mouth wide open.

"What are they doing?"

"I can't tell where his hand is exactly, but from the look on her face, I think I can guess. At their age! And on Grafton Street!"

"No!"

"Of course not, you moron! They're just talking."

"Caroline!"

"Now they're moving away. Don't turn around — they're passing right behind us. Now they're gone."

When I do turn around, I search for them again. For a second I think they've been swallowed up in the crowd but then I spot them. "Right, come on."

"Where?"

"After them, of course."

"Rosie, this is seriously weird! I'm not going following your colleague —"

But I dump all the bags on her and take off. At first I think I've lost them but then at the junction with Suffolk

Street, I see them again standing at the taxi rank. I watch as he says something to her. I see her smile. Then he gently touches her arm. He bends down, talks to the taxi driver, turns back to her, then he kisses her on the cheek before helping her in. After the taxi pulls out, he stands there buttoning up his own coat.

I take out my mobile phone, press the camera function, focus on him and, just as I click, I hear a shout from behind me:

"Rosie! What the hell do you think you're doing?"

Even I've the sense to be embarrassed. "Nothing," I mutter.

"Did you just take a photograph of that man Fay was with?"

I think about lying, about telling her that I was suddenly seized with the urge to photograph the architectural treasure that is Trinity College, which I now notice is in the background, but somehow I don't think she'd buy it.

"Did you?" she demands again.

"Yes," I admit, shamefacedly.

"I don't believe it!" she cries.

"Hush, can't you keep your voice down?" But Fay's mystery man hasn't noticed – he's talking on his phone now.

"You're bloody mad!"

"Probably."

"Have you some older man fetish you haven't told me about?"

"No!"

"Then why?"

"You wouldn't understand!"

"Try me!"

"Okay. Did I ever tell you the story my mum told me about Fay, about how, when she was our age, she ran off to London with a married man?"

"Yes?"

"And how they had a baby together but when the baby died he abandoned her and came home to his first family."

"Yes, yes — of course I remember it."

"Well, I think that's him. That's the man she ran away with. That's Anthony Knowles."

She looks over to where he's standing. Oblivious to our stares and to our conversation about him, he's still talking into his phone.

"What a bastard!" She turns back to me. "But what's she doing with him now?"

"Well, that's exactly what I'm trying to find out. He's just seen her off in a taxi."

"Hmm. But why take a photo of him?"

"I wanted to find out if it definitely was him. My mum would know. I was going to send the photo to her. At least I was thinking about it but it's a stupid idea. I'm not actually going to send it . . ." I trail off.

She's staring at him. "It's funny — he looks a harmless old sort. Who'd have imagined he'd had such an eventful life."

"I wonder if someone will be saying that about us one day?" I think aloud.

She laughs — I'm not sure at what exactly. Maybe she thinks the idea of us being old is preposterous.

"Do you think he's on the phone to Fay now?" I ask.

"Hardly. Not when she's just got into a taxi. Maybe he's on to his wife telling her that . . . I don't know . . . that he's just going to collect that skirt she put aside, or to pick up that ham she asked him to get. That poor woman. He cheated on her with Fay once, and now he's doing it again."

"We don't know that!" I protest.

"That's how it looks from where I'm standing."

We watch as he puts his phone back into his pocket and

then he begins to walk off. If looks could kill, he'd be lying dead on the pavement, his blood puddling around him.

"Well!" Caroline turns to me. "What are you waiting for? If you're going to go around acting like some cheesy private eye taking clandestine photographs, then you might as well go the whole hog. Go on! Press send!"

"Caroline, I don't think —"

"Press send!"

And I do.

19

"Lo♥e is the drug . . ."

I arrive at the boutique at my usual time on Monday morning to find I'm the first. This in itself is a first and I'm a little disorientated to see the place all closed up. In all my months working here, this has never happened before and I stand outside the shuttered shop, with three piping hot coffees, wondering what I should do. I don't have keys, I've never had any need of them, and now I discover that I've left my phone at home too. I hope that Fay or Monica get here soon – it's freezing. I begin to worry that something might have happened to them but, illogically perhaps, I'm reassured by the fact that *both* of them are missing – it's unlikely something bad could have befallen each of them on the same day. I check my watch thinking that maybe I got up an hour early but no, it's 9.15. I wonder if it's some public holiday but it's very unlikely I'd forget one of those and, anyway, I notice, looking around, all the other shops are opening up.

I put two of the coffees down on the window ledge and

begin to sip the third, then take one of the doughnuts from the bag and tuck into it.

But soon I get a funny feeling I'm being watched. I look around and see a guy sitting in the doorway, across the way. His whole body is wrapped up in a sleeping bag like a pupa and he has a woolly hat pulled down over his head so all that's visible are his eyes and these, I now see, are focused firmly on me. I try to ignore him and carry on eating my doughnut and sipping my coffee but then a bite of dough sticks in my throat. I can't enjoy it any more, not with him staring at me with those hungry eyes.

I pick up one of the spare coffees and go over to him.

"Would you like this?"

"Has it got sugar in it?"

"Pardon?"

"Has it got sugar in it?"

"No."

"Okay then." He sits up, wriggles his hands free from the sleeping bag and takes the coffee from me.

"Ta, very much."

I hand him one of the doughnuts.

"Cheers," he says.

I walk back to where I was standing and continue sipping my coffee and waiting.

"You work in that shop, don't you?" he calls out through a mouth packed full of doughnut.

I think before I decide to answer. Giving him something to eat is one thing, chatting to him is another. I'm not sure I want to draw him on me. But he doesn't wait for an answer:

"You're always late."

"Pardon?"

"The fat one arrives first, then the skinny one and then you."

"What? How do you know?"

"I see youse all in the mornings."

"What? Do you sleep here every night?"

"Some nights. You always come rushing around the corner in a right tizzy, carrying the coffees. I'm always worried you're going to spill some on yourself. So where do you think the other two are now?"

"I don't know."

"It's not like them."

"No, it's not."

We fall silent. My toes are numb from the cold. I start on the second coffee to keep warm.

"Here she is," he suddenly announces and I turn to see Fay rushing towards us.

"Oh, isn't Monica here yet?" asks Fay when she sees me standing there.

I shake my head.

"That's not like her," she mutters and begins to search in her bag.

"Hurry on," I mutter. "I'm freezing!"

"I don't think I have my set of keys. I'd better ring Monica and find out what's happening."

She takes out her mobile, punches in the number and then from their conversation I gather that Monica is on her way but she'll be half an hour.

"I can't wait here that long," I moan. "Come on, I'm going to get some breakfast – are you coming?"

She hoists her bag up on her shoulder and we head off.

"I'll tell her where you're gone if she gets here before you're back," my new friend calls after us.

"Thanks," I call back, then notice Fay staring from one of us to the other.

Five minutes later we're ensconced in a cosy little booth

and I'm waiting for the fry I've ordered. Doughnut aside, I've had nothing else to eat in my usual Monday morning rush to get to work so I'm determined to make the most of this unexpected opportunity.

In more ways that one, I decide, looking across at Fay. This, I'm thinking, is the perfect chance to find out more about her mystery man who I'm ninety–nine per cent certain is Anthony Knowles. My mum did get the photo but when she texted back it was to ask why I'd sent her a blurry photograph of some unidentifiable person, so I told her, and then she texted me to say that, yes, it *could* be Anthony Knowles, but, then, it could be just about anyone; and ended by suggesting I should start taking vitamins pills.

"So," I say to Fay now, "aside from Monica's party, did you do anything at the weekend?"

"No, no, not really."

"I came into town yesterday. It was packed! The crowds on Grafton Street were unreal."

I wait. Now an entirely innocent person could be expected to say something like, "You're right. They were brutal. I know. I was in town myself." But Fay sits there, saying nothing.

I go on. "Yeah, I was waiting outside Brown Thomas for my friend at around six and the place was so mobbed I was afraid I wouldn't see her."

Another silence. She just goes right on sipping her coffee as if I haven't even spoken. Okay, I've given her every encouragement to tell me where she was but, still, I'll give her one more chance – but enough with the pussyfooting. Time to drop the kindly Miss Marple act. If I want some straight answers, I need to start asking some hard-boiled Philip Marlowe style questions.

"So what did you do yesterday?"

She looks up and, at first, I think she's going to tell me to mind my own business but instead she answers: "I stayed at home most of the day."

"Doing what?"

She looks a little startled now at such a direct question. "Just the usual sort of stuff," she says, but there's a hint of annoyance in her voice.

"Did you go out at all?"

"Pardon?" She looks over at me irritably. It's like I've finally tested her patience to the limit. "Rosie, why are you asking me all these questions?" she demands crossly. "I really don't think they're any of your business."

"Sorry, I was just – chatting."

"And I'm sorry too, for snapping. I have a lot on my mind."

"Want to talk about it?"

"No."

"Are you sure?"

"I'm sure."

"I'm a good listener."

She doesn't answer. We quickly finish up and leave.

When we arrive back to the shop, we find Monica has opened up and is busy serving a customer. As soon as she's finished, she turns to us.

"Girls, I'm so sorry I wasn't here to open up but I was up half the night worrying and I overslept this morning. Doug has me tormented! If that whole fiasco of a party wasn't enough, he then stayed in his room all day Saturday with some harpy. I swear I had to get out of the house to get away from them. Then, when I did finally come back from town, she was gone, but he was slouched on the couch and the whole place was a complete mess again after I'd spent the morning tidying up so I lost my temper with him and told him I wasn't one bit happy with him sleeping with any old tramp who'd have him, and under my roof too, and then he flipped and stormed out. I haven't seen him since – who knows where he is!"

I think before answering. "Monica, that ah – harpy – is Dana, my friend, the girl I came with to the party."

"Oh, so that's who she was! Of course!" She narrows her eyes and stares at me accusatorily, like I'm personally responsible for the whole situation.

"Dana's nice," I tell Monica.

"What's she doing with my Doug then?"

I'm about to say that I've been asking myself the same question but remind myself that he *is* Monica's son. It's all right for her to criticise him but it mightn't go down so well if I start.

"And you needn't worry about Doug. He's over at our place."

"Is that so?"

"Monica, Dana really is nice."

"Humph!" She's not convinced.

"You'd like her if you got to know her," I tell her.

"I doubt that somehow."

Another customer comes to the counter and Monica goes to serve her but, every now and then, I notice her scowling over at me. It's like she really does blame me for what's happened. I've a good mind to tell her that I've no worries about her lump of a son, Doug. He's big enough to take care of himself. It's Dana I'm worried about.

Later, when Fay goes for lunch, I decide to tackle Monica on the subject of Fay. I want to find out what she knows but I figure it might also distract her and keep her off the topic of Doug and Dana.

"So, I see Fay has a boyfriend," I say quite casually.

Immediately I see this is news to her.

"No! She never told me. How do you know?"

"I've seen her around town with him a few times."

"But how come she hasn't said anything?"

"I don't know. Maybe she wants to keep it a secret."

"Whatever for? If I had a new boyfriend I'd be driving around in a pick-up truck with him propped up in a chair on the back for all the world to see, and I'd be blaring the news over a loudspeaker to make sure nobody could miss him."

I laugh.

She goes on: "Wait until she gets back after lunch – I'll have a few questions for her."

I regret saying anything now. If Fay finds out I've been gossiping about her, she'll go mad. "Monica, maybe you shouldn't say anything to her."

"Not say anything! Are you joking?"

"If she wanted us to know, I think she'd have told us."

"Hmm." She thinks for a moment. "Maybe you're right. But I am glad for her. I don't think she's had anyone since . . ." she trails off.

"Since?"

"Well, let's just say, for a very long time."

"How long have you known Fay?"

"Since our school days and then, when I opened the shop, she came to work for me. She'd never worked in a shop before but I knew she'd be great."

"What did she do before?

"Office work mainly, here and in London too."

"She lived in London?"

"For a few years. God love her, she had a very rough time there. It took her a long time to get over it."

"Why, what happened to her?"

"It's a long story but it's all in the past now. I don't think Fay would like me talking about it. But what I will say is that there isn't a person alive who deserves a little happiness more than Fay. She's had more than her fair share of heartbreak. Now, come on, I need you to put that new stock out on the floor while the shop is quiet."

When I arrive home that evening, the house is in darkness and I think there's no one there. I decide to have a long soak in the bath and an early night. But when I try the bathroom door it's locked.

"Caroline, are you in there?"

No answer, but I can hear someone shuffling around inside. "Dana?"

"I'll be out in a minute."

I wait and it's a good five minutes before she finally unlocks the door and, when she does come out, I see her face is all red and puffy from crying.

"Whatever is the matter?" I ask.

"Nothing," she snaps and hurries off to her room. She closes the door and I hear the lock turning

My bath isn't quite as relaxing as I might have hoped. My mind refuses to be calmed by the warm, aromatic bubbles and insists on flitting from one thought to another. To Dana, and just why she was so upset – the whole thing with her parents, or did she already have a falling-out with Doug? No good can come of him and her, I just know it. And to Fay and Anthony Knowles. What is the story there? It must be twenty years since all the stuff in London happened? Have they been having an affair all this time?

And to Mark too. I guess I expected him to ring me today, but he didn't.

20

"I'll have to say I lo♥e you in a song . . ."

My stomach is in bits. I look at myself in the mirror and think I look okay. Or okay-ish. Maybe I have too much make-up on. Or maybe I don't have enough. Oh, I don't know. You see, Mark rang and asked me if I'd like to meet him for coffee in town and to then go on to a movie or for a bite to eat. A movie, a bite to eat, a wander around a car accessories outlet – like I *care* what we do!

"Ah, why not?" I said on the phone with truly remarkable composure. "So, when?"

"How about in an hour?" he said. "Would that suit?"

"*Yes! Yes! Yes!*" I cry, with my hand over the receiver. Then I take it away: "An hour? Sure. I think I can manage that."

Oh, I like this guy – a lot. True, this whole business with Finn is unfortunate but there's nothing I can do about that. I'm not so big-headed as to think that Finn won't get over it. And I can't *not* see Mark for fear of upsetting his friend.

I arrive into the coffee shop expecting to see him sitting

there, waiting, but he's nowhere to be seen. Disappointed, I sit down. I look at my watch. I'm five minutes early. I order a coffee.

Five, ten, fifteen minutes pass. I begin to feel self-conscious. Anyone watching me – like that surly waitress behind the counter – must know from the way I keep glancing towards the door that I'm waiting for someone. She probably thinks I've been stood up. I too am beginning to think I've been stood up. Should I just go now, head hanging in mortification, or will I have another coffee? I decide to give him the time it takes me to drink one more coffee and then I'm out of here. I get up, go to the counter, order from the waitress who manages to get through our entire exchange without saying a single word to me, apart from muttering "€2.50" as she slaps my coffee down on the counter. No please, no thank you, no have a nice day.

I sit down again, and sip as slowly as possible. The waitress is mutely staring at me. I think of things I'd like to say to her, like, "So, what attracted you to the service industry? Let me guess – you love working with people."

But I can't make the coffee last forever and, after I've drained the last, I decide I've had enough. I've waited as long as I'm going to wait, longer than I would have waited for anyone else. I begin gathering my things together but then, just as I'm about to get up from the table, Mark comes rushing in.

"Hi, there! I'm sorry I'm late." He bends down and gives me a kiss on the lips. "Hmm-mmm," he sighs and then, before I've managed to recover from the surprise of the first, he gives me another, much-much longer kiss. When he finally pulls away, I'm staring at him dumbfounded. Wow! This man sure can kiss! But then I know that already.

He sits down opposite me. "I hope you're not mad,"

he says.

"Mad at what," I ask, genuinely puzzled – the kiss having given me a sudden attack of amnesia.

"That I kept you waiting."

"Oh yeah – that!" I laugh. "It doesn't matter. I haven't been here that long," I lie. But it really doesn't matter, now that he's here.

He goes on: "I got into this stupid argument with Finn just as I was going out the door."

"What about?"

He takes a breath, as if he's readying himself to launch into some big tale of woe but then he shakes his head. "Nothing really, just some boring band stuff – you wouldn't want to know."

"It must be hard living with someone and then playing with him too."

"Not usually. Finn and I go way back. I guess we're more like brothers. Even though we're the same age, I've always looked out for him – like a big brother. His mother died when he was little and he spent most of his time in our house when we were growing up so we've always been very close."

Just how close? Did Finn tell him he asked me out? I think about asking but decide against it. Why tell him now, if he doesn't already know?

"Besides," he goes on, "it's not like we're together twenty-four/seven. He works with his dad and I work in a call centre during the day but hopefully that will all change soon and I'll be able to give up, even though I'm a supervisor there, in fact the chief supervisor."

"When the band takes off?"

"Yeah. So, another coffee?"

I'm kind of feeling all coffee-ed out but I nod: "Yeah,

go on."

He goes up to order and I sit back, feeling all delighted and excited, with myself, with him, with being here with him, with life itself. I look to where he's leaning against the counter and just the sight of him sends a thrill through my body. And then I see I'm not the only one he's having an effect on. The surly waitress is no longer surly but now has this beam on her face and is chatting away as she fills the cups. I think about standing up and shouting: "Hullo, he's with me! You saw us kissing, didn't you?"

But I can't blame her. He *is* gorgeous. He's gorgeous and he's with me!

He comes down carrying the two coffees.

"For you, Princess."

Princess? *Princess?* Who's he calling princess? Okay, okay, it's just a term, I tell myself; people use it all the time. He sits down again but, before he does, he puts his hand to his crotch and unselfconsciously rearranges his bits. Lots of men do that, I remind myself and, remembering back to the other night, I'm thinking he has more need to than most.

"What are you grinning at?" he asks.

"Ah, nothing."

"Did anyone ever tell you, y*ou* have a *very* sexy grin?"

There's really no answer to this cheesy – although not entirely unwelcome remark – but it seems he doesn't expect one. He picks up his jacket, searches in one of his pockets, takes out a little round tin, then taps out two little pills into his coffee.

"Sweet 'n' Low – they're a sugar substitute," he explains, seeing me looking.

But I don't need him to explain *what* they are – I've seen my dad use them often enough but, what might be of more use is an explanation as to *why* he's using them. He's not fat, or old, or in danger of having a heart attack as far as I'm aware, so what's he doing with these?

"Oh, right." I see no way of asking him without seeming rude.

"Why did you leave so early on Sunday morning?" he suddenly asks.

"Pardon?"

"You left before I woke."

"I'm sorry," I stammer. "I just needed to get some things done."

"On a Sunday morning?"

"Ahh, yeah. You see my parents are on holidays in Australia and we have this arrangement that they ring me early each Sunday before they go to bed." A lie, to be sure, but a good one I think.

"So you didn't have any regrets then?" he's asking me.

"No, oh no. Definitely not!"

"Good. I was afraid you might. I don't usually move so fast . . ." He reaches across the table and begins to gently stroke my cheek with the back of his fingers. "But then I don't often meet someone like you." He's staring at me. "In fact I've never met anyone like you. You really are something. You are so beautiful, Rosie. You know, I can remember the very moment I first saw you."

"You can?"

"You were sitting near the front of the stage. You were wearing a purple top and had on this big shiny silver medallion."

It wasn't *that* big. It was more pendant than full-scale medallion but I leave it pass – now's not the time for nitpicking.

"Mark?"

"Yes?"

I *have* to ask him. "Did you write that song about me?"

He takes his hand away, sits back in his seat, and stares at me for a very long time. "If I said I did, would you mind?"

"Mind? Of course not. No, I think it's lovely. I'd be – flattered."

He begins to hum gently.

"Da-da, da and light bouncing off a silver pendant. No reason, no rhyme, it takes no time, just a first glimpse of you . . ."

I hold my breath, thinking of what comes next ...

". . . to fall in love."

We both sit there staring at one another. Then he reaches across the table and takes my hand again.

"You looked so beautiful that night! You know, I – I –"

I lean forward but then he pulls back.

"It's great news about Damien Rice, isn't it?" he says.

"Great," I say, a little confused by this sudden change. What was he going to say?

But the moment has clearly passed. He goes on: "I can't believe it."

"It must be all very exciting. Things are really beginning to take off for the band, aren't they?"

"Yeah. Did I tell you that he's even thinking of recording one of our songs?"

"No way! But I thought he wrote all his own songs?"

"Usually, but he's really interested in doing this one."

"Which one?"

"Day Without a Future."

"Is that the one about the day stretching out before you, after your girlfriend went away and took all your dreams with her?"

"Yeah," he nods.

"I love that song."

"It's one of my favourites too."

And then it's like a cloud passes over his face. Suddenly he looks terribly sad.

"Mark, what's the matter?"

"Nothing, nothing. I'm just a sentimental old fool. It may sound odd but I can never sing that song without all the feelings I felt that day flooding back."

"You must have really loved her?"

"It was years ago, I was only nineteen, but I thought I did. I was certain we were going to be together forever."

"What was her name?"

"Isabella, or Bella, for short."

"Where is she now?"

"Living on the Isle of Man, the last I heard."

"Do you write all your own songs?"

"Yeah."

"You've very talented."

"I don't know about that." He shrugs.

"You are! Don't be so modest."

He smiles. "I don't know whether it's talent or luck – luck more likely – but EMI are interested in signing me up."

"You're kidding!"

"But there's a catch. They only want me."

"Not the rest of the band?"

"No."

"Oh!"

"I don't think I can do it. The band means everything to the guys."

"But this is such an amazing opportunity for you."

"I know, I know. But I've never been that ambitious. The

band is just a bit of fun for me. I have lots of other stuff going on. But with Finn it's different. The band is his whole life and if I go . . ." he trails off.

"There's no band?"

He shakes his head.

"So what are you going to do?"

"Stay, I guess and wait until someone is ready to take all of us together."

"But what if that never happens?"

He shrugs. "As I say, it wouldn't really matter, at least not to me." He smiles. "Listen to me, going on and on about myself. Am I boring you?"

"No, it's all fascinating."

He takes a sip from his coffee and begins humming that song again. *"Da-da, da . . . just a first glimpse of you to fall in love."* He looks up at me. "You know I never wrote a song without meaning every single word. It's so much easier to say what you really want to say in a song than in real life."

I swallow. So just what *is* he saying?

"What I'm saying is, I think I have fallen in love with you."

I sit there staring at him, stunned. He isn't looking at me, he's looking at my hand in his and, then, with one of his fingers he begins tracing the lines on my palm. What can I say? I don't think anyone in the history of the world has ever said those words without hoping to hear them back. But I can't say them. I've never, ever said them to anyone. I like him, yes, but I don't love him. How could I? Caroline is right – I hardly know him. And he doesn't know me – yet he's saying he loves me! This is only the fourth time I've met him! The first time we didn't even speak, the second time, no more than a few sentences, the third time was the night we slept together and yes, it was probably one of the best nights of my life but it wasn't our in-depth conversation that made it so — we didn't speak an awful lot that night either, now that I recall. But, now, here he is, saying he loves me! Whoa — steady on. Maybe I should pretend I didn't hear him, and carry on the conversation as if those words had never been spoken but I've lost my chance to do that. No doubt the shocked expression on my face has told him that I've heard

Then he laughs. "I shouldn't have said that but I couldn't not. I just wanted you to know. I don't expect you to feel the same but I can't play games, Rosie. I wear my heart on my sleeve. What you see is what you get. That's the kind I am."

"But how can you say you love me? You hardly know me!"

"I feel I do — I feel like I've always known you — that I was just waiting to meet you. You are everything — *everything* — I have ever wanted."

I look at him, wondering if he's just feeding me lines but it doesn't feel like he is.

"Mark — I'm sorry. I just can't say the same back."

"Not yet. I don't expect you to."

"It's just that if I told someone I loved them I'd have to be hundred per cent certain that I meant it. They're such big words."

"I know. But they're the only ones to express how I feel. I've never felt like this before about anyone."

"Not even Isabella?"

"Who."

"The woman who took all your dreams away?"

"Not even Bella."

"Mark, I like you too," I tell him. "A lot but . . ."

"Rosie, relax, don't feel you have to say any more. I just want you to understand what I'm thinking. I'm not trying to put pressure on you. But as I say, I'm not capable of playing games. That you like me is enough." He grins. "For now. Anyway, enough of the heavy stuff and back to this evening – what do you want to do for the rest of the night? Movies or dinner or the pub? Or then again, we could just go back to my place?"

"Now that sounds like a very good idea."

21

"I lo♥e you just the way you are . . ."

I see the sleeping-bag guy sitting in the doorway opposite the boutique again this morning. He hasn't noticed me yet and I'm thinking whether to slip past or say hello when he looks up and spots me.

"Hiya!" he calls out.

"Hi." I go to pass on. And then I think, maybe I should give him one of the coffees. It's a bitterly cold morning and it strikes me that he could do with it more than me.

I hand it to him.

"Hey, thanks."

And I carry on inside.

The shop is busy all morning but the rush eases off around noon and Monica asks Fay to go and collect some display props she's ordered.

Well," says Monica, once Fay has left, "I met your friend Dana last night. Doug brought her for dinner to our house."

"Oh, yes?"

"Doug has never brought any girl to meet me before!

You know, I think I was wrong and you were right. She does seem like a very nice girl. She's doing Doug the power of good. I haven't seen him this happy in a very long time. And they seem to get on so well together. Honestly, Doug couldn't keep his eyes off of her and she seems very fond of him too. She was telling me she's studying psychology.

"Yeah, she's doing her Master's."

"She must be very clever."

"I guess."

"You know Doug was very bright at school but then he seemed to lose interest in his final years. He has been working with this decorating company these past couple of months and seems keen on it, not that he says much, and I have to admit I've been worried that it would go the way of all his jobs, that he'd just decide to give it up one day but maybe he'll stick at it this time. She's a good example to him – she seems very dedicated to her studies. I think she'll be a good influence on him. Maybe all the bad times are finally behind him. For the first time in I don't know how long, I don't feel so worried about him."

I wish I could feel as optimistic about their relationship as Monica. There's no doubt Doug is lucky to get someone like Dana but I can't help feeling Dana has got the short end of the stick. Obviously I don't say as much to Monica but if we go on talking about them, I'm afraid I will. Instead I change the subject.

"By the way, you didn't say anything to Fay about that man I told you I saw her with?" I ask.

"I told you I wouldn't."

"Good."

"But I've been dying to. Was he nice? Tell me what he looked like?"

Suddenly I have a brainwave. I still have his photo in my

phone. The resolution must be better on mine than on my mum's because he's pretty clear on my little screen.

"I can do better. I can show you."

I take out my phone and scroll until I find the image, then hand it to Monica.

She stares at it for a long time. "I don't believe it! I can't believe she could be so stupid to get involved with him again after all this time. How could she be so bloody, bloody, *bloody* stupid!"

"Who?"

We both swing round. It's Fay. What the hell is she doing here? She shouldn't be back for ages yet.

"Nobody," says Monica and she goes to put the phone behind her back but, at the same time, I go to take it off her and, suddenly, it goes crashing to the floor and lands right at Fay's feet.

All three of us swoop down to get it but it's Fay who reaches it first. She picks it up, stares at the photo, and then at me.

"What is this?"

"I can explain."

"How dare you!"

"Fay, look, I'm sorry —"

She looks down at the picture again, and then back at me. She's trembling with rage.

"Why do you have a photo of this man on your phone?"

"I —"

"Why did you take it? When did you take it?"

I shrug. "I —"

"I'm asking you a question, Rosie! When did you take it?"

"Ahhm — last Sunday."

She stares at me for a long while, like I'm a piece of dirt

on her shoe, and I'm kind of feeling that's exactly what I am.

"Why did you take it?"

"I . . . I . . ." There's no point in saying I can explain, because I can't. "I don't know."

"You don't know!" She's still staring at me. I feel wretched. "So," she goes on, "the other morning, when Monica was late, all those questions you were asking me about how I spent my Sunday they weren't just idle nosiness, were they? You wanted me to tell you that I spent the afternoon with this man? Am I right?"

I nod.

"What business is it of yours?" she demands.

"None. Look, Fay, I'm really, really sorry." And I am. Who do I think I am, prying into her life like this?

"Sorry for what? For taking the photo? For showing it to Monica? For being such a nosey little cow? Or sorry that I caught you?"

"For taking the photo. For everything."

"Fay," interrupts Monica, "please don't tell me you're seeing Anthony again!"

Now Fay turns to Monica again. "That's nobody's business but my own."

"But I'm worried about you –"

"Well, don't be, and now, if it's okay with you, Monica, I think I'll go on my lunch break." She doesn't wait for an answer but begins heading back out. But then she turns back to me. "You know, I'm really, really disappointed in you, Rosie. I expected more from you."

The rest of the day in the shop was truly awful. I expected Fay to have another go at me when she got back after lunch but she didn't – she just ignored me completely – which very effectively kept me feeling as worthless as I deserved to feel.

When I get home, things don't get any better. Dana and Doug are sitting on the couch. I groan when I see him and walk straight back out. I'm just not in the mood for him tonight – or any night. And he does seem to be here so much that we should be asking him to pay rent.

Dana comes marching out after me.

"How dare you!"

"What?"

"Treat my boyfriend like that! How can you be so rude?"

"Hey, I'm sorry. Look, I wasn't being rude. I'm just tired."

"Just what is your problem? Why can't you be nice to Doug? You never talk to him."

"It's a little difficult."

"Pardon?"

"Well, it's not like he says an awful lot himself."

"Why should he? You've never asked him so much as a single question. The fact is, he is my boyfriend. I think you should be nice to him. I can't think of the number of losers we've had to entertain because of you, including your current one, and quite frankly, he's about the biggest loser of all."

"How can you say that? Mark is normal whereas Doug . . ." I trail away.

"What's wrong with Doug?"

I shrug. "Do I have to spell it out?"

"Yes, you do, actually!"

"Okay, he's rude, he's a loser, he flits from one job to another –"

"No, he doesn't. He's been in the same job for months now."

"Dana! He even steals from his own mother!"

"What? What on earth are you talking about?"

"I should have said this to you earlier but Monica once told me he stole a €100 note from her purse."

"Doug has never stolen anything in his life. Never! Not even –" But she shuts up.

"Not even what?"

"Nothing! Look, his problems are all behind him now."

"What problems?" And then I remember Monica too talking about the bad times being behind him. What was she, what is Dana talking about? "What problems?" I demand again. "What exactly are we talking about here?"

"None of your business!"

Suddenly, the penny drops. "He's a druggie, isn't he?"

"No, I don't know what you're talking about!"

"Yeah, you do. Jesus, Dana, what the hell *are* you doing with him? He's such a loser! You're going to get hurt, you must see that!"

Dana suddenly looks to the door. Doug is standing there, listening. I wonder how long he's been there, and how much he's heard. I could bite my tongue off

"Don't mind her, Doug. She doesn't know what she's talking about. Look, Rosie, I don't expect you to understand what we have but I love him, he loves me!"

"Love him! You barely know him!"

"I know him better than I know anyone. What we have is real."

"Like what you thought your parents had was real!" It's out before I know it. "Look, I'm sorry – I didn't mean that."

Dana is standing there, staring at me, looking too stunned to speak and it's Doug who reacts to my words.

"Don't you *ever* speak to my girlfriend like that again!"

Then without another word, he takes Dana's hand and they leave me standing there.

I feel so bad I could cry.

Just then, my phone beeps.

I take it from my bag. It's a text from Mark, I see.

– *Are u @ home? Will I come over?* –

I text back.

– *Yes. And do please* –

The sooner, the better, I think.

22

"Addicted to lo♥e . . ."

Despite or maybe because of Fay's reaction, my obsession with Anthony Knowles is growing. After another day spent with her refusing to make eye contact, I go home that evening to an empty house (thank God – I couldn't face Doug and Dana after last night) and find myself picking up the Golden Pages. I flick through it until I come to the section with all the ads for legal practices and, there, in the middle of them, I spot a big ad for – Haughton and Knowles. They specialise in corporate law, I read. Very lucrative, I imagine, lucrative enough to have offices in Merrion Square. I see that Anthony Knowles is now listed as one of the partners.

Then I look up his name in the white pages. There it is: *Anthony and Elizabeth Knowles, 14 Sycamore Road, Donnybrook, Dublin 4*. Nice, very, very nice. I pass that way on the bus home every day. I don't know the exact house but I know the kind: detached redbrick, granite steps leading up to a front door painted in some glossy primary colour with a shiny brass knocker in the middle, and flanked on either side by globe-

211

shaped topiaries with long narrow trunks rooted in matching, slightly weathered terracotta pots; some flowering creeper making its way up the brick and inching over towards the plant-filled conservatory at the side of the house; a piano or cello visible through a front sash window that also provides just a glimpse of the drawing room interior and out to the fine gardens beyond.

That little blip – Anthony's stay in London with Fay – obviously didn't interrupt the trajectory of his life.

And that makes me mad.

I know Fay isn't well off. Her flat is in a nice part of the city, but it's a flat, she rents it, and she lives there on her own – not with the daughter she and Anthony had together, not with the other children they might have had, and not with him. Now she lives a life so far removed from what she must have imagined for herself when she headed off with him to London. Her time there changed the entire course of her life.

Yet Anthony who was married – who was more at fault than she was – slid back into his own life and picked up the pieces exactly where he'd left off. His children, quite young back then, probably don't even remember that he was ever away. When they're browsing through old photo albums they probably don't even register his absence in photos taken during the years he was gone. Then again, maybe there weren't any photos taken that year – maybe his wife was too despondent to take them. For there is a wife too, and I know nothing about her, except that for the second time in her life, he's not all hers. But she took him back like a fool that first time. Why – how – could she have done that? And has she any idea that her husband and Fay are seeing one another now?

And then, I find myself picking up the phone and keying in their number. Out of curiosity only. I'm not going to do anything – or say anything.

"Hello!" The voice on the other end sounds like a young child.

"Hello," I hesitate. Maybe it's the wrong number – his children would be grown up by now.

"Do you want to speak to Granny or Granddad?"

"Ah – your granddad."

"One moment, please."

As I hold the receiver up to my ear, I can hear the sound of her running down the hall. "Granddad! Granddad!"

"Yes, pet?"

"There's a lady on the phone for you."

I hang up.

When I do, I see a text has come through from Mark.

– *On my way over* –

23

"Lo♥e on the rocks . . ."

For the next two weeks I don't see much of Caroline and the others. Mark and I are living in our own little wonderful love bubble. It's like being on a little love holiday, most of it spent between the sheets. Practically the only time I see him vertical is when he's on stage. I love watching him sing, knowing he's singing to me. Then, afterwards, as soon as the band is through, when Finn and the others plus assorted hangers-on head off to a nightclub or to a late bar, we head away. We've got better things on our minds.

Besides, I don't like being around Finn much. In fact, I'm beginning to really dislike him. I've tried and tried to be nice but I get nothing in return. He's never outright rude but he seems to go out of his way to avoid me and talks to me only if he has to, and even then he keeps it to a minimum. Sometimes, when I'm sitting there, looking up at Mark singing to me, I can feel Finn staring at me but I don't give him the satisfaction of looking back.

I was getting so sick of the way Finn was carrying on that, the other night, I finally told Mark what had happened between Finn and me at the party. Mark wasn't surprised. He said that Finn had pulled that stunt before – asking a girl out *because* Mark was interested in her.

In fairness to Mark he hasn't fallen out with Finn. In fact, he says it's Finn who's odd with him. I don't see why he should be that way. It's not like Mark *stole* me from him. The thing is, Mark and Finn have been so close for years, you'd think Finn could get over it especially when Mark is being so magnanimous. When I say as much to Mark, he just shrugs and tells me I shouldn't worry, that it will all work itself out in time. But then, one night, he goes on to tell me this story about the two guys in The Ramones. One of them, Johnny, I think who was the guitarist, slept with the lead singer's girlfriend and she then left Joey – that's the singer – for Johnny and they eventually got married. They stayed married and even though the two guys played together afterwards, year after year, and had hit after hit, not a word ever passed between them again. But there's more, Joey penned a song called the 'The KKK Took My Baby Away,' and, night after night forever after, Johnny had to strum away knowing that he was the KKK of the song.

But I was never Finn's baby to begin with, as Mark reminds me.

Tonight we're not going straight home, we're going out. It's Caroline's birthday and she's booked a table at some favourite restaurant of hers, some fancy place on Dame Street where she goes to a lot on business. Mark was reluctant to go so, as a compromise, I decided to give the meal a miss and just join them for dessert instead. When I told Caroline she was a bit miffed but, anyway, we're here now. Our taxi has just pulled up so we climb out.

"Is this the restaurant?" Mark stands on the pavement, looking up.

"Yep, that's it," I say.

"And whose birthday is it again?"

"Caroline's."

"Who else is going to be there?"

"Just the usual crowd. Come on!" I pull his hand. "It's about time you got to know them."

"Look, why don't we give it a skip? We could go back to your place."

"No, we can't. Not tonight. That's what we do every night."

"I've never heard you complain before."

"I know, but we can't go on like that forever – nice as it may be." I smile. "You're not nervous about meeting them, are you? I know you don't really know them but don't worry. They're all lovely. You'll be fine. They'll love you. We'll have a great night!"

He begins nuzzling into my ear. "But we'd have a better night at home."

"Mark! Stop! Cut it out! Come on, we'd better go in. We're late enough as it is."

They're all there – Caroline, Mick, Shane and Loretta, and Dana and Doug, all sitting at a table by the window. They're in boisterous form – clearly the evening has been going well, helped no doubt by quite a few bottles of wine. Mick is telling some joke and the rest of them are falling around laughing. Suddenly I'm excited. It seems like ages and ages since I've been out with them. I grab Mark's hand and we make our way over.

"Hi, everyone. You all know Mark, don't you?"

They all nod and call out hello.

I wish Caroline a happy birthday, give her a kiss on the

cheek, and go to sit down but see that there are only two free places, one next to Caroline, one next to Doug. Oh God, I don't want to sit next to Doug, but I can't possibly inflict him on poor Mark, so I end up taking my place beside the Sullen One.

"Hi, Doug," I say as I sit down

"Hi, Rosie," he says.

He doesn't smile at me and I don't smile at him.

By now, they've all finished their main courses and the waiter comes to hand out dessert menus but he has to shout over the laughter to get any attention – Mick is in the middle of some other story and has them in stitches again, even Doug. I'm not really following what he's saying, I'm looking over at Mark. It's strange to see him there, surrounded by my friends. We really have been cocooned this past fortnight. I'm surprised to see him looking so uncomfortable. It never struck me before that he might be shy but now I see how uneasy and fidgety he is out of his own environment. I watch as he unfolds his napkin, refolds it, unfolds it again and then places it on his lap. Then he pours himself a glass of water. He turns to Caroline and asks her does she want some but she doesn't notice him – she's busy talking to Doug, telling him some funny story, and I see Doug is smiling back at her, looking at ease, looking like he belongs. Unlike Mark. Why doesn't Caroline turn to him and put him at ease? Since when has she become so fond of Doug? Still unnoticed by Caroline, Mark now puts the jug down, and takes a sip from his glass, then sets it back down again. Then, he nervously fiddles with his place setting, straightening up his dessert-spoon and fork and fixing his cup and saucer just so. He picks up the jug again and pours some more water into his still almost full glass. I wish I was sitting beside him. I don't like being so far away.

He looks up and sees me looking at him. "Love you, babe!" he calls over — right at the exact moment the table happens to fall completely silent. All heads immediately turn to him. I cringe but, then, I notice Caroline look towards Mick with a smirk and suddenly I feel defensive. What's wrong with my boyfriend telling me he loves me? Okay, I'm not gone about the 'babe' part, I'd have preferred if they hadn't heard that, but so what if he is open about his feelings?

"And I love you too," I suddenly announce, surprising myself more than anyone. I hadn't meant to say it. I've never said it to him before even though I know that's what he's been waiting to hear ever since he first told me he loved me. I've never said it to anyone — ever. The awful truth is I don't mean it. I didn't say it out of love but — well — out of pity, I guess. I just couldn't have them smirking at him like that. The words were out before I could stop them.

Mark is staring at me with a great big grin on his face like all his Christmases have come at once and I'm compelled to smile back though I don't feel like it. I'm so shocked I just said what I said. The others are staring at me too but I don't care about them. I look around at each of them, daring them to comment but then the waiter interrupts with perfect timing:

"Are you ready to order dessert now?"

"It's your birthday, Caroline. You should go first," says Mick.

Mark is still beaming over at me and the enormity of what I've just said is beginning to sink in. How can I ever take it back?

"Okay . . . ah . . . hmm," I hear Caroline hum and haw, "I'm going to have the . . . ah . . . the peach tart with home-made vanilla ice cream and a coffee."

Mick goes next, then the others, and then it's my turn.

"I'll go with the hazelnut meringue cake, please, and a coffee." I notice Mark hasn't ordered yet. "Are you having dessert, Mark?"

He pats his tummy. "I'll skip – I owe it to my fans."

Everyone erupts with laughter, including me. I probably laugh louder than anyone – partly it's nervous tension and partly it's because I'm just so relieved that he's relaxed enough to join in the fun, but then I see he's looking around the table, totally bewildered. Oh God! He didn't mean it as a joke. I immediately shut up but everyone else is still laughing so hard that he has to shout over their laughter to order his coffee

"Oh, that's a good one!" cries Caroline, wiping her tears. "I owe it to my fans!"

Jesus! Would she shut up! How much wine has she had to drink? Poor Mark. To his credit, he's managing to put on a brave face – he even manages to smile, a little, like he might have meant it as a joke, but he must be mortified. He doesn't deserve this. I stretch my leg out under the table and manage to connect with his. He looks up and I smile at him. He blows me a kiss.

Our desserts come and then our teas and coffees. Caroline takes some cubes of sugar from the bowl, then goes to pass it to Mark.

"Sugar?"

"Ah no, not for me," he tells her, then picks up his jacket and begins searching in his pocket and I cringe – I know exactly what he's going to do next *and* I know exactly what Caroline's reaction is going to be – unless I can distract her.

"Caroline, so did you get any nice presents?" I call over to her.

"What?" she asks, but she doesn't look around. She's staring at Mark as he taps his little sugar substitutes, his little pensioner pills, into his coffee. I can't have her teasing him!

"*Caroline!* Did you get anything nice for your birthday?"

"Jesus! Rosie! No need to shout! Do you want to get us kicked out and, yeah, since you're so interested, I did – some good CDs, a couple of books and – that's about it really. Okay?"

She turns back to Mark. He's now stirring his coffee and I relax back, thinking the moment has passed. But then Caroline's beady eyes spot his little tin on the table and she picks it up.

"Sweet 'n' Low," she reads out, then looks at him.

"Sugar substitute," he explains.

"Why do you need them?"

"I just use them sometimes. You know, when the dial is edging up into the danger zone."

I could die. I look around the table. Everyone is gaping at him. Maybe if I start laughing, they'll all think he's joking again and join in but, right now, I don't think I can find it in myself. And Mark has *no* idea. He finishes stirring his coffee, then puts the spoon down and takes a sip.

"Hmm," he smacks his lips.

Caroline is looking over at me and I just know what she's thinking: you are going out with a man who doesn't eat dessert because he owes it to his fans *and* who carries a tin of Sweet 'n' Low around with him *and* who probably weighs himself more often than any girl sitting at this table.

I turn away from her. "Mark, can you pass me the milk please?"

"Sure!" He hands me the jug.

I take it from him and say as brightly as I can manage: "Thanks, darling."

"Do you want these?" Caroline asks and, smirking, she picks up the little tin and shakes them at me.

I should just ignore her, but I don't. I can't.

"Just leave it out, Caroline! It may be your birthday but that doesn't give you the right to be a bitch."

"Calm down, Rosie! I was only having a bit of fun. Wasn't I, Mark?"

Mark looks at her. I don't think he gets what's going on at all.

But it gets worse, oh so much worse – and so quickly too when Mark suddenly leaves out a groan.

"Are you okay?" I ask.

"There's a woman heading over here with a bunch of flowers."

I glance around and see that there is indeed a woman with an enormous bunch of flowers coming in this direction *but* what I don't see is what his problem is with that. But I soon find out.

"I guess she must be a fan," he sighs.

I stare at him. Yes, he is a talented and gorgeous singer. Yes, he could be the next big thing to come out of Dublin. Yes, EMI want to sign him up. *But* I can't *believe* he thinks for one second these flowers are for him. Does he think this 'fan' was passing along the street, happened to glance in through the window, managed to spot him in the throng of people, hurried away, woke up some florist, insisted she make up a bouquet there and then, and rushed back here, to present it to him?

Does he think he's Bono? Is he *that* deluded?

The bouquet-carrying woman reaches the table, passes by Mark and presents the flowers to – Caroline.

"Caroline, the management and staff just wanted to wish you a happy birthday. You're in here so often, you're more like a friend than a customer."

"Gosh, Catherine, thanks. They're beautiful!"

Then the lights go down, one of the waitresses emerges from the kitchen with a birthday cake lit up with candles and, as she leads the staff over to our table, they all sing 'Happy Birthday', with everyone in the place joining in.

"Happy birthday to you! Happy birthday to you!"

Even Mark is singing along. But I can't.

"Happy birthday, dear Caroline, happy birthday to you!"

How could I have been such a fool! And I told him I loved him too.

24

"Have I told you lately that I lo♥e you?"

I stare at the enormous didgeridoo my dad is holding out to me.

"It's a didgeridoo," he explains, his head nodding excitedly.

"A didgeridoo?"

I *do* know what a didgeridoo is. What I *don't* know is what prompted him and my mum to select this, above all else in the tourist emporiums of that vast continent that is Australia.

I look over at Mum, still dressed in the tracksuit she wore on the plane but with a frilly apron over it now, to protect it from the spitting frying pan. I look to my dad: jeans, slippers, yellow polo-shirt taut over a little pot-belly on his otherwise skinny physique. He's still standing there, still holding out that didgeridoo like it's a peace offering and he tribal chief, me white man.

My mum and dad. This is the woman who carried me for nine months, breast-fed me, brought me to and from school every day until I was old enough to cycle. This is the man who taught me how to ride that very bike, who cleaned my knees when I fell off, who taught me how to sing dirty limericks and who patiently listened to all the childish nonsense I spouted.

These are the two people in the whole world who might be expected to know me best and they bought me a didgeridoo.

"Thanks, I don't know what to say," I say because I really don't.

"You play it," explains Dad.

"Ah – right."

"See –" Dad brings one end right up to my face, then taps it with his finger – "You blow into it here and then" – he turns the whole thing around and taps the other end "– the sound comes out here." Like this is all complicated stuff. "The Aborigines made it."

"*All* of them?"

He doesn't hear.

"There's even a CD to go with it that teaches you how to play it. Nora –" he swings, I jump back "– do you know where I put it?" But Mum's not listening. He swings back again. I jump again. I image the chaos he caused in Melbourne airport: "Excuse me, excuse me, excuse me," I see him shouting as he rushes for the plane, a trail of dazed people in his wake, stumbling around, clutching their temples.

"I don't know how you managed to bring it back," I say.

"Well, it wasn't easy."

"I appreciate it."

And I realise I really do appreciate the effort it must have taken Dad with his bad back to lug this contraption halfway around the world just for me.

"Ah, there it is." He hands me the CD.

"Thanks."

But – does he *really* expect me to spend my evenings, holed up in my room, cross-legged on the bed, brow furrowed, ears cocked as I listen to the CD, cheeks bulging as I blow? Does he see future Christmases with my aunts and uncles gathered around, feet a-tapping as I impress them with my amazing didgeridoo-blowing skills? Does he envision a time when he'll be proudly introducing me, as, "My daughter, Rosie – she plays the didgeridoo, you know. I was the one who got her started."

"And wait until you see this, Rosie!" Dad laughs, and from the mess of bags on the table, he unearths one of those hats with corks hanging from all around the rim.

I stare. Oh dear God! Is this for me too? Does he actually expect me to wear it? And if so, when and where – exactly? Maybe when I'm taking to the stage of the National Concert Hall.

But Dad plonks it on his own head. "What do you think?"

I stare at him. Dad is shaking his head from side to side causing the corks to swish away non-existent flies. What's there *to* think?

"Come on, Will, take that stupid thing off and let's sit down and have some supper," snaps Mum.

She clears some space on the kitchen table and serves up three mountainous fries, plates piled high with rashers, sausages, eggs, mushrooms, tomatoes, beans – lamb chops even. I had tried suggesting on the way home that we might all go out to eat but she was having none of it. She was sick of eating out. She wanted some decent Irish cooking. She wanted a good Irish fry. She missed her kitchen.

Holidays are wasted on some people.

As we eat, Mum picks up again some story I'd forgotten she'd even started before Dad got so excited over the didgeridoo.

. . . so there we were at the foot of Ayers Rock –"

"Uluru – that's what you're meant to call it these days if you want to be all PC," interrupts my Dad.

"All right, Uluru then, and you wouldn't believe it but . . ."

Is there anything worse than listening to tales of other people's holidays? No matter what exotic location they go to, there's always a sameness about their stories. The holiday goes well and those of us back home are subjected to accounts of fabulous sunsets, great meals out, lovely people met, fantastic sites visited, and wonderful hotels stayed in. If the holiday has been a disaster, then we have to listen to a litany of disaster stories: bad plumbing, cheating taxi-drivers, rude locals and oh, worst of all, stories of food poisoning. Why do people subject other people to such intimate details that are really best kept private? Nobody wants to hear how another human being dealt with the problem of simultaneous diarrhoea and vomiting. Ever. Ever, ever, ever. It just does not conjure up good images. At least my mum isn't talking about that. I think. But what is she talking about? I've lost track.

". . . thousands of miles away from home, can you imagine that?"

"Imagine what?"

"Bumping into these two people from Kilkenny?"

"Who?"

"This couple from Kilkenny."

"What couple? People you knew?"

"No, no, but they were from Kilkenny, from Ireland, like us! And we bumped into them in the middle of Australia, thousands of miles away from home."

Well, knock me down with a feather! What an amazing coincidence! My parents bumped into two people they'd never met before – it's worthy of penning a letter to some *Life's*

Like That section of a magazine. "What on earth do you think they were doing there?"

"What?" I'm annoying her now. "They came on a bus tour out from Alice Springs, same as us."

"They were both doctors," says Dad, as if that might answer my question

"That's right," says Mum. "He was a paediatrician and she was a GP."

"No, no, he was the GP and she was the paediatrician."

"Are you sure? I thought she was the GP and he was a paediatrician –"

Arghhhhh!

"You're wrong! I distinctly remember him telling me about his drive to work. Even though he had to go through the town to get to the hospital –"

"Don't call it a town. It's a city. He was very particular about that –"

"All right, the city then – anyway, it only took him fifteen minutes."

Stop! I want to scream. I don't care! I don't know these people. You don't know these people. You'll probably never set eyes on them again. So why are we talking about them? But I don't say any of this. Instead I listen.

"And best of all," Mum goes on, "and you won't believe this, Rosie. Didn't they know Michael Green?"

"Who?"

"Michael Green."

"I don't know any Michael Green."

"Course you do. He used to run The Mill Bar years ago – actually it was probably before you were born – but, anyway, he sold up when he married a Kilkenny woman and he moved down there. They run a café now – it's supposed to be one of the best places to eat in Kilkenny. Rosie, if you're ever down there you should give it a try. Rosie, are you even listening to me? Anyway, they were saying –"

"Who were saying?"

"This couple from Kilkenny – try to keep up, Rosie – that Michael's mother died a couple of years back and his father went to live with him; I was wondering why we hadn't seen him lately. Michael has three sons now – one works with him in the business, another works in New York – what is it he does again, Will?"

"Something to do with real estate."

"That's right. And their youngest is in college here in Dublin studying catering –"

"Engineering."

"No, you're wrong. Cathal Brugha Street is a catering college, you can't do engineering there."

I have to remind myself why we're discussing whether or not the son of a man who my parents haven't set eyes on, or even thought about, in over twenty years is studying catering or engineering in college – oh yes, it all goes back to that couple they met from Kilkenny.

As my mother goes on, I find myself smiling as I envision her and Dad and this other couple in a huddle, chatting and laughing, ignorant to those around them, those who have travelled so far to see the spectacle, wonder at the magnificence, and relish the quiet out there in the desert. Instead, they got to hear about Michael Green and all belonging to him.

"Rosie, are you listening to a word I'm saying?" snaps Mum.

"Yes, yes, go on." But then, before she does, impulsively I reach out and take her hand. "I'm glad you're back. I missed you when you were away."

And it's true. I'm glad we're sitting around the table like this. I'm glad to be hearing all these stories, even if I don't listen to every word. I'm glad they've come home safe. I heave a contented sigh. All is well. I pick up Dad's cork hat and plonk it on my head and turn to him:

"So, do you think it suits me, Bruce?" I say in an Aussie accent.

For some reason he thinks this is hilariously funny and for some reason this makes me very happy.

25

"Careless lo♥e . . ."

After having listened to one thousand billion holiday stories *and* having successfully managed to divert all Mum's many attempts to have a 'So how are things with you?' conversation (by *things*, she means boyfriends primarily, plus my Plans-For-The-Future) I get into Caroline's car and hightail it back to the city. I'm feeling pretty satisfied with myself, I have to say. The last thing I wanted was to get into a discussion about Mark. Thankfully, it was pretty easy to distract her this evening. Anytime it looked like she was going in that direction, I just headed her off by asking her about some detail of the holiday, like, "Where *did* you say you met those two doctors from Kilkenny again?" And she was off.

Caroline's the only one at home when I finally get there. She's sitting on the couch, reading the paper.

"How are your parents?" she asks.

"Madder than ever."

"Did they have a good time?"

"Yeah, they had their ups and downs but overall they really

enjoyed it. It's done them a power of good. They're in great form. They're even talking about taking a trip to the States."

"What about your dad's fear of flying?"

"Well," I laugh, "Mum is talking about taking a trip to the States."

"So I guess they'll be going then?"

"I guess."

"Mark rang when you were out. He said he tried you on the mobile a few times."

"Oh, it must be switched off."

Which is a lie. I got his dozens of calls but I didn't want to talk to him after last night. I was so busy all day between work, going to the airport, collecting my parents and then catching up with them that I didn't get a chance to sit down to try to figure out what to do about him and I didn't want to talk to him before I did. How could I have been so stupid? How could I not see what he really was like? True, we didn't exactly talk that much and most of our time together was either spent in bed or at one of his gigs. But am I really that superficial? Was I so blinded by his looks, his songs, and the most amazing sex ever?

It seems I was and it doesn't make me feel especially proud of myself.

"Rosie?"

"What?" I look over at Caroline.

"Nigel? Dan? Philip?"

"What?" It takes me a moment to make the connection between all these names: they're all old boyfriends.

"Paul? Anton? Jude? Need I go on?" she goes on.

"What have they got to do with anything?"

"It can't be long before Mark's joining that sad list. Shane gives it until the end of the month but, after his performance last night, I'd doubt he'll last until even then."

231

"You and Shane were discussing me and Mark?"

"Of course, we were. We're your friends, aren't we? That's what friends do: discuss the ones that aren't there."

"Bitch behind their backs, you mean?" I'm annoyed now. "Well, both of you are way off. Me and Mark are rock solid."

"Come on, Rosie, you've got to be joking! Surely you can see it? The man is an idiot – a very good-looking idiot, but an idiot nonetheless."

She's right, of course, but I'm really hating her for saying it. Like, who the hell does she think she is? If she wasn't being quite so bloody superior, I'd be sitting with her on the couch by now, half-laughing, half-crying, because I was stupid enough to get involved with someone so ridiculous and who thinks he's head-over-heels in love with me even though he doesn't know the first thing about me. I'd be sitting here with her, planning the best way to split up with him.

"You've dumped a lot nicer fellows for a lot less," she ploughs on. "Remember poor Anton. He was positively – "

"For the record, I have no intention of dumping Mark."

"Really?"

"Yes, really."

"So I can tell Shane that he was wrong?"

"Most definitely."

"And you'll still be together at the end of the month?"

"Yes, and for a lot longer. *Not* that it's any of his business, or yours for that matter."

"Do you want to bet on it?"

"On what?"

"That you won't have split up with Mark by the end of the month?"

"Don't be insane! I'm not betting on something like that!"

"You're frightened of losing, I suppose."

"No, I'm not! Give over."

"How about a weekend in Prague for everyone?" She points to the double-paged spread in the travel pages of the newspaper that lies open on her lap.

"A weekend in Prague for everyone?"

She nods. There's a look in her eye. She's daring me to say no, and I don't like it.

"Right, you're on!"

"Right then."

We look at one another for a moment or two, then we do a mock spit and shake on it.

She goes back to her paper and I pick up one of her discarded supplements and begin to browse through it but I'm paying little attention to what's before me. I'm thinking over this stupid bet. To win, all I have to do is stay with Mark until the end of the month. That's not that long. Today is the 8th so that means I only have to stay with him for twenty days. And it's not like I'd have to meet him every day but, say, three times a week, max, for two and a half weeks, that's about eight times. Eight times! Bloody hell! Still, I could manage that. Or could I? I could end up shooting him. But up to last night we got on fine. But that was before the blinkers came off. Now that they have, it'll be impossible to ignore the blatantly obvious.

Suddenly I have what I think is a brainwave.

"What if he splits up with me?"

She laughs. "Ah, I can see your crafty game plan: behave so atrociously that he'll be forced to break it off. No, the deal is you and him have to be together at the end of the month."

"Well, we will."

"Good."

She goes back to reading. I go back to mulling over this

whole deal. It's okay for her, she has pots of money – pots. I doubt she's ever gone to a cash machine, keyed in the amount she needs and found herself faced with that awful message – *you have insufficient funds to meet your request* – and then keyed in a lower amount, and then a lower one still, to be met again and again with the same awful message. I doubt she's ever had to take her card, walk away from the machine, mortified to know that everyone in the queue knows she's broke. Unlike me. And that was just this very afternoon out at the airport. I couldn't afford to send them all on the bus for a day trip to Wicklow, not to mind fly them to Prague for the weekend.

"Ahh – who exactly would the loser have to take to Prague?" I ask.

"Like I said, everyone: me, Mick, Shane, Loretta I guess, and Dana. And Doug too, they're getting pretty serous and he's a nice guy."

Seven people, six if I don't go myself. "But that would cost a bloody fortune!"

"Why are you worrying if you're so confident you're not going to lose?"

"I'm not. I'm just trying to establish what exactly our bet entails."

"Well, now you know." She goes back to her paper and I go back to worrying.

I feel a tinge of guilt. Going out with someone for a bet is not exactly a nice thing to do. But he won't know. And it's not for that long. Where's the harm? It's not like anyone is going to get hurt.

"Prague would be lovely this time of year," Caroline points to a picture on the page in front of her. "Look, there, the old town. Isn't it like something out of a fairytale, so romantic?" And then she smirks. "Speaking of romantic, what are you and Mark going to do for Valentine's Day then?"

Oh no! I'd forgotten about that. I shrug. "We haven't made any plans but something especially romantic – it is our first Valentine's together after all." If she can be a bitch, then I can be a bitch. "And you? The usual, I guess. Pity you won't have Dana to keep you company on the couch this year."

"That's pretty low."

"I'm sorry." And I am.

Just then, the doorbell rings.

"It's late. I wonder who could that be?" I say.

"Mick, maybe. He said he might call over but you don't need to sit up if you don't want to. You look tired. Why don't you go off to bed?"

I've a feeling I'm being got rid of and, out of spite, feel like plonking myself on the couch and not budging for the rest of night. But she's right. I'm tired. I head to bed.

As I'm about to hop into bed, my phone beeps. I know who it is.

R u back from ur parents? Will I come over –

No, going to stay there 2nite –

Two seconds later, there comes another beep-beep

Luv u. C u 2morrow

I don't bother replying.

26

"How deep is your lo♥e?"

Because Mark rings and texts me so much, I've taken to switching my phone off and, now, when I turn it back on again, I see I've missed a string of calls from him but also from Mum. She's such a text fiend these days that I wonder what has her ringing me now. It must be something important. I'm about to call her when my phone rings. It's Mum again. I pick up.

"Mum, hi!"

"Rosie . . . I . . ." She breaks down. I hear a great sob.

"Mum, what is it? Whatever's the matter?"

"Where-were-you?-I've-been-trying-to-ring-you.-What's-the-point-in-having-a-mobile-if-you-never-turn-it-on?" Her words come out in a torrent.

"Mum, I didn't know you were trying to reach me. I only just switched it back on. Please, can you tell me what's the matter?"

But now all I can hear is her weeping on the other end.

"Mum, Mum, you're really freaking me out." And she is

– this is so unlike her. "I can't help you unless you tell me. Did something happen to Dad?"

"Yes," she manages.

"What?"

"He's being taken to hospital. I'm in the ambulance with him now!"

"Oh my God!"

"Oh, Rosie! He's unconscious. He looks so ill!"

"Can you tell me what happened?"

"Well . . . well . . ."

"Take it slowly, Mum. I'm listening."

"Well, all evening he'd been feeling bad. He was complaining of pains in his chest and in his tummy and he was sweaty and weak and I should have called the doctor but he wouldn't hear of it – you know how stubborn he can be – and he said it was nothing, that it would be gone by the morning but then I managed to persuade him to go to bed but then he must have gone out to the bathroom when I was trying to get hold of you on the phone because when I went back upstairs – oh God! – I found him collapsed on the floor, Rosie! I thought he was dead!"

"Do they know what's wrong with him?"

"No, but he looks awful. What if he's had a heart attack? What if he goes and dies on me, Rosie?"

"Mum, don't think like that – you can't! It won't do either of you any good. He's in good hands now. Just hang in there, all right? What hospital are you going to?"

"Beaumont."

"I'll be there as soon as I can, okay? And don't worry Mum, okay?"

Which is a stupid thing to say but whoever knows what to say in a crisis?

I hang up the phone. Shane's standing in the doorway.

"My dad – "

"I heard." He already has his own coat on and he's holding mine out for me. "We'll be there in no time," he says, as I slip in my arms.

I see Mum sitting all alone in a waiting room crowded with people and their own worries. She's hunched over, and has her arms wrapped around herself.

"Mum?"

She looks up. "Oh, Rosie, thank goodness you're here."

I go to hug her and she hugs me back tightly.

"How is he?"

"I don't know. They're with him now. They're doing tests on him."

"Mrs Kiely, is there anything you need me to do?" asks Shane. Mum looks up at him blankly. "Do you want me to ring Sarah in Australia, and your sons?"

Mum looks to me for guidance.

"I think we should find out exactly what the situation is first," I say.

"But what if they never get a chance to say goodbye to him?" cries Mum.

"Mum, let's just wait to see what the doctors say and then we'll ring them straight away."

"I'll get you both coffees," says Shane. "There's a vending machine out in the hall." He's about to go, but then he hesitates. "Mrs Kiely?" Mum looks up. "My girlfriend, Loretta, works here as a doctor. She's on call at the moment. Would you like me to ask her if she can find out any more for you?"

"Please. If it wouldn't be too much bother."

Despite everything, I almost smile at her diffident choice of words but at the same time I almost cry too – she sounds so meek, so powerless, so different from her usual feisty self.

"No bother," says Shane.

When he goes, neither of us talk. There's a cold breeze whipping through the waiting room and, noticing Mum doesn't have a coat, I take mine off and throw it over both our shoulders. And we just sit there in silence, huddled together, for support, for comfort: that age-old and universal pose – like refugees who've lost their country, earthquake victims who've lost their homes, famine victims who've lost their will to live, rape victims who've lost their self-respect, plane crash survivors who've lost a loved one – as we might do before the night is out. As Mum begins to rock back and forth, I can't help thinking how fragile is our existence, is our happiness: a moment can take either away forever.

But I don't want to think about the what-ifs. I can't. I won't.

"Oh Rosie," sobs my mum, "what if he dies? I couldn't bear it, I just couldn't bear it!"

"Mrs Kiely? Rosie?"

We both look up. It's Loretta. I barely recognise her. She's wearing a white coat, a stethoscope hangs around her neck, and her hair is tied up in a bun. But she seems so ridiculously young, like she's playing at doctors and nurses. How can someone this young be the real deal? How can she be charged with dealing with life and death every day?

She sits down on the empty plastic seat joined to my mum's. "Mrs Kiely, we haven't met. I'm Shane's girlfriend. I work as a doctor here in the hospital. Shane asked me to see if I could find out what's happening with your husband. Now, I'm afraid they don't know just yet what's the matter with him. It could be an ulcer, or pancreatitis, or he may have had a heart attack. His blood pressure is very low. There's a possibility he may have had some internal bleeding. They're carrying out tests and I'll let you know the minute they know more." She roots in her deep pockets and takes out a notebook and a pen. She scribbles, tears out the page, and hands it to my mother. "Here's the number for my pager. Now, I'm on all night so if you're worried about something, or feel you need to ask me anything, then make sure to page me, all right? Or if there's any news I'll come and tell you."

"Okay," Mum says meekly.

After Loretta leaves, I try ringing my brothers and my sister. I manage to get on to Sarah and Con but not William. Con says he'll keep trying William's number. Both he and Sarah say they're going to start making arrangements to fly home immediately. But I know they're worrying – like I am – that even immediately just might not get them here soon enough.

"Do you want to ring anyone else, Rosie?" asks Shane once I've hung up. "Mark, maybe?"

"Mark?" I shake my head. "No."

"What about Caroline and Dana?

"Will you do it for me?"

"Sure."

An hour later, Loretta comes back. She sits down again beside Mum. She looks very serious.

"Mrs Kiely, Rosie, I wish the news could be better but Mr Kiely is going to theatre. They suspect he has a perforated duodenal ulcer. He's had a lot of internal bleeding and he will have to have a blood transfusion. His condition is serious and the operation he's going to be undergoing is high risk but absolutely necessary."

The outsized white-faced clock hanging on the wall opposite loudly ticks out the dragging minutes and the waiting room gradually empties of everyone bar us, their situations resolved more quickly than ours, for better or for worse. I try to persuade Mum to get some sleep, but she's adamant she needs to keep awake, in case . . .

Shane dozes off and, just as I find myself beginning to too, my mum starts talking.

"You know, not long after we started going out, he arrived up at the house one day with a present for me. I remember tearing it open – it was the first present he'd ever bought me. It was a pair of shoes!"

"Shoes?"

"Yes, a pair of blue, high-heeled dress shoes with little sparkly bows. To this day, I don't know what possessed him to buy them but I loved them. They were the prettiest things. My mother didn't know what to make of such a present. 'Shoes? Shoes?' she kept repeating as if the very concept of shoes was alien to her." Mum laughs. "I remember your dad explaining to her like she was a child or a simpleton, 'Yes, Mrs Moore, shoes! They're this great new invention. You just put them on your feet, one on each, and you can go out in all kinds of weather.' I remember he looked over at me then and we both burst out laughing. I think that was the moment I decided he was the man for me. Poor Mammy, I think she thought he was some kind of pervert with a shoe fetish. I don't think she ever fully trusted him after that. She always tut-tutted under her breath whenever she saw me going out in the shoes. I still have them, you know, in a box somewhere."

Then she lapses back in silence, lost in her own thoughts. From time to time, she gives voice to them.

". . . they weren't even the right size but I wore them anyway. They were so gorgeous . . . he bought me a bread-maker for our twentieth wedding anniversary but the only loaf that stupid thing saw was your father's when I nearly threw it at him. A bread-maker – I ask you, where's the romance in that? . . . It was the hottest day for years the day we got married. 33 degrees. Your Grand-aunt Chrissie nearly died of heat stroke but it was her own fault. What was she thinking wearing that famous fur coat of hers on a day like that? And, of course, nobody could persuade her to take it off . . . I never saw him cry, you know, except the day you were born. You were the only one he saw coming into the world. I wasn't even sure I wanted him there, I don't even know if he wanted to be there – he was more of the old school, but the matron on duty practically bullied him in to it. I was afraid he might faint but the last thing I expected him to do was to burst into tears . . ."

"Rosie? Mrs Kiely?" Loretta gently shakes us awake and both of us immediately jump to our feet, as does Shane.

"I just want to tell you that Mr Kiely is out of theatre now and down in recovery. Everything went fine. There were no complications. It was a perforated duodenal ulcer, as suspected. He's lost an awful lot of blood and he has had to undergo several blood transfusions. He's on a ventilator now and still heavily sedated from the operation. He'll be in recovery for some time yet but, as soon as they're satisfied, they'll be moving him up to Intensive Care. He's still in a serious condition but he is stable."

"Oh thank God!" Mum brings her hands together palm to palm.

"The next twenty-four hours will tell a lot." Loretta looks at the clock on the wall – it's 3.30 in the morning. "Mrs Kiely, I think you should go home and get some rest."

"But –"

"He's in safe hands. He'll need you more when he wakes up. Shane can drop you home, can't you, Shane? And Rosie too."

"I think I'll stay here," I say.

"Dana and Caroline said to let me know if you needed them," Shane tells me. "Will I ring them and ask them to come in. It'd be better than being on your own."

I nod.

Mum and I hug again and then Shane takes her by the arm and they head towards the door.

Loretta's still here.

"Thanks," I say. "For everything."

"Don't mention it. It's my job. Besides, I'm happy to be of help to a friend."

27

"Lo♥e is a many-splendoured thing . . ."

"Rosie!"

I open my eyes to see Caroline rushing through the double doors of the waiting room, laden down with half-a-dozen plastic carrier bags, looking like she's bought out the entire stock of some nearby twenty-four hour SPAR.

"Have you found her?" I hear Dana's voice echoing in the long corridor outside, and the doors swing back on her just as she's coming through, nearly sending her and the big bundle she's carrying to the floor. She regains her balance and pushes the doors open again using the heavy load.

"Rosie!"

The sight of the two of them suddenly releases all my pent-up emotions and I begin blubbering like a baby – surprising them, but myself too. They quickly dump their loads on nearby seats and gather around me.

"Hush now, hush," murmurs Dana.

"Have you got bad news?" asks Caroline gently.

"No, no," I say between sobs. "He's fine. He's in recovery. I'm just so pleased to see you."

"Well, you a *very* funny way of showing it," mock-scolds Caroline.

I wipe away the tears. "You have no idea how glad I am you've come."

"Of course we've come," protests Caroline indignantly. "What did you expect? That we'd stay cuddled up in our beds, leaving you sitting here on your sad old lonesome-ownsome, like some unfortunate Orphan Annie? You know us better than that!"

"What's with all this stuff," I ask.

"I brought you a sleeping bag," Dana picks it up and hands it to me. "I thought you might need it, plus your own hot-water bottle but it's not so hot any more and you may want to get one of the nurses to refill it."

"Thanks. I'm sure they're just sitting around, waiting for something to do," I joke.

"Plus a flask of tea – very strong, the way you like it. I made some sausage sandwiches too –"

"*Some* sandwiches," I laugh, "That's a whole sliced pan's worth! And half a pig!"

"I guess I got a little carried away. I put lashings of Ballymaloe Relish on them – the way you like, and, oh, a box of tissues, in case –" she looks a little embarrassed here "– well, in case you need them.

It's Caroline's turn now. She reaches for the SPAR bags and begins unpacking. "Let's see. Magazines, loads of them – all the trashiest – check. Bars of chocolate – half a dozen – check. Two litre bottles of Coke – check. A packet of your favourites, Lemon Bonbons – check – though, if you ask me, they should come with a health warning on the pack, *guaranteed filling remover* – not that tonight's the night to be worrying about things like that." She roots some more. "Ice cream – check. McDonald's double cheeseburgers and fries multiplied by three – check. Which poses a dilemma – *if* we eat the ice cream first then our McDonald's will go cold *but* if we begin with them, the ice cream will melt even further. Maybe we could alternate between bites – that would be an interesting gastronomic experience. And let me see, what else is there? What's this?" She pulls out a bottle of Lucozade and stares at it as if she's never seen it before. She hands it to me.

"Caroline, I'm not actually *in* hospital," I protest.

"I don't even remember buying that!" She shakes her head. "I guess the word hospital must have lodged itself in my brain."

She reaches deep down into the bag in her hand and pulls out three Cadbury's Creme Eggs. *"Da–da!"* she cries, like she's a magician pulling rabbits out of a hat. Then she upturns the bag. "That's all."

"This is outrageous!" I cry. "Has World War III suddenly broken out? Are we under siege or something?"

"What?"

"I do intend leaving here one day, you know, and in the not-too-distant future."

I stare at the sinful mound of food now spread out over several of the plastic chairs and am reminded of that programme on telly where all the junk food some fat person goes through in a week is laid out before them, in an effort to shame them into eating more healthily.

"What would Gillian McKeith make of this?" I wonder aloud.

"'How can you feed slop like this to your friends?'" Dana startles us with a surprisingly good imitation of the red-haired, habitually outraged, telly nutritionist's Scottish accent. *"'It's tantamount to food abuse!'"*

"Well, at least," says Caroline, "no one is going to prod

our livers, examine our tongues or send us off for a colonic irrigation when we're finished."

"We *are* in a hospital." Dana looks around, warily. "Do you think they do that sort of thing here?"

"Now you mention it, I did see a sign for the Colonic Irrigation Department on the way in," says Caroline. "Plus a queue of very bloated, very uncomfortable-looking individuals all the way down the corridor and around the corner."

It's the absurdity of this image that sets me off. I start laughing. And, once I start I find I can't stop. I laugh like I haven't laughed in ages, with tears actually rolling down my face, while the other two sit there, stony-faced, no doubt thinking I've truly lost it. I don't even know why I'm laughing, not really – maybe it's just a necessary letting-off of steam.

"I think I saw them," I manage to say between the laughing, "lined up, wearing nothing but their hospital gowns, the wind blowing around their ankles and wafting up their gowns."

This starts the pair of them off and soon they're as bad as me. I think how it would look if anyone – Loretta, for instance – walked in to see the three of us like this, laughing our heads off like crazies while my dad is lying somewhere close by, recovering from major surgery. So what? I think. I'm not going to *not* laugh out of guilt. There'll be enough scary moments in the days ahead. I'm going to enjoy this precious moment while it's here. There may not be another for quite some time.

"You're lunatics, the pair of you! And I love you both." And it's then I see that all this – the food, the sleeping bag, the hot water isn't so much about taking care of my physical needs, but it's their way of showing me they care.

It's a good ten minutes before we finally calm down.

"Come on, let's tuck in!" says Caroline. "Before everything gets ruined."

"I am stuffed!" announces Caroline, stretching back in her chair, and rubbing her belly.

"Are all the bonbons gone?" asks Dana. I pass her what's left and she pops two of them in her mouth and begins to chew, her cheeks bulging. "I can't *believe* how much we've eaten!" She goes all Scottish again. "'*Do you know the damage you've done to your bodies*!'"

"You really ought to get out more," sighs Caroline.

Dana ignores her. "Who wants a magazine?"

"Yeah, pass me the *Hello*," says Caroline.

"But that's the one I was going to read," I whinge.

"Well, tough!"

"But it was *my* father who nearly died tonight."

"Oh very nice – trading on your poor dad's misfortune."

"He wouldn't mind. He'd be pleased to think he was helping me."

She gives me a doubtful look. "Go on, then, Dana. You'd better give it to her."

We're the only people in the waiting room and, apart from the loud ticking clock and Dana chewing on bonbons, quiet reigns.

Until:

"Ah, *come* on!" cries Caroline. "I have never read *such* rubbish!"

We both look over.

"Who *are* these people?" she cries.

"What people?" Dana asks, unwisely.

"These people who place these personal ads!" Caroline flicks the page in front of her. "Listen to this: '*65-year-old deep-thinking, wine-loving gastronome WLTM kind, sensual woman (22-25) with an interest in cooking.'* Just *who* would reply to an ad like that? Some masochist who wants to live out her days dishing up big dinners to some fat old fool who sits there all evening, getting sloshed, pontificating on 'important' matters *and* salivating over the delights that await him in the bedroom later with a woman a third his age."

She falls silent and carries on reading and, when we seem safe from further outbursts, so do we – but the silence doesn't last long.

"And," she erupts, "they all think they're so clever with their little play on words! *'Aisle be there for you'* from someone who's openly desperate to snag a husband; *'Grape expectations'* from a wine-guzzling phoney, and this one from some amateur who probably thinks he earns the right to call himself a painter after one painting holiday to the Dordogne: *'Paint necessarily so'*."

"'Paint necessarily so', that's a good one!" chuckles Dana.

Caroline throws her a dirty look.

"Why are you bothering to read those ads if they annoy you so much?" I ask.

"Because she enjoys a good old rant," answers Dana for her.

I think Dana is probably right. Caroline pays neither of us any heed but carries on:

"And have you ever noticed how so many of the women call themselves *ladies*?"

"What's wrong with that?" asks a baffled Dana. She looks to me for enlightenment but she's looking to the wrong person. Frankly, I have no idea.

"And nobody is fat. Oh, no! They're either 'full-bodied' or 'curvy'. And the hills of the country must be positively crawling with lonely-hearts. '*Outgoing attractive female (34) loves theatre and walks . . . Stocky muscular male (55) loves the outdoors and going for walks . . . Sincerely yours (22) loves films and walks . . . The real deal (29) loves walks, eating out and . . .*' You'd wonder why they even need to advertise when they must be falling over each other up there in the hills!"

She gives a big sigh, then falls silent. Dana and I look to one another, both wondering if the storm has passed.

"Just listen to this!"

Alas, no, it was just the eye of the storm."'*Attractive female, 20's, chemistry student seeks floppy-haired sensitive Mr Darcy for relationship.*'" I mean, *come* on! This girl doesn't know *what* she wants! Has she not seen *Pride and Prejudice*? Does she not know that Mr Darcy is the very opposite of sensitive? I pity poor Elizabeth Bennet being stuck with him. Can you imagine what he was like *after* they were married, when his courtship veneer wore off?"

Suddenly, I'm annoyed.

"Why must you always assume the worst?" I demand crossly. "For all you know they could have been deliriously happy for the rest of their lives." I am aware that I'm talking about fictional characters who don't actually have lives after the credits roll but it bugs me the way Caroline is so quick to consign them to a unhappy-ever-after just because she looks at every relationship through doom-saturated glasses.

"Oh come on! And he was just *so* boring!"

"I'd put up with boring if I got to look at Matthew Macfadyen across the table every morning, even if he was wearing breeches."

"Now you're just mixing up the character of Mr Darcy with the actor who plays him," interrupts Dana.

I turn to her. "Your point being?"

"Well, you see, in the book –"

I wave a hand dismissively. "I've never read the book. Give me Jilly Cooper any day and what's-his-face – Rupert Campbell Black."

"Have you really never read *Pride and Prejudice?*"

From the look of incredulity on Dana's face, you'd swear I'd just told her I'd never read any book, ever.

"So? What's the big deal?"

"It's one of those books everyone should read. Like *Wuthering Heights* –"

"Well, I did read that. I did it for the Leaving but I don't remember it very well," I confess and she gives me this withering – or wuthering even – look. "Dana, it's just a book!"

"*Just* a book! How can you say that?"

"Because it is. It's got a cover, pages and –"

"But it's the best book ever written. I must have read it over thirty times."

"Thirty times? I don't think I've ever read any book more than once."

"Don't you understand, *Wuthering Heights* is not just *any* book!"

"I don't get it? Why do you love it so much?"

"Two words: Cathy – Heathcliff."

"But Heathcliff was an animal, I remember that. Didn't he string up someone's dog?"

"He wasn't an animal but he was treated like one. By Mr Earnshaw, and then by Hindley. And who knows what happened to him before that? You know, when I first read it I used to lie awake at night crying, thinking of what he must have gone through when he was a parentless little boy, living like a wild animal in the slums of Liverpool."

She looks like she's not far off crying now.

"Dana, he's not real, you know."

"Well, he feels real to me," she declares passionately

"O-kay." Over Dana's shoulder Caroline is making "loony" signs. I ignore her and go on: "But still, there's no excuse for stringing up a dog."

"He was *crazed* with love!"

"Oh yeah, I remember, he and Cathy tormented each other."

"They had no choice. 'Nelly, I *am* Heathcliff!'" Dana suddenly cries in an anguished Yorkshire accent. Then just as suddenly she reverts to her own again. "You know, the first time I saw Doug at his party, I couldn't believe it. He looked exactly how I pictured Heathcliff in my head."

I think of making a joke about Doug sharing the same personality as Heathcliff but then I stop myself. First, because I know Dana wouldn't appreciate it, but then because the most awful of awfully awful of awful thoughts comes to my head. I can't believe I'm even thinking it but I could imagine Doug doing something cruel like that. There's something about him that's always made me uneasy. Now I try to put my finger on exactly what it is. It's not his sullenness. I imagine a lot of people come across as sullen when they're really just shy. But Doug isn't shy. There's not some awkward but nice Doug hiding behind the surly façade whatever Dana and the others might like to think. I just *know* Dana is going to get hurt, I just know it. I shiver involuntarily but then I tell myself to get a grip, I hardly know him. I've barely spoken two words to him.

"Look!" says Caroline. "The sun's coming up."

"Rosie?"

We all swing around.

It's Loretta. "Your dad is out of recovery now and they've taken him to the intensive care ward. Would you like to go and see him?"

"Yes." I turn to Caroline and Dana. "You go home and get some rest. I'll be fine now."

"Are you sure?" asks Dana..

I nod. "And thanks, girls."

"No problem," says Caroline. "That's what friends are for. You'd have done the same for us."

28

"Lo♥e hurts . . ."

Dad looks so old and frail, in a gown that hangs loosely around his sinewy neck, with the pink blanket – like a baby's oversized cot blanket – covering him but clearly delineating his thin frame and little pot belly. There must be half a dozen tubes coming from him – from his nose, his mouth, his neck, from his thin, freckled arm, from the back of his hand, even from his tummy. There's a bank of monitors surrounding him. I sit down and take his other hand in mine and for a long while I just look at him. It's hard to believe but he was once *the* strongest man in all of Ireland, you know.

When I was small he would hoist me up on his shoulders and then gallop around the kitchen, while my mother gave out in the background.

"Be careful, Will. Don't drop the child!"

But my dad would laugh and say something like: "Don't be silly, woman! Tell your Mum why she's being silly, Rosie."

"Because Daddy won't drop me. Don't you know, he's the strongest man in all of Ireland!"

Then he'd prompt: "Stronger than . . ."

"Sugar Ray!"

"Stronger than . . ."

"Joe Louis!"

"Stronger than . . .

"Muhammad Ali!"

I hadn't a clue who these men were. I think maybe I thought they were neighbours.

"And what do they shout when they see me coming?" he'd cry.

"Mercy! Mercy!"

"What kind of nonsense are you filling that child's head with?" Mum would grumble.

I was at least eight or nine before I began to suspect Dad might not in fact be the strongest man. Which, given that he was hardly ten stone, marks me out as a very gullible child.

I don't know how long I've been sitting there when I hear the door open. I turn around.

It's Mum, and Auntie Joanna, my mother's sister, and Shane; I guess he must have collected them. Mum goes straight to the bed and stares down at Dad's sleeping face for a long time. Then she reaches out and pushes some strands of hair back over the patch where it's thinning.

"You promised me you'd finally make a start on trimming those Leylandii at the end of the garden this morning," she says aloud, without turning around. "Will you ever be able for them now? Trust you to pull a stunt like this to get out of it!"

I smile at her weak joke. "That's Dad for you.

Then she turns to me, a sort of odd puzzled look on her face, like she can't comprehend all that's happened, can't comprehend how everything could have changed so much in less than twelve hours

"Oh, Rosie!" she wails and suddenly all the strength goes

from her body; it's like the bones have been stripped from it and, without support, she's turned to jelly. I reach out and steady her before she falls. Then I put my arms around her shoulder and draw her in close to me and hold her tight.

"Oh Rosie, Rosie, Rosie!" Her arms are around my waist now and her face is resting against my chest. I can feel her body heave up and down. I rest my head lightly on her fluffy hair and breathe in the familiar smell of her musky perfume.

"Shush, Mum, shush now. Everything will be all right. He's on the mend."

We stand like that for a long time and then she pulls away.

"Rosie, you go home and get some rest now. You need it. I'll stay with your dad. Joanna will keep me company.

"Are you sure?"

She nods. "Come back when you've had a sleep."

"Come on, Rosie. I'll take you," says Shane.

29

"Nothing's gonna change my lo♥e for you . . ."

The last thing I want to do is sleep and when I say as much to him, Shane suggests we go and get something to eat and I agree – anything is better than going home.

We drive to the shopping centre, park in the carpark, and find a little coffee shop. I sit down while he goes to the counter.

I look around. The place is full even at this early hour: mothers with young children, pairs of old ladies, men in work clothes having an early break, solitary men reading the newspaper, and couples the same age as my parents. That's what my parents should be doing now – having coffee, looking over the photos they've collected of their trip to Australia, my mum planning their next trip to the States, bullying my dad into going. They should be sitting here or some place like it – not one sitting, watching over the other in a hospital bed.

Shane comes back with a tray laden down with two fries, a heap of toast and a pot of tea for two.

It's strange to see everyone going about their business as usual. Nobody knows anything. If we register in any of these people's consciousness at all they probably assume we're like them, carefree – up early to hit the shops. Maybe they even envy us – a nice young couple, just starting out in life, everything before them. Or maybe they think: he looks a fine fellow but, God, I don't envy him. The one he's with is a right mess! Wouldn't you think she'd go to the trouble of combing her hair before coming out?

"I must look a right state," I say.

"You look fine."

Given all I've eaten during the course of the night, I'm surprised I'm hungry but I am, and I eat in silence until my plate is clear, then I push it aside and pick up the cup of tea and sit there while Shane finishes his food.

"Shouldn't you be at work?" I say.

"It's Saturday."

"Oh yeah." I look over at him. "Shane, listen. Thanks for all you're doing."

"You'd do the same for me."

"You wouldn't need me to. You'd have Loretta."

He shrugs. "You can't have too many friends at a time like this."

"Loretta was brilliant last night," I tell him.

"Yeah, well, I guess she's used to dealing with this kind of situation," he says and for some reason his obvious pride in Loretta niggles me but I push this mean feeling aside. Why wouldn't he be proud of her?

We lapse back into silence. I fill up my cup again. I find my bag on the floor, and take out my phone to check my messages. There's a couple from Dana and Caroline from earlier last night before they came in, and a whole string from

Mark. I sigh. I really don't want to talk to him now. Or ever. That stupid bet is the reason I haven't got rid of him. I don't need the added complication of him right now. I need to focus on what's important. And then I realise what I need to do, and decide that there's no better time than now.

"Shane, have you time to take me over to Mark's house?"

"Sure, no problem."

He doesn't ask why, and I don't tell him.

When we get there I ask him to hang on, then I get out of the car and walk up the narrow little path and ring the doorbell. While I'm waiting, I look back towards the car and see Shane is on the phone. To Loretta, I imagine. I wonder if he's telling her where he is right now. He may be doing everything he can to help me out but Loretta is the one he'll be lying with in bed tonight, recounting it all back to. I'll just be part of his day, one of the anecdotes he shares as they lie, spooned together, drifting off to sleep. Shane is Loretta's – I just have him on short loan to get me over the crisis. All I have is Mark and that won't be for much longer.

I press the doorbell again.

Finn, barefoot, in boxers and T-shirt, answers the door and stands there for a moment squinting in the bright morning light, scratching his bed-tousled hair.

"Oh, it's you."

I spare the niceties. There seems little point in making an effort now. I won't be back here again.

"Is Mark home?" I ask.

"Yeah."

As soon as I step in, Finn closes the door and then, without a word, he goes over to the fridge and takes out a carton of juice. He pours himself a glass, sits down at the table and begins flicking through a newspaper. It's like I'm not even here.

I climb the stairs and knock on Mark's door.

"Mark?"

"Come in!"

He's lying in the bed. I walk over to him.

"Hey, this is surprise!" he says, pulling me towards him and, suddenly, I feel sorry for him. He has no idea what's coming and it's nothing like he's so obviously expecting. And why shouldn't he be expecting me to hop into bed with him? After all, that's about all we ever did.

I manage to pull away from him and sit myself down on the side of the bed. Immediately he sits up and begins to nuzzle my neck.

"Not now," I say but he goes on nuzzling. "Mark! I said, not now!"

"What did you come here for so?"

"To talk."

"To talk?" he repeats, as if he's testing out the word, considering what it could mean.

"Actually not to talk, but I guess for me to talk and for you to listen."

"Okay." He's smiling at me. He really hasn't a clue.

"The thing is, I don't think this is working out."

"What?"

"I like you, you know I do, but I think we're too different to make it work and, now, well, my dad could have died last night. He underwent major surgery, and it'll take him a while to recover so I really need to focus on him." I feel a bit cheap bringing my dad into this but I think somehow it will make it sound better, a little softer. Besides, it is true. I do need to focus on him and Mum.

Mark is staring at me.

"But I don't understand," he says finally. "We're perfect for each other. Anyone can see that."

"I don't think we are."

"But I love you and you love me."

"I'm sorry, Mark – I don't."

"But you said you did!"

"I was wrong," I say. I don't tell him it was because I felt sorry for him. Could there be a more foolish reason?

"How can you be wrong about something like that?"

I shrug. "Because I'm stupid," I tell him.

"So you're breaking up with me?"

"Yes."

"But we had such good times together?"

"We did."

"Is there anything I can say or do to change your mind?"

I shake my head. "I'm sorry, Mark."

He sits there, shaking his head, like he's refusing to believe what he's hearing but he doesn't say anything and there doesn't seem to be any more for me to say. I get up and go towards the door.

"Goodbye," I call out but he doesn't reply.

Once outside, I heave a sigh of relief. That wasn't as bad as I'd expected.

I walk down the stairs, pass Finn who's still sitting in the kitchen hunched over his newspaper, and head out to the car.

"So where to now? Home?" asks Shane.

"Yep. I think I'm finally ready for bed."

But I don't get to bed as soon as I thought I might. As I

climb the stairs I hear what sounds like crying coming from Dana's room

"Dana?" I knock. "Are you okay?

"Yes."

I push the door open.

She's sitting in the middle of her bed, her arms wrapped around her legs, hugging them to her chest. She has her coat and scarf on.

"Are you going out somewhere, or have you just come back?"

"What? Yeah." She seems distracted.

"Is something the matter, Dana?"

"Nothing, nothing's the matter," she says crossly but then she asks, "How's your dad?"

It's then I see she has this deep red mark on her wrist – like someone has grabbed it and twisted the flesh around it.

"What happened to your wrist?" I reach out and try to push her sleeve up to have a closer look but she pushes me away and quickly shoves the sleeve back down again.

"Stop!"

"Dana, what happ –"

"Nothing, all right! I must have just hit it against something. So go on, tell me how's your dad? Is he any better?"

"But Dana –"

"It's nothing, Rosie. Stop fussing and just tell me about your dad."

"Dana –"

"Rosie! Tell me how your dad is!"

"He's okay-ish. He was still sedated when I left this morning. Mum is with him now. I'll go back in later when I've had a sleep."

"You must be exhausted."

"I am."

"Come here," she says and I sit down on the bed beside her. She reaches out and hugs me.

"Mark just rang," she says after a while.

"Like earlier?"

"No, just now. The phone was ringing when I was coming in the door."

"Oh!"

"What?"

I think about telling her that I've split with Mark. But I couldn't bear it if she started teasing me about dumping yet another boyfriend.

"Nothing."

I didn't even tell Shane when we were in the car on the way back here. Even more so than Dana, I didn't want him teasing me.

". . . and you know all of us are here for you . . ."

I realise she's talking to me.

". . . so just remember that you have your friends."

"I know," I nod. "I'm lucky."

I notice her wrist again. You don't get a mark like that from hitting yourself. It's more like a Chinese burn. I should know – I got enough of them when I was little from the school bully.

"So you and Doug are happy?"

"Yep."

"You really like him, don't you?"

"I sure do."

"But . . ."

"But what?"

Like she said, I have my friends. But I'm her friend too. I need to look out for her. But I need to tread softly.

"But what do you and Doug have in common? What do you ever do together? What do you ever talk about?

"What are you getting at, Rosie?"

"Nothing. I'm just wondering what the pair of you talk about?"

"Everything."

"Everything?"

"But –"

"But what? Rosie, I know your dad is in hospital. I know you're probably in need of sleep but I really don't want to have a conversation about Doug with you. I already know how you feel about him."

"I just –"

"It doesn't matter that you don't like him. What matters –"

"It's not that. I'm just trying to understand why you like him. Don't you think that maybe you fell for him because you were feeling vulnerable after your father left your mum? I don't think he's the right person for you."

She's staring at me.

"I'm just trying to figure out what it is between you and him," I tell her.

"Well, don't bother *trying*. I don't expect you to understand what Doug and I have."

"But I want to understand."

"Why do you dislike Doug so much, Rosie?"

"I don't –"

"You do. Of course you do. Is it because you think he doesn't like you? You're used to everyone fawning all over you and you don't like the fact that he's not like that."

"That's not it at all. Come on, Dana, let's face it –" I bring my hand up in a fist and knock a couple of times against the side of my head "– with Doug, there's not a lot going on inside, is there? And I'm just wo –"

"Rosie, I am sorry about your dad, I am, and I know you must be tired and emotional but I'm just not going to have this conversation with you, all right?"

"But Dana I'm only try –"

"Goodbye, Rosie."

"Dana, pl –"

"Get out of my room, *now*!"

30

"Hello, I lo♥e you . . ."

When I open my eyes, the room is in darkness. All that's visible are the illuminated numbers on the clock, flashing 6.00 – 6.00 – 6.00 – 6.00 – 6.00. I stare at them. The alarm is beeping. I'm disorientated. The duvet is tight around me like I haven't moved an inch as I slept. I struggle to pull my arm out from underneath it, then stretch out and switch off the alarm and on the bedside lamp. I hear the sound of the television in the living room. What's that doing on at this hour of the morning? Because it's not morning! It's evening! Dad! I need to get to the hospital!

An hour later, Caroline drops me but she doesn't come in. She can't stay. She has a late meeting with some clients. When I arrive up to Dad's room – he's out of ICU now – I find his brother Dave sitting at the bedside.

"Hi, Uncle Dave."

"Hi, Rosie, love."

I look at my dad in the bed. He seems peaceful. Most of the tubes are gone. He's off the ventilator but he has a saline drip still attached to his hand.

"How's he been?" I ask.

"Fine. He was awake a lot of the afternoon. Your mother was here up to ten minutes ago. Margaret took her home," he says, meaning his wife.

I sink down into the low plastic armchair beside Uncle Dave. Perched up on a high, hard, antiquated chair, he towers over me. I wonder if there are even two chairs the same throughout the wards.

We sit in silence. Dave isn't a big talker. And I don't feel like talking either.

After five, ten minutes he gets up.

"I'll head off," he says. He pats me on the shoulder, a gesture that reminds me of my dad. "Don't stay here all night, now."

"I won't."

"You need to get your sleep too."

"I know. Goodnight, Uncle Dave."

Soon after Uncle Dave goes, Dad stirs. He smiles when he sees me.

"Rosie, hello, my love."

"Hi, Dad. You gave us all a fright!"

He reaches out and takes my hand. "Have to keep you on your toes, don't I?" he smiles again.

"How are you feeling?"

"Sick and sore but glad to still be here."

"I'm sure."

"Your mum was here. And Uncle Dave. Is he gone home?"

"Just gone."

"I must have fallen asleep on him." And then he gives a little laugh. "I've always said he'd sent anyone to sleep!"

I smile.

"So how are you?" he asks.

"Happy, now that I have you back."

We don't say much after. He still seems tired and weak. Now and then, a nurse comes bustling in to check on him. The television is playing in the corner of the room and we pass most of the time watching that but all the time I'm conscious of the tight hold he's keeping of my hand. When the nurse comes in at around nine to settle him down for the night, I decide it's time to go home.

"See you tomorrow." I bend over and give him a kiss on his forehead. Then I turn to go.

"Rosie?"

"Yeah?

"Take care of yourself now. You know, good people are hard to come by."

I smile at him. "Well, then you'd better take care of yourself too," I say, then blow him a kiss. "Sleep tight."

As I go back down the long echoing empty corridor I'm lost in my thoughts and when I swing through the double doors at the end, I don't even see him standing there.

"Rosie?"

"Jesus! Mark! You gave me a fright! What are you doing here?"

"I came to see your dad."

"What? But . . . but you don't even know my dad." And have you forgotten we broke up this morning? I almost add.

"No, but I know what it's like being in hospital. He'll appreciate the company. Besides I feel I do know him – you know, through you. I bought him these." He holds out a bottle of Lucozade and a bunch of green grapes. "Here, take them."

I'm so surprised that do I take them. I look at him. He's smiling kindly at me.

"That's very kind but –"

"And I thought you could probably do with the company. It can be hard having someone you love in hospital."

"Ah – thanks."

"Maybe I'll just pop in to him for a minute or two."

"Mark – visiting hours are over."

"Maybe I'll call tomorrow then."

"I'm not sure that's such a good idea." Just what *is* he doing here? Okay, I guess he's being kind but . . . but . . .

"Should I wait until he's better then?" he asks.

"I'm not sure when that will be."

"Oh, my poor Rosie." He reaches out to take my hand but I pull it away. This is all *very* strange.

"Would you like to go for a coffee?" he asks.

Coffee? "No, no, I wouldn't."

"It would be good for you to have someone to talk to. Or we could go for a drink maybe – anywhere you like. I have the car."

I look at him. He's smiling at me. It's like this morning simply never happened. Maybe it didn't. Maybe I was so tired and emotional that I dreamt the whole thing but then how would he know my dad was here if I hadn't told him? Of course, it happened! Why am I even thinking this way? Because this is all so weird.

"Mark, why are you really here?"

"Because you need support."

He goes to put his hand on my shoulder but I pull away. I don't want his support. I just want him gone.

"So come on, let's go for that drink."

"Mark, I don't want to go for a drink. Okay?"

"Sure, no problem."

Did I tell him this morning what hospital Dad was in? I don't think so.

"Mark, how did you know which hospital my dad was in?"

269

"I rang around – I didn't want to bother you."

"And they told you?"

"Yeah. When I said I was his son – I don't think they would have otherwise. Now come on. Let me take you home."

"I'm fine, Mark. There's no need. I'm going to take the bus."

"Don't be silly. My car is in the carpark."

"I'd prefer to be on my own.

"Sure, sure, that's understandable."

I walk away but he quickly catches up and walks alongside me. "So how *are* you bearing up, Rosie?"

"Fine."

We reach the front door.

"Are you sure now about that lift? Like I say, it's no bother."

"I'm sure."

He reaches up and suddenly strokes the side of my cheek, just once. "Goodnight then," he says and then turns and walks away, leaving me staring after him. This is just too weird. He looks back and gives me a wave.

I walk towards the bus stop and stand there. It's dark, damp and there's no one around. I feel uneasy. It begins to rain. Five minutes later, Mark pulls up and rolls down the window.

"Last chance to change your mind?" he calls cheerily.

I shake my head.

"We're both going in the same direction . . ."

"Mark, I'm fine. You go off home."

"I'm afraid I can't do that."

"Pardon?"

"Not until I see you onto the bus. It's not safe for a woman to be standing here like this. Anything could happen to her. Look around – the place is deserted. What if some pervert was lurking around and saw you standing there all on your own? Who knows what he might decide to do. You read some terrible stories. Who would you call to for help? No one would hear your screams. No, I'm going to wait here until I see that bus pull up."

I look at his face. It's relaxed, open – he's smiling at me. I don't know what to make of all this.

"I'll just sit here," he tells me in this cheery way. "You can pretend I'm not even here if you like but I can't go off and leave you. I couldn't have it on my conscience if something happened to you."

I can't *make* him go away. I stand there. He sits in his car. Through his open window I can hear the radio. It's lashing rain now. Why doesn't he put up his window? He must be getting almost as wet as I am. Five minutes later, he pops his head out again.

"Are you sure you won't even sit in while you're waiting? You're getting soaked."

"I'm sure."

I stand there another ten minutes. I'm drenched now. Maybe I should call a taxi. Or maybe I should just take that lift. But the last person I want to be with is Mark. I don't want to give him false hope that there may be a chance we could get back together again if that's what he's thinking.

But just then, the bus comes around the corner. As I'm about to climb on, Mark shouts out: "I'll give you a call tomorrow, okay?"

I slip in home, too weary to face meeting anyone but, as I climb the stairs to my room, I hear Caroline and Mick. They're in the middle of an argument.

"Why not?" I hear Caroline demanding crossly. "Loretta

went to a lot of trouble. *I* went to a lot of trouble."

"Did I ask Loretta to? Did I ask you? Did I ask either of you to interfere?"

"All I'm asking you to do is to meet him, that's all."

"No!"

"You're refusing to meet Kevin North? What kind of idiot are you? Any other actor would *kill* for the opportunity to work with him."

Kevin North? My ears prick up. Mick has a chance to work with Kevin North? So what's his problem? Kevin North is just about the best director ever to come out of this country. If all Kevin North wants Mick to do is dress up in a ladybird costume for one of his daughter's parties, or wants to employ him to shine the Oscar he received for *Catcher's Peak,* then Mick should be jumping at the chance.

"Why are you being so stubborn?" Caroline is demanding but Mick doesn't answer. "Mick?" she repeats. "Mick! I'm asking you a question!"

Okay, I need to get in there and find out what's happening. I go back down the stairs and when I walk in they are standing at opposite sides of the room looking daggers at one another.

"Hi!"

They both turn around.

"Hi, Rosie," says Caroline. "Jesus! You look rough! You're soaked!"

"How's your dad?" asks Mick.

"Much better."

"Mark rang – a couple of times," Caroline tells me. "He wants you to ring when you get in."

"Oh!"

"He said he tried you on your mobile too."

"I have it switched to off."

"Are you okay, Rosie?"

I don't feel ready to talk about Mark. I need to think about it, figure things out in my head first. "So what's all this about Kevin North?"

"Were you eavesdropping?" asks Caroline.

"Hardly. You weren't exactly whispering. So what's the story?"

"Okay, well, have you heard of *Fate Farm*?"

"The book?"

"Yeah," says Caroline.

"Course I have – who hasn't? Shane gave it to me at Christmas but I haven't got around to reading it yet."

"Well, it's about this farmer and his son who get taken hostage by these two druggie inner-city thugs when they walk in on them burgling their home."

"Right?"

"And then the four of them, the two farmers and the two thugs, are holed up in the farmhouse for a week only because the thugs don't know what to do with them."

"It's a comedy, isn't it?"

"Not really," Caroline goes on, "though there are some hilarious bits in it. But it's more than that – way more. It's kind of like *The Field* crossed with *I Went Down* and the ending is just incredible – you'd never, ever see it coming. It's a brilliant book and it'd be a great film and Kevin North thinks so too. He's bought the film rights."

"How do you know?"

"Because he was one of Loretta's patients a while back. He lives in London most of the time now but he has a house down in Wicklow too. When he was staying there, he fell ill so they brought him into hospital and Loretta was looking after him. Anyway, the pair of them got quite friendly and, one day, she noticed that he was reading *Farm Fate* so they started talking about it and he happened to mention he was

273

planning to make it into a film."

"I see."

"So it struck her that Mick would be perfect for the part of Lenny."

"Who's Lenny?" I ask

"The farmer's son who gets his brains blown out at the end," mutters Mick.

The penny begins to drop.

"Has all this got to do with the morning I caught you and Loretta conspiring in the kitchen?"

Caroline shrugs.

It has, even if she doesn't remember. I guess the rest. "So Loretta told you about North and his plans to direct *Fate Farm* and you went to try to convince him that Mick would be perfect in the role of Lenny."

"Exactly. Course he was reluctant to meet Mick to begin with but because he liked Loretta so much and because I was so persistent he's finally agreed to, now that he's out of hospital. He's not promising any favours – but meeting him is all the favour Mick needs. The minute he sees Mick, I just know he's going to think he's perfect for the part."

"So I don't understand – why don't you want to meet him, Mick?"

"He thinks it's that butter ad all over again," answers Caroline.

"That's not it!"

"He's afraid of being typecast."

"Are you listening, I said that's *not* it!"

"Cameron Diaz doesn't go, 'Oh no, not another role for a beautiful blonde female – I can't do it in case –'"

"Hello – didn't you see her in *Being John Malkovich*?" I interrupt.

But Caroline goes on: "This role could be written for

Mick. I swear even the description of Lenny in the book is him – big, blond, and handsome in an outdoorsy way. I don't know why he just can't see that Lenny *is* the role he was born to play but, instead he's, like, holding out until someone decides to do a remake of *Mission Impossible* and seeks him out to cast him in Tom Cruise's old part and –"

"Don't be stupid! I'm not!"

"Good, because you're no Tom Cruise. But you *are* Lenny." She looks over at me. "All the other roles have been cast already and they're all big names – Brendan Gleeson is playing one of the gangsters but Kevin North is still looking for someone to play Lenny and that person could be Mick – if he wasn't so bloody stupid! North is flying back to London tomorrow – Mick is going to miss the opportunity of a lifetime."

I look at Mick: "I really can't see why you won't go and talk to him."

He doesn't say anything for a while, then he turns to Caroline. "Why do you care so much whether I get this role or not?"

"Because you were born for it!"

"But why does it matter to you so much if I get it?"

"Because you're my friend!" she says, staring at him crossly.

He's staring back.

Oh for God's sake, I suddenly think – this *thing* between them has gone on long enough! Someone has to do something about it and, if they won't, then I guess it's up to me.

"She's doing it because she's in love with you – you idiot! She probably has been since she first met you on the train when you shared your sandwiches with her but she's too stubborn to admit it. And you're in love with her too, even

275

if you don't know it."

"Of course, I know it!" Mick shouts. "Of course, I know I'm in love with her!"

"Oh!" I say.

Caroline doesn't even manage that. She's just standing there, mouth wide open, staring.

"And you're right. I think she does feel the same way but, until I make what *she* considers a success of my life, she's not going to admit it even to herself. Of course, I'd die for that role. I *don't* think it's like that stupid butter ad all over again, whatever she might think. The part of Lenny is a once-in-a-lifetime role. Jesus! It's . . . it could . . . it is . . . it's . . . it's up there with Richard Harris's role in *The Field*. But, say I do meet Kevin North and say if, by an extraordinary stroke of luck, he does decide that I'm perfect for the part – excellent! Fantastic! But what if he doesn't? What if he takes one look at me, and says – 'Nah.' What if I have to spend the next ten years, the rest of my life even, broke and struggling – are you," he's talking only to Caroline now, "going to go on telling yourself that you don't love me? Are you going to hold out for someone you consider successful enough to deserve your love? I don't need you trying to make me into the kind of man you think you want. This is it, Caroline! This is what you get! Take it, or leave it."

And, with that, he storms out of the room.

31

"Lo♥e you inside and out . . ."

"Mum?" I call as I come into the hallway.

"In the kitchen, Rosie!" she shouts out.

I sniff. The house is thick with the smell of disinfectant – no chance of survival for any hospital bug so brazen as to *dare* use Dad as a vehicle of escape. I can see Mum going around, dowsing the place in preparation for his arrival: "Not in *this* house – no, sir!"

I go into the kitchen. Mum's standing at the table spooning a boiled egg from a saucepan into – "your father's eggcup" – so called by all in homage to her daily requests to us as children to "Set the table for breakfast and make sure to put out your father's eggcup," or "Rinse out your father's eggcup. His egg is ready". Nothing else in the kitchen has a title. Plates are just plates, cups are just cups but this innocuous-looking blue and white striped eggcup has been called 'your father's eggcup' ever since I brought it home to him from a school tour. No, there's nothing special about it. No name of the town I bought it in (Wexford, I think) painted on the side.

It's not an example of fine craftsmanship but a very ordinary, mass-produced blue and white striped eggcup – the likes of which can be seen in many homes up and down the country. My reason behind my somewhat (as Dad put it, when I presented it to him) 'unusual' choice of gift that day is long gone from me.

Mum looks up. "Hi, Rosie, love."

I go to kiss her. "How's Dad?"

"He's settling in nicely. Everything is set up for him. Your Uncle Dave was a great help. Himself and Margaret stayed all morning." She picks up the tray. "I'll just bring this in to him. He's slept a lot today but I might wake him now for a bite to eat. Just something light – I don't know whether he'll have much mind for it."

"Will I take it in to him?"

"Ah no, I'd prefer to do it myself."

She takes a last look at the tray to make sure everything is just so. I see she's even put a few early snowdrops from the garden into a little bud vase. "Can you open the door for me, there's a pet?"

I do, and when she goes through I follow after her.

We go into what's usually the living room but has been changed into a temporary bedroom. Or at least there's a bed in it, so incongruous-looking that it could have dropped down from outer space. With Dad in it. He and the bed are in the dead centre of the room, without apology to the resident furniture; the couch, the coffee table and the telly have all been pushed aside, discommoded but proud – determined to ignore this brazen interloper and go about their business as usual: this *is* a living room after all, lest we forget.

He's sleeping but I go over to him. Lying there, in the bed, pale, mouth open, head back, eyes closed, without glasses, and wearing pyjamas (blue and white striped too), he looks like a little old man – he could almost be any little old man. I lean forward and give him a kiss on his papery cheek. He smacks his lips but goes on sleeping – dreaming, maybe, of the boiled egg to come.

I look around. On the mantelpiece there's some scented candles alight and, on the coffee table, an upturned library book – *War Artillery, 1910-2005* – the kind of book Dad's forever getting out of the library. Mum's glasses are folded on top of it. I picture Mum, the staunchest pacifist in the world, reading it for him when they're here all on their own. In the corner, between the couch and the wall, I see a bundle of bedclothes and a folded-up camp bed – all ready for Mum to sleep here tonight (How will the coffee table *et al* like that then? – "Humph! You let one in, and see, see, what happens!").

"Mum, you don't have to do everything on your own. I'm more than happy to stay with you, you know that?"

"I know, I know, but I'm fine. Don't worry. The neighbours are in and out all the time. Mrs Price has been a star. She's been in twice already today. If I need to get anything from the shops, she'll get it for me when she's going for herself. No, Rosie, it'd be madness for you to stay here – you'd be hours getting to work in the morning with all the traffic. Just come out in the evenings when the roads are quieter – that's when we could do with you most."

The mute telly catches my eye and I see a fat, curly-haired, red-faced, slack-jawed actor in a woolly hat, wellies and a knitted jumper talking to two stooped elderly people – his parents? – in an old-fashioned kitchen. They're all talking animatedly and then the son points to the table and a slab of butter in a dish comes into focus, and then a caption – *Cork Glory*. I smile. Mick was right to turn down his chance at this role. Nobody's going to mark this rural Frank Spencer out as the next Richard Harris. I haven't seen Mick or Caroline since the big fight. Caroline's down in Cork on a business trip and, between everything, I haven't had a chance to catch up with Mick. He rang yesterday to check how I was doing and how my Dad was but he wasn't very communicative otherwise. We didn't get into talking about him and Caroline, or whether or not he went to see Kevin North. I've a feeling he didn't.

My dad wakes up and smiles when he sees me. "Ahh, Rosie," he says, and he reaches out to take my hand and gives it a squeeze. Between us, Mum and I manage to prop him up and then she begins to feed him, spooning the egg into his mouth, talking all the time as she does. About Mrs Price being a star. About Dave and Margaret and what a help they've been. And about my brothers and sister:

"Oh yes, and by the way, Sarah rang to see how you were doing. You know, I'm glad she was able to cancel her flight and didn't come rushing home. Now the whole family are going to come over at Easter instead. That's a much better plan. You'll be well enough to enjoy them more then, especially the little ones. It would have been madness for them to come any sooner. And Con is talking about coming over in the summer for a couple of weeks, so that's something else to be looking forward to."

When the egg is all gone, she hands him another finger of toast and he holds it in his hand and nibbles at it like a hamster. She picks up a cup of tea, puts a straw into it and, for some reason, the sight of that damned straw makes me want to cry and I have to fight the tears back. If Mum can cope so well, then there's no way I'm going to sit here blubbering like a baby – upsetting everyone. Right at that moment, Mum happens to look over at me, and I'm afraid she'll see I'm upset and I just know that if she says anything solicitous, I'll burst into floods of tears. But she doesn't. She just gives me a little smile and carries on holding the straw for Dad until he's finished.

Exhausted from his efforts, Dad falls back to sleep. Mum gets up, takes the end of the toast from his closed fist, puts it on the tray and goes to bring the whole lot back into the kitchen but, not used to the changed configuration of the room, she bumps against the coffee table and the tray goes flying to the floor and the eggcup smashes into a dozen pieces. Immediately, we both stoop down to clear up the mess.

"Damn," she mutters – staring at the shards of blue and white in her hand.

"Never mind," I say. "We can get another one."

"But it won't be the same, will it? He's had that one for years."

"Come on, Mum. It's just an eggcup."

"It's not *just* an eggcup – it's your father's eggcup. And now it's gone."

And then, sitting there on her haunches, she begins to cry. Great big tears start rolling down her face.

I go and put my arms around her. "Mum, Mum, hush now," I say, though there isn't a sound coming from her – nothing but these silent tears. The only sounds are my dad's little snores.

"Rosie, just look at him! How am I to cope? Will he ever be right again?"

"Mum, he's on the mend. Give him a couple of weeks and you'll see great changes in him."

"What if the same thing happens again? Or worse?"

"Oh Mum, don't think like that."

But she's not listening and I see she's not ready to take comfort in anything I can say. Instead she needs to talk.

"Oh, I know everyone thinks I'm the one in control, the one who organises your dad, and bosses him around but I can't do a thing without him. I need him. He's part of who I am. I just want him back – the real him – not the one who feels he has to thank me when I prop up his pillows or help him out to the bathroom. I want him back doing all those things that used to drive me mad, all the little things I used to complain about. I want to see him coming through the front door, throwing his coat over the banister. I want to see him standing there, taking all the coins out of his pockets and lining them up in little stacks on the mantelpiece as he tells me whatever bit of news he has. I want him back, the way he was. I don't want him to be someone who suffers the indignity of having to put up with me having to take care of him, and having to feel he has to thank me for doing so."

"Mum, Mum, come on now. He's doing great. You both are."

She looks up at me. "But are we, Rosie? Are we?" She sighs. "Remember when we were away and I kept sending you all those texts telling you to take care?"

"Course I do." I smile.

"But I think it was really him I was worried about. All the time I was afraid something would happen to him. That awful turbulence on the plane on the way over frightened the life out of both of us. But I was the one who had persuaded him to go in the first place. I couldn't let on. I felt responsible. I just wished I'd never made him go. Then over there, it was so busy – we were going non-stop, and with the heat and everything, I swear I was terrified he'd have a heart attack or something. The day we visited Uluru was the worst. I thought he'd keel over and die on me. He insisted on climbing to the top at midday when it was in the high thirties – talk about mad dogs and Englishmen! Mad Irishmen, more like! I can tell you I was so relieved when we bumped into those two doctors from Kilkenny – I kept thinking that if anything happened to him, at least I'd have someone there who'd know what to do, that I wouldn't be on my own – Sarah and Rod were back in Melbourne, you see, too far away to be of any use. After that, I swore to myself that if we ever managed to get home again in one piece, I'd never pester him to go anywhere ever again. I'd just be happy to let him – us – enjoy the rest of our retirement in peace."

"And you will too. He's on the mend."

But she's not finished talking. "But do you know something – when we'd landed back in Dublin again – safe and sound – didn't he turn to me and say: 'You know, Nora, we should think about going out to the States next. The boys' families are growing up without us knowing them.'" She shakes her head. "Now I don't suppose we'll ever get there."

"Maybe you will, Mum. He's getting better."

She looks at me. I get up and hold my hand out to her and pull her to her feet. "Come on," I say. "It's about time we had something to eat ourselves."

By the time I eventually leave, it's late, nearly eleven, and Mum tells me to borrow Dad's car instead of getting the bus. He doesn't need it – as she points out. I find the keys, say my goodbyes, and as I'm heading out to the car, I realise I'm happy. Mum's better now after her cry, more upbeat, and I'm thinking maybe things will be okay for them again. In fact, I know they will. And then I notice I'm humming a Bee Gee's song I heard playing on the radio earlier on in the day, 'Love you inside and out,' and I think of my mother and think how she does love my father inside and out, backwards and forwards, with her heart hanging. Okay, those wouldn't be the words she'd use but I now know that is how she feels. And I think how lucky they are to have one another.

I get into the car but then, just as I'm about to start up the engine, the passenger door opens and I turn, thinking it's Mum come to give me something I've forgotten, but instead I see Mark looking in at me, smiling at me.

"Jesus! Mark! You gave me the fright of my life! What the hell are you doing here?"

Before I can do a thing, he gets in, then slams shut the door.

"Hi, Rosie," he says, ever so calmly, ever so normally – like we'd arranged to meet and I was just sitting here expecting him to come along at any minute.

"Mark, what are you doing here?" I ask again.

"I've been waiting for you. So how is he?"

Before I can manage an answer, he leans towards me. "You know, you look like you might need a hug."

I lean back. "Don't, Mark!"

He sits back but keeps staring at me. Then he reaches out to touch my face but I push his hand away.

"Stop!"

"Hey, come on. Rosie, don't be like that." He sits back in the seat. "Your mum looks like she's holding up okay."

"Huh?"

"She seems like she's coping – although she did lose it a little when she dropped that tray."

Oh my God! He was standing out here in the dark all this time, for hours, looking in at us and we had no idea. He reaches out and puts a hand on my knee.

"Mark, take your hand away! What are you doing? Can't you understand we're not together any more!"

He doesn't let go of my knee, but begins to squeeze it ever so tightly as he starts talking ever so gently to me:

"Rosie, I know you've a lot to deal with and that's why you're not thinking straight. I just want you to know that I'm here for you. I can see you're upset and, of course, you would be with all that's going on. You're worried about your dad. You're not thinking straight. I know that."

"Mark, please, let go of my knee. You're hurting me."

"I love you, Rosie, and you love me – that's what's important – we mustn't lose sight of that."

"I *don't* love you, Mark."

"Of course, you do. You do. You told me. So you see the connection is there. Me and you, Rosie. Me and you. Two sides of a coin. And when this is all over and your dad is back to normal, then we can get back to normal. In the meantime, I just want you to know that I'm here for you. I'm not putting any pressure on you – that's the last thing I'd want you to feel. I just need you to know that I'm here for you. That I love you."

"But I don't love *you*!"

"Don't say that, Rosie!" His voice is as low as ever but there's no softness there now. It's as sharp as flint. His fingers are digging into my flesh. I think about what I should do. If I hop out of the car, he'll be out as soon as I am. If I blow the horn, the only person that's going to be alerted is Mum. I can see her now through the window, moving around in the kitchen, oblivious to what's happening out here in the dark. But what could she do? I don't want to involve her. I can't. I tell myself I'm overreacting. I know Mark. I can handle him.

"Mark, I'm sorry but I don't love you! You've got to understand that."

"Don't say that, Rosie. I mean it. Just don't say that!" Then he squeezes my knee so tightly that I scream out.

"Mark! Let go!"

He does. But there's worse to come.

"I'm sorry," he murmurs. He roughly pushes apart my legs, then bends down, and kisses either side of my knee where he'd been gripping it. "Oh my poor Rosie! I'm so-so sorry." And then he begins gently planting little kisses all along my inner thigh.

I have never been so terrified in my life. I can hardly breathe. What's coming next? He stops kissing me, lifts his head back up, then reaches out and takes hold of my chin with one hand and cups it so tightly that I can't move my mouth. He's really hurting me. Then, with his other hand, he starts tidying a loose lock of my hair behind my ear.

He lets go of my chin and sits back in his seat.

"Okay. Now, Rosie, I want you to start driving."

If I don't? If I blow the horn, then what? Mum comes running out. How's that going to help? That could make things worse – escalate matters maybe. He's acting so weirdly. Could I jump out of the car? Could I get to the house before him?

"Start up the car, Rosie!"

To go with him would be stupid. Could I open his door, push him out of the car and drive off? Not a chance. But even if there was, I couldn't leave him here with Mum and Dad.

"Rosie, come on now – start the *fucking* car!" he suddenly shouts.

Okay, I tell myself, I just need to keep calm. I think I can handle him. I know him. I do as he says. I start up the car and begin reversing out of the drive. I see Mum at the window now, washing up, and she gives a wave but she's just waving into the night. With the headlights shining in, she can't see me – or him. She has no idea what's happening.

We drive into town – all the time he has his hand on my

knee. He's stroking me now where he hurt me. He starts singing that song, softly, over and over and over.

"*Blue eyes upturned, blonde hair flicked, tight jeans crinkled, purple shirt gaping, and light bouncing off a silver pendant. No reason, no rhyme, it takes no time, just a first glimpse of you to fall in love. No reason, no rhyme. Light bouncing off a silver pendant.*"

Over and over and over.

And then he starts talking.

"You and me, Rosie. We're soul mates. Kindred spirits. We're the same. We're lucky, we have something so special – how many people in the world are lucky enough to have what we have? To have found their other half? Two halves of a whole – that's us. Sometimes when you're lying there sleeping, I look at you and think we must have known each other in another life – in all our other lives – since time began, and that we'll go on loving each other until the end of time. Something this big can never end. Nothing could ever keep us apart – not even death. The first time I saw you, I knew you were for me. I remember you sitting there, looking up at me – Jesus, you were so beautiful. I've never felt like this about anyone – ever. And neither have you. The looks that passed between us that night we first talked, before we even talked – they were electric, remember? Remember the first time I told you how I felt about you and you said you liked me but that it was too soon to say you loved me too. But I knew you did – even then. You were just frightened of what was between us – it was so powerful, so deep. And I was happy to wait until you were ready, as I knew you would be. Remember when all your smart-alecky friends were smirking at me when we went out to dinner with them, especially that bitch Caroline? But you just came out and said it. Told me that you loved me in front of them all. Remember how they all stared? They were sick with envy – I could see that. And they could see that special connection – anyone could just by looking at us, and they wanted the same for themselves. What fucking idiots – people like them can only dream about having what we have. Yin and Yang, that's us. Rosie and Mark."

And he keeps repeating all this same kind of freaky stuff again and again and in between he hums, "*No reason, no rhyme, it takes no time, just a first glimpse of you to fall in love.*"

After the longest drive of my life, we finally hit the city proper and I see we're coming up to the junction where I'll have to decide to go left for his house or right for mine. I don't know which way to go. I don't want to ask. I don't want to think about what's going to happen. What if he tells me to keep driving? What will happen when we get to wherever it is he's decided we're going.

But then he turns to me: "Hey, why don't we go for a drink? I know it's late, but what do you say?"

And I manage to answer calmly, as if I'm seriously considering it as something I might like to do: "I don't think so, Mark. I have work in the morning. I should go home."

"Of course!" He slaps the side of his head. "I forgot. No problem – we can do it later on in the week. Okay, well, you can drop me off here at the junction. I don't want to put you out. As you say, you have an early start."

I hardly dare believe that that's it, that this whole awful nightmare could actually be coming to an end. But there's still more to come. Before he gets out, he leans over, roughly grabs my face and turns it to his and then he kisses me, forcing his tongue into my mouth. Then, just as abruptly, he lets go of my face.

"I'll ring you tomorrow, okay? Night, sleep tight. And try not to worry about your dad – he'll be fine."

The second he's removed his vile presence from the car,

I pull out from the kerb like I'm Eddie Irvine but as I drive the rest of the way home, I can't stop shaking and when I turn into the driveway and see the lights are on I almost weep in relief – Dana or Shane must be at home. Thank God! I need to talk to someone. I get out of the car and walk to the front door on shaky legs. I go to put my key in the lock but I'm trembling so much I can't manage to get it in, but then, just when I finally do and I'm struggling to turn the key, I'm yanked forward as the front door is suddenly pulled open from the other side. It's Doug. He hurries out, and nearly knocks me down as he brushes past.

"Hey, why don't you watch where you're going!" I shout after him

He grunts, in apology maybe, but he hasn't the manners or intelligence to offer anything more meaningful and then he runs off down the driveway.

"What's your bloody hurry?" I mutter. I'm really beginning to hate him.

I go straight into the living room to see if either Shane or Dana are in there, but the room is empty. The television is on and I turn it off, then I go back out and climb the stairs. I go to Dana's room and knock.

"Dana?"

There's no answer. But I know she must be in. I knock again. Still no answer. But I really need to talk to her.

"Dana?" I call again, then open the door.

"Go away, Rosie," comes a muffled voice from beneath the duvet.

"Dana, what are you doing?" I try to pull back the covers but the lump underneath them is gripping them tightly.

"Dana, I need to talk to you." I pull harder and this time the duvet comes flying off. "Jesus!"

She's looking up at me, or at least she's looking at me

with one eye – the other she can't open. She turns away to hide her face.

"The bastard!"

She immediately sits up. "What? You think Doug did this? Doug didn't do this!"

"I know you think you love him but you can't make excuses for him, Dana! He's a monster!"

"Rosie, are you mad?"

I've had this conversation, or variations thereof many times in my head. I don't even need to hear her responses – I've already answered for her many times already. I have a lot of theories about Dana, Dana and Doug, Doug – particularly Doug – and now she's going to hear me out, whether she likes them or not.

"You can't let him away with this! Sure, he had no father growing up but lots of men without fathers turn out to be perfectly decent – not animals like him!"

She's staring at me like I'm deranged, though I have to say with just the one eye open she's looking fairly deranged herself. But I go on. All this needs to be said.

"And don't try blaming this on his mother either. I know Monica, remember? I know she was the best mother to her sons –"

"Rosie! Stop it right now! Are you insane? Doug wouldn't hurt a fly!"

"You've got to face it, Dana. He's a scumbag! A loser!"

"Rosie, I'm warning you – stop it! You haven't a clue what you're talking about!"

"You probably feel like you have to cover up for him. You're frightened. But you can't let him –"

"I am *not* covering for him!"

I don't believe her.

"He'll keep doing it, you know. But then, he's done it

before, hasn't he? I just knew something like this would happen! I knew it! You need to go straight down to the Garda Station and report him. I'll come with you!"

Suddenly she grabs me by the shoulders and starts shaking me. "Watch my lips – *Doug – Did – Not – Do – This – To – Me! So shut the fuck up!*"

"Okay," I say – trying to be calm in the face of her craziness. "I'm a little lost here. I come home, I nearly get knocked over by Doug flying out the door and then I come up here and find you like this. Can you please explain all this to me?"

"Okay." She's calm now too – very calm. She takes a deep breath. "This isn't easy to talk about but – my mum did it."

"Your mum?" Is she crazy? Has the blow made her lose her senses? "What on earth are you talking about?"

"Since Dad left she's done nothing but drink and drink. She's a mess – she doesn't know what she's doing. Whenever she used to get like this before – and it wasn't often, but she used to from time to time – never violent, but drunk, yes – my dad could handle it. He was able to sort her out. He was always able to persuade her to check herself in to dry out. And then when she'd came back out, she'd be fine, everything would be back to normal. But I can't handle her on my own. And she won't let Dad inside the door. Then this evening, when I called over, she was in a really bad way. I tried to talk to her but maybe I should have left it until the morning – she's never her best in the evenings when she's like this – I should have learnt that from of old and tonight she just left fly verbally and –" she points to her eye, "– physically. She's never deliberately hurt me before – pushed me, shoved me, grabbed me, yes – but never set out to actually hurt me, but then I've never seen her as bad as she was tonight. Then, as soon as she saw what she'd done, she started crying and saying she was sorry and calling me her baby but I wasn't ready to tell her it was all okay, so she started screaming at me to get out and not to come back, that she didn't need me, she didn't need my dad, she didn't need anyone. The minute I left there, I rang Doug and he met me on my way back here but now he's going over there again with Dad. They're going to try and talk some sense into her – I can't deal with her on my own any more."

"Oh Dana, I'm so sorry!"

She shrugs.

"And sorry for being such an idiot!"

"You should be, because you are an idiot."

Right now, it seems like I've a lot to apologise for.

"And I'm sorry about all that stuff I said about Doug too."

"How could you think that about him?"

I shrug but, fortunately for me but unfortunately in every other respect, she's more preoccupied with her mum.

"You know, the night Mum found out about Dad, I wanted to stay with her but she wouldn't let me – she was the one who insisted I come back here. She said she was fine, and that she needed to be on her own but now I think she was only trying to get me to go so that she could slip down to the off-licence as soon as I was gone. Maybe if I had stayed that night it wouldn't have got to this stage, maybe I could have got her over the worst and it wouldn't have got to this point."

"Come on, Dana, you can't blame yourself."

"I'm not – I'm just saying." She looks so sad.

"Come here." I give her a hug.

Her phone rings and she picks it up. "A-huh . . . A-huh . . . Okay . . . Yeah, okay . . . Okay . . . Well, keep me posted . . . Yeah, I love you too . . . Bye." She hangs up. "That was

Doug. He and Dad are over at Mum's – she won't let them in but they're going to stay there until she does. He'll ring me again and keep me posted." She looks at her watch. "It's 12.15. You'd better go to bed. You have work in the morning."

But something in her voice makes me ask: "Do you want me to stay here with you until he rings again?"

"Please. I think I'd go out of my mind with worry if I was left on my own."

We climb in under the duvet and, as we lie there side by side, with just the light from the street outside, she begins to talk.

"Partly the reason why Dad used to ring her so much during the day was to keep an eye on her. I don't know how he put up with it for all these years. She was brilliant when she wasn't drinking, the best mother in the world, but then there were times it was chaos. Monday mornings and my uniform would still be in the washing machine or hadn't even got that far. Then some days, I'd come home from school and she'd be lying at the table – drunk as a skunk – but she'd pretend everything was normal and I'd have to sit there watching her trying to make tea, dropping the eggs or whatever on the floor – smiling when she laughed and said, "Oh clumsy me! I'm a right butterfingers today!".

Dana's phone rings again. It's Doug telling her that her mum has finally let them into the house and now her mum and dad are in the kitchen talking.

"You know, I meant what I said about them loving one another. During the good times they were the best. And he's always been there for the bad. I wonder if he'll come back to her. I know he wants to. But I don't know if she'll take him back. But the fact that she let him in tonight is a good thing, don't you think?"

I nod but I don't really know. I'm beginning to think I know nothing about love.

"You know, I'm sorry I've never told you any of this before. It was just that I'd have felt like I was betraying her. My parents used always to pretend to neighbours and family that there was nothing wrong, that we were a normal family. When she had to go away Dad would always say she was just visiting someone. I guess I took my lead from him. I never, ever told anyone – all the time I was growing up."

"That must have been hard."

"It was."

She's silent for a while and just as I'm about to check if she's gone to sleep, she begins talking again.

"But I told Doug. That first night we met, we just talked all through the night, talked and talked about everything. He told me from the outset that he'd had trouble with drugs in the past. Back when he'd been feeling shit about not having a job, he fell in with the wrong crowd but he's clean now. He's really sorted himself out. It's his brother he's worried about now."

"Which one?"

"Tim, the youngest one. Remember when you told me that Monica thought Doug was stealing from her?"

"Yeah?"

"It wasn't him, it was Tim. But Monica wouldn't, couldn't believe it could be him. He's always been her golden boy. She was so sure it was Doug. And I guess because Doug had been so honest with me about his past, it made it easier for me to tell him everything – all the stuff I'd kept bottled up for years."

Now her phone rings again. It's Doug again, ringing to tell her that her mum has agreed to check herself in first thing in the morning and that her dad is going to stay with her until then. Doug says he's now on his way back here.

"So what about you and Mark then?" Dana finally asks, relieved now I guess that her mum is being looked after, and having said all she needed to say.

"Well . . ." I think about telling her everything – but I'm not sure what everything is. I need to think about things myself first. He hasn't done anything to actually harm me but his behaviour isn't normal either – far from it. I need to figure it all out myself. Weirdly I feel guilty. Like Dana with her mum. I don't blame myself exactly but I do feel if I had acted differently then things between us wouldn't have come to this; that he wouldn't be acting the way he is. But now's not the time to get into all this with Dana. She has enough on her plate right now. If things get worse, I will tell her, but tonight's about her and her mum.

"We split up," I say instead. That will do for now.

"Oh!" she laughs. "What was it this time?"

"You know what Caroline always says: never trust a man who spends more time in front of the mirror than you do?"

"And Mark does?"

I nod.

She laughs. "That figures."

We hear the door open and we both lie there, listening as Doug comes up the stairs. We're presuming it is him – he hasn't actually called out hello.

"So can he actually – like – speak?" I whisper.

She laughs. "Don't be mean!"

"I'd better get out and make some room for him."

On my way out, I meet Doug on his way to Dana's. He looks at me but doesn't say anything.

"I hear you've been brilliant," I say, a little shamefaced.

He gives me what I think is a smile and then he grunts, before turning and disappearing into Dana's room.

And in Doug language, I take the grunt to mean something

like, "Why, thank you for noticing. I know you've never liked me so I guess you saying that really means something. You know, maybe we could make a stab at being mates – of sorts. You are one of Dana's friends after all, and I love Dana and I'm kind of figuring on being around for a while yet."

Then again, maybe it is just a grunt.

32

"That's when I'll stop lo♥ing you . . ."

Everything considered, I had a surprisingly good night's sleep and as I take the bus in to work on the bright, crisp morning that it is, I'm feeling better about everything. First thing this morning, I got a call from Mum saying that Dad slept well too. When I asked Mum if she managed to get any sleep on the camp bed, she told me it was even more comfortable than her own bed – a lie for sure but I guess that's where she feels she needs to be right now. I told her I'd call out this evening. Dana's dad rang too at breakfast and they'd a long chat about her mum and everything.

Doug was still there this morning. As a matter of fact, there were four of us sitting at the table: Dana and Doug, and me and this life-sized teddy Doug had given Dana for Valentine's Day. Humph! Valentine's Day, indeed! This will *not* go down as one of my better ones. To be honest, I felt a little sorry for myself sitting there at the breakfast table with Dana and Doug all loved up, canoodling and whispering sweet nothings to one another with me and Teddy looking on. That said, I do get a warm feeling when I think of Dana and Doug and what I now see they have. How could I have been so wrong about him? I really am an idiot sometimes. Okay, so he and I are never going to be best buddies but I'm thinking that, in time, we'll move beyond the grunts. Even this morning we made a little progress – he asked me to pass the milk. One small step but give it a couple of weeks and he may feel ready to have a fully fledged conversation with me. I might even get to know the Doug that Dana so clearly loves and, if she loves him, then he's worth knowing. I'm beginning to think Dana's a lot wiser than me. But then, I'm beginning to think everyone is a lot wiser than me. Who, but a fool like me, would get tangled up with someone like Mark?

That whole business with him is the only dark cloud looming, but in the crisp winter light of this sunny morning, I'm even able to put it into some perspective. Yes, his reaction to our break-up has been way over the top but we did have a very intense couple of weeks together. Yes, it's all been very, very frightening. *But* he hasn't harmed me or even threatened to harm me. Maybe after last night he'll finally understand that I mean it when I say there is no 'us' and, if he doesn't, I'm thinking maybe I should get Finn's number from Shane and ask him to have a word. True, Finn and I have never got along but he is Mark's friend. Mark might listen to him. But maybe it won't come to that. Maybe I'm worrying too much.

I get off the bus and stop off for the usual coffees on the way except now the usual three have evolved into four – the fourth being for the sleeping-bag guy. He's here most mornings but when he's not I just drink it myself. This morning he's here, still asleep but as I stoop to put it down on the pavement beside him, he stirs and then sits up.

"Hiya," I say. "Room service!"

He takes it from me. "Ta very much." I walk on but then he calls out: "Can you come back at noon to do my room?"

I look back, laugh, but keep walking.

"Hey!" he calls out.

I turn around.

"So, what's your name?" he asks.

I'm reluctant to tell him. But why? What's my problem? It's not like it's classified information.

"Rosie!" I shout back. "What's yours?"

"Seán. Pleased to meet you, Rosie."

He smiles and I catch a glimpse of even white teeth with a gap in the middle – he's got a nice smile. It occurs to me that he's way younger than me. Up to now he's just been a homeless guy of indeterminate age in a sleeping bag. If anyone asked me to describe him (in exactly what circumstances this should happen, I don't know) that's all I'd have been able to say about him. Now I see that he's young, nineteen or thereabouts, and underneath the grime and stubble I think he's probably quite good-looking.

I walk back towards him.

"And pleased to meet you, Seán," I say.

"Can I say something to you?" he asks.

"Ah, yeah – I guess."

"Would you ever give me a shout when you're leaving the coffee down? Do you not know how awful it is to wake up, get that lovely smell, reach out and find it's bloody cold?"

I'm annoyed. I guess I was expecting him to thank me again and tell me what a kind and thoughtful person I am.

"Maybe I should stop bringing it altogether!" I say crossly.

"Here, come on now, I was only having a laugh with you.

299

Listen, I appreciate it, all right?" Then he smirks and adds in an American accent, "Now y'all have a nice day, d'ya hear?"

But I don't go. For once I'm on time for work. Why change the habit of a lifetime?

"Now, can I ask you something?" I say.

"As long you're not asking for money."

"Huh?

"It's a joke!"

"Oh right."

"Fire ahead. What do you want to ask?"

"What are you doing sleeping here?"

He smirks. "Cos – duh – I'm homeless."

"Okay, okay – stupid question. But why are you homeless? Like how did you become homeless?"

He looks at me. "Do you really want to know or are you just taking the mick?"

I nod. "Yeah, I do want to know."

He looks at me for a moment, really looks at me, as if he's carrying out some private evaluation. I guess I pass. He begins to talk.

"I used to have a home, you know – a flat with the girlfriend and the two little ones."

"You have two kids?"

"Yeah?"

But he's just a kid himself. "But what age are you?"

"Seventeen."

"Seventeen? *Seventeen*? And you have two kids? What age were you when you had the first?"

"Fourteen."

"Fourteen?"

"Yeah, fourteen."

"Fourteen?"

"Yeah."

Now he's looking at me like I'm stupid. "It comes after thirteen. You know like thirteen, fourteen, fifteen, sixteen. Can you not count?"

"But why did you have children so young?"

Now he's looking at me like I'm so stupid he actually feels sorry for me.

"Ah, we thought it would be cheaper than spending the money on a condom," he jokes. I think.

"So where are they now? The kids?"

"In care."

"Oh! And their mum?"

"Hilda's at her mum's. It's driving her mental. We moved in together after Julie was born because we didn't want the baby being around that psychotic bitch – it was bad enough for Hilda to have to put up with her when she was growing up."

"So why is she back there then?"

"It's a long story?"

"I have the time."

"Are you sure you want to hear it?"

I nod.

He looks at me again, for what seems like ages, and then he starts:

"She ran into a bunch of fucking skangers at the end of their night out when she was on her way to one of her cleaning jobs and they beat the shit of her – just for laughs."

"God! That's awful! Was she badly hurt?"

"You could say that! She ended up in hospital. She was there for months. They fractured her skull and did some brain damage and she has to relearn a load of stuff. She's not back to her old self yet but she's getting there."

"So that's why she's staying at her mum's?"

"Yeah. The flat we had was on the top floor and because the lifts never worked she couldn't stay there. She wasn't able for the stairs but before she ever got out of hospital the social services got involved. They didn't think I was fit to look after the kids on my own – which is crap. I was always the one who minded them. But they took them away. I was trying to get them back but then I lost the flat. Without the money Hilda was making I couldn't make the rent. I couldn't get a job. I'd never worked what with minding the children and all and I'm not, like, the most educated person going. Now I'm on the streets no one is ever going to give me a job."

"Why don't you sleep in a hostel?"

"Nah, I prefer to stick on my own. There's too much drinking going on in them and if I start at that lark, I'd never stop. I have to keep focused. You know what I'm saying? When she's better we'll try again to get a place from the council and all four of us will be back the way we were. Do you want to see a photo of them?"

I nod and his hand disappears down inside his sleeping bag and, rather than the creased snapshot I guess I was expecting, he pulls out a studio portrait in a large wooden frame that belongs on a mantelpiece, not buried deep in a sleeping bag. He hands it to me.

"That's me with Hilda and the two little ones. Julie's the dark one and Queenie's the blonde – she's the spit of her mum. Same personality too. Fiery, but as bright as a button."

"They're lovely-looking kids." And they are. So is his girlfriend. She looks about fifteen and he about the same. Clean-shaven, with a neat haircut, and in clean jeans and a T-shirt – I'd hardly recognise him. He looks like, well, like a non-homeless person, I guess. Just a regular teenager. But with a family.

And I thought I had problems.

"You know it's kinda weird but most people see me – and I don't know – I think they think I was, like, born, this way or something. Or that's it just what I do – in the same way they go into an office." He gives an embarrassed laugh, like he suddenly thinks he might have said too much. "Here, you better get to work – their coffees will be cold."

"You're right." I hand him back the photo.

"Thanks for the chat."

"No problem."

When I get to work, I hand Monica and Fay their coffees. Monica takes a sip then screws up her face.

"This is cold!"

"Sorry, I got delayed. Do you want me to go and get fresh ones?"

"No, no – it doesn't matter."

Fay picks up the coffees and goes into the back to throw them down the sink. Monica goes to attend to a customer who's looking for help. I scan the shop, to see what needs to be done.

Fay comes back.

"Sorry about the coffee," I say.

"Don't worry."

The door pings again. It's another customer and she comes straight to the counter to Fay, looking for advice.

Things are okay-ish again between Fay and myself, or at least as okay-ish as they're ever going to be. After she saw Anthony Knowles on my camera, it was all very, very strained. She's never said another word to me about it since, nor a word to me about anything else much either although, since my dad got sick, she hasn't been quite so hostile – but I do hate knowing she thinks so little of me.

The morning flies. It's the busiest the shop has ever been since I started. All morning the door is pinging and the tills are chinging. Now the place is packed. There's a queue outside the changing rooms and another at the counter. I look over at Monica: she's in her element, rushing around dealing with this person and that person. She must be relieved with this sudden upturn in business. But for the fact that she owns the building and doesn't have to pay any rent, this shop could never survive – even I can see that. With its heyday long gone, it's now something of a dinosaur breathing its last, surrounded by chain stores that probably make more in a single day than this place does in a month. Caroline says Monica should capitalise on the building and sell up, or else lease it out to someone who can really make it pay, and then sit back and enjoy the rent cheques; she'd make more money that way for far less effort. Caroline says that the problem with Monica is that she's too emotionally attached to the place. I think she's probably right.

"Rosie, do you want to go for lunch first?" asks Monica now.

I look at my watch, surprised to see that it's that time already. It's better when the shop is buzzing like this. The mornings drag when it's quiet.

"Sure."

But just as I'm about to get my coat, the door opens and a guy comes in carrying an absolutely enormous bouquet of yellow roses.

"Rosie Kiely?" He looks around to see if such a person is here.

"That's me," I say and he hands me the great big bunch of roses – there must be three dozen of them. I put them down on the counter and take out the card, not with excitement but with dread – I know who it's from. I read it.

"It took just a first glimpse of you – Happy Valentine's Day, my darling."

304

My heart sinks.

Fay holds back, but Monica goes into raptures when she sees the flowers, and keeps saying things like, "Isn't it great to be young?" and "Aren't you the lucky one?" If she only knew. All I want to do is shove these flowers head first into the bin but if I do that then I know I'll have Monica demanding explanations. It's easier to just stick them in a vase so I do and stand them on the counter. Then I go for lunch.

As soon as I come back, the phone calls start coming from Mark. Every ten to fifteen minutes he rings but I don't answer and, eventually, I switch my phone off. The afternoon is nearly as busy as the morning and by the time six o'clock comes I'm absolutely exhausted.

I leave work and start heading to my bus stop but I haven't gone more than fifty metres when I feel a hand on my shoulder. My heart thuds. I swing around. It's Mark.

"Two seconds later and I'd have missed you!" He's beaming at me.

"Mark, will you please just stay away from me?"

But it's like he doesn't even hear me.

"So, did you get my flowers? I was going to send you red ones but then I thought you'd prefer yellow seeing as how it's your favourite colour."

"It's not."

"Yes, it is."

I stare at him. How can I argue with someone who thinks they know me better than I know myself.

"So, how are you, my love?"

"Mark, I'm not your love. Can't you just get it into your head that I don't love you!" I decide the time has come to be cruel to be kind. I really need to spell things out to him. "Look, the only reason I said I loved you that night was because I was embarrassed for you. I didn't want my friends sniggering at you. I felt sorry for you. We went out for a couple of weeks – that's it. The special relationship you seem to think we had, or have, is all in your head. Now just leave me be! I only stayed going out with you as long as I did because . . ." but I don't go on. I stop short of telling him about Caroline's bet.

I walk away. He shouts after me.

"Even if I believed what you say, even if you never loved me, that doesn't mean I can just stop loving you! You can't turn love off, Rosie!"

Then he comes running after me.

"Rosie, just tell me what I need to do to make you love me. For God's sake, Rosie, just tell me!"

He grabs my arm.

"Let me go!"

"Rosie if you don't love me then I swear I'll kill myself!"

"Don't say that – it's not funny."

"It's not meant to be."

Suddenly he pulls up both his sleeves and I see cuts criss-crossed all the way up his arms.

"Jesus!"

"I couldn't bear the pain in here!" He pounds his chest. "I had to take it away somehow."

"Rosie, are you all right?"

We both swing around. It's Seán, the homeless guy.

"Is he bothering you?" he asks.

"Yes."

"I'm not, so fuck off back to whatever hole you crawled out of and leave me and my girlfriend talk in peace."

"I am not your girlfriend!"

"Can't you leave her alone?" persists Seán.

Mark stares at the pair of us, and then suddenly storms off.

"Are you okay?" asks Seán.

"Yeah, I think so. And thanks for that."

On the bus home I'm still feeling rattled. I think the sight of Mark's slashed arms upset me more than anything. No one sane would do that to himself. Now I keep half-expecting him to hop on at the next stop, or to turn around and see him sitting there, in the seat behind me. But the bus arrives at my stop without incident and I get off and walk around the corner. I see our house is in darkness. I wish the others were here. And then I notice the car sitting outside the house, and a figure sitting at the wheel. It's Mark. Shit!

But I go up to him. He rolls down the window.

"If you don't leave, I'm going to call the police. I mean it," I tell him.

"I'm not doing anything illegal. I'm just sitting in my car on the public road."

"You're not. You're stalking me. Leave me alone, Mark. Can't you just leave me alone?"

"Like I said, Rosie – you can't just switch off love. I'm not a machine."

"Mark, for the last time, listen to me! I *don't* love you. The reason I said I did was because I felt sorry for you – can't you get that into your head?"

"I can't. Because it's not true!"

"It *is* true! Listen to me, I'd have ended things sooner except that Caroline bet me that it would never last between us and I wanted to prove her wrong."

"You're lying. You're only saying that."

"I'm not. Think about it, why would I?"

"I don't believe you!" He's shaking his head now. "You can't have given me all that you gave me, allowed me to love you, let me believe you loved me and then expect me to go on like nothing happened when you decide to take it all away from me!" Suddenly he reaches out a hand and grabs my arm. "I've booked a table for two in Dino's for seven. If we go now, we could get there in time."

"What? Are you completely mad! Have you not heard a word I've said?"

I manage to pull away and I make a run for the house. He doesn't come after me and when I reach the door, I turn around and shout out:

"If you set one foot inside our gate, I'll call the gardaí, I swear I will!"

Inside the house, I pull the curtains and start phoning. I ring Caroline first but I'd forgotten that she's in Cork. Before I can get a word in, she tells me she's with clients and she can't talk and immediately hangs up. Then I ring Dana but there's no answer. I ring Shane next but his phone is switched off and I remember now that he told me he and Loretta were meeting to go to a movie after work and for a meal afterwards. I ring Mick but he doesn't pick up either. All the while, I'm going from one room to another, peering out between the curtains. He's still there.

But then when I check for what's probably the hundredth time, I see his car is gone. I look up and down the street – there's no sign of it. I decide I have to get out of here. I'll go to my mum's – she was expecting me but I can't take Dad's car since the battery has run down – I'm so used to driving Caroline's flash car that I forgot I needed to manually turn off the lights in Dad's. I decide to ring for a taxi.

Twenty minutes later the taxi pulls up outside the house and I rush out but, just as I'm getting into it, Mark's car appears around the corner and he cruises by slowly, looking at me.

"Where to, love?" asks the taxi-man.

I can't have Mark following me out to Mum and Dad's, no way.

"Come on, love, the meter is ticking."

"Ah – town please." I don't know why I say that but I can't think of anywhere else.

All the way into town, I keep glancing back, and all the time he's right behind us.

"Where in town?" asks the driver.

"Ah, Dame Street, please."

"Going somewhere nice for Valentine's?"

"What? Ah – yeah."

What am I going to do if he's still behind us when we reach Dame Street? Tell the driver to go somewhere else, or get out and try to lose him amongst the people. I don't know. I just don't know what to do. Then my phone rings. I look down at it: it's Mark. I ignore it but I turn again and look out the rear window. He's so near I can see the mad intense expression on his face.

"Can you hurry up?" I ask the driver. "I think the guy behind is following us."

The driver laughs. "What do you think this is, love, a Hollywood movie?"

I see him looking at me in the mirror. No doubt he's thinking he's got a right one on his hands, but it'll make for a good story to tell his mates back at the base.

Mark rings again. I ignore it.

"Jesus! What's the idiot behind me doing? He's right up my arse!"

"Look, I'm not some mental woman and he *is* following us. He's an old boyfriend – since I split up with him he's been acting crazy."

He looks in the mirror again. "Fucking brilliant!" he mutters.

When the phone rings for a third time, I pick up. "Mark, will you leave me alone! You're freaking me out!"

"Tell me you love me!"

"No!"

Suddenly I'm thrown forward. The car has been hit from behind.

"Christ!" cries the taxi driver.

There comes a second jolt.

"What the fuck!"

The driver speeds up. He's in a panic now. "Call the guards," he's shouting at me. "Call the fucking guards!"

As I'm keying in 999, we're hit again and my phone goes flying to the floor.

The driver is driving as fast as he can go now but we keep hitting traffic lights. He's on to the base, explaining what's going on. Now he takes a sharp right to get out of the heavy traffic and away from Mark but Mark is still right behind us. The driver breaks a red light, makes a whole load of other turns but we still can't shake off Mark. I've no idea where we are now – coming down onto the docks, I think. The driver makes another right turn and, this time, Mark doesn't make it. His car goes careering forward, across the road, skids, then crashes into a concrete wall.

33

"I'd do anything for lo♥e . . ."

The others went to Mark's funeral but I couldn't face it. I just couldn't. I can't face much since it happened. For the whole week since Mark's death I've moved between my bed and the couch in the living room. I just keep going over and over that night. I can't stop thinking about it. I can't stop thinking about Mark, and how he's dead now, and how it's all my fault. I keep thinking that if only I'd handled things differently then it wouldn't have happened. I can't stop thinking up these 'what if' scenarios. What if the battery in Dad's car hadn't been flat? What if I hadn't called a taxi? What if I'd told him I loved him in that last phone call – like he so desperately wanted me to? What if the taxi had pulled over instead of racing off like that?

For the first couple of days, the others really mollycoddled me – listened to me when I needed to talk, prepared meals for me, bought me magazines, books, newspapers, videos – anything to distract me. As if they could. Nothing can.

But the others are moving on, getting back to normality. I wish I could. It's early evening now but they're all still out at work – I haven't been to work since.

Now my tummy is rumbling. Apart from a bowl of cereal and a couple of packets of crisps I haven't eaten all day. I've just spent it under my duvet, staring up the ceiling but, now, hunger drives me from the bed and I get up and mooch down to the kitchen. I go from one press to another, trying to think of what I want to eat but I don't know what I want. I take out a tin of tuna thinking I'll make a sandwich but it seems like far too much effort. I open the tuna, bring it with me into the living room, turn on the telly and eat directly from the tin with a fork as I flick from channel to channel.

I hear the front door open.

"Hello!" It's Shane. He comes into the living room.

"Hi."

He sits down on the couch beside me but then stands up again and picks up the empty tin and fork and takes them into the kitchen. He comes back in again but doesn't sit this time, but just stands there looking at me.

"You're blocking the television," I tell him.

He bends down and turns it off. "You didn't go back to work today, I take it."

I shrug.

"I thought you told Monica you would."

I shrug again.

"Did you even ring her?"

I shake my head.

"Did you even go outside today?"

I shake my ahead again.

"Rosie, you haven't set foot outside the door in a week."

So, what's so brilliant about outside? "Can I turn the telly back on – I was watching something?"

He sighs. "Since when have you been interested in the business news?"

His phone rings. He looks at the number and goes to

take the call out in the hall. I put the telly back on but I can hear him talking. I know by the soft sound of his voice that he's on to Loretta. I wish I had someone to talk to me like that. "Listen," I hear him saying, "can we give tonight a skip. Well . . ." He's whispering now but I can make out some of what he's saying and I can guess the rest. He's talking about me, saying he doesn't want to leave me on my own. Good, I don't want to be on my own.

He comes in.

"Listen, why don't I go and get a DVD and a takeaway? And you can go and have a shower while I'm gone."

"Does it look like I need one that much?"

"You're not looking your best, Rosie, my sweet."

A half-an-hour later I come down in my dressing-gown, towelling my hair. I go back into the living room and take up my spot on the couch. I see Shane's tidied things up. He's even set two places on the coffee table and there's a bottle of wine open and two glasses standing beside it. He comes back, puts the pizza and garlic bread on the table, then bends down and sticks in the DVD.

He sits down beside me, hands me a glass of wine and a plate with a couple of slices of pizza.

"Thanks." Suddenly I feel like crying again. It seems like just about anything can set me off these days, like this little act of kindness.

"It's *Breakfast in Pluto*," he tells me as he clicks on the remote control.

The trailers play but I don't watch them. Now that I've started eating I can't stop. I reach out for another couple of slices of pizza and fill up my glass again. Before the movie's even started I've eaten more than half the pizza. I reach out for the wine again. I see Shane looking at me but he doesn't say anything. I hold the bottle out to him but he shakes his head. He still has a full glass in front of him.

For the first half of the movie I'm fine. Better than I've been for ages – I'm not thinking about Mark. Despite myself I'm really getting into the drama on the screen. It's all about this guy who calls himself Kitten and who's a misfit in this drab dreary town he lives in. He spends his time dreaming of going to London to find his mother who abandoned him as a baby, dressing up in women's clothes, and hanging out with his friends – all misfits themselves in their own way. The story feels familiar and then I remember Finn talking about it to me, at that party, the night I got together with Mark.

I'm not sure if it's the thought of that night, or if it's all the wine I've drunk, or if it's what's now happening in the film – probably a mixture of all but, suddenly, I start bawling. On the screen, Kitten's young friend – a Down's Syndrome boy – has just been blown to smithereens. It seems like the saddest thing I've ever seen and I watch it with the tears running down my face.

"O-kay," says Shane. "Maybe this wasn't the best choice of movie. I'll turn it off."

"No, no!" I need to see what happens. "Don't turn it off now!" And for the rest of the movie I sit there, crying, watching all the awfulness that happens to Kitten but then, in the end, he finds happiness of a sort.

That's what I want to be – happy. When is all this misery going to end? I wish I could go back to a happier, uncomplicated time – like before I met Mark, or even before that again – maybe as far back as to when I was young, and growing up with my own friends, in my own small town. I was happy then. I was definitely happy then. Not just happy but I had no comprehension of unhappiness. I remember Shane telling me that a friend of his parents had committed suicide – we must have been about eight. I remember not being able to understand why anyone would do that. If things had gone so wrong for this man, why hadn't he just moved away and started afresh? I had no notion that it was *inside* people that things went wrong, that there was no getting away from their troubles.

"Are you okay, Rosie?" Shane looks over at me.

"No."

He moves closer and gives me a hug and, with my head now lying against his chest as the credits roll, I think back again to those times when Shane and I were the best of friends, when we used to walk home from school every day together. I think how he's always been part of my life. I no longer have any meaningful contact with any of my other friends in school but even back then all I needed was to have Shane as my friend. Other friends have come and gone but he's always been part of my life, and I always assumed he would be. Except lately. Since Loretta, we haven't been as close as we were, but we will be again. We can't not be. We've know each other too well and too long.

"Remember how we used to walk home from school every day?" I ask him.

"Course I do. I had to listen to you, yapping, yapping, yapping." He's rubbing my back now. I like that. I don't want it to stop.

"You were as bad," I laugh.

"Never!"

"Remember when we were about eight maybe, and one of the Gordons went cycling past, one of the older ones, and he shouted out to you, 'Ohooo, holding hands with your girlfriend!'"

"Yeah," says Shane and I can hear it in his voice that he's smiling at the memory.

"We used to hold hands every single day before that," I say.

"Yeah, but we never did again," he laughs.

"Remember how the minute we'd get home, we'd ring each other?"

"It used to drive my mother mad."

"Mine too. 'What do you want ringing him for? Haven't you just left him?' What used we to talk about?"

"Who knows?"

I wish I could go back, as a fly buzzing around us as we walked home, listening in to all those childish, innocent chats.

"Remember, when we started secondary school, everyone thought we were going out together," I laugh. "I remember hearing your friend Ben going on at you one day when he didn't know I was listening. 'Admit it, she's your girlfriend! Go on, you fancy her, don't you? Why else would you be hanging around with a stupid girl all the time?'"

I'm still nestled against Shane's chest but I know he's smiling.

And that's when I do it. I don't even think about what I'm doing. I just sit up, lean over and kiss him on the lips, a long lingering kiss, and I think I begin to feel his lips respond to me but then he pushes me roughly from him.

"Jesus! Rosie, are you fucking insane?"

"Shane, I'm sorry – I didn't know what I was doing."

He's sitting there, like he's in shock, like he can't believe what I've just done.

"Look, I'm sorry. I'm not myself. This whole thing with Mark has really got me addled. I'm sorry, Shane!"

Silence still. He goes on staring at me with that shocked look.

"How many times do you want me to say it? Okay, what

I did was wrong, stupid, but it was only a little kiss! Stop looking at me like that! I'm sorry!"

"Rosie, look, we all know what you've been through but this isn't going to make things better."

And it's then I say it because I figure it's what we've both always known anyway.

"It's not like you can't have wanted me to do it. You've always loved me, you know you have." I say it because somewhere, deep inside, I've always believed it.

Shane's staring at me, like he just can't believe what he's just heard.

"You are un-fucking-believable!"

"Okay, then, say you don't love me."

"I *don't* love you!"

"You do. Remember the time you kept coming up to ask me to dance? You must have asked me like ten times and each time we danced I knew all you wanted to do was kiss me but you couldn't work up the courage."

"I remember. Yeah, I remember I was thirteen. I remember I'd never snogged a girl and, yeah, I thought I'd better do it someday soon if I didn't want to be a laughing stock, and yeah, I thought it might as well be you, seeing as how you were already my friend."

"No, no, it was more than that!"

"Rosie, I'm a man – of course I can see how gorgeous you are. And of course from time to time, I've thought about you and me, and what if? But that was before I met Loretta. I love Loretta."

"You don't love Loretta!"

"Of course, I bloody love her!"

"But I thought –"

"You thought what? That I was just going out with her to pass the time, because I couldn't have you?"

I guess that's exactly what I thought. Somewhere in the back of my mind I've always believed that all I had to do was click my fingers and Shane would come running.

He gets up. "I need to get out of here before I say something I'd really regret."

He leaves the room but then, seconds later, he comes back in again.

"You know, I'm sick of this – this isn't all about you! You barely knew Mark a couple of weeks. All this lying around the house is just you indulging yourself. Have you ever given Mark's parents a second thought? They've lost their only son. They've every right to stay in bed, crying for the rest of their lives but even they manage to get up in the morning and put on their clothes. Finn says Mark's Dad is even talking about going back to work. So stop your wallowing and get a grip!"

34

"What's lo♥e got to do with it?"

If you think snogging my childhood friend was bad, there's worse to come, and if you don't already think I'm a stupid, selfish, careless child, then you soon will. And I can't offer any explanations.

The next morning, I do finally pull myself together enough to go into work. Both Fay and Monica are just lovely to me. They don't say much but when I turn up without my usual coffees, Fay runs out and gets them and a big bag of doughnuts. While she's gone, Monica says that if I'd like to talk about 'things' then both she and Fay are here for me but they both understand if I don't want to talk. Then, all day, they tiptoe around me, letting me go to lunch first, making sure I'm busy but not too busy, chatting about this and that, just to keep my mind occupied. But, when closing time finally comes, all I want to do is go back home and crawl into bed.

When I get off at my bus stop, I call in to a restaurant at the corner to get something to bring home with me from its deli and, as I'm queuing at the counter, out of the corner of my eye I suddenly spot Anthony Knowles – Fay's Anthony Knowles – except he's not with Fay. He's sitting at a table across from a woman about his own age and I think it must be his wife. Neither of them are talking. They're just sitting there in silence, eating.

"Next, please," says the woman behind the counter and I manage to drag my attention away from them and back to her.

"Can I have a portion of lasagne, please, and some of the tomato and cucumber salad to go with it?"

"Have here or take away?"

"Ah – here please," I say, quickly changing my mind. "And I'll have a Coke too."

"I'll bring it down to you."

When I've paid, I sit down at the table across the way from Anthony and his wife. The restaurant is busy and because of all the noise I can't hear what they're saying, but then, they're not saying much. They just go on sitting there in silence, eating – not looking particularly happy, but then they don't look unhappy either. Slightly bored, maybe, even a little resigned. Every now and then, I see one of them ask the other to pass something – the salt, a napkin – but that's as far as conversation between them goes.

Sensing me staring at him, perhaps, Anthony looks over at me and I don't bother to look away. I just stare at him coldly and I can see he's puzzled why a stranger should be staring over at him with such hostility. He clearly doesn't have any memory of meeting me. I can feel his wife now looking from one of us to the other, wondering just what's going on. She calls his name, he looks away from me and back to her and I see her asking a question, probably asking him does he know me. He shakes his head. They both look back at me. I don't bother to look away.

Suddenly I feel so mad. What is this man playing at? Who does he think he is? Just what does he think he's doing? Here he is, with his wife, the woman he left for Fay years ago yet he's still seeing Fay *but* he's still with his wife. What exactly is going on? Has he been stringing his wife along all these years? Stringing the pair of them along? What kind of a man would do that? And how dare he! How does he get away with it? How does this very ordinary middle-aged man get away with stringing along two women all these years? Surely Fay, surely his wife, deserves better than that? Fay looked so happy that day I saw the pair of them on Grafton Street together and it seems grossly unfair that she's had to survive on the scraps he's thrown her over the years. And though I don't especially like the look of his wife – she's too humourless-looking, too stern-looking to warm to – doesn't she too deserve better?

The pair of them are whispering to one another now, wondering just what is the story with me but I don't care. Then, suddenly, his wife gets up and I see she's coming over to my table. I quickly look away

"Excuse me?" She's now standing at my table.

Reluctantly, I look up.

"Do we *know* you?" she demands.

"Pardon?" I stammer.

"I'd like to know why you're staring over at my husband."

For a split second, I think about telling her exactly why, but I manage to hold my tongue. "I'm sorry," I say. "I don't know what you're talking about."

She stands there for a while, clearly not satisfied with my answer. Does she think there's something going on between me and him? Does she have reason to believe there could be? Maybe Fay is just one of a long line of indiscretions. Maybe she thinks I'm another. Maybe she thinks I'm a spurned girlfriend.

I don't really care what she thinks. She's still standing there. I pick up my fork and begin eating and try to ignore her. Finally she turns away and goes back to her seat.

After maybe five minutes, she stands up again, as does Anthony, and the pair of them start putting on their coats but then I hear her telling him to hold on a moment, that she's going to use the bathroom. She makes her way down to the toilets while he resumes his seat.

I look over at him again and I think of Fay. While he's here with his wife, what's Fay doing? Is she sitting all alone in her apartment, waiting for him to call? Is she looking forward to the next time he can spare some time for her out of his real life? Suddenly, I push my meal aside, gather together my coat and bag, get up and go over to him.

"Hello!"

Startled, he looks up. "Ah – hello," he says, looking a little puzzled, like he's trying to place me.

"Anthony, isn't it?"

"Ah – yes."

"And that must be your wife?" I nod in the direction of the toilets.

"Yes." Now he gives an apologetic smile. "I'm sorry, you have the advantage on me. You are?"

"Rosie Kiely. I work with Fay O'Neill. I think you know Fay."

I watch as the colour drains from his face. He doesn't answer immediately. He looks like he's figuring out how he's going to play this. Then he smiles at me, and shrugs.

"I'm sorry. I think you've mistaken me for someone else. I don't know any Fay O'Neill."

He's staring at me now, daring me to contradict him and all I can think is what a rotten little weasel – denying he even knows her.

"Ah Elizabeth, there you are!"

We both look around as his wife comes over to us. He quickly gets up again from his seat, goes to his wife, puts his hand on her arm and tries to guide her out as speedily as he can, but his wife isn't quite as anxious to go as he is. She's staring at me again.

Then she turns to her husband. "Do you know this girl, Anthony?"

"No, no, I think she's mistaken me for someone else."

She looks back at me. I should just go and leave things as they are but I think of Fay, and how happy she looked with him that day on Grafton Street, and I think how now he denies even knowing her. Fay doesn't deserve that.

"Your husband is right. I guess I have mistaken him for someone else."

Out of the corner of my eye, I notice Anthony leave out a sigh of relief. He thinks he's got away with it. Maybe he even gets off on the buzz of his double-life.

"I thought I met your husband in town not so long ago with my colleague, Fay O'Neill, but obviously I must have been mistaken."

And, shaking, I walk away but not before I see from the expression on Elizabeth Knowles' face that the name Fay O'Neill most certainly means something to her. She looks furious.

35

"Everyone lo♥es somebody sometime . . ."

The next day is Saturday and, when I wake up, the first thing I remember is the incident in the restaurant. I can hardly believe what I did. If only I could take the last twelve hours back. But I can't. In less than one minute I quite possibly changed the lives of Anthony and Elizabeth Knowles forever and there's nothing – not a single thing – I can do to change it back to the way it was before. I don't want to – can't bear to – imagine what's going on in that house right now.

I go downstairs. Loretta is making tea to take upstairs for Shane and herself.

"Hiya," she smiles at me.

I don't know if Shane told her what happened between him and me. I can only pray he didn't. It's hard to tell with Loretta. If she does know, and if she was another person, then she'd most definitely take this opportunity to tell me to stay the hell away from her boyfriend. But Loretta is different. I can see her trying to see things from my perspective. Unthreatened, secure in the knowledge that she and Shane belong to one another, I can see her feeling sorry for me. I don't want Loretta to feel sorry for me. I'd prefer her to scream at him, call me the bitch that I am, but Loretta is bigger than that. Even if she knows, she'll still go on being nice to me. Because that's what she's always been to me – nice. That's what she is – a nice, thoroughly decent human being, who's always been far nicer to me than I have been to her. Take when Dad was in hospital, and afterwards, she was brilliant then and in the days after Mark died too. She was willing to put up with listening to me even more than any of the others. So why have I always had such a problem with her? Was it because somewhere in the back of my mind I was afraid of what she really meant to Shane?

"See you," she says, picking up the two cups of tea.

"See you," I say.

She knows. I just know she knows.

I sit down at the table and pour out a bowl of cornflakes. There's a paper from yesterday lying on the table and I scan through the already out-of-date news. I think what I'm going to do for the day. I have no work. Maybe I should have asked Monica if I could go in today but it's too late. The Saturday staff would already be in by now. There's no one in the house only Shane and Loretta and somehow I don't think he'll want me hanging around with them for the day. Dana stayed over at Doug's last night. And I know Caroline isn't due back until Monday evening. She's in London, on business. I heard her going out at the crack of dawn to catch her flight. Maybe I'll give Mick a ring – he hasn't been around much of late. I think he's avoiding Caroline ever since he told her he loved her.

I could go out to see Mum and Dad. I haven't been there in a while but I decide to put it off until this afternoon. Mum said Uncle Dave and Auntie Margaret are calling out this morning and I don't want to meet them. I know my mum will have told them all about what happened to Mark and, even if they don't talk to me about it, it'll still be in the air. I know they'll be thinking about it.

I think about Mark's parents. Since Shane accused me of not having given a thought to them, his words have stuck with me. I've been thinking a lot about them since. I wonder what they're doing now? Talking about him? Thinking about him? Trying not to think about him? If I had been in love with their son then, maybe, I'd now be planning to call over there, to offer them comfort and to be comforted by them. We could sit around talking to each other about how we loved him, how we miss him, about all those things that made him so special to us. But I didn't love him. I hardly knew him. And if I did love him, he wouldn't be dead.

So what would be the point of me even calling to their door? What could I say? "Hi, I'm the girl your son was following when his car went out of control. Yeah, I'm the one who's responsible for his death." I have thought about writing them a letter, but it's the same problem – I don't know what I would put in it. There's nothing I can write to them that will allow them to feel that the death of their son was anything other than the stupid awful thing it was. I have nothing to offer them.

I think about if Mark was alive and I wonder what he'd be doing now? Still in bed or up having his breakfast, maybe sitting at the table with Finn chatting about band stuff. Mark's death must be awful for Finn. He practically grew up with him and they were living together; everywhere he looks there must be reminders of Mark. I wonder if Finn too is sitting at his breakfast table now, wondering how he's going to get through the day. Maybe I have something to offer Finn. Maybe I should ring him. But could I? But the more I think about it, the more it seems like a good idea. The worst he can do is tell me to go shove my sympathy. I could even talk to him about Mark's parents, ask him if he thinks writing a letter is a good idea.

I take out my phone, scroll until I find Mark's home number (still listed), press call and, almost straight away, Finn answers. Suddenly, I feel nervous.

"Finn, hello, it's Rosie Kiely."

"Oh hello!" He sounds surprised

"Look, I wanted to call you to say I'm sorry about Mark. I know how close you were."

I wonder if he blames me for what happened.

"Yeah, well, thanks – that's kind of you."

Encouraged by his words, I go further than I meant to and suddenly find myself saying: "I know we haven't seen eye-to-eye but I think we probably both could do with a friend right now. Do you want to meet for a coffee?"

I can hear his hesitation.

"Yeah, okay, I guess we could."

Walking past the window, I see him sitting there – a head of black curls bowed over a newspaper. I open the door and go in.

"Hi!"

He looks up but doesn't smile. "Hi there." He looks pale and tired.

"I'll go and get myself a coffee. Do you want another one?"

"Okay so."

I go to the counter. As I'm standing there, waiting for the coffee, I look down at Finn. He's hunched over the paper again. What am I doing here? I hardly know him. But I know that this is where I want to be right now. I'm not ready to move on, not ready to draw a line under everything just yet.

I come back with the coffees and sit down.

"Thanks," says Finn.

In silence, he pours in some milk and takes a sip. Now I'm here, I don't know what to say.

Finn looks like he has nothing to say either but then he glances up. Now he smiles at me – the first smile since I got here. It's not a hundred-watt smile or anything, more like ten-watt, but it is a smile. I realise I'm relieved. Maybe I half-expected that he was going to use this opportunity to tell me what he thought of my part in Mark's death.

"I thought about ringing you too," he says now, "but I'm finding all this pretty hard myself."

I nod. "Thanks."

"For what?"

"Well, that you even thought to ring."

He shrugs.

"How are Mark's parents?" I ask.

"As well as can be expected – which is pretty bad. Mrs McCarthy especially is finding it very difficult. She and Mark were very close."

"She must really hate me." Inside, I cringe. What would Shane say if he heard me – that I was bringing it all back to me again?

Finn looks up at me. He thinks for a moment and I think, as I watch him, that's what he's going to say, that it isn't all about me. But it's not. He talks slowly, as if he's really weighing up his words: "I guess she wishes Mark never met you. But I don't think she hates you." He shakes his head. "No, Mrs McCarthy doesn't really do hate. She's kind of special. If anything, I think she feels sorry for you. I think she's imagining how all this must be for you."

"No! You're joking!"

"Like I said, they were close and Mark talked a lot to her about you. I think she worried about him right from the beginning. She knows – knew Mark. Mark had always been – well – very emotional, putting it mildly. Mrs McCarthy was afraid of what might happen if you ever broke it off with him but it didn't seem like that was about to happen. She – I – thought you were as much into him as he was into you. He talked an awful lot about you to everyone but he never told anyone that you and he had split up. Even the day he died, he stormed out of the house after we'd had our huge row and I was worried about him then."

Row?

"He was in a right state but because he said he was on his way to meet you I wasn't as concerned as I should have been. In a way, I'm as much to blame as you –"

"How can you say that! He died because he was chasing me! Because I was so horrible to him!"

"Yes but if I hadn't –"

"Finn," I interrupt, "look, I had this crazy idea of sending the McCarthys a letter just to let them know I was thinking about them. Do you feel that's a good idea, or do you think it would upset them?"

He thinks for a long while. "No, I think you should."

"Okay, I will." Now I have made the decision, now that Finn is being so nice to me, I relax a little. "So how are you?"

He shrugs. "Not so good. Sometimes I feel that I wouldn't get through it all without the McCarthys. Sometimes I feel they're the ones giving me the support I should be giving them." He takes a sip of coffee. "You know, I was working myself up to sorting out all Mark's things when you rang so I was glad to have an excuse to put it off for another day. I just don't have the heart for it. I don't know when I will." He takes another sip. "It's weird. Mark's been part of my life since I remember. My very first memory is of him. Our two mums were very close. When she was alive and we were toddlers, my mum and his mum used to go out for long walks with us in our buggies. One day when we were about two or three we went to Stephen's Green. While they sat on the bench chatting and chatting, we were running around exploring everything. But then one of us – and I think it was Mark but he always said it was me – decided we should go for a swim in the little lake. I guess we knew we shouldn't because we hid behind a bush and took off all our clothes and then went creeping down into the lake on the far side where they wouldn't see. But I guess someone – some stranger who had spotted us – must have asked our mothers did the two naked skinny little boys belong to them? I remember looking up and seeing my mum and his running towards us, shouting their heads off. They killed us that day." He smiles. We're at about a forty-watt now. "Anyway, what am I like? Going on and on. You're probably bored out of your mind."

"No, I'm not," I shake my head. "You know, it's kind of weird. I know Mark and I went out together for a short while but I never really felt I knew him. It's kind of nice hearing about him now."

We drink our coffees. We're coming to the end of them. I don't want it – this – to end. I like being here but then Finn puts down his empty cup, gathers up his paper, and looks around for his jacket.

"I guess I should get going," he says.

"Yeah, me too." I reach down for my bag at my feet.

We stand up and, as we walk out, he holds the door for me.

"Well, thanks for the chat," he says.

"And thank you."

He seems reluctant to move off. Maybe he's thinking of the job that lies ahead of him – sorting out Mark's belongings. In the middle of this crowded street of normal people, all laughing, chatting, shopping, it seems like a very sad and lonely thing to have to do.

And then I hear my own voice saying: "Finn, I know this might sound strange but if you want someone to help you, or to even just keep you company while you're going through Mark's things, I could."

"Ah, no, you're fine," he says. "It's something I need to do myself."

"It's not like I have anything better to do."

He looks up at me. "Are you sure?"

"Sure, I'm sure."

We take the bus back out to Finn and Mark's. It's weird being back here, especially in Mark's room. As it turns out, I don't really do anything much. I think Finn needs to do it himself. But I think by just being here I'm a help. I'm someone to whom he can verbalise all the emotions and memories Mark's belongings are bringing back to him.

Every now and then he passes me something – mostly photos. Like a photo of their class, about thirty boys in matching grey. Immediately I spot the pair of them, standing side by side, smack bang in the middle of the middle row. They're about nine-years-old. Neither has really changed much. Mark is by far the best-looking boy in the class and already it's like he knows it. Most of the other boys (Finn included) have silly grins on their faces, some aren't even looking in the direction of the camera, but Mark is standing up straight, staring right into the lens. He's very composed. *But* what he doesn't know is that Finn is making rabbit's ears with two fingers at the back of Mark's neatly groomed hair. Finn hasn't changed much either. He has exactly the same cheeky grin he has now – not that I've seen much of it today. The one difference is his hair. It's short-ish and still curly now but, in the photo, it's a mass of thick black curls – too big to be conceivably real.

"What's with the wig?" I laugh.

He takes the photo back from me, looks at it and laughs too. "When Mark's mum saw that photo she was so mad. First, because I was making fun of Mark but also because of the state of my hair. She said I was a disgrace. She tried to persuade my dad to take me to a barber but my hair would have had to have been around my ankles for Dad to see the need to intervene." He laughs. "So, she decided to take matters into her own hands. I remember her chasing me around her kitchen with a scissors, with Mark sitting at the table in the middle of it all, laughing his head off, shouting, 'Catch him, Mum. Catch him!'"

"And did she catch you?"

"Yeah."

Suddenly he looks very sad.

"What's the matter, Finn?"

"She caught me but she didn't cut it because I started shouting at her: 'You're not my mum! My mum is dead! You can't make me cut my hair!'"

Finn's phone rings now. He picks it up from where it's lying on the bed. "It's Mrs McCarthy – I'd better take it." He goes out into the hall and talks to her for a long time, then comes back in.

"She's not doing too well today," he tells me as he kneels down on the floor, in the middle of Mark's things. "I said I'd call over later."

"It's kind of weird, isn't it? You lost your mum and Mrs McCarthy was like a mum to you when you were growing up and now she's lost her son and –"

"Rosie! Don't go there! I'll never replace Mark, no more than she ever replaced my mum."

"Sorry, I didn't th –"

"But I will be there for her. I will do everything to make things better for her."

I look down at the photo again. "Finn, what was Mark really like?"

He thinks for a while. "He was just Mark. He was just like my brother, like family. Even when we had our differences – and we did, a lot, sometimes he drove me mad – but he was always part of life. It wasn't a choice thing. It just was."

He falls silent. I look at him from where I'm sitting on the bed. I'm wondering what he's thinking. Then he looks up at me.

"I've never really thought about what he was like before but he definitely was kind. He was very kind to me. Another child might have had problems sharing their mum but he never did. If ever their family were going on a day out he'd always want me to come along. He was gentle too, too gentle for his own good. Guys at school were always picking on him but he'd never rise to them. Sometimes I ended up having to beat them up to get them to leave him alone." He laughs. "And he was vain – boy, was he vain! But, you know, he'd a good sense of humour but he lost some of that as we grew up, especially after we left school. He hated working in that call centre. I think he couldn't believe that was all life had in store for him. Maybe that's why when we set up the band he was so desperate for us to really make it. For the rest of us, the band was a laugh. We'd lots of other stuff going on. I'm happy working with my dad in his DIY store, doing my paintings, even doing up this house, but Mark saw it differently. He saw the band as this big opportunity. When we split up –"

"What? The band split up?"

"Yeah." He looks confused. "I thought you knew."

"No, I didn't. When?"

"The day he died. That's what our big row was all about."

"I see. But why?"

"We may have been like brothers, but brothers fight too and before he died we hadn't been getting along. So the band split. He was gutted."

I look down at the photo I'm still holding. "What a waste! He was such a talented singer and songwriter."

"What?" Finn asks.

I look up at him. "What, what?"

"What did you say?"

"I don't know – that he was a gifted singer and songwriter."

"He wasn't a songwriter. I wrote our songs."

"Yeah, I know you helped him but –"

"Helped him? Why would you think that?"

"I don't know – because he told me?"

Finn looks mad though he's trying not to. It's hard to be mad with someone who's dead.

"I don't know why he would say that. I wrote all our songs."

"All of them?"

"Yeah."

I've having a problem with this. Even "Just a First Glimpse of You to Fall in Love"? I think of asking, but I don't.

Then Finn gets up from where he's kneeling on the floor and looks around at all the boxes and black plastic bags he's filled during the course of the afternoon. "I think we're more or less through here. I guess I could take all this stuff over to McCarthys'."

"Yeah, I should be going too."

I help him load everything into the car.

"So will I drop you home on my way over there?" he asks.

"You're all right. I feel like a walk."

And I do. I have a lot to think about.

That night, I take out a sheet of paper and a pen. After the day spent with Finn, I think I know Mark a little better. Like Finn said, he was kind and gentle, I'd almost forgotten that. He had been like that with me too, before I broke up with him and he turned all psycho.

But what I keep thinking about is how odd it is the way Mark pretended to write those songs, and odd the way he took aspects of Finn's life, and made them his own. I remember Mark saying that he looked out for Finn, but I see now that it was the other way around.

I look upward, to where heaven is supposed to be, and think: Mark, I hope you're happier where you are now.

One other thing I do know about Mark is that he meant an awful lot to Finn and to his mum and dad. I know that he was loved. I know that he is missed. And that's the gist of what I write in my letter.

I go to bed and try not to think about a lot of things. I try not to think about what if that's the end of Mark – forever – that there is no heaven. I try not to think about the fact that Finn wrote that song about me. And I try not to think about the incident in the restaurant with Anthony and Elizabeth Knowles.

36

"Lo♥e's got a hold on me . . ."

I leave the coffee down on the pavement.

"Seán?" I call.

He opens his eyes. "Thanks, Rosie. You're a star."

Knowing what lies ahead, I'm in no hurry to get to work, so I stand there looking down at him.

"What?" he asks, grinning.

"You really have the life, don't you?" I say, half-jokingly.

"What do you mean?" He's puzzled now.

"Not having to get up on a Monday morning and face going into work like the rest of us? Having me deliver your coffee before you even get out of bed?"

There's a sudden flash of annoyance. "Yeah, well – take a look around. This ain't no fucking bedroom, is it? Why don't you try it sometimes if you think it's so good? See how you like it when some drunks decide to wake you up in the middle of the night because they feel like a game of 'kick-the-shit-out-of-the-down-and-out'!"

"Hey, Seán, I'm sorry – I didn't think."

"Don't worry about it," he says gruffly.

But I feel awful. I don't know what made me say it. I can't just go, having so obviously upset him.

"How are Hilda and the girls?" I ask, guessing that no matter how annoyed he is with me, he won't be able to pass up on the opportunity to talk about them.

He smiles. "The girls are doing great. I got to see them yesterday. And Hilda's much, much better. Another few weeks and I think she might be able to move out of her mum's place. Maybe then we can start trying for a council house."

"Good. I'm glad. Anyway, I'd better get to work."

"Bye then."

Since I woke up this morning, my stomach has been in knots at the thought of going into work. I've been sick with dread, but now here I am. As I hand Fay her coffee, she takes it, but doesn't say thanks, and doesn't look me in the eye. This is not good. Does she know about what happened in the restaurant or doesn't she? I can't tell and, all morning, as customers come and go, I find I'm looking for signs. She is very quiet in herself, but then she's always quiet and it's hard to know if she's any quieter than usual.

"Fay, Rosie, I think I might just pop out to the post office while it's quiet," Monica announces around midday.

"Do you want me to go?" I ask and want to add – please, please, I don't want to be left on my own with Fay.

"No, you're fine. I could do with the fresh air."

Monica goes into the office and, moments later, she comes back out wearing her coat and carrying a bunch of brown envelopes. She glances at her reflection in one of the shop mirrors, fixes her hair, calls out goodbye, and then she's gone.

Now it's just Fay and me.

For maybe five minutes, Fay stands at the counter staring out the window. I keep glancing over at her trying to figure out what's on her mind. Is she just idly considering the passers-by? Or is she trying to work out exactly what she's going to say to me.

"Did you meet Anthony Knowles and his wife on Friday night?"

The shiny blade of Arthur's Excalibur couldn't have done as swift and neat a job of slicing the silence.

She's staring at me but I don't say anything. I don't need to. She wouldn't be asking me this question unless she already knew the answer. Besides, that answer is clearly written on my guilty face.

"Have you any idea what you've done?" she asks, in a voice even lower than her normal one. It's barely a whisper.

"Fay – look – I'm sorry!"

"You interfering little cow! What possessed you? What have I ever done to you?"

"Look, I happened to see them in a restaurant together and I suddenly felt sorry for you and –"

"I don't need your sympathy!"

"– and for her and –"

"Sorry for *her*? Believe me, she's one woman who doesn't need your sympathy."

"How can you say that? Her husband is having an affair with you!"

"An affair?" She looks like she's considering the word. Then she looks at me. "I don't know how much you know about me and Anthony Knowles but –"

I see no point in pretending. "I know about you running away to London, and having a baby together. And I know that when the baby died, he came back to Dublin and back to his family."

She nods her head as if thinking about this, as if she's weighing up whether it's a reasonable account of their history.

Then she begins to talk. "Do you know that when our baby died, that she and the other babies I might have had if there hadn't been complications took with them any future we had together? Do you know that without a future, Anthony's past suddenly became so much more appealing to him? A good career, a lovely home with three beautiful children and a woman who might have treated him like dirt but who rang him every single day pleading with him to come home again – not out of love but because he was her husband. All that versus a hand-to-mouth existence in a dingy flat in a strange, friendless city with a woman so deranged with grief that she couldn't manage to dress herself in the mornings. Do you know that the last memory I had of our time in London was lying in my bed in the early morning, watching him sneak out the door with his suitcases in hand, no doubt thinking he'd managed to get away without me seeing him. Do you know any of that?"

She looks like she's expecting an answer.

I shake my head. "No, I don't."

"Well then, you don't really know anything, do you? But still you took it upon yourself to meddle."

"Fay, loo –"

"Don't interrupt! You know, I swore that day after I'd seen him sneaking out on me that I would never let a single word pass between us again. And I didn't. Over the years I passed him on the street – sometimes on his own, sometimes with Elizabeth and the kids – and I didn't so much as make eye contact with him. I just got on with my life, such as it was. Until, a while ago, I got a phone call from him out of the blue. Maybe you remember the call – you were the one who took it. Do you remember?"

I nod.

"He sounded desperate on the phone. He needed to talk. He was crying. Could we just meet up for coffee, he pleaded. So I agreed. I figured enough time had passed. I figured I was strong enough.

So we met for the first time in over thirty years and, as I sat there, he told me how that morning his granddaughter had died unexpectedly at two weeks of age, exactly the same age that our own baby had died and, suddenly, all those emotions and feelings he'd had back then came flooding back and I was the only one he could talk to about them. None of his other children knew about their half-sister and he couldn't talk to Elizabeth.

And the emotions and feelings I had for him came flooding back too when I met him that day. It didn't matter what he had done to me in the past. I still loved him, every bit as much, but then I'd never stopped. It didn't matter that he didn't deserve my love, he had it anyway, always had. That first day we talked for hours and hours and then, afterwards, we fell into a routine – meeting up once or twice a week, the odd stolen night together. I didn't feel I was taking anything from Elizabeth – their marriage had never been about love and I think our meetings probably kept it going through those hard times after their granddaughter's death. I think Anthony would have left her for me then if I'd wanted him to, but I didn't want to take him away from her a second time. It may sound stupid but I always felt that when our daughter died it was like a punishment for Anthony and me because of what we'd done. I was never proud of the fact that I had stolen someone else's husband. But these little meetings – they were enough. I reasoned to myself that I deserved them, after everything. But now they've been taken away from me because of you and your stupid interference.

Elizabeth has made Anthony make a choice and, like he did the last time, he chose her."

"Fay, I'm sorry. I never knew. Look —"

"Frankly, Rosie, I don't need to hear anything you have to say right now. You've said enough."

I'm hurrying blindly through the lunch-time crowds, desperately trying to think of somewhere I can go, somewhere private, before the tears that are surging up inside break their banks.

"Hey! Look where you're going!" shouts one of a group of office girls in matching uniforms when I hit against her.

"Sorry," I mutter. I scurry on, with my head down.

I have to find somewhere — and quickly. The toilets in Brown Thomas maybe? But will I get there in time? I can't burst into tears, here, now, on the street! I can't!

"Rosie?" I hear a voice call my name from behind. Oh God! Who is it? I can't, won't turn around. I keep my head down and plough on through the crowds.

"Hey, Rosie!"

Go away, go away, go away, go away! I silently plead.

"Rosie?"

I feel a hand on my shoulder. I know it's Finn. I freeze but don't turn and he has to walk around me.

"I thought it was you!" He's smiling — but not for long. The dam has broken. Now he's staring at me in alarm as I stand there, great big tears surging forth and streaming down my face. "Hey, hey, Rosie — what's the matter?"

I try to stop these ridiculous tears, conscious of how I must look to him, to the passers-by, but they're only gathering momentum. I'd have more luck pushing back the tide.

"Here, here, come on, now." Finn takes me by the arm. "Come with me."

We turn around and he brings me back in the direction he came from. As we walk along, I keep my head bowed, depending on him to negotiate our path through the crowd. I don't even know where he's taking me and I can't ask. I've managed to stop the tears but it's taking all my efforts just to do that. Talking is beyond me.

We turn a corner and then come to a stop. I raise my head enough to see we've standing outside a vacant shop. Without a word, Finn pulls a set of keys from his pocket and unlocks the door.

"Come on," he says, and leads me inside.

The inside of the place is in the throes of being renovated. He turns off the beeping alarm then lifts a couple of old paint cans from a beaten-up chair and wipes away the dust.

"Come here," he says. "Sit down.

And I do.

"I'll get you something for those tears." He goes into the back and brings out a ball of tissue paper. "Here," he says and hands it to me and I wipe my face.

"Now blow your nose," he orders.

I do. I look at him, slightly embarrassed by the sheer volume of my efforts.

"And again," he says.

I manage a smile. "What are you, my mother?"

He smiles too. "Now, do you want to talk about what's the matter?"

I shrug. "No!"

"Okay." He looks at me. "Listen, I was on my way to get a burger and chips. Why don't I nip out and bring some back for the pair of us? What do you say?"

I don't say anything.

He gets up. "I'll be back in five minutes. Now, don't go anywhere."

When he's gone, I sit there for a while, listening to the hum of the street outside. A happy, girlish laugh rises above the background noise and I think I want to be her, whoever she is. I just want to feel the way I used to before – disgruntled every now and then but happy over all. I get up, walk to the back of the store, find a little toilet and, in the grimy, paint-splattered mirror, I see my face. It's red, puffy and mascara-smudged. I look a sight. I tear off a strip of toilet paper, dampen it and wipe away the black.

I hear the front door open again and I hear Finn call out my name. I go back out.

"Hope you're hungry," he says.

He pulls up a box and sits down and when I sit down on the same old chair, he hands me the bag of takeaway food. Together we eat our burger and chips in silence. He passes me my Coke and I drink it. I'm glad he isn't trying to talk to me and, maybe because he isn't, I'm the one who speaks first.

"So how come you have the keys for this place?"

"I got them from the builders. I needed to deliver some stuff for them but they're off on another job so they dropped the keys in to me this morning."

We're both silent again. I take another sip from my Coke.

"Do you want to tell me what's wrong?" he asks. "You don't have to, but I'm happy to listen if you do."

"Where would I start?" I ask. I sigh, but then I do start, with this morning. I tell him about Fay and her relationship with Anthony Knowles and how my stupid interference has changed everything, and how upset Fay was because of what I did. All the time he's looking at me, listening. ". . . and I don't know why I did it, I really don't," I finish. "But I just

343

couldn't bear the thought of him stringing her along, denying he even knew her, being so relieved when he thought he'd got away with such a narrow escape."

When he doesn't stand up and declare I'm the vilest bitch he's ever had the misfortune to come across, I find myself carrying on.

I tell him about Shane. How he's my best friend, but how I've ruined everything by kissing him. "We've known each other since we were three and never before would I ever have dreamt of doing something like that. I still can't explain why I did it."

Again he doesn't stand up and shout at me that he can't listen to all the evilness that I'm spouting. He just nods, impassively. But it's encouragement enough for me.

I tell him about Mark and how I still feel guilty about what happened. "I know it's not my fault in the sense that I didn't actually drive his car into that wall but it wouldn't have happened, he wouldn't have died, if it wasn't for me."

He nods. I go on.

"I just want to feel like I did before. Since Mark died I just feel so awful. It's not that I miss him – terrible as that might seem, but I didn't know him well enough to miss him. But I miss *something*. Everyone is carrying on with life as normal but I feel I'm not like them anymore."

"I kind of know what you mean. I feel like that too."

"Do you?"

"Before, I felt like – I don't know, just like everyone else, I guess – but since Mark it's like there are two types in the world. Ordinary people with ordinary concerns and people like me and the McCarthys – damaged people who are just managing to hold it together."

"But I didn't know Mark like you did. I shouldn't feel like this. I feel like I'm indulging myself. He's dead and here

I am wallowing in self-pity – doing all these awful things, ruining things for Fay, trying to snog Shane, and excusing myself for doing them on the basis that I'm just not myself."

"And maybe you're not." He thinks for a second. "Rosie, you're being too hard on yourself. Okay, you're not carrying the loss of Mark like his parents, or even I am, but you're carrying the guilt. An awful thing happened. Mark died. You feel responsible. You need to give yourself time to cope with that."

"So you don't think I'm mean and evil?"

He smiles and shakes his head. "I don't. Of course I don't, because you're not. And you're not responsible for Mark's death either. If the band hadn't split up, maybe he wouldn't have acted the way he did that day. I could blame myself, say it was my fault, just like you're saying it's yours. But things like that – relationships, bands even, breaking up – happen to people all the time. Disappointments are part and parcel of life and yet most of us don't react like Mark did. You can't blame yourself."

I look at him. He's looking at me, and smiling ever so kindly.

"Why are you being so kind to me?" I ask.

"Why not? Besides, you've been the same to me."

I look at him, not knowing what he means.

"You rang me when you didn't have to – I really appreciated that, especially . . . well, let's face it, I've never been that nice to you. And on Saturday afternoon, you sat there listening to me talking on and on when I needed someone to listen. I don't think I could have sorted out Mark's things on my own. You were a friend when I needed you. And now you need a friend."

I nod.

"And you're not as evil as you make out. Far from it. You're a nice person, Rosie."

"How can you say that after all I've just told you?"

"Now stop it, Rosie! Haven't you been listening to a word I said? Stop beating yourself up all the time."

"Okay, Okay."

"And you do good things as well. I got a phone call this morning from Mark's mum – they got your letter."

"Oh!"

"Relax – she was really pleased to get it. It meant a lot to her. So, see, you're not all bad." He stands up. "Now, come on. Do you think you can face going back to work?"

I shrug. "I guess. But what am I going to say to Fay?"

"Apologise to her again. Be as nice as you can to her. And prepare yourself for the fact that she might not forgive you, at least not for a very long time."

That night, when I get home after truly the worst day at work, everyone is in the living room.

"So what's going on?" I ask, looking around at the beaming faces. They're all there: Caroline, Mick, Shane, Loretta, Doug and Dana.

"Oh Rosie!" cries Caroline. "Mick got the part of Lenny in Kevin North's film *Fate Farm*, can you believe it?" She couldn't be happier than if she herself had won the Lotto.

"Congrats, Mick!" I go to give him a hug. "That's the best news ever."

He grins. "It's pretty cool all right. And it's all down to Caroline." He looks over at her, like he's dead proud of her. And she's looking at him, like she's pretty proud of him too.

"But I don't understand – I thought you two weren't even talking?"

"We weren't," Caroline tells me, "but, when I found I had to go to London on business, I rang up Kevin North and told him that I was coming over with Mick and asked him would he meet him. When he said he would, I booked two seats on a Saturday flight to London."

Laughing, Mick carries on the story. "She turns up outside my apartment block at five-thirty in the morning and rings up from her car, telling me to get dressed and come down straightaway, that she's taking me somewhere but won't tell me where."

"He refuses to come down but –"

"– but then she starts beeping the horn!" Mick is still laughing. "So all the neighbours start opening the windows, shouting down at her to shut up, that it's the middle of the night, but she won't let up. The only way to get her away from there was to do as she says and get dressed and come down."

"I just pretended I'd booked a second seat by mistake and – you know what – he believed me."

"Come on! I did think it was a bit fishy."

"I didn't tell him why I was really taking him to London until –"

"You didn't ever actually tell me. I kept asking what were we doing there exactly but –"

"Remember you nearly walked out on me in the Victoria and Albert Museum? But then you realised you didn't know the address of our hotel and you had to come straight back!" She laughs. "But anyway, the next day –"

"– we pulled up in a taxi outside this mansion in Mayfair and Kevin North himself opened the door. I swear –"

"Mick nearly collapsed!"

"There was North, shaking my hand, and saying I must be Mick –"

"I didn't tell him before that because I thought he'd get too nervous, or, worse, get all stubborn on me and refuse to see Kevin. Anyway, I guess Kevin must have liked what he saw. The next day, he asked us around again, only this time there were some more people there, the producer and a whole bunch of others and the rest, as they say, is history – they loved Mick!"

"If it wasn't for Caroline –"

"– and Loretta. Remember if she hadn't taken such good care of Kevin in hospital, then none of this would have happened. Anyway, Rosie, what I was about to say to the others, just before you came in, is that I'm planning to have this big celebratory dinner here tomorrow night for all of us!"

"Here?" I ask.

"Yeah."

"But who's going to cook?"

"Me!"

"But you can't cook!" cries Dana.

"How do you know? You never saw me?"

"Exactly – doesn't that say it all?" says Shane.

I go to bed early, leaving the others all still chatting below. As I lie in the dark, I hear my phone beep. I lean over and pick it up from my locker and look at it. It's from Finn.

– Hope you're feeling better now –

Am I? In a way, yes. Hearing Mick's good news has certainly lifted my spirits and the talk with Finn today did me a lot of good – at least in one way. I can't change anything I did. I can't magic Mark alive. I can't fix my meddling in Fay's life. I can't take that kiss I give Shane back.

But I can learn from my stupidity.

For a start, I'm not going to text Finn back. On Saturday, he needed a friend, and I was there for him. Today, I needed a friend, and he was there for me. But that's an end to it. There can be no more. But ever since I left him this lunchtime, I haven't been able to think about anything but him. How kind he was, how gentle he was, and how much I really like him. And he is kind and gentle and I do like him; I should think these things about him. But the problem is, my thoughts don't stop there. Oh, but that they would. You see, I keep having to block out all these totally inappropriate thoughts, like what it would be like to be held by him, to be kissed by him, to wake up and see his tousled black curls on the pillow next to me. Such thoughts are inappropriate and I'm not going to let myself think that way. I know now I'm just vulnerable, just lonely – I'm not going to morph his kindness and affection into something more than that. I've already done that with Shane. No, my stupid days are well and truly behind me.

37

"Perhaps lo♥e . . ."

I may have resolved to put my stupidity behind me, but it's harder to avoid Finn than I thought, as I find out the very next evening.

At eight o'clock, I come down to the kitchen to find it looking like a tornado has swept through the place – it's a disaster zone with the debris of Caroline's cooking littering every surface.

"Out of the way!" she cries, rushing between cooker and counter with a bubbling pot in hand. I clear away a space and she sets it down. She too looks like she was a victim of that selfsame whirlwind – her hair is caught up in this mad bird's-nest bun and, overall, she's just a right mess – a chef-detective could probably figure out exactly what this evening's meal is going to be by the many stains on her old tracksuit. (But is there such a profession as a chef-detective? What kind of crimes would they investigate? Death by Chocolate?)

"Watch it!" Caroline warns, rushing back with the same

pot to the cooker again. "Out of the way, Rosie, out of the way!"

Come to think of it, I guess *she* is the tornado. But what exactly is she doing with the pot, I wonder, watching her take it off the cooker again and set it down on the counter for a second time. Now, she's staring at it, like even she's not quite sure. She lifts up the pepper mill and begins to grind.

"Did you need a hand?" I ask.

"No, no, everything is under control," she tells me as she keeps grinding and grinding.

"Is it?" I ask looking around at the chaos.

"Yes, everything is just perfect. I think I've outshone myself. All the effort has been worth it."

"So there's nothing I can do then?"

"Well, I guess you can set the table so if you want to be useful."

I clear off the mess, wipe the table down, and then go to the drawer and count out the knives and forks.

"Set it for eight, by the way," she tells me.

"Why, is there someone else coming?"

"Yeah, Shane's invited Finn along."

"Oh!"

She looks at me. "Come on, Rosie. He's been through a bad time. Shane thought it would be nice for him. Mark was Finn's best friend."

"I know that."

"Is it because he'll remind you of Mark? Is that the problem?"

"I don't have a problem."

"Good! Now, when you've finished the table, will you whip up some cream?"

"Sure."

"Okay, I think I'm on top of things," says Caroline,

looking around. She picks up the pepper mill and begins grinding again. "They should be arriving any minute now. I just need to clean the place up a little."

"How about cleaning yourself up and I'll sort out here?"

"Oh yeah, you're right. I am a state. Okay, I'll go and get changed so."

After I've whipped the cream, I begin tidying.

Somehow, miraculously, I've restored order of a sort to the kitchen by the time the first ring on the doorbell comes.

"I'll get it!" shouts Dana.

"Oh, hi, Finn," I hear her say. "Great you could make it."

"Thanks for inviting me," he replies, causing my heart to leap into my mouth – which is not good – not good at all.

"Come on into the living room. You're the first to arrive."

I stay in the kitchen. As the number of people increases, so too does the volume coming from the living room. I listen to them all laughing and talking over one another. I can hear Caroline telling someone – Finn, I guess, as he's the only one who doesn't know – about Mick's big break. I hear Shane laugh – at something Loretta is saying to him, maybe. And then I hear Finn laugh too, but I try to ignore it, try not to think how he looks as he laughs. Someone turns on the CD player and John Denver begins to sing. John Denver means Dana has taken charge of the remote control.

"Ah no, Dana – not that!" cries Caroline. "We're not listening to *him!*"

But Dana wins out: it plays on.

But I think poor John is unheard by all but me as they chatter. I can't hear the words of the song but I know them anyway. I've heard Dana play that album often enough. "*Perhaps love is a like a resting place, a shelter from the storm. It exists to give you shelter, it is there to keep you warm. . .*"

Caroline comes bustling into the kitchen. "What are you

doing out here?" she cries when she sees me but doesn't wait for an answer – she's in busy-busy hostess mode. She goes to the cooker, stirs one of the pots, grinds some more pepper in, then takes a bottle of wine from the fridge.

"Are you coming?" she asks, looking back at me as she bustles out again, not waiting for an answer.

"Yeah, sure," I mumble.

But by the time I do make a move to follow her, I meet them all on their way in.

"Wrong way, wrong way, turn back!" cries Caroline excitedly and so I find myself leading them all back into the kitchen.

We stand around the table. From across the room, Finn gives a little wave. "I was wondering where you were," he says.

I smile back but don't have to say anything because now Caroline is pulling me by the sleeve.

"Okay, we're going to do – boy, girl, boy, girl. Here, Rosie, you sit here – then Doug, you go next to Rosie. Loretta, I'm putting you there. And Finn, this is your spot – and Dana, you sit here – and Shane, you go beside Dana. And Mick, you're here and so that leaves me – I guess I can squeeze in beside Mick."

Soups set out before us all, Caroline passes behind Mick, rests her hand on his shoulder for a second, puts the empty soup pot on the counter, passes back behind Mick again – another opportunity to touch his shoulder – and then she takes her place beside him. It's just as well she's forgotten to light the candles in the centre of the table or the place would explode with all the electricity their looks and secretive little touches are generating. It seems there are three couples here tonight, plus Finn and me. Mick and Caroline may not officially be a couple but something's obviously going on between them. So three couples and me and Finn. I hope Finn doesn't think I've set this up, but then why would he? He doesn't know how I feel about him.

"Okay, tuck in," says Caroline and we pick up our spoons and do.

It's a thick lentil soup, quite tasty at first but as I get beyond the first couple of spoonfuls my mouth begins to burn. This stuff is hot! Gram for gram it has got to have more pepper in it than lentils. I reach for the jug at the same time as Finn does. He lets me take it but he fans his mouth and I know I'm not the only one suffering. I look around the table. Shane is blinking back the tears and poor Dana's head looks like it's about to blow off. Doug nudges me and tells me to hurry up with the water. And then the jug quickly goes from person to person as they all dowse the fires raging within but, when it comes to Caroline, she passes it on without pouring a glass for herself. I see now she's not eating. She's sipping her wine and looking preoccupied with hostess concerns, like she's working out if there's anything she needs to be doing.

Suddenly, she jumps up. "Oh, I forgot to light the candles." She hurries to get some matches.

"Are you sure you need to light them?" asks Shane. "I think it may be hot enough in here as it is."

He could mean the carry-on between Mick and Caroline, but I think he means the soup. Whichever, suddenly I burst out laughing. That does it for the others – straightaway, they all join in.

"What? What's the joke?" Caroline asks, looking around in puzzlement, but we all manage to hold in any further laughter and just mutter, "Nothing" and carry on pretending we're eating these bowls of lava, and Caroline is too preoccupied to persist with her line of enquiry or to notice that we are all just pretending.

"Are you not having soup?" Dana asks Caroline.

"No, no. I already had some when I was cooking it."

Perhaps. But before she ground the entire contents of the pepper mill into it.

"So, you have actually tasted this?" asks Mick.

"Yes, yes." A momentarily look of concern flashes across her face. "It's not too hot, is it? I think I might have been a little heavy on the pepper."

"No, no," we all murmur.

"Hmmm, it's lovely," Mick even goes so far as to say.

"Good, finish up quickly then and I'll start on the mains."

She stands up and goes to the cooker. The minute her back is turned, Mick gets up first and then Finn and, with all the precision and stealth of a well-planned nocturnal military operation, the pair of them scurry back and forth, back and forth, between table, bin and counter – lifting, emptying, then stacking the soup bowls. Mission complete, they resume their places just as Caroline turns around.

"So, I'll just clear away the bowls and –" she stalls, and looks around the table at our cleared places. She turns to the counter and sees the empty bowls stacked on the counter. "Boy! You lot were hungry! I hope you have room for this," she says.

"What it is?" asks Mick tentatively.

"Hungarian goulash," answers Caroline. She begins ladling great big spoonfuls of it onto our plates. And I mean great big spoonfuls – like she's the boarding-house landlady and we're a bunch of starving navvies who've just come off the building site after a hard day's graft. She hands Doug a near-overflowing plate of this brown concoction and somehow he manages to pass it on to Loretta without spilling it.

"Mind now, it might be a little spicy," she warns.

We lift our forks and, bearing in mind her warning, we take a cautious first taste but, after the soup, its relative blandness comes as a welcome relief.

"Hmm, tasty," murmurs Mick – maybe out of love, maybe out of relief, but then he begins to chew.

Tasty is *not* a word to describe what's on our plates. How would I describe it then? Tasty, no. Tasteless, yes. What it looks like I won't even get into, not if I hope to keep on eating. But to keep on eating is easier said than done. I chew on. Tough and hard would perhaps be the most fitting description. The meat is like a proverbially old boot and the vegetables are like stones. If this is what the Hungarians have to live on, then my heart goes out to them. It really does.

There's no sound in the room. We're all just sitting there, chewing and chewing our heads off and not daring to look at one another, knowing the ridiculous sight of each other – like cows chewing the cud – will cause us to erupt again.

"What kind of meat *is* this?" ask Dana.

"Beef," Caroline tells her.

"Did you – like – buy it in the butcher's?" asks Shane.

"Of course. Where else?"

Too many possibilities spring to mind.

"Road kill," Finn is mouthing at me. "Road kill." And when I finally get what he's saying, I erupt laughing.

"What's the joke?" asks Caroline

"Nothing. I was just thinking of something that happened at work today."

"It must have been very funny."

I can't answer but I make the mistake of looking over at Finn again. Now he's miming Caroline manically driving a car.

Caroline spots him.

"And what are you doing?" she demands.

"Nothing – I was just asking Rosie does she want a lift home later."

"But she lives here! And why now, in the middle of our meal?"

She stares at him. I guess she's wondering if Shane was wise to invite him along. After all, only Shane really knows him. But determined to play the good hostess, she decides not to badger the guest.

Finally I manage to chew a piece small enough to swallow and, as I sit there, studying my plate, deciding which lump I'm going to tackle next, Caroline pipes up.

"I guess the meat is a little on the tough side."

"Ah no," we mutter.

"Tough? No, no," we mumble.

I'm trying not to look at anyone, I am *this* close to bursting out laughing again but I can't do that to Caroline. It's just as well I don't have any meat in my mouth or I think I'd choke. Then I notice Finn across the table from me furtively bringing his napkin up to his mouth. It takes me a moment to cotton on to what he's doing but I realise he's spitting some inedible lump into the napkin. And I take his lead. When Dana spots me, she follows suit. Soon we're all at it. Every couple of seconds a napkin surreptitiously goes up to one of our mouths and we're a step nearer to getting rid of the foul mess from our plates.

Caroline is staring at her own plate now – wondering, maybe, just what went wrong. She forks an ambitiously large lump into her mouth. She chews and chews and chews. And chews and chews. Then chews and chews some more. We're all sneaking glances at her but not daring to look at one another. Finally she audibly swallows – *"Gulp!"*

"No, it definitely is on the tough side," she concedes but then glancing around at our empty plates, she adds, "But maybe I'm being overly-critical."

If my napkin wasn't full of Hungarian goulash I'd be stuffing it in my mouth right now.

It's Dana who breaks first. And the minute she starts laughing it's like some air-borne laughing virus sweeps around the table going from one person to the next. Doug catches it next, then Finn, then Loretta, then Mick, then Shane, and then me. Only Caroline is immune but that makes it all the funnier. She's staring at us with that expression people always wear when they just don't get the joke – bemused, anxious not to look like they don't get it, and keen to join in but not exactly sure just what it is they'd be joining in with. We keep on laughing, laughing and laughing. If the Grim Reaper were to glide into the kitchen right now and point his bony finger at one of us, I don't think we could stop.

Caroline sits there looking from one hysterical person to another. And slowly even she joins in. "What am I even laughing at?" she cries through her tears. And that really cracks us up. The laughing goes on and on, coming in waves – just when we think we've finally recovered, one of us starts again and it sets us all off.

But, finally, we manage to hold it together and Caroline stands up. "Now, I'm afraid I didn't stretch to dessert, but –"

"Thank God!" Shane lets out.

"Pardon?" asks Caroline.

"I couldn't eat another bite!"

Caroline smiles in satisfaction. "Good! And I'm glad you all liked it. It's the first time I've ever cooked a proper meal for so many people."

"You don't say!" says Shane.

"Honestly – I'm not joking," she says proudly. "Maybe cooking is something that's in your blood. My mother's a great cook. You know, I didn't even have to follow a recipe."

"I bet you didn't," says Dana, but her take on what Caroline says goes right over her head.

Her moment of glory is impervious to everything

"No, no. Well, I did take my ideas from one of Shane's cookbooks but then I improvised, added my own few touches. Isn't that what all the best chefs do?"

"Caroline, my love, Jamie Oliver has nothing on you," says Mick. He leans over and gives her a fond hug but then she notices us all watching and she shrugs him away and stands up.

"So, I'll just make some coffees and teas."

Someday we probably will tell her what we really thought of her meal, but not tonight. She's too chuffed with the success it's been.

"No, no, you've done enough." Dana jumps up. "I'll sort out the teas and coffees."

Maybe she's concerned with what Caroline might do to them.

"And I'll clear off the table," says Shane, getting to his feet. "Loretta can help." Maybe he's thinking that he needs to get rid of all these napkins bulging with Hungarian Goulash before Caroline finds them and we're all rumbled.

"Okay," says Caroline. "Then shall the rest of us retire to the drawing room or, in other words, go back into the living room and settle ourselves on the couch?"

Back in the living room Mick is recounting the finer details of his meeting with Kevin North to Loretta and me but I can't concentrate – my stomach is rumbling so much I get up and go back into the kitchen. I go to the press and reach for a packet of biscuits and take out as many as I can hold in my fist. As I'm loading them into my mouth, Finn walks in. He takes one look at my bulging cheeks and the packet of biscuits in my hand and laughs.

"Looks like you have the right idea. I'm starving!"

My mouth is too full to say anything but I hold out the packet to him and he takes a few.

"I have to say that meal in one of the most memorable I've ever had. Has Caroline ever cooked before?"

"Not that any of us are aware." And then I grin. "That was *so* mean of you making me laugh like that in the middle of it all. I was just about holding it together but when you started on about road kill, I thought I'd actually choke trying to hold in the laughter."

He laughs now. "Remember when Shane asked her did she actually get it in a butcher's – I swear I thought I'd explode."

I suddenly realise we're standing very close together and I take a step back.

But then, without even realising it, I think, he steps forward again so we're as close as ever.

"So you're feeling a little better?" he asks.

I nod. "And you?"

"Yeah – I'm getting there."

"Good."

He's smiling at me. And before I know it, he's leaning over and then he kisses me. Just a small sweet kiss on the lips.

Immediately I step back. "I'd better go in to the others," I mumble and hurry away.

Back in the living room, I squeeze in on the couch beside Dana. Soon after, Finn comes in and finds a space for himself on a footstool. I can feel him looking over at me but I won't look back. I focus all my attention on the conversation that's going on. Shane is grilling Caroline and Mick.

"So come on, tell us what really did happen in London?"

"How do you mean?" asks Caroline. "You all know what happened. We met Kevin North and –"

"Yeah, yeah, we all know that Mick got the part but what we all want to know is what happened between you and Mick?"

"What are you trying to say, Shane?"

"Come on, Caroline, there's no point in denying it.".

"I don't know what you're talking about. There is —"

"Give over, Caroline!" Mick interrupts and then he suddenly grabs Caroline and gives her a big sloppy kiss on the lips. "Caroline, they all know. Stop trying to pretend otherwise. Tell them. Go on. Tell them!"

"Tell them what?" she asks crossly, shrugging him away.

"If you won't then I will! Caroline and I are in love! Aren't we, Caroline?"

"Mick — stop! Don't be such a blather-mouth!"

"I just knew it!" shouts Shane.

"But you can't be," teases Dana. "Remember, Caroline doesn't believe in love! There's no such thing, is there, Caroline?"

"Stop it, all of you! Mick doesn't know what he's saying. You know these actor types, you know the way they go on — it's all, 'darling this' and 'lovey that' — it doesn't mean anything."

"So Mick is lying then and nothing happened?" asks Dana.

"Okay," Caroline concedes defensively. "We have come to an understanding but —"

"An understanding?" laughs Shane. "What age is this? The Victorian? Simple question, are you, or are you not, going out together?"

"And are you, or are you not, in love?" adds Dana.

"Well . . ."

"Yes or no?" demands Shane.

"Well, yes, I guess, *technically* you could say that."

There's a whoop from all of us and then Dana begins singing: *"Caroline and Mick up a tree, K-I-S-S-I-N-G —"*

"Stop it. Stop being so childish!" shouts Caroline.

Childish it most definitely is, but soon we're all joining in Dana's little ditty, all chanting like seven-year-olds in the playground:

"First come love, then comes marriage, then comes a baby in a baby's carriage!"

"Come on, stop now! There's not going to be any of that. We're just going out with one another."

"That's not quite what you said in London," Mick reminds her. "Didn't you say you always thought a Christmas wedding would be nice, and maybe two children, a little boy and a —"

"Jesus, Mick! Do you have to tell everyone our business?"

"But I thought you said you wouldn't go out with anyone," Dana interrupts, "unless — what was it you said again — they were seriously rich?"

"Exactly, and now that Mick has got that part he will be seriously rich. So you see I am following my principles."

Mick's grinning now. "Principles—shinciples! I know you have a reputation to maintain but all this happened between us *before* I got the part, remember?"

"Whose side are you on?" Caroline demands crossly.

"Yours, my love, always yours!" And he leans forward and kisses her again.

At that moment, I happen to glance over at Finn and I see he's looking over at me. I immediately look away but, as I do, I see that Shane is glancing from one of us to the other. I turn away from him too and back to Caroline and Mick.

38

"Just a first glimpse of you, to fall in lo♥e . . ."

For the next couple of weeks, there's only two things on my mind: one – Finn; and two – keeping him right OUT of my mind. I am NOT going down that route. Yes, yes, I do have feelings for him, but so what? If I've learned one thing it's that my feelings are NOT to be trusted. Nothing can ever happen between him and me. It can't. It won't. Because I'm not going to let it happen.

In the days following the dinner I did get a few *seemingly* innocuous texts of the 'How are you?' variety from him. But did I reply? I most certainly did NOT. I know how these things work. A few innocent texts back and forth, and then, next thing you know, he's ringing up to ask me out. And there's NO WAY that's going to happen.

To keep my mind off *things*, I keep as busy as possible. Every evening I badger Caroline and Dana to come out with me to the pub, and there I stay until whichever one of them I'm with insists that it's time to go home. If both of them refuse to come out with me (which happens more than I'd like, because they're so busy with boyfriends these days) I stack up on DVDs and sit watching them long into the night and, then, when I can't keep my eyes open any longer, I climb into bed, too shattered to think about *things*.

In the mornings, I wake up exhausted, but that doesn't stop me getting up immediately (busy, busy, busy – that's the key) and then I shower, dress, skip breakfast, and hurry for the bus. When – two mornings in a row – I arrive to work before Fay and Monica, I ask Monica to give me a set of keys of my own, and she does so reluctantly – perhaps distrusting this new me and not expecting it to last. Ha! She of little faith!

Because I'm now always in before the others, there's no point in stopping off to buy coffees any more so, instead, I've brought in a little coffee percolator from home that we don't need any more, and I keep a pot of coffee on the go all day, bringing out a cup to Seán at his usual time, if he's there.

Buoyed up with all this coffee, I work every day like a slave. One day, I reorganise one corner of the shop that's been in need of sorting out for a long time. By the time I'm through with it, all the stock is displayed much more effectively and there's even room for a whole new rail. I show Monica a picture in a brochure of the rail I think we should get and she says she'll think about it. Another day, I go through the catalogues and come up with a few new lines that I think will attract a younger clientele. You see, what I feel we need to do is expand our customer base and the way to do that is to go for some cheaper and younger lines. That's where the money is. I read somewhere that women are spending far more money on clothes these day but now they tend to buy lots of cheaper outfits rather than investing in a couple of good ones. They spend more money on accessories too and I tell Monica that I think we should get into jewellery, and bags, and even shoes maybe. Then our customers could buy a complete outfit from us, and the cost of all the different bits would really add up. Monica says that she can see where I'm coming from and that she'll have a think about it – and maybe she is *still* thinking about it – and the rail – but I'm beginning to get the impression that she's not as enamoured with my bright ideas as I might have expected. But that doesn't deter me. No, no, busy, busy – that's me.

So, this morning, I reorganise the space behind the counter to make it more streamlined. The problem with it before, as I tell Monica when she arrives in, is that we were always bending down to get at things but, now, everything we regularly use is within easy reach. No more disappearing underneath the counter looking for something when there are customers waiting. Sure, initially it's going to be difficult to remember where everything is but it's just a matter of getting used to it.

"Hmm," says Monica now, surveying the changes.

"And look, I've moved the large carrier bags down to the third shelf because we don't use them as much as the medium-sized ones. I know it's confusing now but we'll get the benefit in the long term."

"I'm afraid, Rosie, there's not going to be a long term."

"Pardon?" I ask, still surveying the counter, to see if there is any more I can do to make things even more efficient. Maybe if I bring the tissue paper over to the left-hand side . . .

"Fay, can you come here a moment?" Monica calls.

Fay walks over.

"Yes?"

"And Rosie, can you put down the tissue paper and listen up?"

I do and the two of us wait to hear what she has to say, but she just stands there, looking all serious. Well, it can't be because of anything I've done. But I am kind of anxious that she gets on with whatever she has to say – there's a lot I need to do.

She takes a deep breath.

"I'm thinking of closing the business and leasing out the premises. Actually, I'm not just thinking of it, that is what I am going to do. I was trying to find the right moment to tell you but I guess now is as good as any. Look, the shop hasn't been doing well these past few years. If I'd been smart, I'd have closed it down a long time ago. I'm sorry. And I do appreciate all your hard work." She turns to me. "Rosie, you've made some nice changes these past two weeks, and you've come up with some good ideas, but I'm afraid it's too late. This place is haemorrhaging money."

"So we're closing down?" asks Fay. She looks like she's in shock. I guess it's not going to be easy to find a job at her age.

Monica nods.

I feeling shocked myself, far more than I could have imagined I would. I know I've always regarded this job as temporary but I guess I felt it was temporary until I decided I was finished with it. I never expected it to finish with me first.

"When?" I ask.

"The end of the month. Of course, I'll give you the holiday money you're due, plus severance pay, and more besides. And, needless to say, I'll write you excellent references."

It seems like everything is happening in the same day and when I head out for lunch, I find Finn standing outside the shop, waiting for me.

"Rosie, can we talk?" he asks.

"I don't think so. I have a lot of things I need to do."

"Please?"

"Really, Finn, I'm very busy, very busy." I go to move on, but he puts his hand on my arm.

"I need you to hear what I have to say. It won't take long."

"Finn, look —"

"It would be the fastest way to get rid of me," he grins.

I look at him for a moment and, foolishly perhaps, I give in.

We go to a coffee shop around the corner. I sit down while he goes to the counter. He comes back with two coffees and two sandwiches.

"Rosie, I want to talk to you about what happened at Caroline's dinner. In the kitchen."

"No need! I understand. These things happen."

"But —"

"I understand it didn't mean anything."

"But the fact is, it did mean something. I wanted to kiss you that night."

I open up my sandwich and begin inspecting it.

"Rosie, do you hear what I'm saying?"

"Yes, well," I say, "I won't hold it against you. Take it as forgotten — it's like it never happened."

"You're not listening! Please, stop inspecting your sandwich and just listen to me! I *don't* want to forget about it. Look, I've done a lot of thinking before coming here. To be honest, I've been trying to forget you. I felt I owed it to Mark."

"That's right. We mustn't forget about Mark."

"And I haven't, believe me! But I've wanted to kiss you since the moment I saw you."

"Look at all the mayonnaise on this sandwich!" I tut-tut.

"Rosie, put the sandwich away and listen to me! Didn't

you hear what I just said? I wanted to kiss you from the moment I saw you."

I look up. "And what do you want, a medal? Why do you feel this great need to tell me this? Do you think I want to know? Really, I can't be doing with this right now. I need to think about important things." Like – losing my job, but I don't tell him that. I don't want to give him a reason to act all sympathetic.

"Remember the song, 'Just a First Glimpse of You'?"

I pretend to think, then I shake my head. "No, I don't think so."

"Well, I think you do! And that song was about you!"

"Yes, well, you have to take your inspiration from somewhere, I understand that. You see a girl in the audience that you like the look of. She presents a nice picture. Maybe you remember how, say, some singer-songwriter fell in love with his girlfriend when he first spotted her at one of his concerts. You combine these two scraps, and you have a song, a story. I can see that the image of me in my purple shirt was a catalyst."

"So you do remember! And you weren't just a catalyst – the song is about *you*."

"No, no. I was just the subject. Like the way a bowl of fruit is to a still-life artist. Painters have to have something to paint. And I guess songwriters have to have something to write about. Now, can you please pass me a napkin? I've spilled some of this mayonnaise on my lap."

He sighs, grabs a fistful from the holder and passes them over and I begin rubbing the stain. I can feel him staring at me. I keep my head down and keep rubbing. "Hmm, maybe I need to dab it with some water."

"Will you please stop rubbing and look at me?"

"Yes, well, I can't go back to work looking like this."

He leans over, grabs the tissues away. "It's a speck. Nobody will see it. I can't even see it." Then he sits back again.

I begin looking around. "It's busy here, isn't it?"

"I don't care if it is or not."

"Yes, well, I'm just sayi –"

"You're really being impossible!" He sighs. "Okay, do you remember me asking you out that night of the party?"

"Yes, yes – I *think* I remember that. But well, I imagine you've asked a lot of girls out. Isn't that what guys in bands do? Isn't that the reason why you form bands?"

He shakes his head. "I'm really not getting through to you at all. Okay, the only reason I had that party was because I hoped that Shane would bring you along. *You* were the reason for the party."

Hah! I have him here. "No, no," I tell him. "The reason you had that party was because Damien Rice asked you to play support!"

"That was just the excuse! *You* were the reason."

"Stop pointing at me. It's rude!"

"Jesus! Okay, let me tell you the reason why the band split. Again it's you. You are the reason. I couldn't bear the way Mark kept talking about you all the time. I couldn't bear the sight of him singing my words to you. It was hell! And I didn't know then that he'd gone so far as to pretend he'd written those words but, in a way, it hardly mattered. The way you used to sit looking up at him, it was like he'd already made those words his own."

"No, no, that's not right. You're changing things around. It was finished between Mark and me by the time the band broke up."

"But I didn't know that! Mark never told me! The way he was still going on about you I half expected him to buy you an engagement ring on Valentine's Day!"

Instead he died. Okay, I think I've listened to enough of this.

"Look Finn, I don't like the way you're talking about Mark. Mark was your friend. You may have broken up the band because you couldn't handle the fact that you fancied his girlfriend, but Mark – well – he was better than that. He cared a lot more for you than you seem to have cared for him. Did you know that EMI wanted to sign him separately but he wouldn't entertain the notion because he didn't want to let you guys down?"

"Did Mark really tell you that?"

"Yes."

Finn shakes his head. "Poor Mark was a fantasist. EMI never approached him."

"They did. But he didn't tell you because he didn't want to upset you."

"He didn't tell me because it never happened. If it had, Mark would have been crowing about it from the rooftops. He couldn't have kept it a secret! And do you think for one moment he'd have put the band above a solo career? Are you joking me? You really didn't know Mark at all."

"Excuse me but –"

"Look, Rosie, you feel bad because you ended up not liking Mark when he was alive, now you're trying to endow him with all these characteristics which, quite frankly, he never had."

"Oh please! Leave the psychology to Dana. She's the one studying it!"

"What I'm saying is true. It's time to take your blinkers off. Let me tell you a few nasty truths about Mark."

"Isn't that what you've been doing all along?"

"I haven't even started! Just because Mark is dead doesn't change what he was. I want to tell you a story."

I get up to go. "I'm sorry. I don't have time for stories. I don't have time for any of this."

He grabs me by the arm and pulls me back down.

"Take your hand off me!"

"Well, sit down then, and listen!"

Unless I want to make a bigger scene than we're already making, I have no choice. I sit down and stare at him truculently. He begins to talk.

"A couple of years ago, I wrote a song about breaking up with a girlfriend – 'Long Day, No Future'. One night this girl turned up at one of our early gigs. I mentioned that the song was about her to Mark and, after the gig, he made a beeline for her. Afterwards they went out a couple of times which pissed me off because Mark knew how I still felt. As it turned out, she soon broke it off with him too, but he didn't take it very well. He started ringing her all the time, and pestering her until, one night, she rang me in a state and asked me to get Mark to back off. I spoke to him and he did ease off for a while, but then it all started up again. He couldn't accept the fact that she didn't want him. In the end she moved to The Isle of Man. She had family there but I always felt that at least part of her reason for going was to get away from Mark.

Now, maybe I should have told you all this before. I wish I had now. I wanted to but I didn't think there was a need when you seemed to like him as much as he liked you. And I guess I thought you'd think I was being jealous. Which I was. Mark certainly thought so. The first night he was going out to meet you – a few days after that party – we had this huge fight. I said he was only seeing you because he knew I liked you – that he hadn't even noticed you until he overheard me talking about you to the other guys at the break. But he told me to stop being ridiculous. And maybe I was. He did seem crazy about you. He talked about you all the time. It used to drive me bats." He sits back. "You know, in a way, you're right and I wrote that song knowing nothing about you only that you were so lovely-looking. But I think I know you a little better now."

"Don't be stupid. You don't know me any better than Mark did!"

"I know that you're beautiful!"

"See! You're just the same as him! So, you like the way I look, big deal! How deep is that!"

"I can't help if that's what attracted me to you first but, the fact is, I think I do know you now. You're warm, funny, a little bit awkward sometimes, and you babble. You're unhappy right now – part of that is to do with Mark and partly it's because everyone around you is blissfully in love."

"Oh please!"

"And you're kind. Remember you phoned me when you didn't have to, and you sat listening to me when I was going through Mark's things. And you didn't have to write that letter to the McCarthys but you did, and you were sensitive enough to say exactly what you did say. Mrs McCarthy showed it to me. It was the loveliest letter I've ever read."

"Yeah, well, anyone would have done the same."

"I don't think so."

"If I am this lovely person you seem to think, what about all the other stuff I did? The kiss with Shane, my meddling in Fay's life –"

"Old chestnuts." He flicks his hand as if waving them aside.

"But there's other stuff." And I start pouring it all out. I tell him all about the night I told Mark I loved him. "I only did it because I was embarrassed for him. That night was the worst. The way he actually thought Caroline's birthday bouquet was for him. I knew that Caroline and the others were sniggering at him, especially when he took out that tin of Sweet 'n' Low and then —"

"Everyone who knew Mark mocked him because of those!"

"But I shouldn't have told him I loved him."

"Maybe, but you weren't being malicious. You did it out of kindness."

"That's no better. Besides, there's more I haven't told you. Did you know I was going out with Mark for a bet! Hmm? That's the kind I am. You may think I've put Mark on a pedestal but I think you're doing the same with me!"

"How do you mean you were going out with him for a bet?"

Finally I've managed to come up with something that he won't find so easy to forgive.

"After that birthday dinner I knew I wanted to break up with Mark but, before I summoned up the courage, Caroline bet me that I'd dump him, because that's what I always do. If I was still with him by the end of the month, she'd take everyone to Prague. If I wasn't, I'd have to take everyone. What I didn't know then was that she'd already booked the flight for this weekend coming, long before she made that stupid bet. She'd got some obscenely big bonus and she'd decided to treat us all"

"Okay." He thinks about this for a moment. "But you didn't keep going out with him, remember?"

Jesus! Is there anything I can say to put this guy off? He's like a dog with a bone.

"Rosie, will you please just try to understand how I feel about you?"

I snort. "You said you loved that girl, Isabella, too, remember?"

"Hang on. I'm not saying I love you. You're right, I did write that song without knowing you but I'd like to think that, maybe, what I was feeling back then was the start of the real thing. And yes, I did love Isabella. If she loved me back, maybe I'd still be loving her, but she didn't, and I don't love her now." He pauses for a second. "How did you know her name?"

"You must have said it." Now's not the time to tell him that Mark told me his own version of the story of that song, and how he came to write it.

"Look, Rosie, why can't we just go out for a few dates, and see how things go, that's all I'm asking."

I can feel myself wavering – just for a second – but then I think of another reason.

"What about Mark's parents? How do you think they'd feel if we were seeing each other?"

"Upset at first. But I've thought about that a lot too and I think they'd understand. They're good people. Look, Rosie, all I'm asking you is to give us a go."

"Okay, say I do, say we start going out. We have a great few weeks together and then I start finding things wrong with you – small things. Next thing you know, I'm breaking it off and then we never speak to one another again. So let's go straight to that point and cut out the middle bit."

He shakes his head. "I give up." He stands and puts on his coat. "Nobody says there are any guarantees but I'm willing to take the chance. I've said what I wanted to say. Now it's up to you."

It is up to me and I'm not willing to take the chance. I let him walk out the door.

39

"I can't stop lo♥ing you . . ."

It's Friday of the following week and I'm on my way to work but, having reverted to type, I'm late. After Monica's announcement, there seemed little point in keeping up my efforts. The percolator I brought in from home has died a death so I've collected four coffees from the customary place but now, as I arrive at the shop, I see there's no sign of Seán in his usual spot. I try to think when was the last time I saw him, and I figure it was probably at the start of the week. Maybe he's moved on. Maybe that council house he talked about has come through for him and Hilda.

The shop window is festooned with great big red and white CLOSING DOWN SALE banners and, since we put them up on Monday, it's never been busier. Even at this hour of the morning the place is packed. When I hand Monica her coffee, I see she's in bad form.

"Pity they weren't all so keen to buy before," she mutters, looking at the line of women outside the cubicles, all clutching stuff they neither want or need, but the sale price has convinced them otherwise.

The constant stream of buyers means our coffees go cold, and for the next six hours I'm run off my feet. We all work through our lunch break, eating the sandwiches Monica brings in from the nearby deli. At around four in the afternoon, there's a temporary lull in the onslaught and I'm about to use it to nip to the loo when my phone rings. It's Dana.

"Rosie, Hi! Look I'm not going to get time to go back to the house and pack for Prague so could you throw some things into a bag for me and bring it with you to the airport."

"But Dana —"

"Ask me why I'm going to be delayed, go on!" she demands all excited.

"But —"

"Go on, ask me!"

"Okay, why are you going to be delayed?"

"Well, my mum and dad have decided to get back together again! I'm with them now."

"That's brilliant. I'm really delighted." And I am.

"Isn't it the best? My mum has come to her senses and realised how much she needs and loves my dad. I don't know if she's ever going to be able to forgive or forget entirely, and I don't think she'll be having baby Cathy and her mother around for tea but I think she accepts that he has another daughter and that he's determined that she's going to be part of his life. I think she understands that there has to be more give and take and, in a way, she's always been the one taking. Doug and I have talked about things and I'm going to try and spend time with Cathy as well. None of this is the child's fault. And you know, growing up, I always wanted a brother or sister, and now I have one."

"I really am pleased for you all."

"So will you pack a few things for me and I'll meet you at the airport?"

"The thing is, Dana, I'm not going."

"What? You're kidding!"

"I'm not."

"But why?"

"I think I have a flu coming on. No point in going and then passing it on to all of you. We'd all end up having a miserable time."

"I see."

"So have a good time, okay?"

"Rosie, are you okay?"

"I have a temperature and—"

"No, I mean are *you* okay? You've been very down in yourself lately."

"Yes, well, I guess that would be the flu coming on."

"Then it must be coming on for a long time."

"Okay, well, I have to go," I tell her brightly. "We're tearing busy here. Make sure you all have a good time." I hang up.

Before I put my phone back in my bag, I notice there's a string of messages on it from my mum. I begin to open them and smile as I read.

1.55 p.m. – U'll never believe it! Ur Dad booked us on flight to Washington to c ur bros–

2.05 p.m. – Can u believe it?

2.08 p.m. – We're going in 2 wks time –

2.12 p.m. – U'll have to come shopping with me –

2.28 p.m. – Rosie, where r u?–

3.35 p.m. – Rosie, r u getting my messages? –

I think about texting back but see that will only trigger off another string of messages. I decide to wait until I finish work

Ten minutes later, my phone rings again – enough time

for the bush telegraph to kick into action – as I knew it would. I was expecting it to be Caroline but I see it's Shane calling. I let it go to message. Two minutes later it rings again. Again, I ignore it.

"Rosie, there's a call for you," Fay tells me almost straight away.

I hesitate, think about asking her to tell whoever it is – Shane no doubt – that I'm busy and that I'll ring back, but I'm reluctant to ask Fay for a favour. True, she's been nothing but civil these past weeks but it's a cool professional civility, like she's not going to let the fact that she hates me interfere with our work relationship.

I pick up the shop phone. It's Shane, as expected. He launches straight in.

"Dana says you're not coming."

"Yeah, I think I have this awful flu coming on," I say in what I think is a weak flu-like voice. "I'm feeling sweaty and weak and I'm running a temperature. I've taken something for it but as soon as I get home I'll go straight to bed."

"Bullshit!"

"Excuse me!"

"Why aren't you really going?"

Good question. The last thing I want is to be stuck in the house on my own all weekend. Actually, that's the second last thing, the last being stuck with three loved-up couples in a foreign city. But I answer: "I told you. I have the flu."

He doesn't say anything and, as the pause goes on, I give a little cough for effect but then I think, why bother, what does it matter whether he believes me? Who does he think he is, ringing me up like this, like he cares about me, like he's my friend? Barely a handful of words have passed between us of late. The relationship we used to have is long gone. We're just on the periphery of each other's lives now.

"I know you've been avoiding me lately but –" he begins.

"Me avoiding you? Don't be silly!"

"I'm not going to get into all that right now, but I want to know if the reason why you're not going, and the reason why you've been acting so weird lately, has got to do with Finn."

"I haven't been acting weird! I don't know what you're talking about!"

"Finn has told me how he feels about you. Now, I don't know how you feel about him but I do know that if you even feel a fraction of what he does for you, then you'd better wise up, take your head out of the sand, and tell him."

"Look, I have to go now."

"Rosie, don't hang up! Let me say one thing to you: don't let the guilt of what happened between you and Mark stand between you and Finn."

"Hey, hang on here! What's any of this got to do with you?"

"It's got to do with being your best and oldest friend, which you seem to have forgotten. And it's got to do with me wanting you to be happy."

"I have to go now – we're really busy with this sale and everything."

"Ring him, Rosie. Just ring him!

"Thanks for calling – have a nice time in Prague."

"Rosie –"

I hang up.

By closing time, my feet are aching and the shop is a complete mess. I start tidying up.

"Leave it, or we'll be here all night," says Monica. "I'm getting the Saturday girls to come earlier than usual. You go on off home. You must be wrecked."

"Monica, do you want me to come in tomorrow?"

"I thought you were going to Prague?"

"Yeah, well, there's been a change."

"Thanks for offering but Fay said she'd come in and I'll be here myself so we should be okay."

When I leave the shop, I don't get far. I just stand outside, not knowing which direction to go in. Left or right? It hardly matters. Not when I have nowhere to go. I look across and see Seán's empty doorway. Maybe things have finally worked out for him and Hilda and the two children. Maybe – at this moment – they're all sitting in the warm cosy living room of their new council home, in front of a roaring fire, with their family portrait back where it belongs, sitting on the mantelpiece.

Only because I don't want to be still standing here when Fay and Monica come out, I turn left. The others will be leaving for the airport soon and the house will be empty but I don't want to go back to an empty house. Instead, I stop off to buy a paper and head in the direction of McDaid's. I might be able to find a quiet corner there, and I'll have a read of the paper, have a glass of wine and then I'll head home. I could collect a DVD on the way.

"Can you spare the price of a cup of tea, love?" I hear someone ask and I look around.

Two homeless guys are sitting on the pavement. I'm about to walk on, but then I pause and go over to them. I reach into my bag and take out my purse but see I have only a few coppers and some notes. I think of Seán and take out a twenty and hand it to one of them.

He stares at it for a second, then quickly shoves it into his pocket – before his mate gets his hands on it, maybe, or in case I see that I've made a mistake.

I walk on. But then I think, one of these fellows might know about Seán. I turn back. The two men are squabbling now – over the money I gave them, maybe.

One of them looks up and is about to ask me for the price of a cup of tea again but when he sees it's the girl who just gave them the twenty, he suddenly starts looking at me warily, the two of them do, like they're worried that I've realised my mistake and am about to demand the note back.

"Do either of you know a homeless guy, a young guy called Seán? He's about seventeen – he often sleeps outside Elegance Boutique."

"Where?" The one wearing the red hat turns and asks the other.

His buddy shrugs. I guess a boutique for middle-aged women isn't the best marker to use in the situation.

"Maybe she means Psycho Seán," the fellow in the red hat says now to his friend. "Ask her does she mean Psycho Seán."

His buddy nods and then turns to me. "Why do you want to know?"

"He's – a – friend."

He looks me up and down, and I guess he's satisfied that I'm not some undercover cop or whatever it is he suspects me of being.

"Do you mean Psycho Sean?"

I shake my head. "No, I don't think so."

"Ask her is she talking about the fellow who sleeps down by the old lady's shop," Red Hat tells his buddy.

"Are you talking about the fellow who sleeps down by the old lady's shop?"

"Yeah." I guess. I wonder how Monica would feel about this description

"Well, that's Psycho Seán then, and we do know him but he's gone back in."

"Back in where? Prison?" I don't know why I say that except I can't think where else they could mean.

"No, back into the loony bin. He had one of his turns."

"No, no, I think we're talking about two different people. The fellow I'm looking for wasn't a loony. He was a normal fellow. Good-looking, young –"

"Yeah, well, Psycho seemed normal enough – most of the time. Didn't even drink – though if I were him, I'd never be off it."

Going by the mound of empty beer cans heaped by his side, it kind of looks like he's never off the drink as it is. Why am I even asking them? They're probably talking about a totally different person.

"Yeah, remember all that stuff that happened to his girlfriend?" Red Hat is saying to his buddy now.

Then I know we're talking about the same person.

The other one turns to me: "Yeah, she was coming home from work one morning and was set on by these drunks – they kicked the living daylights out of her. She never recovered – she's been in a hospital for over a year."

"Tell her how she's a vegetable now," Red Hat urges.

"She's a vegetable now. She's never coming out."

"And tell her how they took Psycho's kids away from him."

"Yeah, they took his kids into care after that. He's never been right since."

40

"Let's fall in lo♥e . . ."

I go to McDaid's because that's where I was heading and I'm not up to thinking of anywhere else to go. And I stay here, because I'm not up to leaving. And I order the wine because that's what I came here to do, and it gives me reason to stay. But it stands before me untouched. For a long, long time, I sit thinking of Seán and his need to invent his own reality – and not a glorious exotic one either but simply a story, a life, that offered the hope that his own didn't.

I sit there for so long that the seats around me fill and empty, an ever-changing flux of people I hardly notice but now the girl sitting beside me hits against me as she gathers up her things to leave and I look up. She kisses her boyfriend goodbye. He kisses her back. They both smile. They kiss again. She says something to him, they kiss, they talk for another short while, they kiss goodbye again, then he calls her back again and says something more to her. They grin at one another. Now she hugs him, they kiss again, he smiles again and says something else to her, and now the pair of them are both hugging, with big silly grins on their faces.

It's beginning to seem like they'll never be able to bear to part, and I decide it's time for me to go. I stand up and, as I'm putting on my coat, I see a flower-seller passing by the window. As I'm on my way out, he comes into the pub.

Instead of going, I find myself standing where I am and watching as he goes from table to table. Mostly, people don't even see him, he's just part of the busy background but then he stops by the table of an older couple, in their seventies. The man takes a flower and hands it to the woman he's with, and she reaches out and plants a kiss on his lips. She stands the single cellophaned red rose up in a glass, and they sit back again, looking at the flower, not feeling the need to talk. And I think of the history, the story that's between them.

I think of the flower-seller going from pub to pub, restaurant to restaurant. I think of all the couples he will meet tonight, and all the stories that lie behind each couple who take a flower from him.

For every couple there is a story. The lucky ones have happy stories. Caroline and Mick. Shane and Loretta. Dana and Doug. Her mum and her dad. My mum and my dad. The unlucky ones have not so happy stories, like Fay and Anthony Knowles. Sometimes, one of the couple leaves before the story ends, like Trevor left his and Monica's story; like Hilda left her and Seán's, yet, still, their stories aren't over. How can they be? When Monica, when Sean, live them every day.

The young couple are still saying goodbye to one another, still hugging, still grinning at each other and, as I witness one of the early chapters of their story, I find myself grinning too.

And, suddenly, I'm filled with the most enormous sense of happiness, love, joy, hope, every good emotion there is because I see now that my own love story has to be the story of Finn and Rosie; it was never going to be any other story. And what a wonderful story it could be and I see, really see, that love is one of life's wonders, and life, love is wonderful; wonderful enough to take a chance on. And that's what I've learned about love. Who knows why people fall in love with one another, but they do – all the time – and, now, as luck would have it, it's our turn.

So, if you'll excuse me, there's someone I need to see, to tell him that I'm willing to take a chance.

THE END

Published by Poolbeg.com

Who Will Love Polly Odlum?

Anne Marie Forrest

Polly, the ugly duckling; Davy, who masquerades as a student and hides an ugly past; Michaela, so very beautiful but desperately unhappy; Colin, with bottle blond hair and dodgy connections.

Four characters inextricably linked by love …
Polly loves Davy … Davy loves Michaela …
Michaela loves Colin … And Colin loves – well, anything in a skirt and like spreadable margarine his love goes a long, long way …

When a weekend away with one of his girlfriends leads Colin straight to Polly's door, things start to get dangerously entangled. Attraction and distraction lead to problems for one and all. So who will love Polly Odlum?

ISBN 1-85371-976-5

Published by Poolbeg.com

Dancing Days

Anne Marie Forrest

Ana: a little girl intently dressing up in her old
friend Celia's jewels ... a young woman walking
alone to the church in her bridal gown . . . a
loving wife who suffers tragic loss but survives
and travels to Africa to fall in love . . . an aging
woman who still has an eye for form and likes to
take a risk, ride pillion on a motor-bike, and sing
in a woodland glade with a handsome gardener.

Ana, who twice in her life has found true love,
who twice in her life has lost that love. So, will
Ana, who always depends on life's
unexpectedness, risk falling
in love a third time?

ISBN 1-84223-045-X

Published by Poolbeg.com

Something Sensational

Anne Marie Forrest

'These are the very first words of my travel diary.
Who knows what the last will be …'

Maeve, Genevieve, Laura and Debbie, connected by
little more than the fact that they were at school
together, head off on the holiday of a life time to spend
three months backpacking around South-east Asia.

To mark the great event, Genevieve has bought each of
them a diary to record their marvelous adventures.

As the journey progresses, the girls' account of events
take dramatic turns as each diary reveals a very
different story.

Personal journeys. Personal stories. Sometimes
dangerous. Always sensational!

ISBN 1-84223-072-7